RAVENS IN FLIGHT

BECK TODD

Copyright © 2022 by Beck Todd

First paperback edition January 2022

Book design by Kelly Carter

ISBN 978-0-578-30816-6 (paperback)
ISBN 978-0-578-30815-9 (ebook)

For my family.

Contents

SEA OF WINDS

CEOL

WALLACH RIVER

SAETHYR

LOWYRN

NERIN RIVER

TEYRNAS

JEMAYRT

VOGEL MOUNTAINS

BYYAR

AVERIL

THARYS OCEAN

KEREU

NORTHERN REALM
OF
ELTRIAR

MADAN OCH

NORTH SEA

WALLACH RIVER

GALION

COLD SEA

TIRSHAY

NOWAN

*SALVATION
SEA*

MALLR RIVER

BRAN MARO

*GULF OF
MARO*

TREILEAN

NERIN RIVER

TAROD

*GULF OF
SYKERIA*

1

Springtide

Realta Haar lost sight of her father as she walked through the bustling marketplace. Hundreds of merchants and travelers had arrived in the small village for the annual Springtide Festival, the mark of the new year and the start of trade season. Vendors, occupying every available space in the market, cried out their wares, claiming their goods were better than the ones in the neighboring stall. People, more than she could count, crowded around her. Elbows jostling. Strangers staring.

She maneuvered through the crowd, breaking away at the market's edge. Breathing room.

Where could her father have gone? He had been by her side just a moment ago. And what of Master and Mistress Loy? And her aunt and uncle, for that matter. She had only turned away for a few seconds.

She glanced back at the market. People flooded her vision. Some were dressed in simple farming clothes and wore familiar faces. Others wore colorful cloaks and dresses made of fine silk. Wealthy merchants from the eastern side of the river hoping to be the first to cross Caman's Pass.

A creeping feeling seized Realta, like vines growing over her skin. A feeling she got whenever somebody was watching her. Of course somebody was watching her, she rationalized. Hundreds of people were in the market alone, and likely hundreds more in the village. A few were bound to be looking in her direction. She shouldn't be so paranoid.

She turned and locked eyes with a tall man standing on the other side of the main road. The man had closely cropped black hair and wore a dark blue, knee-length coat. A patch with a flying raven was sown on the coat's left shoulder. At his waist rested a scabbard painted black and blue. He had one hand on the hilt of his sword. The man stared at her, eyes wide and... Confused? Yes, confused. The emotional melted away, replaced by a predatory smile. Realta was suddenly grateful for the crowd.

The man broke away his gaze and continued down the road. A red earring pierced his ear. He headed for Tolman's Inn, sparing a single glance over his shoulder. Realta shivered.

"Realta!"

She screamed, jumping and spinning around. Behind her stood Charity Loy, hazel eyes bright with her ever-present smile.

"Found you." Realta's best friend folded her arms in triumph, as though this had been a game.

"Did you see that man?" Realta asked, her voice shaking. Why did Charity have to sneak up on her? "The man with red earrings?"

"No, but I did see a man with a hawk tattoo on his forehead. Why?"

"He looked at me weird." Realta's face grew warm. Where had her father gone? She scanned the crowd. Hundreds of faces. Perhaps that was a good thing. With so many people in Vala, her odds of running into him again were quite low.

"Weird how?"

The creeping feeling returned, crawling up the back of her neck. "Do you know where my father is?"

"I heard my father mention having business in Tolman's Inn. Your father must have gone with him."

Of course. Master Loy would want his servant with him while conducting business, as a witness if nothing else. Tolman's Inn. The same place that creepy man went. Well, if he tried to start something, Callum Haar would end it.

"Let's go over there," Charity said, grabbing Realta by the arm and leading her to a nearby vendor. Realta spied a girl with a blue ribbon in her black hair watching over a younger boy. Daisy and Rain Nortine, her and Charity's closest friends in the village. Well, Daisy was their friend. Her younger brother just tagged along.

"Look at this thing!" Rain exclaimed, taking a strange implement off the merchant's table and waving one end in Daisy's face. The implement was made of two cylindrical pieces of smoothed wood held together by a short length of rope, about as long as a man's hand.

"Hey lad!" yelled the merchant, a scrawny man with a patch of hair missing. His accent gave him away as Lowyrnic. "What on this world do ya think you're doing?" He snatched the object out of Rain's hand.

"He was just looking," Daisy retorted, hands on her hips.

"Just looking? Ya think this is a toy?" He shook the object in their faces.

Rain shrugged. Daisy acknowledged Charity and Realta's presence with a quick nod, then turned her focus back on the merchant.

The merchant called over to the vendor, a fruit seller, in the neighboring stall. "Hey, Jiselle, lemme see one of them sun melons."

The other merchant, a stout woman with gray hair, glared at him.

"Don't give me them eyes, woman. I'll reimburse ya."

Jiselle rolled her eyes and handed the man a pale melon about the size of a person's head.

"Ya see," the merchant explained. Realta stepped closer to get a better look. "These are Sykerian strikers. The deadliest weapon in the South Lands. Used by the personal guards of the Empress herself." Holding onto one piece of wood, the merchant raised the strikers over his head and slammed the other end down onto the melon. The unsuspecting fruit burst open, bits of rind and juice splattering on the small crowd.

Realta jumped back, wiping the orange remains off her face and dress. Rain screamed, clutching his older sister by the arm. Daisy glared at the man. Likely, he'd be paid a visit by Mistress Nortine before the day was done.

"How much?" asked Charity, pointing at the weapon.

"Charity!" Realta exclaimed.

"What?"

"You really think your parents would let you have something like that?"

"Why not? You're the one complaining about people staring. With those, nobody will ever bother you again."

Realta studied the strikers. Bits of melon dripped off one end. "But still..."

"Spies! Assassins!"

Heart leaping into her throat, Realta hid behind Charity. Daisy, grabbing Rain by the hand, took off running. Others froze in their steps. Travelers and merchants exchanged worried looks and searched for signs of danger. Locals merely stopped to watch.

Across the street, the village healer, Darran Zall, had burst out of his small house, the door slamming against the wall. Dozens of eyes fixed on Zall, watching him attack insects with a rolled-up piece of paper.

"They'll kill us all! Assassins!" He slammed the paper onto the porch railing, smashing a fly to bits.

"Stars above," said the Lowyrnic merchant, his voice barely audible over the screaming. "The mad healer lives."

"You assumed he was dead?" Charity questioned.

The merchant muttered something in Lowyrnic, wiping away the melon and placing the strikers along with his other wares. He called out to the crowd, which had lost interest once everyone identified the source of the screaming.

"Let's go to Tolman's Inn," said Realta, struggled to keep a steady voice. She had known Darran Zall her whole life, but like everyone else in Vala, did her best to maintain a healthy distance. Most people, men and women, went to her aunt for medical help, though Esme Haar primarily worked as a midwife. But Esme lived outside of the village. When it came to emergencies, Zall was usually the only choice. "Maybe your father finished his business."

"Good idea," Charity replied with a smile. She crossed the main road and headed straight for the healer's house.

"What are you doing?" Realta whispered.

"I have a question."

"Does it have to be for him?" Zall continued swatting bugs, adding colorful swears to his accusations of spies. Realta noticed the blacksmith's wife speaking with Esme and pointing at the healer. With a quick nod, Esme hurried towards him. She was one of only a handful who could calm the man.

Realta then looked down the road to the inn. She could leave right now and look for her father by herself. Aunt Esme would make sure no harm came to Charity, and she had gone to the inn numerous times. Mistress Tolman was always kind and even-tempered. Nothing to fear.

What if Red Earrings is still in there?

Gritting her teeth, she kept pace with Charity. Mindful to stay one step behind her.

"A joyous Springtide to you, Healer Zall," Charity said at the same time Esme reached the house. She eyed the healer warily.

The rolled paper raised, the grizzled man glared at Charity with piercing, dark eyes. He pointed at her and said, "You. The Loy girl. And not the rude one. Yes, that is joyous." He lowered the paper, noticing Esme.

"I have a small question."

"What?"

"Why do you consider flies to be assassins?"

Zall smiled, baring his perfect teeth. "Have you ever been in a surgery, girl?"

Charity shook his head. "Not yet."

"You see," Zall said, walking down the short steps. Realta moved closer to her aunt, wishing Charity would do the same. "When a wound isn't cleaned and bandaged properly, it risks infection, and that attracts flies. After the flies begin biting the wound, it starts to fester. Now, if festering occurs on an arm or a leg, the limb can be amputated and the patient lives. Most of the time. But a torso wound, that can't be fixed by the same method. Infection spreads. The patient dies. A surgery full of flies is the last place you want to be."

Charity nodded, smiling. "Thank you, Healer Zall. That was very informative."

And very gross. Can we go now?

"And what of you, midwife?" Zall asked Esme. "Is that Seltachai husband of yours around here?"

"Yes, and we are quite well. How are you today?" Healer Zall's addled mind had associated Realta's uncle with a blood drinking creature from folk tales that read people's minds for reasons that were purely his own. Most of his respect for Esme came from the fact that she was married to a monster.

"It's the flies," he replied, eyes wide. "Every Springtide brings flies. And people call today joyous. It's insanity!"

"Do you want help?" she asked, walking towards the steps.

"From you?" The healer shrugged. "Better than half these idiots," he gestured towards the marketplace. He disappeared into his house, muttering under his breath.

Esme gave Realta and Charity a quick nod, as though to say, "I will take it from here", and followed the healer inside. Realta wished she had an ounce of her aunt's bravery.

Charity, bouncing on the balls of her feet, headed for Tolman's Inn.

"Why did you talk to him?" Realta asked, keeping her voice low. She could have easily asked Esme the same question and gotten the same answer.

"Why not?"

Realta sighed. She ought to know better than to question Charity Loy.

A steady stream of people entered and exited Tolman's Inn. The inn contained over twenty rooms, and at three stories, it was the tallest building in Vala. But during Springtide, too many people visited the village for the inn to hold. Latecomers had to rent spare rooms in the nearby tavern or in people's homes and barns. The Loys sometimes hosted people, but not often. Merchants did not want to stay that far from the village center.

The common room was completely full, every table occupied. Some had to stand while eating their midday meal. Vera Tolman, a lithe woman with sharp brown eyes, moved about the common room, checking on guests and making sure the serving girls were not being overworked.

A lanky young man with a shock of dark brown hair exited the kitchen door. Lok Tolman, Vera's only son, balanced two plates of food, one in each hand. Quickly scanning the room, he scurried over to a table where two men sat, passing the roaring fireplace.

Odd. The day was quite warm for Springtide. That fire did not need to be so large.

Lok placed the food in front of the men, Sardic Loy, Charity's father, and Symund Ritt, the village's master carpenter. So that's who Master Loy had business with. Likely discussing repairs for the farmhouse's front porch steps. She and Charity walked over to them.

"Hello, my dear," said Master Loy, seeing his youngest daughter.

The large man smiled, nearly splitting his bearded face in two. His hazel eyes, the same mixture of green and light brown as Charity's, shone in the light. "Had your fill of the market for today?"

"Not yet. Realta wanted to know if you'd seen her father. And a joyous Springtide to you, Master Ritt."

The balding man returned the greeting.

"Callum was in here a moment ago," said Master Loy, glancing around the crowded space. "Well, he can't have wandered far."

"Hello, Charity and Realta. How are you today?" asked Vera Tolman, walking up to the table.

"Very well, thank you," Charity replied. Realta merely nodded. Being surrounded by people in the open market was one thing, but the enclosed common room was making her feel claustrophobic.

"Wonderful. And you, Sardic and Symund? Did that project up in Lothian pan out?"

"Still waiting on the letter," Master Ritt replied.

"Can't ask for a better day for Springtide," replied Master Loy. "Blue skies, warm sun. But do you have to have the fire so hot?"

"Fire?" Mistress Tolman turned towards the fireplace. Lok, in his awkward way, ambled between people, passing the fireplace. A man stopped him, asking a question. Lok shook his head and pointed at the kitchen door, but the man was insistent. The flames leapt up. A crack sounded as a log split in half. "Lok!"

The boy jumped, turning wide eyes towards his mother.

"Why have you got the fire going? Put it out."

Lok complied, grabbing the empty water bucket and ducking into the kitchen. He nearly collided with a serving girl in the process.

"Sorry about that. You know Lok," Mistress Tolman said with a pained smile.

"Not a problem."

"Realta," Charity nudged her with her elbow, "didn't you say that weird man had red earrings?"

"Yes." Oh, no.

"He's over there, talking to your father." Charity pointed towards the back corner. Sure enough, Red Earrings took the seat opposite Callum Haar. Her father seemed more interested in his pint of ale than the other man.

Realta contemplated her next move. She had wanted to find Callum, and she had. But she also wanted to avoid Red Earrings, avoid his predatory stares. But why had this man taken an interest in her father? Curiosity overriding fear, she walked towards the small table.

"Can I help you, sir?" asked Callum, taking a sip.

"I need to hire a guide to take my team through Caman's Pass," Red Earrings explained. His voice was not as deep as Realta imagined. Instead, it was a bit raspy, and he spoke with an odd inflection.

"I'm sure there are plenty of guides up for the task."

"I hear you're one of the best."

Callum sighed. He had worked as a guide before working for Master Loy, helping merchants and travelers cross the mountain pass. As custom, Caman's Pass opened today and would remain open until Autumntide. Conditions up in the mountains were too dangerous during winter. "I'm retired."

"I will pay you however much you want. Name your price." The man leaned forward, eyes fixed on Callum.

"That's not possible." Callum rolled up his sleeve. On his left wrist were tattooed two thin bands, the width of Realta's little finger. Inside the bands were two diamonds, the mark of an indentured servant. "I'm under contract."

The man grimaced. "I'll buy you out. My employer promised to pay any expense, so long as our task is complete."

"No thanks. My master is a good man. And if this task is so important, why am I speaking to you and not your employer?"

"My employer is back in East Bridge. A thief has stolen invaluable items from his house and his best horse. My team was hired to track her down, and I fear she's going through the Pass. If I don't hire a guide by this evening, we will lose her."

Callum calmly took another sip of ale. "Is that the best story you can come up with?"

Red Earrings looked at him, aghast. "You think I'm lying?"

"Come on. You claim a thief stole something from someone and now said thief just so happens to be right here in Vala, or close enough."

"It is the truth. Most of it." The man's face grew red, his blue eyes burning. "Look, I have it on damned good authority that this thief is heading through Caman's Pass, and it's my job to catch her and bring her to justice in Teyrnas."

"I thought it was East Bridge," Callum smiled.

Realta inched closer to her father. Red Earrings grew angrier by the second. She knew Callum could handle himself in a fight, but she had no desire to see one start.

Red Earrings collected himself. "She was originally in Teyrnas. She stole one of the king's horses, and my team was hired to find her. A week later, that horse was discovered in a stable belonging to a silversmith in East Bridge, his own horse having been stolen."

"So she's wanted in both East Bridge and Teyrnas. Why not just say that?"

"This information is sensitive, and..." The man finally noticed Realta standing at Callum's side. That leering smile returned. Imaginary vines tugged at her skin, crawling up the back of her head, down her arms.

Father is right there. He won't let anything bad happen.

"Is this your daughter?" the man asked.

"Yes." Realta's presence did not surprise Callum in the least. All those years as a guide had trained him to notice small details and changes.

"I can see the resemblance." Not that their resemblance was hard to miss. Realta and her father had coal black hair, dark brown eyes, and a ruddy skin tone that was common in the Hinterlands. As well as angular faces and slightly oval eyes.

Callum polished off the rest of his ale and stood. "I must be going. My master has finished his business here." Realta turned and saw Master Loy shaking hands with the carpenter.

"Please reconsider." The man stood, placing a hand on his sword hilt. Realta stiffened, but he made no move to draw the weapon. A reflex, then. "The reward for this thief's capture and return will be enough for you and your daughter to live in comfort for the rest of your lives."

"I'm sure it is," Callum replied with a hint of sarcasm. "Wait. Did you say return?"

"Well, yes."

"So not only do you want me to leave my master without any notice to go traveling in the Pass, but you also want me to journey all the way to Teyrnas. Sorry, no deal, Master..."

"Kanton. Dane Kanton, Captain of the—"

"A joyous Springtide to you, Master Kanton." He turned to leave, placing a gentle hand on Realta's shoulder. "Come, Realta. Let's see what your cousins are up to."

"Master Haar!" Kanton called out. Several eyes looked his way.

"That is not my title."

Red faced, Kanton stormed out of the common room. Two other men wearing the same dark blue coats with a raven insignia met him at the door.

"Well?" asked one.

Kanton shoved him out of the doorway, exiting the inn. The other man shrugged, and the two quickly followed Kanton. The crowd murmured about the incident briefly, then resumed their normal conversations. It was none of their business.

"What was that about?" asked Master Loy, cocking a thumb towards the door.

"A child who doesn't like hearing the word 'no'."

Master Loy laughed, a deep-chested sound that echoed off the common room's walls. Everyone turned to see him, many smiling in return. Any lingering uneasy dissipated. "Well, to the Abyss with him, then. Come! Let's see what the rest of the family is up to." Master Loy paid the serving girl and led the way to the main road, Callum walking in step with him. Realta and Charity trailed a pace behind.

"What did the Earring Man want with your father?"

Realta told her about the thief.

"That's so weird. Why not contact the guardsmen at Watchtower? They have the final say of who can enter the Pass."

"Good point." Dane Kanton could have traveled the extra fifteen miles to Watchtower, given the guardsmen the thief's description or a drawing, and they would have taken care of the rest. All Kanton and his team had to do was wait. No need to single out her father. Callum hadn't gone through Caman's Pass since Realta was a baby. Ask one of the younger, and not to mention active, guides.

"There's Mother," Charity pointed. Aida Loy and Charity's two older sisters, Nina and Bridget, stood in front of a vendor's stall. Leather-bound books were stacked all over the table. Realta's Uncle Kel and her cousins, Gareth and Estrid, were with them, though Kel stood off to the side with the hood of his cloak up. The collection of scars on the left side of his face tended to draw stares.

Charity waved at the group.

Mistress Loy waved back, motioning them to come closer. The merchant smiled, seeing the crowd double.

"Look at this, my dear," Mistress Loy said to her husband, holding up a book. "Tobert's *Complete History of the Kings of Teyrnas*. And only priced at one silver piece."

"Only one silver?" said Master Loy as he inspected the book. "Why, that's a steal!"

All the books in the world would not be enough for Mistress Loy. Every shelf at the farmhouse was bursting with them. Esme and Kel, both educated at the Academy and eager to keep learning, took full advantage of the reading material.

Esme glided over, wrapping her arms around Kel's thin shoulders.

"I hear Zall's in another one of his moods," Kel whispered.

"You have good hearing, my love."

"Think it will help if I talk to him?" A hint of a smile crept into his voice.

"I doubt that."

"Esme," said Mistress Loy, handing the book over to her, "this is an extended volume. It includes King Logan."

"Really?"

As Esme flipped to the end of the book, Callum whispered in Kel's ear, too faintly for Realta to hear. The scarred man nodded.

Realta caught a flash of movement on her left side. She spied Dane Kanton standing several yards away, glaring at her and her father, that predatory smiled plastered on his face. One hand gripped the hilt of his sword. Realta reached for her father.

Before she could draw Callum's attention, Kanton had disappeared into the crowd.

2

The Hayloft

In the early morning light, Realta selected her cloak from off the rack and donned it. Her uncle sat in a nearby chair, adjusting the straps on his leg brace and grimacing. He had shattered the leg in an accident long before she was born, and the bones never healed correctly. Most of the time, Kel also used an elbow crutch, but yesterday he decided to experiment. He hadn't realized how long they would be in the village.

The Springtide festivities had lasted well into the night. Singing and dancing on the village green. Even a fireworks display. Mayor Gan must have paid a small fortune for those. It wasn't every year they saw fireworks.

Realta had been on the lookout for Dane Kanton, fearing the man would reappear and force Callum to lead him into the Pass. But he never did. She hoped Kanton had wised up and gone to Watchtower, the more sensible method to catch his thief.

The moons were high in the sky by the time they returned to the Loy farm, where both families lived in the sprawling farmhouse. Realta wished she could have slept in to make up for the lost hours, but the chores would still be waiting. Besides, the two farmhands, Ander and Lon Millar, were up and about an hour before Realta had dressed and braided her hair. Not to mention Mistress Loy was already preparing breakfast. No room to complain.

"Are you all right, Kel?" she asked. The simple act of walking out here and putting on the brace left him winded.

"Just this leg," he smiled, though his blue eyes reflected pain. The scars crisscrossing the left half of his gaunt face added to the effect. They were a souvenir from the same accident that ruined his leg. "Don't tell your aunt?"

"Only if you will."

"Deal." Picking up his crutch, Kel stood and made his way to the kitchen.

Realta walked out the door and down the porch steps, mindful of the broken step. The sun had just risen over the horizon, yellow light hiding behind the trees. She pulled her cloak closer as she made her way to the barn. The nightly chill lingered. Mornings would not be considered warm for another month.

At least it isn't snowing. She smiled, recalling the freak snowstorm two years ago. An entire foot of snow in one day! All the adults claimed to have never seen anything like it.

A flash of black movement caught Realta's eye. She turned and saw Shadow, the Loys' black gelding, grazing on the dew-covered grass. Next to him stood Dust, Kel and Esme's painted mare. Odd. Why would both horses be out at the same time? Ander knew better than to let the horses wander, especially Shadow.

Looking around the yard, Realta did not see anyone. Ander had left the house no more than half an hour ago. Where had he gone?

He's just in the barn cleaning out the stables, she assured herself. He tied up Shadow, but the horse chewed away the knot. And Dust did the same? Not likely.

Realta continued towards the barn. The sweet scents of hay and worked leather greeted her. But it was strangely still. The milk cows, Dona and Deirdri, should have been lowing. Both animals were silent. She walked over to inspect them. They appeared to be well. They were eating and moving about in their stalls. Albeit silently.

Invisible vines crept over her skin. Someone was watching her. Probably Ander or his brother. Ander was nice, though he preferred to keep to himself. Lon, on the other hand, had a tendency to jump out and scare people. The action had once earned him a broken nose from Callum. Steeling herself, she turned to face the source.

In the far corner, Ander laid face down, motionless. A small pool of blood surrounded his head.

Heart racing and legs going numb, Realta rushed to his side. Had he fallen? Hit his head? Neither possibility made sense. The farmhand was next to the empty stall, the one Master Loy reserved for a spare horse. There was nothing to fall from. Nothing to hit his head on.

Realta placed a shaking hand on Ander's forehead. Still warm. A soft groan escaped his lips. She breathed a quiet prayer of thanks. Ander was alive. But how extensive was the injury? A simple scalp laceration was one thing. Esme could bind that in minutes. But what if he had a concussion? Healer Zall might help, unless he was in one of his moods...

Screaming.

Realta froze, heart beating in her ears. Heavy boots shuffling on wood. Up above. The hayloft. This was no accident.

The screaming came again, followed by a man's voice.

Realta found herself walking towards the ladder. How many people were up there, and why were they fighting.

"Come here, you little... Oh!" the man cried out. The shuffling grew louder, more frantic. They were fighting. She needed to call her father or Master Loy. Lon ought to be outside by now. She needed to get someone who could help, but she couldn't let them come in blind. She had to get a better look.

Glancing around, Realta spied the milk pail. Not the best weapon, but she had no skill for knives or arrows. And it wasn't like she wanted to join the fight. All she wanted was a quick glance to see who they were up against.

With her free hand, she gripped the siding and began to climb, pausing between each rung, listening to the fight. They were exchanging blows. The hayloft's wooden floor creaked under the excess weight.

This is stupid, this is stupid...

"Aah!"

Realta pressed against the ladder as a large object fell past her, hitting the ground floor with a sickening thud. Forcing herself to look, she saw that the object was a man. A man wearing a dark, knee-length coat. One of the men who had been with Dane Kanton.

"Oh, Great Creator..."

Realta's head shot up at the sound. Standing at the hayloft's edge was a young woman, not much older than herself. She wore ragged men's clothes, and her pale, gaunt face sported fresh bruises. Her sandy brown hair had been hacked short, midway to her shoulders. And her eyes...

Her eyes were the same shade of blue as Kel's. In fact, her hair was the exact same color as his, as well. And her face. That was Kel's face!

How could this girl look just like her uncle? Gareth and Estrid both resembled Esme, with dark hair and ruddy faces, though Estrid had inherited her father's blue eyes. It could not be real. A trick for the light. She saw what she wanted to see.

Of Ander's attacker?

"Please," she said, drawing in ragged breaths. She crouched down, meeting Realta at eye level. "I didn't mean..." She slowly reached for her belt. A knife!

Panic flooding her, Realta swung her pail upwards, bringing it down on the girl's head, metal contacting flesh and bone. She collapsed in a heap, one arm hanging listlessly over the side.

Realta rushed down the ladder, forcing her arms and legs to move. She took the steps one at a time. Two at a time. She lost her balance, dropping the pail. It clattered onto the floor and rolled towards the fallen man. Jumping the last three rungs, she took off running. Out of the corner of her eye, she saw Ander propping himself up on his elbows.

But what about the other man? Was he still alive? Realta didn't think to check.

"Father! Master Loy!" she yelled, running towards the house, her mind racing. Why had the girl and that man been fighting? Who started it? Why were they in the Loys' barn?

And why did that girl look just like Kel?

Please... The girl's plea echoed in her mind.

"What's going on?" asked Master Loy, bursting through the front door, Callum right on his heels. "Are you hurt, Realta?"

"No," she said, taking deep gulps of air between words. She pointed towards the barn. "Ander's hurt. There was a fight. A man and a woman. A girl. In the hayloft. The man fell..."

"Are they still in there?" asked Callum.

"Yes. The girl is knocked out, I think. I don't know about the man." She had never seen someone fall from that height before. Growing up, everyone had warned her to be careful in the hayloft. A fall like that could kill her... Her hands were shaking. Was that normal?

Callum dashed off to the barn without another word.

"Come inside, dear," said Master Loy, placing a protective arm around her shoulders. "Sit down, calm yourself. Your father will take care of it," he said as they entered the house.

"What happened?" asked Mistress Loy, rounding the corner from the dining room. Esme and Gareth poked their heads around the corner.

"An intruder in the barn. Esme, there's an injured man. Fell from the hayloft. Callum is already there."

"Stars above," she muttered. She headed for the door.

"Should I stay here?" Gareth asked her.

"Yes." Esme rushed out the door. Gareth breathed a short sigh of relief.

"Lon!" Master Loy called out. Ander's younger brother emerged from the dining room.

"Yes, sir?"

"Saddle Shadow and ride into the village. Tell Mayor Gan to bring the guard. And the healer, if he'll come. Your brother's been injured."

Lon paled and obeyed, running for the yard.

The village. A ten-minute ride if Lon rode at a gallop. Then fifteen or so minutes to convince the mayor to ride out. Another ten, no fifteen minutes on the return trip. The mayor was an older man. He would not want to ride so fast, even in an emergency. So that was forty minutes minimum. Might as well be an hour.

Realta felt herself being guided to the dining room. Charity and Estrid, setting the table for the morning meal, froze. A plate slipped out of her hand and clanked on the wooden table. Estrid, the youngest of the household at twelve, looked to her father for assurance. Kel, standing off to the side, stared at Realta, blue eyes wide. She had to look away from him. Charity's sisters emerged from the doorway leading to the kitchen.

"Realta, are you all right?" asked Charity, her face turning white.

"Did you say there was an intruder, Father?" asked Nina, drying her hands on her apron. "Where's Ander?" She looked around frantically.

"Callum and Esme are helping him, and Lon's gone to get more help," Master Loy calmly explained. He motioned for Realta to take a seat. She hadn't realized that her legs were numb.

"Looks like she saw a Shade," Bridget muttered. Mistress Loy gave her a disapproving glance.

The front door opened with a bang. The family jumped and whirled around. Callum entered the room. He propped up Ander, who was still bleeding from his head wound. Callum's other hand gripped the girl by the shirt, forcing her forward. Her hands were bound in front of her, and her mouth was gagged. She glanced around the crowded room, eyes wide and frightened. Realta must have only stunned her.

"Ander!" Nina cried, rushing towards him. She took the farmhand by the arm and escorted him to the far end of the dining table, helping him take a seat. "Bridget, get some water and a washcloth," she said, gingerly pushing back his hair.

Bridget stared at Ander, frozen. Realta did not blame her. Blood coated one side of Ander's face, matting his hair and staining his shirt a deep crimson.

Mistress Loy instructed her middle daughter to sit and hurried into the kitchen for the water.

"Should I help?" Estrid asked Kel in her quiet voice. Kel nodded, and the girl hurried after Mistress Loy.

Callum shoved the girl forward, forcing her into the seat opposite Realta. Callum and Master Loy flanked her sides. Kel slowly made his way towards her. Gareth had disappeared.

Realta could not help but stare. This girl looked exactly like her uncle, and those bruises on the left side of her face were helping.

"Now, what do we have here?" asked Master Loy, getting a better look. Did he see the resemblance, too? "A thief, perhaps?" The girl looked away, staring down at her battered shoes. "What did Esme say?"

"The man who fell is a member of the King's Guard. He's unconscious and has multiple broken bones." Callum hesitated. "He might live."

Master Loy's expression darkened.

Ander cried out as Nina applied a damp washcloth to the side of his head. The white fabric was instantly soaked red.

"He might need stitches," Charity said, inspecting the gash. The color had returned to her face, and her eyes shone brightly.

"I will heat up a needle if it comes to that," replied Mistress Loy. She gave her husband a weary look, and he replied with a sigh. They were fine with Charity learning what they called 'practical medicine' from Esme. Her wanting to learn more concerned them.

"The fact that he regained consciousness so quickly is a good sign," Charity continued, oblivious to her parents' concern. "Prolonged unconsciousness would have indicated a serious brain injury. And wounds to the scalp tend to bleed heavily, even the small ones. Perhaps he won't need stitches after all."

"Please tell me you hear this from Esme," said Nina, giving her youngest sister a weird look.

Charity bit down on her lower lip and averted her eyes. She seemed to shrink. "I read it in one of Healer Zall's books."

"The healer?" Bridget blurted out. "Why are you reading his books?"

"I was just curious."

Mistress Loy placed her hands on Charity's shoulders. "We have plenty of books here. And you can ask Esme all you want about medicine. Isn't that right, Callum?"

Callum replied with a quick nod. His sister, after all, had studied medicine at the Academy.

Ander groaned and looked around the room. He jabbed a finger at the girl. "Her! That little bitch hit me with a shovel!"

The girl winced, as though Ander had slapped her.

"Why?" Realta heard herself ask. The girl looked at her with her uncle's bright eyes. Why hadn't Kel...? Realta studied her uncle. All of his focus was on that girl. Not on Ander. Not on his own children. Nor had he gone to assist his wife.

He sees it, too. And he can't explain it either. Realta was not sure what to make of that fact.

"The mayor and the village guard will find the reason when they arrive," said Master Loy.

"Or we can ask her ourselves," replied Callum, exchanging a quick glance with Kel. He saw the resemblance, too. He must have.

Master Loy stroked his beard. "I don't see a problem with that. Gan might not like it, but we'll say it was a way to verify the lass's story."

An acrid scent wafted into the room.

"Drat," said Mistress Loy. "Bridget, get that food off the stove. Nina, Charity, help me move Ander to the couch. And Estrid, see if you can find your brother." Three of the four girls did as instructed.

"Can't I stay here?" asked Charity.

Mistress Loy gave her a pained look. "They're just going to ask the girl some questions. There's no reason—"

"But Realta is staying."

Realta shot her best friend an accusatory glance. She had hoped the three men would forget she was there until halfway through their questioning. Many times people forgot she was nearby. A benefit of being quiet. She wanted, needed to know who this girl was and why she resembled Kel so strongly. Now, she might be forced to leave.

"The girls can stay," said Callum. *Thank you.* "She can't do anything with her hands bound. If that's all right," he looked to Master Loy.

The bigger man nodded. "So long as they sit at the other end of the table. Just to be safe."

Mistress Loy sighed and muttered disapprovals under her breath. She joined Nina and Ander in the living room. Charity beamed, thanking her father. Sometimes, Realta did not understand Charity at all. They sat at the table's far end.

Callum untied the gag, tossing the cloth onto the table. Part of the blue fabric was stained red. The girl's lower lip had been split during the fight.

"What's your name?" asked Master Loy, crossing his arms. Kel sat opposite the girl, studying her.

"Serena," she whispered.

"Why were you in my barn, Serena? Were you trying to steal something?"

"No. Just wanted a place to..." Serena hunched her shoulders, growing smaller. "Place to sleep."

"Then why not ask? Plenty of farmers rent out their barns this time of year."

"I didn't want to be seen."

"Why's that?" asked Callum. "And why were you fighting with a member of the King's Guard?"

Serena shook her head, biting down on her lip.

"How old are you, Serena?" asked Kel, his voice calm and soft.

"Twenty-one."

The men exchanged knowing looks. "Girl, if you're twenty-one," replied Callum, "then I'm an Averillian spice merchant."

"Seventeen," Serena sighed. Kel leaned back in his chair, deep in thought.

"Where are your parents, lass?" Master Loy asked.

"Dead." Her eyes glistened.

Master Loy sighed. "Sounds like she didn't have much of a choice."

"Perhaps." Callum reached down and removed a pouch from Serena's belt. He spilled the contents onto the table. Half a dozen coins of different values.

Realta's heart sank. It wasn't a knife. Serena was trying to buy her silence, hoping a handful of coins would be enough to forget that fight.

"Seems like enough to rent a room," said Callum, picking up a gold piece. More than enough. Serena could have rented a room at Tolman's for a full week with that coin.

"But not enough to get me where I'm going," Serena replied.

"Which is where? The other side of Caman's Pass?"

Serena shrugged. Sandy brown hair obscured her face.

Callum leaned down, meeting her at eye level. "Serena, did you steal a horse?"

No reply.

"Have you ever been to Teyrnas?"

Charity leaned closer to Realta and whispered, "Why ask about Teyrnas?"

Realta's mind clicked. "The man in Tolman's Inn yesterday. The one with red earrings. He's looking for a horse thief from Teyrnas, claims she stole one of the king's horses."

"Your father thinks that girl is the thief?"

"Seems like it." Realta paused, wondering if she ought to ask this question. "Charity, doesn't she look familiar?"

Charity studied Serena. "Not really. Why?"

"No reason."

"The king's horse?" asked Serena. "How would I steal the

king's horse?"

"Have you ever met a man named Dane Kanton?" asked Callum.

All the blood drained from Serena's face. Her mouth opened, but no words formed.

"Is that the man from Tolman's Inn?" Master Loy asked.

"Yes."

"Kanton?" Kel questioned. "You didn't tell me his name was Kanton."

Serena struggled against the rope tied around her wrists. She bit at the knot like a wild animal caught in a trap. The rope began to fray. Callum placed a gentle hand on her shoulder.

"Are you really telling me the truth, Serena?"

"Answer me, Callum." Kel met his brother-in-law with a level stare, a strange tension leaking into his voice.

"Sardic," said Mistress Loy, "Lon's back. He's brought the mayor and some guardsmen."

"That lad has good timing, I'll give him that," replied Master Loy. "Send them in."

A moment later, Mayor Helfin Gan, a man with graying hair and a purple earring in his right ear, entered the dining room with three men dressed in blue overcoats. Each was armed with a small dagger and a cudgel. The mayor shook hands with Master Loy and Callum. He gave only a passing glance at Kel who returned the favor.

Realta studied Mayor Gan's earring. It was an odd piece of jewelry. Very few people, men or women, in the Hinterlands wore earrings. But Mayor Gan had a reasonable explanation for it. He claimed the Hiraeth had kidnapped him as a boy and gave him the earring as a reminder not to trespass in their lands. The story was a bit fantastical, but no one questioned Gan. Not even Kel, who actually was Hiraethi.

Did Kanton receive his earrings from the Hiraeth, too? But Kel did not wear earrings. Though his earlobes contained jagged tears, as if earrings had been ripped out.

"So, this is your thief," said Mayor Gan, looking Serena up and down. The girl continued to struggle against her bonds. The knot was partially loose. "And a lively one, at that." Gan motioned one of the guards forward. He held a pair of manacles in his hands.

"Any damage other than what she did to the Millar boy's head?"

"Yes," replied Master Loy. "She attacked a member of the King's Guard. Hurt him pretty badly."

Gan paled.

Esme entered the room with Gareth in tow. The boy halted, seeing so many unfamiliar faces in the house.

Gan greeted her and asked about the guardsman.

"His right arm is shattered, and his shoulder is dislocated. I suspect he has several broken ribs, as well. Possibly a concussion."

"Not bad, from a fall like that," replied Gan.

"He got lucky. His arm took the brunt of the fall. If he'd landed on his back..." Esme merely shook her head.

"Is he conscious?" asked Callum.

"Yes, but he won't answer any of my questions."

"Don't worry," said Gan. "I'll have one of my men—"

"Aah!" The guardsman recoiled, clutching his hand. "She bit me!"

A second guardsman backhanded Serena across the face, nearly knocking her out of the chair. Gareth fled from the room.

Realta spied blood seeping between the first guardsman's fingers. Charity stood and rounded the table, her eyes fixed on the wound. Realta groaned inwardly and trailed behind her friend.

Serena spat bloody saliva onto the guard's face. He raised his hand, preparing for another hit. Master Loy moved between him and the thief.

"Now that's enough, Alam Mund." Master Loy's face grew red. "Or do I have to involve your mother?"

The guardsman blanched, instantly lowering his hand. "No need for that, Master Loy. But you saw what she did to Mak's hand."

"Guardsmen do not right wrongs with wrongs. Isn't that right, Mayor Gan?"

"Yes," said the mayor, who acted like he had been lost in a reverie. He glanced around the room, getting his bearings on the here and now.

"May I help you?" came Mistress Loy's voice from the front room. The door opened with a bang, forcing everyone's attention away from Serena. The third guardsman went to investigate.

"Who do you think you are," Mistress Loy demanded, "barging into my house!"

No one replied. Heavy footsteps echoed through the silent house.

Dane Kanton appeared in the doorway. He looked at Serena and smiled.

3

A Boon

"Master Haar," said Dane Kanton, sauntering into the room, all eyes fixed on him. "I see you found my thief."

Realta, white knuckling the back of a chair, studied everyone's faces. Better to look at them than face Kanton's stares. The three guardsmen looked at each other, baffled. Mayor Gan picked at his fingernails, forcing himself not to look Kanton's way. She sensed they had spoken earlier, and it had not ended amicably. Mistress Loy, hands on her hips, scowled at the man. Master Loy moved in front of Serena, who had gone as white as a sheet. Callum and Kel glared at Dane, the latter rising to meet him at eye level.

"It was chance, nothing more," Callum replied, his voice low. Three other guards in the same coats as Kanton entered the house, two men and one woman whose hair was cut just above the shoulders. Esme trailed them. She and Kel exchanged worried looks.

Kanton smirked and addressed the mayor. "Your services here are no longer required. Call off your men and sign this." He removed a document from his coat pocket. The royal seal, a raven imprinted on dark blue wax, rested at the top and bottom of the document. The same shade of blue as Dane Kanton's coat.

Mayor Gan read over the paper, nodding. "Do you have a pen?" he asked the Loys. Charity ducked into the next room and returned with pen and ink, placing them on the table. Realta raised an eyebrow. Charity shrugged.

Well, the faster this is over, the sooner Kanton can leave. Wait, did that mean Serena was leaving with him? How would she get her answers?

The mayor signed the document. "Mak, Alam, Leaf," he addressed the village guards, "time to go."

"What about her?" asked Leaf, cocking a thumb towards Serena.

"She's in the hands of the King's Guard now."

The three guards looked at one another in awe. The King's Guard. Soldiers personally selected by the king himself. Realta had only heard it mentioned in history books. The guardsmen shuffled out of the house, saluting Kanton and his cohorts while saying their goodbyes to the Loys and Esme. Mayor Gan moved to follow.

Dane Kanton placed a rough hand on the mayor's shoulder. "That earring. Where did you get it?"

Gan paled. "Why, from the Hiraeth." He licked his dry lips. "Kel's one of them. He can explain. They kidnapped me as a boy, and—"

"So I've heard." Kanton rolled his eyes and motioned for the mayor to leave.

Once the door closed, Master Loy asked, "So what is this really about?"

"Pardon?" Kanton asked as two of his guards rounded the table towards Serena.

"Did you really come all this way for a common horse thief?"

"That thief is far from common, and thanks to you, she will be brought to justice. In fact," Kanton motioned for Mistress Loy to come closer, "I would like to reward you for your service to the kingdom of Teyrnas."

"That isn't necessary," replied Mistress Loy. "There was no damage done. And our farmhand is already recovering."

"What about Patyn?" asked the female guard. "You said he was injured."

"He's still in the barn," replied Esme. "I didn't want to move him in case his spine was injured."

"Take me to him."

"One moment, Marsh," said Kanton. He addressed the Loys. "This is a small village. Only seven hundred people live here, according to the latest census. What is there in terms of education?"

The Loys looked at one another, a little confused. Realta had no idea where Kanton was heading. Education? How did that factor in?

"How old are your daughters?"

Marsh shared a confused glance with her colleagues.

Callum moved so that he stood between Realta and Charity, eyes fixed on Kanton. The dining room felt uncomfortably small. Too many people.

"Well," Master Loy hesitated, "Nina is twenty, Bridget is eighteen, and Charity is fifteen."

"And Master... Kel, is it? That boy I saw earlier. Is he your son?"

"Why?" Kel leaned against the wall, the scarred half of his face directed at Kanton.

"Answer the question."

"Yes."

"And his age?"

"I don't see what my son has to do with anything."

"His age." Kanton's blue eyes burned like fire.

"Sixteen."

"Excellent. And how old is your daughter, Master Haar?"

Callum glared at him. Kanton knew very well that Callum was a servant without any title of his own, yet he insisted on calling him by one.

"Fifteen," Callum acquiesced.

"Have the boy and the two fifteen-year-olds undergone testing by the Scholars yet?"

"No," replied Mistress Loy. "They aren't due back in Vala until Autumntide." Every five years, Scholars from the Academy came to each village in the Hinterlands, administering tests to see if any child between the ages of fourteen and nineteen qualified for admission. Very few passed the tests, and even fewer completed their education. Esme had been one of the lucky few the Scholars accepted.

"Here's what I'm thinking," said Kanton, relaxing his shoulders and placing a hand on his sword hilt. "We have to transport this thief back to Teyrnas to stand trial. The journey will take at least fifteen days, and I need someone to help." The three guards exchanged looks once again but remained silent. "Master Haar, if you wish to change your mind, come with me. And as a boon, I will take these three children to the Academy for testing. What do you say?"

Marsh stepped over to her colleagues and whispered. The two men were as equally confused.

"Um, Captain Kanton," said one. Kanton raised a hand, silencing him.

Callum gritted his teeth. He looked to Master Loy for guidance.

"Why just me?" Charity piped up. "Why not my sisters as well?"

"My dear," Kanton said with a pained smile, "you wouldn't want your parents to be all alone, would you? Besides, the Academy rarely accepts students who are over nineteen."

Charity and Realta exchanged glances. Attending the Academy was prestigious. The greatest minds in the kingdom studied there. Nobles, historians, scientists. And attending did not mean saying goodbye forever. Esme, after all, had returned home.

Realta's gaze fell on Serena. The girl looked so much like her uncle. She even had hints of Estrid in her face, glimpses of the girl's future self. She might be able to pry an explanation from Kel, but the man was so secretive, rarely talking about his life before attending the Academy. He outright refused to talk about the accident that left him scarred, though Realta did not blame him for that. And if Serena left, any potential answers left with her.

"I'd like to go," Realta whispered. She had no doubt that Charity would say yes. That was another reason to go. She did not want Charity traveling with Kanton for that long, even if they were with other guards.

"If Realta agrees, then I want to go, too," said Charity, her bright smile beaming.

"Gareth!" Kel called out, covering the right side of his face. Odd. Why cover that side but leave the scars visible?

Gareth peered into the dining room. His eyes widened, seeing so many unfamiliar faces at once. He turned to run, but Esme caught him by the arm and guided him to rest of the way into the room.

"Gareth," she said, her voice gentle. "These people want to take you and your cousin to the Academy. What do you think?"

Eyes wide and trembling, Gareth looked to his mother, then his father. "I don't know," he stammered.

"This is the wonderful opportunity," said Kanton. "It would be unwise to let it pass you by."

"How long?"

"Try it for a few months," replied Kel. "They don't force you to stay if you don't want to."

"Okay."

Kanton grin, white teeth flashing.

"Are you sure it will be safe?" asked Mistress Loy, casting a weary glance at Serena, flanked by a guard on both sides. The girl sat with her head hung, manacled hands resting on her knees. Had Mayor Gan left the keys for those?

"Of course. The route from here to Teyrnas is a very safe one. Thousands travel it every day. And the Academy takes good care of its students."

"Is this really what you want, Charity?" her mother asked.

"I can study medicine at the Academy, right? How to perform surgery?" she asked Kanton.

The man smiled. "The best doctors and healers come from the Academy, my dear. You won't be disappointed."

Charity's eyes shone brightly, like a small child receiving a puppy or a kitten for her birthday. "Yes, more than anything. May I?"

Master and Mistress Loy smiled their patient smiles. This way their youngest daughter could study beyond practical medicine to her heart's desire and do so miles away from Healer Zall. They gave her their blessing.

"Thank you!" Charity hugged her parents and ran off to tell her sisters the good news.

Realta looked up at her father. His expression was clouded. "Is it all right with you, Father?"

He let out a heavy sigh. "I've only wanted the best for you. And if this is the best, then so be it."

She thanked him, wondering if she had made the right choice. Yes, Esme had returned to Vala after graduating. But she had been gone for eight years. The headstrong teen had returned as a mature, educated woman, who was also married and expecting a child. None of the love between Callum and his sister had disappeared, but those years were gone. Along with any experiences they might have shared.

"At least she's going with friends," Esme added. Callum nodded, a bit of his mood lightening.

"So, you are going with us, Master Haar." Dane Kanton smiled.

"You've left me without a choice."

Realta felt a small pang of guilt. Had this all been a ploy to get Callum's help?

"Captain, I don't think that's necessary," said one guard, the younger of the two men. "We already have the thief in custody, and—"

"Have you forgotten something, Tock?"

"Sir?"

"Patyn is injured. We are down one man. Master Haar will be a fitting replacement."

"Can we see Patyn now?" asked Marsh. Kanton motioned for her to go, and Esme led her to the barn. Gareth seized the opportunity to run out of the room.

"I ought to be back by the start of next month," Callum told Master Loy. "I'll miss the first planting, but..."

"Think nothing of it," replied Master Loy. "I will have the Taft boy help. So long as you're back before harvest," he added with a jovial smile.

Mistress Loy motioned for Realta to follow her into the living room. She walked around the table, keeping an eye on Kanton. He was too focused on Callum and Kel to notice her. She wondered if he saw the resemblance, too.

Ander sat on the couch with Nina and Estrid by his side. The bleeding had stopped, and he rested his head on Nina's shoulder. Lon stood off to the side, glaring at the dining room. Knowing him, he'd like to knock Serena unconscious as pay back. Bridget sat in a chair, her face solemn.

"You better go upstairs and pack," Mistress Loy instructed her. "You have a long journey ahead of you." She pulled Realta in for a quick hug. "Your mother would be so proud."

Realta went up to the small room she and Charity shared. She caught Bridget saying, "Why doesn't he want to take me, too?"

Mistress Loy comforted her middle daughter, assuring her that the Scholars would arrive in a few short months, and she could take the test then.

Bridget wants to go to the Academy? Realta never viewed her as being academic. Bridget's mind often wandered during one of Kel's mathematics or history lessons. Perhaps she didn't know what she wanted until she realized she couldn't have it.

Entering the room, Realta saw Charity laying out a series of dresses and books on her bed. Each book had a medical title. But not all of them belonged to Mistress Loy.

Perhaps it was a good thing Serena hid in their barn, Realta thought as she walked towards the wardrobe. If not, Charity would have to settle for learning the basics from Esme or study under Healer Zall.

Vala needed a new healer. Esme had volunteered to work as Zall's assistant when she returned home. At first, the healer allowed it, especially since Kel's injuries were still fresh and he needed surgery on his leg. Then Zall began growing suspicious, claiming that Kel was recovering too quickly and that odd things happened around him. It was nonsense. The fact that Kel required a leg brace to walk more than ten feet was proof. But not to Zall's addled mind. He began limiting Esme's work time and shut her out completely within a year. Though he grew to respect her in a way, all attempts to repair their working relationship eventually ended in failure.

"What are you going to pack everything in?" Realta asked, removing a dress from the wardrobe. Neither of them had traveling cases or trunks.

"I'll borrow Mother's old trunk. And I'll make sure to pack light, that way we can share. Do you know if we will be traveling by horse or in a cart?"

"Good question." Realta folded her arms. A sickening thought crept into her mind. "How do we know this offer is real?"

Charity left a dress halfway folded. "It has to be. That document Red Earrings showed the mayor was legitimate. It had the king's seal. And that girl recognizes him. Why would he lie?"

Realta shrugged. Kanton's predatory smile flashed in her mind. She pushed the image away. "I don't know. Sounds too good to be true."

"That's nerves talking. Come on, I'll help you pack."

Fifteen minutes later, she and Charity carried Mistress Loy's old trunk out of the room and placed it down at the top of the stairs. Charity went down to fetch Lon and her father. There was no way they could carry it down on their own.

Realta glanced down the hall to her father's room. He sat on the bed, looking at the drawing of Realta's mother. Kiana Haar had died when Realta was two years old, during an outbreak of crimson fever. Growing up, Callum had shone her that drawing until she memorized every detail, saying she ought to know what her mother looked like.

Callum placed the drawing in a book and walked out of Realta's line of sight.

She hurried down the stairs. Nina, Bridget, and Estrid had disappeared. Ander was lying down on the couch, a damp cloth pressed against his head. Charity stood over him.

"His breathing is regular," she whispered. "Nothing to worry about."

"Where are the others?" Realta peered into the empty dining room.

"They're outside."

The stairs creaked as Callum walked down. Slung over his shoulder was a leather satchel. His eyes were narrowed, lost in thought.

"How long will the trip take?" Kanton had said fifteen days, but Realta wanted confirmation from someone she trusted.

"About fifteen, maybe twenty days. No sooner than Alet fifteenth." Callum noticed Master Loy and Kanton talking in the yard and went to join them. The door closed softly behind him.

Twenty days. Two full weeks. Realta had never traveled for longer than one day in any direction. What would two weeks on the road be like? Was it too late to change her mind?

You want to know why Serena looks like Kel, don't you? You can't get those answers by staying here.

Charity grabbed Realta's hand and led her out the door. The rising run had warmed the air, banishing the nightly chill. Master Loy and Lon were attaching the cart to Shadow, and half a dozen other horses were tied to the railing next to the barn. Just inside the barn sat the fallen man, Patyn. Esme bound his arm in a sling while he stared into the yard, looking at nothing. Marsh stood nearby, asking questions.

Dane Kanton monitored the yard, one eye on Serena. The girl sat on one of the horses, her hands tied to the saddle's pommel. The manacles had been removed.

Gareth came up from behind, leading Dust by the reins. Locks of black hair obscured his solemn face. He paused next to his father and sister.

"I don't know about this," he said.

Kel reached into his shirt and removed his necklace, a pendant with two ravens soaring into the sky. He handed it to Gareth. "Your mother gave this to me when we were students. Think of it as the two of us being with you. No matter what."

Gareth sheepishly put on the necklace. Estrid embraced him, followed by Kel.

Not wanting to intrude, Realta continued towards the cart. Callum placed his satchel in the cart and turned towards Master Loy. He handed her father a piece of paper. Realta glanced at the heading. "Rite of Passage". With that, Callum was free to travel throughout the kingdom. He folded it and placed it inside the satchel.

"We'll purchase more supplies in the village," Kanton announced. Callum ignored him as he checked to make sure the saddle straps were tight.

"We each get a horse?" asked Charity.

"Not exactly. Ideally, we will have extra horses so we can switch riders. If only we had something other than a cart," he muttered.

Marsh walked over to him, her face ashen. "Sir, Patyn is in no condition to ride. We can't just leave him."

Kanton glanced at Esme and the wounded guardsman. "Yes, we can."

"But, sir—"

"Do you think that woman is a competent healer?"

Marsh hesitated. "From what little I've seen, sure. I guess."

"It will be better for him to recover here than on the road. Is this clear?"

"Yes, sir."

Realta turned her attention to Callum. He stood beside Serena. "Is that too tight?" he asked her, pointing at her bound wrists.

Serena shrugged.

"Let me know if they are."

"If I..." Serena swallowed a lump in her throat. "If I had asked your master permission to sleep in his barn, would he have let me?"

"No."

Serena sighed, as though she expected that answer.

"Mistress Loy," Callum continued, "would have insisted that you slept in the house."

Tears fell freely from Serena's eyes. She hung her head, turning away from Callum.

Realta felt another pang of guilt. Had she done the right thing in capturing her? Yes, she had fought a guardsman and nearly killed him, but how much of that was in self-defense? *And why does she look like Kel? Why? Who are you?* she wanted to ask. The words refused to leave her mind.

Turning away, she saw Mistress Loy enter the yard, trailed by Nina, Bridget, and Ander. The latter was propped up by Nina.

"Write me the moment you arrive there," she said, giving Charity and Realta hugs.

"We will."

Tears brimmed in her eyes. She placed a hand on Callum's arm. "Watch over them."

"With my life."

"We will send you a portion of the reward," said Kanton, climbing into his saddle, the three guards following suit, "once we reach Teyrnas. King Logan will be more than grateful."

The Loys thanked him. Callum said his goodbyes and climbed into the driver's seat while Charity and Realta climbed into the back of the cart. They sat with their legs swinging off the edge. Gareth mounted Dust, a little uneasy in the saddle. He glanced back at his parents. They gave him reassuring smiles.

Callum flicked the reins, and Shadow took off, eager to go anywhere. Kanton maneuvered his horse into the front, with the horse carrying Serena tied to the back of the saddle. The girl kept her head low.

Realta waved goodbye to the Loys and her aunt and uncle, taking in one last view of the farm. Her home. It felt like a dream. She and Charity were heading to the Academy together, had a chance at a proper education. She thought she would be happier.

She glanced over her shoulder. Kanton's head moved in tandem, facing forward. She still felt his eyes watching her.

4

The Tolman Boy

"Stay here while we gather supplies," Dane Kanton ordered. They had stopped outside the marketplace in Vala. A good number of vendors already had their stalls set up for the day. Travelers would be coming through the village regularly for the next week. Nobody wanted to miss out on extra sales. Kanton, Tock, and Marsh dismounted and headed for the vendors. The third guardsman, Wills, stayed behind to watch Serena.

Once they were out of sight, Callum climbed off the cart.

"Where are you going?" Wills questioned.

"To chapel to pay my respects. Is there a problem with that?"

Wills mulled it over. "Find. Don't take forever, though."

Callum thanked him and said to Realta, "Do you want to come?"

Realta glanced over at Wills. The guardsman did not object. She quickly jumped off the cart and joined her father.

"Charity, Gareth," he called out. Charity stood up in the cart, and Gareth jolted, as though someone had grabbed him. "Help watch that thief and whistle as loud as you can if there's any trouble."

"Yes, Callum," Charity replied. Gareth merely nodded.

"What if he gets mad?" Realta asked, trying to keep up with her father's long strides. What if Kanton went back on his promise? She recalled how quickly Kanton became enraged at Callum, storming out of Tolman's Inn. If he returned and found Realta and Callum gone, would he get angry and leave without them? She doubted the guards would object. They always followed Kanton's orders. That meant Charity and Gareth spending two weeks alone with them. Gareth never did well with strangers. And had Kanton been staring at Charity, too? A shiver ran down her spine, and she quickened her pace.

They entered the village chapel, wind chimes at the front entrance swinging in the breeze. A dozen or so villagers occupied the space, as well as the four chaplains who maintained the building and saw to Vala's spiritual needs. People typically visited the chapel on the first day of the week, seeking prayers and guidance. The Loys always visited at midday.

"You're here early, Callum," said Sister Sabell. She was an older woman with gray hair, tied in a braid that went down to her waist. She wore the brown cloak and robes of a chaplain with a blue cord tied around her waist. The other three chaplains wore a green, red, or white cord, respectively.

"I've a long journey ahead of me. I'm taking Realta and Gareth to the Academy."

Sister Sabell gasped. "That's wonderful. But aren't the Scholars due to visit the Hinterlands this year?"

"Yes, but I've been hired to go to Teyrnas. This way, I'm catching two hares in one trap."

Sister Sabell nodded, seeing the logic. "Very well. Let me know if you need anything."

"Just the Creator's guidance."

Sister Sabell nodded again and went to greet other visitors.

Realta followed Callum downed the aisle to the candle-filled altar. The chapel's walls were decorated with stained glass windows and tapestries, each depicting one of the eight Gadyeni, beings sent by the Creator to protect humankind. To the left of the altar hung Caman's tapestry. It depicted a man with dark hair and tanned skin holding a walking staff. Legend said he created the pass in the Vogel Mountains in order to unite the people in the Northern Realm. Some people claimed that Callum met Caman while working as a guide. Her father neither confirmed nor denied the story.

Callum took one of the lit candles and touched the flame to three unlit ones. Realta listed off the names in her head. Grandfather Drago, Grandmother Mayra, Mother. The smoke from the flames rose to the chapel's vaulted ceiling.

"You are not forgotten," Callum said under his breath. Realta repeated the phrase. Lighting candles for the dead not only prolonged their memory, but also drew the attention of the Creator and His Gadyeni. They looked highly on those who remembered the past. Realta hoped this small act would grant them protection on their journey. She didn't think she could trust Kanton. Or any of the guards, for that matter.

She and Callum exited the chapel. More and more people walked along the streets as morning grew to midday. A small crowd gathered around the cart and horses. Guardsman Wills did his best to deflect people, telling them this was none of their business. Charity, on the other hand, readily answered their questions, explaining their trip to Teyrnas and that her parents were doing very well, thank you for asking.

"Wait, you're traveling with a thief?" asked Ellis, the tavern's head brewer.

"The thief is tied up," Charity replied. "The guards won't let her get away."

"But... Oh, hello, Callum," he said, turning around. "Sardic let you go, too?"

"Who else is going to escort his daughter?"

Realta hurried back to the cart and sat down next to Charity. "Is he back yet?"

"Did you hear me whistle?"

"You were only supposed to do that if there's trouble."

"Well, you never know." Charity looked up and down the street. People milled in front of shops and houses, going about their daily business and greeting one another. The clang of metal and metal rose from the blacksmith's shop. "Look," she said, "it's Lok and Mistress Tolman."

Realta faced the nearby inn. Vera Tolman, a shawl wrapped around her thin shoulders, walked across the street, making a direct line for Callum. Lok remained by the door. He wore a dark cloak that was frayed at the edges and was slightly too big for him. He held a burlap sack in one hand. Realta waved to him. He did not notice, all his attention focused on the ground.

"Callum," said Mistress Tolman, "may I have a word?"

"Of course."

She led Callum off to the side, away from the small crowd.

"Has she said anything?" Realta asked Charity, pointing at Serena. The girl sat motionless with her head down. Her sandy hair hid her face. Kel's face.

Charity shook her head. "No, hasn't said a word. Don't you think it's sad? She's only two years older than us and has to resort to stealing. What do you think happened to her parents?"

"No idea." Serena claimed to be an orphan. A girl in Vala had been orphaned after her mother died from an infection and a year later her father was killed in a riding accident. Unlike the girl, Serena probably did not have any family to take her in, forcing her to fend for herself.

"Oh, no," Charity cried.

"What?"

"Trouble." Charity placed her fingers in her mouth and let out a sharp whistle.

Realta followed her line of sight and saw Dane Kanton heading their way. The other guards trailed behind him, Tock carrying a wicker basket and Marsh leading two bay horses. Kanton did not look pleased. Heart racing, Realta looked for Callum. He was still speaking with Mistress Tolman.

"I see word has gotten around," said Kanton, observing the small group. His eyes flicked over to Serena. "Good. At least some people can keep their word. Girls, get out of the cart."

Realta and Charity did as instructed. Tock placed the wicker basket in the cart next to the traveling trunk. The scent of fresh bread and dried fruit filled the air.

"How much food is that?" Realta thought out loud.

"More than enough to take us all the way to West Bridge," Kanton said proudly.

"What in the world is this?" Callum exclaimed, examining the cart. Mistress Tolman stood next to him.

"Provisions."

"No," Callum shook his head. "We don't need all that."

"Excuse me? What do you expect us to eat?"

Callum sighed, getting his thoughts in order. "I assumed we were traveling one village per day, stopping at night. We'd eat in local inns."

"Really?" Kanton crossed his arms. "And how long would that take to West Bridge?"

"About seven days. Then a full week from East Bridge to Teyrnas. Minimum."

Kanton shook his head. "No. Stopping that often is not good enough. I have a deadline to make. That thief must be brought to justice."

"And justice can't wait a few extra days? Besides, there's another mouth to feed."

"How's that?" Kanton's eyes narrowed. His face took on a reddish hue. Wills motioned for Tock and Marsh to join him, his face a mask of concern. Realta wondered how mad Kanton was going to be. She white-knuckled the edge of the cart.

"You've met Mistress Tolman?" Callum gestured to her.

"Yes, we stayed at her inn. A very fine establishment." He gave her a polite bow.

"Well, she has a favor to ask."

"Master Kanton, I heard you're taking Charity Loy and Realta and Gareth Haar to the Academy. I want you to take my son, too."

Kanton exhaled through his teeth. "Mistress Tolman, I am not doing this out of the goodness of my heart. Master Loy helped me catch a thief. And as a reward, I am taking his daughter to be educated. Now—"

"Lok has no life here." Mistress Tolman blurted out. The group became still. Those not part of the conversation left to go about their business. Realta noticed Lok standing next to the cart, his dark brown eyes studying his mother and Kanton. "He can't speak. He's never said a word and never will. I've done the best I can with him, but he will never have a good life in this village. The things people say about him..." She forced the tears to stay in her eyes. "Please. I don't know if the Academy will accept him, but it's a chance at a better life for my son."

Kanton glared at Callum. "Whose idea was this?"

"Mine, sir," replied Mistress Tolman. "Callum made me no promises, only that you would hear me out."

"And this is your boy?" Kanton pointed at Lok. The Tolman boy's eyes grew wide, and he took a step back.

"Yes. Lok, please come here."

Lok, his pack gripped with both hands, stepped closer to his mother, never once taking his eyes off Kanton.

"How well do you expect your son to perform at the Academy?"

Kanton asked.

"He can read and write, and he knows some mathematics. Please, just give him a chance."

Kanton relented. "Fine. But don't complain to me if the Academy rejects him."

"A chance is all I ask." She turned to her son. "I'm going to get the horse. You listen to Callum and do as he says, okay?"

Lok nodded, his unruly, dark brown hair obscuring his face. Vera Tolman headed for the inn's stables.

"And how many more should we expect?" Kanton spat at Callum.

"Just this one."

"I'm not scouting out the whole damn village."

"I understand. It's just one more. And Lok is fully capable of caring for himself. He's one of the best in Vala with the bow and arrow. Isn't that right, Lok?"

Lok shook his head vigorously.

Callum sighed.

You were supposed to lie, Lok. Realta liked Lok. He was a nice person, but he was not the most astute with people. A result of not being able to speak.

"One of the best with the bow and arrow, is he?" Kanton sneered. "You," he jabbed a finger at Lok, "get in the cart. Now!"

Lok scrambled into the cart, sitting on the trunk.

"At least you're obedient," said Kanton. "How old are you, boy?"

Lok held up one finger and then seven.

"Congratulations. You meet the Academy's age requirement."

Lok beamed a smile. Kanton rolled his eyes. A moment later, Mistress Tolman returned with the horse. Tears streaming down her face, she said a final goodbye to her son. Lok's smile faded, watching her disappeared inside the inn.

"All four of us at the Academy," Charity smiled. She and Realta mounted two of the horses with some difficulty. Neither of their dresses were designed for riding, and Realta had very little practice riding side saddle. They maneuvered their horses closer to the cart.

"Are you excited, Lok?" Charity asked.

Tearing his eyes away from the inn, he nodded.

A blur of movement caught Realta's eye. One of the horses stood with an empty saddle. Frayed bits of rope rested on the ground. Serena raced down the road.

"Hey!" Wills called out.

Pulled out of their conversation, the other two guards ran after her. Kanton took off in a flash. Serena made it halfway to the chapel. Tock lunged at her, wrapping his arms around her waist and pulling her to the ground. Bystanders crowded together, muttering to each other.

"Let me go!" Serena screamed, kicking and thrashing at Tock.

The guardsman, assisted by Marsh, stood and dragged Serena back to the group. Realta stared at them in shock. No movement for an hour followed by a wild burst of energy.

No, not wild. She was waiting, Realta realized.

"What do you think you're doing?" Kanton yelled, grabbing Serena by the shirt and backhanding her. Her lip burst open, spraying blood onto the ground. "How about I break your legs? Let's see how far you get then." Kanton delivered another blow, hitting Serena's already bruised eye.

"That's enough!" Callum elbowed Kanton in the sternum, knocking out his breath.

Realta and Charity watched, frozen. The guardsmen looked at Callum in horror. Kanton stumbled, quickly regaining his footing. He looked Callum in the eye, seething. Callum returned the gaze, his face unreadable as stone.

"Who's in charge here?" Kanton demanded.

"You are."

"I said, who's in charge here?"

"You are, sir."

"It is my job to bring that thief back to Teyrnas, and I will do as I see fit. You will not interfere. Do you understand?"

"I understand. Sir," he added a half second later.

Kanton grabbed Serena and half led, half dragged her back to the horses. He forced her back into the saddle, retying the ropes. Serena winced.

Realta felt anger radiating off Kanton in waves. *This was a mistake. We shouldn't have agreed to go with him.* She looked over at Serena. A female version of Kel. Was going to Teyrnas the only way to find the answer? Could they just—

"I change my mind!" Gareth cried.

Every eye turned to look at him. Realta's heart dropped. Gareth was deathly pale, and he trembled from head to toe. If he wasn't riding Dust, Realta doubted he'd be able to stand.

"Gareth, it's okay," Callum said calmly, walking towards him. "Realta and I will be with you the whole time."

"No. I change my mind." Gripping the reins, Gareth maneuvered Dust over to Realta. He removed Kel's necklace and placed it around her neck. Realta was at a loss for words. This was Kel's necklace. The one he had worn since he was a student. And he had given it to Gareth, his son. Not to her.

"I'm sorry," Gareth said to her, tears glistening in his eyes. He turned to Callum and whispered, "Sorry." Slapping the reins, Gareth rode Dust down the road. Back to home.

"Gareth, wait!" she called out. It was no use. Gareth was gone.

"Well," said Kanton, mounting his horse. "That takes care of one problem. What are you waiting for, Master Haar?"

Callum tore himself away from the road and climbed into the cart.

"Father, aren't we going after him?"

"No."

"But—"

"Gareth is old enough to make his own decisions."

Realta gripped the necklace's pendant tightly and glanced over her shoulder. A part of her told her to ride after Gareth, not to bring him back, but to join him. To stay home, away from Kanton. *But what of Serena?* And Charity and Lok? She couldn't abandon her friends.

"Any other interruptions?" Kanton asked.

Nobody replied.

Kanton flicked the reins, leading them out of the village. Everyone else followed, Charity and Realta keeping their horses close to Callum. Moments later, Vala fell behind them, disappearing around a hill. She had never traveled this far, and it seemed like a long way to go for answers.

"What do you think you'll study?" Charity asked, breaking the silent tension. She did not know what to make of Gareth running away either.

"I don't know. Maybe history. And you already know what you're going to study." Realta managed a smile. The Tolman's horse made a sudden movement. She gripped the reins tighter. She hated riding side saddle. Maybe they could buy some riding dresses in the next village. If Kanton allowed them. The way he had threatened Serena had unnerved everyone, including the guards. They hadn't so much as whispered to one another.

He wouldn't really break Serena's legs, would he?

"Actually, you will study a wide variety of subjects," said Kanton. Realta tensed. He heard them?

"Did you attend the Academy, Master Kanton?" Charity asked, a slight tremor in her voice.

"Yes, when I was not much older than you and your friends." None of his previous anger was in his voice. It seemed to fade as quickly as it flashed to life.

It's because Gareth left, Realta surmised. *He only promised to take us three.* But why would adding another person make him so angry? It wasn't like he was escorting them alone. There were three other guards. And there was safety in numbers. The larger the group, the more daunting it would be to rob.

"What did you study?" Charity asked.

"A little of everything. Writing, logic, history, linguistics. And of course my Thane studies."

"Stars above, you're a Thane," Callum exclaimed, sitting upright. Thanes were individuals with incredible powers, gifted to their ancestors by the Gadyeni. Some were able to move objects with a thought, while others could control the weather with the wave of their hands. Realta had only heard of them in history books. People of great renowned. Kings and queens.

"Took you that long to notice?" Kanton placed a finger on one of his red earrings.

"There aren't any Thanes in Vala," Callum explained. "I had forgotten you marked yourselves with earrings. Which type are you?"

"A Learner," Kanton replied, a touch of pride in his voice. "But just enough to receive good marks in all my classes."

"Wait. Thanes mark themselves with earrings?" Charity asked.

"Yes."

"Mayor Gan, he has a purple earring. Does that make him a Thane?"

Wills muttered something under his breath.

"A purple earring," replied Kanton. "Yes, I recall seeing it. That makes him an Empath, able to read other people's emotions. But a very low leveled one. You see, Thanes receive the earring in the right ear upon entering the Academy. They don't receive the left one unless they graduate. He likely flunked out during his first or second year. That story he tells is to prevent embarrassment."

"So, the Hiraeth don't give people earrings," said Charity.

A spike of pain tore at Realta's heart. Kel had always confirmed Gan's story, saying it was part of Hiraethi culture. And though he never said it, those tears in his earlobes showed where rings had been ripped out. Was it all a lie? And if so, what else had Kel lied about? Her gaze drifted towards Serena.

"Maybe they do, maybe they don't. I personally have no desire to find out."

Realta forced her thoughts away from Kel and focused on Kanton's explanation. It made some sense. Mayor Gan was always polite and had the right words to say. Whether a person was angry, sad, or happy, he immediately knew what to do in each situation. Why hide the fact that he was a Thane?

The last farmhouse disappeared behind a bend in the road. Sunlight shone through the trees. Green draigs, small, sinuous reptiles with a single whisker on the sides of their faces, jumped from branch to branch. One chased after a bird, making a sport of it. The breeze was a bit on the cold side. Realta was grateful for the warmer weather. Some years, there was still frost on the ground until the middle of Alet.

A piece of white flashed in her eyes. Realta turned and saw Lok in the cart, holding out a small sheet of paper. In his other hand was a notebook and a charcoal pencil. She took the note and read it.

"That horse's name is Jak."

"Thank you for telling me, Lok." She placed the folded paper in her dress pocket. Lok had remarkably good handwriting. No wonder. It was his only means of communication.

Lok handed another piece to Callum.

"You're welcome," Callum said, reading it. Realta guessed it read, 'thank you'. Perhaps Lok attending the Academy was not solely Vera Tolman's idea.

"What's the next village, Father?"

"Lothian. We should arrive there in the evening. I have connections there. Are you worried?" Callum added. His dark eyes, almost as black as the pupils, studied her. She knew he was thinking about Gareth's decision. Maybe she should have made the same one. Too late now.

"A little," she admitted.

Callum nodded. "It's normal to worry about a long trip." His attention drifted to Serena. The girl had not said a word since Kanton's beating. Her left eye was swollen shut, and her lip was puffy and crusted with dried blood.

I know Father sees the resemblance. Does Serena see it, too?

Realta thought about asking her father. He knew Kel far better than she did. But the words died in her mouth.

They continued along the road at a steady pace.

5

Lothian

They arrived in Lothian as the sun set behind the trees. The sky had taken on a violet hue, and branches cast long shadows on the road. Dane Kanton led them through the village. People were closing shops for the day and heading home. The majority smiled and waved at them. Travelers, common this time of year, were always a welcomed sight.

Realta studied each building as they passed. Everything seemed so familiar, but at the same time strange. The roads were still hard-packed dirt, and the buildings made of wood with tiled roofs. But the blacksmith's shop was farther away from the marketplace. The chapel closer to the mayor's house. The small, two-story houses spoke of home, but the people living inside were strangers.

Kanton raised a fist in the air as they approached the inn, a three-story building that was much longer than Tolman's Inn. The guardsmen immediately halted. Realta and Charity followed suit, their horses stopping next to the cart. Candles shone in every window.

"Tock, Wills," Kanton order, "ask if they have any vacancies."

The guardsmen promptly obeyed. They returned less than a minute later, their faces solemn.

"Sorry, sir," said Tock. "They don't have any vacancies."

"But the innkeeper said we can eat in the common room, if we want," Wills added.

Kanton was silent for a moment. "Very well. We'll eat and camp on the outskirts."

"Why don't we ask to sleep in a barn?" asked Callum.

"I doubt any farmer would be willing to put up nine people for the night. Especially one that's a thief."

"We're sleeping outdoors?" Charity asked. Realta heard a hint of hopefulness in her voice. So long as it was an adventure, Charity was up for it.

"It appears so. Are you unaccustomed to sleeping outdoors?"

"Oh no. We always sleep outside on warm nights."

Only when we don't get caught. Mistress Loy forbid her daughters from sleeping outdoors, due to wild animals prowling around at night. But that did not stop Charity. Roping in Realta, she'd stuff pillows and clothes underneath their blankets and sneak out through the window, climbing down the tree outside their bedroom. Realta never understood the appeal. Yes, the night sky was beautiful with the myriad stars and the two moons flying across the sky in their eternal race. And the night air had a cool, almost calming quality. But not enough to make Realta forget about the potential dangers. Not completely.

"Good to hear," replied Kanton. "And I assume an accomplished guide would have no trouble sleeping outdoors?" he addressed Callum.

Callum sighed. "No trouble. But what about her?" He pointed at Serena. She had not moved or made a sound since leaving Vala. The evening shadows made her injuries look worse. "Seems like a good opportunity to make a run for it."

"We will see that her legs are properly bound and sleep in shifts. I have no intention of losing her again."

"Again? You mean other than this morning?"

Kanton's eyes narrowed. "We came close to capturing her in West Bridge. The bastard slipped through our fingers. A mistake I don't intend to repeat."

Serena's head shot up, her good eye glaring at Kanton. Realta wondered how much of that story was true. Or if it was just that. A story.

"Very well," replied Callum. He climbed off the cart and led Shadow by the reins to the inn's stable. "You said the common room was open?"

"Yes," Tock answered.

"We should eat before making camp, don't you agree?"

"Of course," Kanton replied. He dismounted and followed Callum.

The two stable hands, a little overwhelmed by the size of the group, took the horses and managed to find a place for them in the nearly full stable, as well as the cart.

Lok jumped out of the cart and stood close to Callum. The Tolman boy was surprisingly tall. Almost a head taller than Callum.

Wasn't his father really tall? She recalled Master Loy saying that Ansonn Tolman was the tallest man he had ever met. Six and a half feet. Seeing his son, Realta believed it.

Kanton and Marsh went to Serena and deftly untied the rope around the pommel while keeping her hands bound.

"Now," he said as Serena stumbled onto the ground. "Are you going to stay put this time or—"

Serena kicked Kanton in the leg, just below the knee.

"You little bitch!"

Serena turned to run, but Marsh and Kanton lunged at her, grabbing her shirt collar. The fabric ripped as Kanton flung her to the ground. He placed his booted foot on Serena's chest. The guards circled them.

"You no good bastard. Your father should have destroyed you the moment you were born!"

"Don't you think that's enough?" Callum asked. The two stable hands, hearing the commotion, stared at them, eyes darting from Serena to the guardsmen to Callum. Realta edged closer to her father, Charity and Lok following suit.

"She's a thief. This is the third time she had tried to run away today."

"Second."

"Excuse me?" Kanton stepped closer to Callum, his eyes burning like hot coals.

"It's the second time."

"It doesn't matter."

"Has it ever occurred to you, to any of you, that she wouldn't run away if you treated her gently?"

Kanton scoffed. "Do I have to remind you—"

"Who's in charge? No, sir. You're in charge. I was merely offering a suggestion."

"Then I suggest you keep your suggestions to yourself."

"Understood."

Kanton waved at the guards, and Tock and Wills pulled Serena onto her feet. Kanton then led the group into the inn. Realta,

Charity, and Lok all walked behind Callum, keeping their distance from Kanton.

Marsh, holding the door open, whispered to Callum, "You need to stop angering him."

"He's always like this?"

Marsh nodded.

Entering the common room, Realta's attention returned to Serena. *Why is she so desperate to run away?* The obvious conclusion: she did not want to stand trial for her crimes. But Realta thought there was more to it. Despite the beatings, Serena gazed at the door, towards the open street. At the people riding on horseback and in carts. She was still seeking a means of escape. Realta hoped to get the truth out of her before reaching Teyrnas.

Forty some odd people milled about the common room, sitting and drinking and talking. A musician played a flute in the far corner, the music just loud enough to be heard. Two serving girls flitted from table to table, ensuring everyone was well cared for. A part of Realta was glad that Gareth was not here. There was no way he could tolerate this crowd for more than a few minutes. Not without his parents close by.

They sat at two tables, one occupied by the three guardsmen and the other by everyone else. Kanton sat at the head with Serena on his left and Callum on his right, the guardsmen's table directly behind Serena. Realta sat next to her father, with Charity across from her, and Lok sat at the end. No one talked. One of the serving girls spied Serena's bruised face and whispered to her colleague.

Callum placed his satchel on the table and pulled out some maps.

"No need for that," Kanton said. "We have everything planned out."

"I like to be thorough," Callum replied, spreading out a map of Teyrnas in front of him.

Kanton rolled his eyes and began telling Callum their route. The guardsmen interpreted this as permission to talk quietly to each other.

Realta glanced over at Serena. Hands resting on the table, the girl looked at nothing, her expression blank. She wished she had the courage to ask about her resemblance to Kel. But would she say anything? What would Callum think? Would asking a simple question make Kanton angry? Marsh warned Callum to stop angering the man. Realta feared Kanton would give her a face to match Serena's.

"Drat," said Charity, pulling Realta out of her thoughts. Charity was inspecting the bonds around Serena's wrists. Some of the fibers were stained red. "These are far too tight." She placed a hand on the ropes and Serena jerked away her hands, eyes filled with dread.

"What do you think you're doing?" Kanton demanded, standing up.

"Her bonds are too tight," she explained, not at all fazed by Kanton's anger. "See. Her wrists are bleeding."

Kanton grabbed Serena's wrists, inspecting them. "I will see to them later," he said, resuming his seat.

"But infection could set in—"

"I said I will see to them later." Kanton's voice echoed throughout the room. All eyes turned to their group. The musician stopped playing. Realta held her breath, fearing Kanton would hit her friend. Callum studied Kanton.

"Is everything all right?" a serving girl asked timidly. She was no older than Realta and Charity.

"Yes," replied Kanton. "A pint of ale for myself and my serving man. Watered down wine for the rest. And put that table on my bill." He gestured towards the guards.

Serving man?! Realta raised an eyebrow. Callum was acting as an escort. He was still under contract to Master Loy. How dare Kanton claim that contract for himself!

Callum made no response. His eyes shifted to the common room's entrance. A lanky young man with wild black hair and piercing blue eyes entered and scanned the room. Seeing Callum, he made his way over to the table, a smile on his face.

"I knew it!" said the newcomer. "Something good had to come balance out this absolutely terrible day!"

"Who are you?" asked Kanton.

"Not talking to you."

"Dane Kanton," Callum introduced, "this is Arnyn Teleran. Arnyn, Captain Dane Kanton."

"A pleasure, possibly," Arnyn replied. His eyes widened as they fell on Realta. "Is this your daughter, Haar?"

"She is."

"Wonderful!" Arnyn looked over at Lok. *If his eyes widen any further*, Realta thought, *they will fall out of his head.* "And who is this boy?"

"Lok Tolman."

"The innkeeper's son, correct?"

"Correct."

"Excuse me," said Kanton, his face growing red, "but do you want something?"

"Only to say hello. Can't people say hello anymore, or has a new law been enacted?"

"You can say hello, but we—"

"Then why are you being a pain in my ass?" Arnyn asked. Kanton glared at him. Realta shrank down in her seat. She prayed this man had the sense to shut up or leave before Kanton lost his temper.

Callum stood and addressed Arnyn, "Why don't we speak over there." He pointed at an empty table. The serving girl arrived with their drinks, placing them on the table. She kept a close eye on Kanton and scurried away.

"If you insist. It was a pleasure to meet your wonderful daughter, and the wonderful son of the innkeeper. And I'm sure the other two girls are good children. You, I'm not so sure about," Arnyn said to Kanton, smirking. The other man balled his hands into fists.

Callum collected his things and led Arnyn away, offering him his drink. Arnyn promptly accepted it, extolling the virtues of free ale.

"One of your father's friends?" Charity asked.

"I guess so. I've never heard of him." Realta watched the two take their seats closer to the musician who now played a cheerful tune. She wished Callum hadn't left them alone with Kanton.

He's close by. He won't let anything bad happen.

Callum glanced over at her and gave a reassuring nod. A small part of her fear melted away.

Kanton flagged down the other serving girl and ordered food

for everyone.

Lok wrote in his little notebook and handed it to Realta. *"Why are you and I wonderful, but not Charity or what's-her-name?"*

"I don't know," she replied. She stole another glance at her father and Arnyn. He smiled at her, warm and kind. The exact opposite of the way Kanton had smiled at her in the marketplace yesterday.

Was that only yesterday? How could so much change in such a short time? She wondered how the rest of her family was doing. Had Gareth made it back home okay?

"I don't know either," said Charity, reading the note. "And her name is Serena."

Serena eyed Charity through locks of sandy hair. They really ought to put some ointment on that eye. Thief or not, she was still a human being.

"May I ask you a question, Serena?" Charity asked.

Serena shrugged.

"Why did you steal the king's horse?"

"Enough of that," Kanton cut in, taking a sip of ale. "You are not to speak to her. Is that understood?"

"But we're traveling together."

"No. You are traveling with us to the Academy. This thief is being escorted to stand trial in Teyrnas. Though you are traveling in the same direction at the same time, you are not traveling with her. Therefore, she is of no concern to you. Is that clear, Miss Loy?"

"Not really." Charity met his eyes. "But if that is the rule, then I shall follow it to the very best of my ability."

Realta knew that tone. Charity hated being talked down to, as though she were a small child. She would find a way to navigate around that rule simply out of spite. The fact that Kanton had a violent temper did not factor in.

"I'm glad to hear it," Kanton said acridly. A moment later, the food arrived. Mutton with potatoes and stewed carrots.

Realta took a small bite. It tasted okay. The meat was cooked well. But it wasn't Mistress Loy's mutton. The spices were different. Too much salt and not enough turmeric.

Charity and Lok quietly ate their food. Every now and then, Charity stole a glance at Kanton. Her mind was working against him, Realta just knew it, even though he was doing them a big favor.

Is he really? Had they waited another six months, the Scholars would have come to test them. If they passed, then the Scholars would take them to the Academy. If not, they would stay in Vala. Realta would learn trade skills from her father and Mistress Loy, and Charity would learn medicine from Esme, and secretly from Healer Zall. What if the Scholars did not accept them? They still had to take the exam. Failing meant this whole trip, Kanton's so-called reward, had been for nothing.

Towards the end of the meal, Callum parted ways with Arnyn.

"I still know that tattooist," Arnyn remarked. "He could cover up that ink in a blink of an eye."

"I appreciate the offer, as always," Callum replied, pulling his sleeve over his servant's mark.

"Suit yourself." Arnyn shrugged with his hands. He then exited the common room. Callum resumed his seat.

"Should we expect you meeting with more friends?" Kanton asked.

"No."

"Good." Kanton stood. The guardsmen stood as well. "Pay the innkeeper and help get this one back on the horse." He pointed at Serena. The girl hadn't eaten a single bite.

They left the common room and retrieved their horses from the stables. Kanton led the group out of the village, the two moons high in the sky and candles burning in windows. They passed Arnyn Teleran as they rode.

"Goodbye, Miss Haar and Young Master Tolman," he cried out. "May the Gadyeni guide your paths."

"What does he mean?" she asked her father. She never liked being singled out. Everybody's eyes focused on her.

Callum stared forward. "It's just a blessing."

They rode until they reached a clearing in the woods outside the village, just off the main road. They made camp, Marsh and Tock seeing to the fire while Wills hitched the horses to a stand of trees. Realta, Charity, and Lok set up their sleeping packs, ones Kanton had purchased in Vala, between the horses and the fire. Kanton and Callum arranged the rest of the packs around Serena.

Serena was bound at the wrists, elbows, and the knees, her back against a tree. Kanton then connected a rope from her wrists to a low-hanging branch. Realta thought the entire process was excessive.

"Where is her sleeping pack?" Charity asked Callum, keeping her voice low.

"She doesn't have one."

Charity chewed on her lower lip, thinking. "We could take a blanket from each pack and give it to her."

"I doubt Kanton would approve. Do yourself a favor and don't anger that man any further."

"Yes, Callum," Charity sighed. "But what about Serena's wrists? If they become infected, then—"

Callum signaled her to hush. Kanton and Wills strolled up to them and inspected the ropes. "Very good. I'd like to see you get out of those." Kanton gave Serena a swift kick in the leg. The girl let out a sharp cry. Realta flinched, and Charity rushed to her. Callum held her back. "I see everything else is in order."

"Master Haar," said Wills, studying the sleeping arrangement, "aren't you worried about that boy sleeping so close to your daughter?"

"I'd bet ten gold marks that boy believes intercourse is kissing underneath a blanket. There's no harm."

"What?" Realta asked. Lok seemed equally confused.

"Nothing," Callum replied. "Go to sleep. We've a long journey in the morning." He paused, looking up at the sky. Ilana, the younger moon, was midway across the sky, with Nalani trailing close behind. "I will always love you, Realta. Remember that."

"I love you, too, Father." There was an odd edge to her father's voice. An aspect Realta could not describe with words. She wondered if witnessing Kanton's harsh treatment of Serena had prompted it.

"Who has the first watch?" Kanton asked the guards.

Marsh raised her hand.

"I'll watch with her," Callum said. "If that's all right."

Kanton allowed it.

Charity giggled under her breath as they walked towards Lok.

"What is it?" Realta asked. She and Charity settled down on

their sleeping packs. Realta pulled the blankets close. The night was growing cold.

"I think I know what your father meant."

"What?" she asked, curious.

"I'll tell you when Callum thinks we're asleep," Charity whispered.

But Realta never got a chance to hear. The moment her head hit the blankets, she was fast asleep.

6

Into the Night

Realta opened her eyes and was greeted not by a forest clearing, but by a narrow hallway with gray stone walls. There were no windows, the only light coming from a lantern on the wall. Three women stood beside a closed door, their faces pained. One woman wore a fine silk dress while the other two wore plain wool dresses, much like the women in Vala.

"Where am I?" Realta asked the woman standing closest to her. No, not a woman. A girl, no older than herself. She wrung her hands, eyes shifting from her two companions to the closed door.

Realta tapped the girl on the shoulder. Her hand went straight through the girl as though she were made of mist. A dream, then. But she rarely remembered her dreams. Not that there was much to remember. Most of them were flashes of color, bits of memory. Never anything this realistic.

Footsteps echoed off the walls, and another girl, a teenager, appeared. She closely resembled the finely dressed woman, sharing her bright blue eyes and dark hair. She wore a light blue cloak over a gray dress.

"Where is he?" the girl asked.

The other girl continued wringing her hands, averting her gaze.

"You shouldn't be here, Sarra," said the finely dressed woman. Realta assumed she was Sarra's mother. "Your brother is very ill."

"That's exactly why I'm here," Sarra replied, her cheeks growing red.

"The physicians won't allow anyone in," her mother said. "Shasta," she addressed the third woman, who was only as tall as Realta's shoulder, "please escort Sarra to her room."

"At least tell me what's wrong with him. Is it crimson fever?"

A chill went down Realta's spine. That disease had killed her mother and twenty other people in the course of a few weeks. If

Sarra's brother had the fever, he would need to be kept separated.

"It isn't..." Sarra's mother shook her head. "I should have never written to you. If your father knew—"

"Knew what? That Car is sick? Shasta, what isn't my mother telling me?"

"I am not in a position to answer that, my lady," Shasta replied diplomatically.

"Where's Lo? He'll tell me." Sarra spun on her heels.

"Sarra, wait," her mother began. A heart wrenching scream on the other side of the door interrupted her. Other voices sounded from inside.

"Lo?" Sarra paled and rushed to the door. Her mother grabbed her by the shoulders, locking eyes with her.

"You cannot go in there."

"Why?!"

"Your brother... Car was injured. Badly."

The screaming froze Realta's blood. Was that Sarra's brother? During the few times she helped Esme, she had never heard such horrifying screams.

Sarra shoved her mother out of the way and pushed open the door. In the corner, a pair of surgeons dressed in blood splattered, white clothes struggled to hold down a young man, his face a mask of pain, screaming at the top of his lungs.

Realta's eyes shifted to the bed, turning in tandem with Sarra's. On the bed lay another young man. His entire face was coated with dark blood. Deep lacerations turned his flesh into a bloody maze. His glassy eyes stared up at the ceiling. Sightless.

Sarra screamed.

Realta turned to run out the door and found herself sitting up on her sleeping roll. She was coated in a cold sweat, her hair and clothes clinging to her. The world around her was quiet and calm as the phantom screams were reduced to echoes. The two moons hung low in the sky, their nightly race almost concluded. The sun would rise in a few hours.

Wiping the sweat from her forehead, Realta tried to steady herself. Every time she closed her eyes, even for a second, the dream repeated itself. Screaming. A dead man covered in blood. What had prompted that dream? The people in it were all strangers.

No recognizable faces. Mistress Loy claimed every dream had a meaning. But what could possibly be the meaning of this one?

A twig snapped. Realta spun around, her eyes adjusting to the low light. A large shadow approached a tree and crouched down next to another shadow, one huddled on the ground. Serena. The larger shadow held something in his hand, the metal glinting in the moonlight. A knife? The shadow raised the knife high, aiming it right at Serena.

"Father!" Realta yelled.

Callum Haar awoke and shot to his feet. He quickly threw a bundle of sticks onto the dying fire. The embers sprang to life, the fire blazing. Realta clearly saw Kanton standing over Serena with a dagger in his hand. Serena stared up at him, helpless.

Callum yelled and ran towards Kanton, knocking the man off balance. They grappled on the ground, the dagger held tightly in Kanton's hand. Callum used one hand to hold off the dagger and the other to grip Kanton's neck. He dug his knees into the man's chest, pinning him to the ground.

"What's happening?" Charity asked in a sleepy voice. Realta turned and saw Lok shaking her awake. His face was a mask of pure terror.

The other guards were awake and on their feet, rushing to help Kanton.

"We have to free Serena," Realta said. Before Charity could reply, Realta ran to the girl. She quickly untied the bonds around Serena's legs, her hands trembling. She wished she had a knife. She looked at her father. Kanton had managed to get on top of Callum, the dagger inches from her father's face. Tock stood next to them, his own dagger drawn. No time.

A burning log hit Kanton on the back, singeing his clothes. Lok grabbed another log and hurling it at the man. Tock ran towards Lok, ordering him to stop in the name of the King's Guard. Marsh ran towards Charity who was untying the horses. Wills looked from one person to another, unsure where to go or what to do.

Realta returned to her own task. The bonds around Serena's hands were tied in an intricate knot. Where was the ending? Where was the beginning? There! The rope unraveled. Realta tossed it into the fire.

Serena sat up and yanked the gag out of her mouth. "Thank you," she said, breathing in ragged breaths.

Callum screamed, Kanton's dagger plunging into the right side of his chest. Realta's heart stopped as she watched her father fall to his knees. The dagger was embedded to the hilt in his flesh.

Another scream sounded. This one from Tock. The man was covered in fire, the flames licking at his clothing, hair, and flesh.

"Help me!" he screamed, running straight into Kanton. The two men collided and fell into the fire. Embers shot upwards, falling around the campsite in tiny yellow bursts. It was Kanton's turn to scream. He pulled himself out of the fire and ran off, desperately trying to put out his flaming clothes. Wills dashed towards his fallen colleague, pulling Tock out of the fire and beating away the flames with his own coat.

Callum pulled out the dagger and stood on shaking feet.

"What did you do?!" Marsh demanded, her sword drawn.

"Run!" Callum yelled, ignoring her. Charity stood frozen, her hands on the reins of a bucking horse. She stared in horror at the blood seeping from Callum's chest. "I said run!" he screamed. He rushed towards Charity, picked her up, and placed her on the only saddled horse. The horse took off into the forest. Lok ran after her, disappearing into the night.

Marsh ordered them to stop and ran into the woods.

Realta dashed towards Callum, Serena right behind her. The girl kept one eye on the remaining guards. Kanton had torn off his dark blue coat, or rather what was left of it. The front had been reduced to cinders. A loose button glinted against the fire. Angry, red burn marks covered his face and arms. Screaming and cursing, he struggled to beat out the flames on his shirt. Guardsman Tock had grown silent. Wills continued to fight off the flames, tears trailing down his face.

"Hurry," Callum said, heading for the remaining horses. Most of them had run away. Realta tore her eyes away from Kanton. She followed her father on shaking legs, her knees reduced to water. "Get on," Callum pointed to Jak. The horse stood calmly next to Shadow, as though witnessing an everyday occurrence. Callum mounted Master Loy's horse without a saddle.

"The saddles..." Realta said, her heart pounding and Kanton's screams filling her ears.

"No time. Get on. Now!" Callum grabbed Shadow by the reins.

Realta scrambled onto the horse's back, Serena climbing on behind her. She had Callum's satchel over her shoulders. Imitating her father, Realta grabbed the horse by the reins. Serena wrapped her arms around Realta's waist. Charity was right about the bonds being too tight. Red lines with thin trails of blood circled Serena's wrists. Realta looked at her father. The entire right side of his shirt was stained red.

"This way," Callum said, flicking Shadow's reins. The horse took off at a gallop, speeding down the darkened road. Realta did not even have to do that. Jak took off after Shadow, like Nalani chasing her sister Ilana across the night sky. Kanton's screams faded away.

***

Branches scratched at her face and tore at her clothes. The cold night wind wiped at her hair as Charity rode deeper into the forest. She clung to the horse, keeping her head low. Tears leaked from her stinging eyes. In the distance, she heard screams.

She had awoken to Realta, her best friend, screaming for Callum's help and Lok standing over her, terrified. Kanton and Callum fought. That brute buried a knife in Callum's chest. All that blood. Charity was not given an opportunity to think, to process their situation. A sharp cry sounded right behind her, causing her to flinch.

The horse reared on its hind legs. Charity tightened her grip on the reins. She had heard what a fall from a horse could do to a person. Some walked away with bruises and maybe a fracture. Others never walked again, their spines broken. The horse landed its hooves on the ground, panting.

Charity glanced around the horse. There was just enough moonlight coming in through the trees for her to see the downed branch. Steadying her breathing, she dismounted. Her legs felt numb, every inch of her body shaking. What did those medical books call this? Shock. Yes, she was in a mild form of shock.

Twigs snapped. Charity spun around, heart pounding against her ribs. A tall figure ran in her direction. Kanton had followed her!

No, wait. This person was too thin and tall to be Dane Kanton. The figure slowed down, taking in deep, ragged breaths.

"Lok?" Charity recognized the silent innkeeper's son. How had he followed her on foot? Did that mean Realta and Callum were close behind?

The figure nodded.

A weight lift from her, adding some strength to her legs. The shock was wearing off, thank the Creator. She needed to be alert. Panicking never helped people in the middle of the woods.

Don't panic, Healer Zall's words echoed. She had once asked him about performing surgery. His advice had been not to panic under any circumstances. *Panicking leads to mistakes, and mistakes lead to disaster.*

"Where are Realta and her father? Are they with you?"

Lok shook his head. Moonlight glinted off his dark eyes.

Charity observed their surroundings. The forest was too dense and dark to see their campsite. Ilana was no longer visible overhead. The sun would be rising in about two hours. They could rest, see if the others caught up with them, and head back to the main road. But what if Kanton was still there? Why had he stabbed Callum? And what about the other guards? All of them had rushed to help Kanton, not Callum. It didn't make any sense.

"Did you see what started the fight?" Charity asked Lok.

Again, Lok shook his head.

"Drat." Charity smoothed down her hair, removing a handful of twigs and leaves. She glanced back at the way she had rode. No sounds, no signs of fire. No one else heading their way.

"What's this?"

Charity and Lok spun around. A dark figure stood on a fallen branch, hands on his hips. The horse flicked its head and stomped its hooves. Charity held onto the reins, steadying the animal.

"Who are you?" she asked.

"Why, young miss, don't you recognize me?"

Charity squinted in the low light. The man was tall and lanky, and his voice... "The inn! You were at the inn in Lothian!"

"Correct." Arnyn Teleran jumped off the branch and approached her and Lok. He had a bow in one hand and a quiver full of arrows on his back.

"What are you doing here?"

"Oh, just doing a little night hunting. Why? Is there somewhere else I should be?"

"In the village, I guess." Charity glanced around. No one was with him. And this man was Callum's friend. She could trust one of Callum's friends. He would not harm them. *You thought Dane Kanton wouldn't harm you, either. Now look at the mess you're in.*

"I never cared for villages. Too many people. Besides, I'm out here as a favor to a friend. Taught me how to properly pick a pocket, after all. So, why are you here?"

"We ran away. The people we were traveling with..." The knife went into the right side of Callum's chest. Just below the collarbone. Buried to the hilt. Blood seeping out of the wound. Charity forced her mind to focus. The forest. Outside of Lothian. Two hours until sunrise. "They attacked us. I think they meant to rob us." Yes, robbing them. That was a logical reason to attack people at night. The whole guardsmen act was some sort of ploy. But why show themselves to people in Vala? Why not just rob sleeping travelers? "Lok and I ran into the woods. We don't know what happened to our friends."

Arnyn rubbed his chin. "I knew that fellow was bad news. Never trust a Learner Thane. They're all too smart for their own good."

"Do you know a lot about Thanes?" Anything to keep her mind away from Callum's stab wound. And learning about Thanes might explain why Kanton attacked them. She had never heard of Thanes using violence. They were nobles and scholars. Men and women of great renown, not murders and thugs.

"Let's walk and talk," replied Arnyn. "There's a small settlement up ahead. The two of you can rest from your ordeal."

"Thank you, sir." Charity led the horse with Lok one step behind her. Arnyn, by the light of the setting second moon and the rising sun, navigated his way through the trees.

"I know a great deal about Thanes," Arnyn said. "Well, not a great deal. I just know them when I see them."

"How's that?"

"The Creator loves balance," Arnyn replied, moving a branch out of the way, "that's how. You see, I'm just a simple son of a whore who got kicked out of the house the moment I was old enough to steal bread. A very bad beginning, wouldn't you say?"

"Yes," Charity agreed. How old did you need to be to steal bread? Six or seven?

"So the Creator, in His infinite love of balance, saw this very bad beginning and gave me the most wonderful gift. The ability to see Thanes."

"Do Thanes look a lot different from normal people?" She formed a mental image of Kanton. Nothing about him, other than his earrings, stood out from other people.

"Of course. Every Thane I've encountered has this Aura around them, like rays of colorful sunlight streaming out of their skin."

"That sounds beautiful."

"It is. That's the way your silent friend looks right now."

Charity halted. Lok stumbled, his eyes wide and confused.

"You didn't know?"

Lok shook his head. He held out his trembling hands, studying them.

Arnyn's smile reflected in his bright blue eyes. "It always astounds me that so many Thanes must be told what they are. You'd think they were born knowing, judging by the way some act. Yes, boy, you truly are a Thane."

Lok stood as still as a statue, processing the words. Charity looked at him in awe. Lok Tolman was a Thane? All the Thanes she could think of were nobles. King Logan and half of the monarchs in the Northern Realm were Thanes. How would the people back in Vala, the ones who called Lok stupid and good for nothing, react to this knowledge?

Fumbling inside his coat pocket, Lok removed his notebook and pencil. He wrote a quick note and handed it to Arnyn. There was just enough light on the horizon to read.

Arnyn gave him a wry smile. "I'm not much of a reader. Perhaps your nice friend can help." He passed the notebook to Charity.

"Lok wants to know which kind of Thane he is."

"That I can do. You're an Elemental. The first one I've ever met. You should be proud of yourself, young man. By the way, what are your names?"

"I'm Charity Loy, and this is Lok Tolman." She was surprised

Callum hadn't told him. She recalled Arnyn addressing Lok by name as they left Lothian. Maybe the man simply forgot or wanted to make sure he had the right names.

"Young Master Tolman," said Arnyn, standing on his toes and placing his hands on Lok's shoulders, "I congratulate you on being not only a Thane, but the first Elemental Thane I have ever met in my balanced life."

Lok sighed. He gently lifted Arnyn's hands from his shoulders and shook his head.

"Is there something wrong?"

Lok motioned for the notebook. Charity handed it back, and he wrote, *"I am not important enough to be a Thane. I can't even speak."*

"Nonsense!" Arnyn exclaimed. "There are plenty of people in this world who speak all the time and say absolutely nothing. The Creator has balanced your life, too, my young friend."

"What about Charity?"

Arnyn studied her. She did not expect to be a Thane. Nobody in her family was one, nor anyone in Vala. That was, until Kanton revealed Mayor Gan's secret. What did he call him? An Empath? Something to do with reading people's emotions. Why had the mayor kept his ability a secret? It seemed very useful.

"Unfortunately, no," replied Arnyn. "You are an ordinary human, Miss Loy. But you don't look disappointed."

"I've been an ordinary human my whole life. I never expected to be anything else."

"That's surprisingly mature." Arnyn raised an eyebrow. "I've told adults twice your age that they're only normal humans, and they've thrown fits to rival spoiled children."

Charity laughed, picturing the scene.

"Laughter. Always a good sign." Arnyn continued walking through the forest. Charity now saw a clear path in front of them. Several branches had recently been broken, marking the way.

"Is the settlement very far?" Charity asked.

"About six or seven miles. Shouldn't take more than a few hours."

Good. They could rest there and wait for Realta, Callum, and Serena to catch up. Charity sighed. It was a nice thought, but the odds were against them.

She looked back at Lok. The young man walked slowly, his face a mixture of confusion and awe.

7

The River Road

Kanton's screams faded as Realta raced down the road, white knuckling the reins, terrified to stop moving. Serena clung to her, taking furtive glances at the abandoned campsite. Realta had no idea where they were going, only that Callum was in the lead. Her father would know what to do, where to go.

We should have never trusted Kanton.

They rounded a small hill. The sun's red and orange rays rose from the horizon. Realta felt like they had been riding for hours, but the morning sky indicated that it had been no more than one or two. On the other side of the hill rested a small village. Callum slowed Shadow to a trot. Realta followed suit, riding next to him.

She glanced over her shoulder. There were no signs of anyone following them. The other guards must have remained behind to help Kanton. Or they were merely waiting in order to give them a false sense of security.

She did a quick head count. Many of the horses had run off, one carrying Charity into the woods. Lok and Marsh had run after her. Kanton and Tock had both been injured by the fire, pretty badly from what Realta could tell. Burns on their arms and faces. How long did a person have to be on fire for the injury to be severe? Neither man might not be in a condition to ride. And Wills seemed too distraught to think clearly. It might be some time before he rode after them.

Realta looked at her father. Callum's face was pale, its usually ruddiness drained away. The right side of his shirt was stained dark red. They passed the first houses. She hoped this village had a healer. A sane one.

"Do you know this place?" Realta asked him, her voice weak.

"Narfalk." Callum's breath wheezed as he spoke. "First village on the River Road." He glanced around. "I haven't been here in twenty years. Did you pass through here?" he asked Serena.

The girl clung to Realta, her wrists raw and scabbing. "Yes," she whispered.

"Where's the healer's house? Do you know?"

Realta's hands trembled. She had never seen her father sick. Cuts, bruises, a handful of broken bones, but nothing this bad. How much blood had he lost?

"Keep going on this road. At the first crossroads, go left. Two houses down on the right," Serena replied.

Callum nodded and followed the directions.

People emerged from their houses, going about their morning routines as the sun rose higher, warming the spring day. Craftsmen headed for their workshops, and merchants to their stores and the marketplace. Men and women exchanged greetings. A group of children ran down the road, laughing and delaying their arrival at the schoolhouse until the last minute.

One woman noticed Callum, bleeding and disheveled. She turned to her husband who then alerted another man. Soon, every eye was on them.

"What happened to you, sir?" asked a village guardsman. His face was pale.

"Bandits."

"I will tell the healer to be ready for you," replied the guardsman. He dashed off down the street, entering a sturdy, two-story house.

They arrived at the same house a minute later. The ride felt surreal, as though Realta were stuck on a raft in the middle of a river, being carried by the current. All she could do was hang on and hope for a safe destination.

Serena dismounted and tied the two horses to a nearby post. Realta followed suit, landing on wobbly legs. The healer, a man with eyeglasses and streaks of gray in his dark brown hair, rushed out and helped Callum dismount.

"Oh Creator," cried the healer, peeling back Callum's shirt to inspect the wound. Dark blood seeped out. He led Callum into the house. A woman dressed in a white apron, the healer's wife Realta surmised, helped Callum into a bed in one of half a dozen small rooms lining the hallway. She quickly ducked into another room and returned with a large, black bag. She removed a handful of medical instruments. All of them shiny and silver.

"What about your children?" the healer asked. "Were they also hurt?"

"Her wrists..." Callum's voice faded. His eyes closed, and his head titled listlessly.

"Father!" Realta rushed to his side. His chest moved up and down. He was breathing. Slowly, but breathing.

The healer unbuttoned Callum's shirt and cut away the undershirt with a pair of scissors. Dipping a cloth into a bottle of alcohol, he began cleaning the wound.

Realta felt herself being pulled away from the bed. Away from Callum. She fought to stay with him, but her body was too tired to comply. The healer's wife led her into a sitting room filled with plush furniture and motioned for her to sit. The guardsman from earlier stood in the corner.

"Guardsman Errick will ask you some questions, young miss," she said, "while we attend to your father and sister. Is that all right?"

Sister? She didn't have a sister. She was an only child, though at times it felt like Charity was her sister. Realta looked up at the healer's wife. Serena stood beside her. The girl who looked like Kel. Why did she look like Kel? She was not his daughter. And it was all her fault that they had been dragged into this mess, that Callum was bleeding out, possibly dying. If she hadn't hidden in the Loy's barn, then Kanton wouldn't have enticed them with his fake reward. They would all be safe at home.

Realta nodded anyway, her head feeling like it was full of iron. Serena was led down the hall. Guardsman Errick sat in the chair opposite her. He was older than she had assumed. Likely in mid mid-forties. Fine lines surrounded his pale, blue eyes.

"Can you tell me your name, miss?" Errick asked.

"Realta Haar. My father's name is Callum." Was that her voice? It sounded hoarse, as though her tongue had been replaced with sandpaper.

"And your sister's name?"

Why did he assume Serena was Callum's daughter? Kel was the one she resembled. Realta suddenly felt very tired. Too tired to explain their real relationship. "Serena."

"And you were attacked by bandits?" She nodded. "Did you get a good look at them?"

"There were four of them. Their leader is about my father's height. Short black hair." No. Those descriptions were too generic. She could be talking about any man in the Hinterlands. *Think, Realta. One good detail. One that people will instantly recognize.* "Red earrings. He had a red earring in each ear."

Errick nodded. "That ought to be easy to track. And the others?"

"Two men and one woman." She gave their descriptions, realizing that nothing about them really stood out.

"Where were you coming from?"

"Lothian."

"Are there any other details you can tell me?"

Realta racked her brain. Details. A hallway with stone walls. A young woman asking about her sick brother. No, that was a dream. Charity's smiling face came into view. Lok standing outside the inn, wearing a cloak that was far too big. "We were traveling with friends. We were separated from them." Tears stung her eyes. "I don't know where they went."

"Okay." Errick nodded sympathetically. "And their names?"

Before Realta could answer, the healer stepped into the sitting room. He dried off his hands with a red stained cloth. "Errick, a word."

"I will be right back." He stood and left Realta alone. She strained to listen but could only hear soft whispers. No distinct words. A form walked up beside her. Serena. White bandages covered her wrists. Callum's satchel was strung over her shoulder.

A knock came at the door. Realta tensed, sitting upright and gripping her dress. This was the first village on the River Road. Kanton and Tock's injuries would need medical attention. Had a twisted turn of fate led them here?

The healer's wife answered the door. A woman's voice complained of a severe toothache. The healer's wife led her into an unoccupied room. Realta relaxed, the tension draining away, leaving her feeling even more tired.

"Thanks for not telling him about me," Serena whispered.

"Should I have?" Realta stood, meaning her eye to eye. "If my father dies..." If her father died, she would be orphaned. She would not be alone. Kel and Esme and the Loys would take care of her, but it would never be the same. The absence would haunt her the rest of her life. And it would be all Serena's fault.

Serena hung her head, sandy hair obscuring her face. "I should have warned you about Kanton. That man is insane."

Realta took a deep breath, steadying herself. If Callum died, his death would be on Kanton's hands, not Serena's. This girl had a reason for stealing the king's horse, and that fight in the barn had been an act of self-defense. But Kanton had a reason to track her down. That left a glaring question.

"Why did he try to kill you?"

"How should I know? Fire and smoke, the man and his cronies hunted me down to the edge of the kingdom. I thought they just wanted justice. Not this."

"You talk as though you know him."

She hesitated. "I ask a lot of questions."

"What does that mean?" Realta crossed her arms.

"Realta, Serena," said the healer. "Your father is ready to see you. And we have a few more questions," he added gravely.

Realta and Serena complied. She did not want to waste another minute.

Callum sat propped up on the bed, the right side of his chest covered in white bandages. His skin retained that sickly pale complexion. But he was conscious, his eyes alert. Esme would say that was a good sign. She hoped Gareth had returned home safely.

"If you could come over here, please." Realta went to Callum's side with Serena close behind. "Do you know what this tattoo means?" The healer pointed at the two bands on Callum's left wrist. Two diamonds, the symbol of indentured servitude, rested in the middle.

"My... Our father is a hired hand," Realta answered. Panic flooded her. The paper, the rite of passage. Where was it? Had they lost it? Left it behind as they ran for their lives?

"Does his master know where he is?"

"Yes," Serena replied. Reaching into Callum's satchel, she took out a folded piece of paper and gave it to the healer. He inspected the paper, nodded, and handed it back. Serena returned it to the satchel. Of course. Callum's satchel. Serena had it this whole time. Her brain was not working right. Too much happening too quickly.

She turned to her father. Callum wore a thin smile.

"Very well. I will send word to Master Sardic Loy of Vala and have him come take you back."

"No!" Serena cried. "Those bandits followed us all the way from Vala to Lothian. They'll be waiting for us—"

"Young miss, your father is under contract to another man, even though it is temporary. And that man must know the damages. You are welcome to stay here free of charge until Master Loy arrives. Please know that this is my duty."

"Healer Tesell," said Callum, "my master gave me leave to journey to Teyrnas and back on business for him. I intend to carry out that business. With your permission, I'd like to write that letter myself and wait for its reply."

The healer mulled it over. "Two letters. One from you and one from me. It will take four or five days for the reply. Plenty of time for you to heal."

Four or five days. If Kanton followed them on the River Road, this village was first on the list. He'd find them in no time.

"Very well," replied Callum. "May I have a private word with my daughters?"

"Of course." Healer Tesell exited the room, closing the door.

Callum motioned for them to come closer. Realta listened to his breathing. He definitely breathed easier, but that wheezing remained. Esme would know what that meant. Damaged lung, her aunt's voice echoed. *Kanton stabbed him in the lung. That's why his breathing is labored.* A damaged lung. Great.

"When I first met Kanton," Callum said, "he claimed to be a captain in the King's Guard. Members of the King's Guard don't kill unharmed prisoners. So, who are you?"

Serena bit down on her trembling lip. She rubbed her bandaged wrists. "A horse thief."

"What else?"

"A bastard."

Callum stared at her. Realta had a dozen questions, but she held her tongue.

"My father was a nobleman," Serena continued. "My mother was a servant. They had an affair. No one knew I was his daughter until my mother told his children everything. She was dying and wanted to make sure I was cared for. They were furious but took me in anyway. My oldest brother, he..." Tears streamed down her face. "I had to get away. They never loved me, so I thought I wouldn't be missed."

"So you stole the king's horse," said Callum.

"They're the fastest animals in Teyrnas." Serena wiped her eyes. "My brothers love watching the races. I left the horse for everyone to find in East Bridge. I thought that would be enough."

"It certainly doesn't warrant killing you in your sleep."

Serena ran a hand through her short hair. "I thought the worst that could happen was being caught and sent to jail. Maybe forced into a contract. Not this. I never meant for anyone else to get hurt."

"I know, Serena."

"Would Kanton really have taken us to the Academy, or was that just a lie?" Realta asked. She knew it was too good to be true.

"I don't know."

"That's not an acceptable answer, not for me," replied Callum. "The King's Guard is stationed in Teyrnas."

"The main garrison is in Norgard. But yes, Kanton and his team were stationed in Teyrnas."

"Then that's where we will get our answers."

"We're still going all the way?" Realta questioned. Would her father be able to ride in his condition?

"I don't see any other way. You want to attend the Academy, don't you? And Charity and Lok were placed in my care. If they aren't at the Academy, it will be my responsibility to find them and bring them home safely."

Realta nodded. When Charity was dead set on accomplishing something, she accomplished it. Even being separated and lost would not deter her. She and Lok Tolman would be at the Academy when they arrived in Teyrnas. Realta bet a gold mark on it.

"How will we get away?" Serena asked.

"You leave that to me."

A knock sounded at the door. The healer and his wife entered, carrying writing material and a platter full of food. They placed both on a small table by the window.

"There's no rush on the letter," said Healer Tesell. "Take as much time as you need."

"I appreciate it," Callum replied. The healers left. Callum leaned back on the bed's headrest and closed his eyes. "You two eat. I got too much on my mind."

"Yes, Father." Realta did not feel like eating either. What if there was something wrong with it? Something to make them sleep or more compliant or... What was she thinking? Yes, Kanton had betrayed them, but that did not mean the Tesells would, too. They were healers. And they were of sound mind. She had no logical reason to fear them.

And she needed her strength in order to travel to Teyrnas. The capital city. That was where she would get her answers.

She joined Serena at the small table. The platter contained three bowls of oatmeal and a variety of dried fruits and bread. She took a small bite of bread, chewing it slowly. Other than being a little sweet, it tasted normal. Taking another bite, she studied Serena. Perhaps it was mere coincidence. Serena's father or mother might have shared the same features as Kel. It was not impossible for two strangers to look similar.

But Kanton insisted on Callum helping them. Not to mention the odd way Kel behaved when the guards were at their home. She sighed. Another thing in her life that did not make sense.

Serena poked at the oatmeal with a spoon but did not eat any. She stared out of the window, facing the street. Neither she nor Realta said a word.

8

Letters

The walk to Arnyn's settlement took much longer than a few hours. Overgrown shrubs and downed branches cluttered their path, forcing them to stop and remove the debris. And the horse had proved difficult to manage. Charity now recognized it as Kanton's horse, a large warhorse with a pure black coat. The creature obviously took after its master.

"How much longer, Master Teleran?" Charity asked. The sun was high in the sky, warm light streaming through the branches. Sweat beaded on her brow. This had to be the warmest Alet in her life!

"Shouldn't be much farther," Arnyn replied. "Unless they moved it. Hmm..." He rubbed his chin. "Let's rest for a moment. Get our bearings."

Thank you. Charity tied the horse's reins on a nearby tree. She and Lok sat on a fallen, moss-covered trunk while Arnyn studied the forest. A small group of green draigs scurried from one tree to another. Songbirds chirped and jumped from branch to branch. A cool breeze rushed past her face, bringing much needed relief.

Lok took out his notebook and jotted down a few words. He handed it to Charity. She read, "What can Elemental Thanes do?"

"The meaning is in the name," Arnyn answered. After a few silent moments, he added, "Don't you go to chapel?"

Lok and Charity nodded, but she did not quite grasp Arnyn's meaning.

"Each chapel is designed to mirror the four basic elements: air, water, earth, and fire. The Gadyeni gave Elementals control over those four things. So, Young Tolman, you likely have control over two or three of them, based on the strength of your Aura."

Lok shook his head, confused.

Charity said, "But I thought the Creator gave Thanes their abilities, and the Gadyeni acted as their teachers."

"Close. The Eight Gadyeni asked the Creator permission to give humans abilities in order to fight the Midnight King, and permission was granted. Each Gadyeni was allowed to give one gift, hence the eight types of Thanes."

Lok wrote, *"Which Gadyeni made the Elementals?"*

"That would be Abhainna." Charity recognized the name. Abhainna was always depicted as a woman in her thirties with dark brown hair, bronze skin, and bright blue eyes. "Are you sure you don't know which elements you can control?" Arnyn asked.

Lok nodded.

"The Academy will test him, won't they?"

"Oh, I'm sure they will. It's their job to teach young Thanes, and young humans."

Charity frowned. "I don't suppose you know the best way to get to the Academy, do you, Master Teleran?"

"No. I tend to stay away from that side of the Nerin. But I might know someone who does, if she's still at the settlement."

"And she'll take us all the way to Teyrnas?" Charity had no idea where Realta and Callum were, or if they were okay. They might be returning to Vala, in which case her family would send help. Kanton and his team would be arrested and questioned. Then again, they might be heading for Teyrnas, hoping to meet them at the Academy. Or maybe Callum had succumbed to his wounds, and Realta and Serena were on their own and lost. Or worse, Kanton had found them.

"Now, why would she take you to Teyrnas?" Arnyn asked, placing his hands on his hips. "I thought you were heading for the Academy."

"We are."

"Well, the Academy ain't in Teyrnas anymore. It's in Norgard."

"What?" Charity shot to her feet. Lok's face went pale. "What do you mean?"

"The old Academy, the one that was in Teyrnas, burned to the ground centuries ago. Struck by lightning, so the history books say. Anyway, the Scholars rebuilt it bigger and better in Norgard. The town was smaller at the time, and closer to the Garrison."

"Kanton never mentioned that." Charity eased herself back

onto the fallen tree, her legs going numb. "Why wouldn't he..."

"When Callum told me about transporting a thief to Teyrnas, I figured the Academy was the next stop. It's only a day or so away. Kanton must have had a change of plans."

Lok rose and stormed over to the horse, rifling through the saddlebags. Charity and Arnyn joined him.

"What are you looking for?" *Think, Charity. It's Kanton's horse.* "Do you think he kept a journal? Or orders?"

Lok nodded. His face burned red, eyes like a furnace. This was the first time she had seen him angry.

Opening one bag, Lok tossed several changes of clothes onto the ground. At the bottom was a notebook filled with various papers and letters. Lok handed the letters to Charity while he leafed through the notebook.

"Anything enlightening?" asked Arnyn. He picked up a letter and looked at it upside down. She figured he had very little schooling.

"Give me a moment." Charity read a formal letter issuing for Serena's arrest. It stated that she had stolen one of King Logan's prize horses as well as money from the stable hands. It gave her description followed by a bunch of legal jargon. She felt a light tap on her shoulder. Lok held out the open notebook for her, and she accepted it.

"What language is this?" The letters were from the Teyrnian alphabet, but the language was wholly unfamiliar. Nothing about it... "Old Eltrian. I think this is Old Eltrian." Her mother had an Old Eltrian primer, but Charity never bothered to read it. Blast it. Why had she been so singular with her education?

"I'm sure the Scholars can translate it," Arnyn chimed in. "Speaking of which, we'd best keep moving. I'm not a fan of these woods at night."

Gripping the horse's reins in one hand and the letters in the other, she followed Arnyn and Lok deeper into the woods. At least these letters were written in Teyrnian.

One letter seemed to be from Kanton's lover. The script and words were flowery, full of outrageous similes and metaphors. The paper smelled faintly of a woman's perfume. Charity had no idea what any woman could see in Kanton. She moved the letter to the bottom of the stack and inspected the next one.

This letter was an order from King Logan himself and had the same seal as the document Kanton had given to Mayor Gan. A flying raven in dark blue wax. The king ordered Kanton to find the thief known as Serena Molyns no matter the cost, and to return her to Teyrnas unharmed.

Unharmed. They why were Callum and Kanton fighting? Had they gotten into an argument? And the look on Realta's face. It was as though she had seen a Shade. Hadn't Serena looked just as terrified? And there was something about Serena that was hauntingly familiar. An aspect of her face or posture. Charity was going to kick herself when she finally discovered it. It was so close yet slipped through her fingers like water.

The third letter was also written in Old Eltrian. A well of good that did!

Lok fell back and walked alongside her. Turning to a blank page, he wrote, *"I think Realta and Callum are okay."*

"I hope so, too." The knife piercing Callum's chest, driven to the hilt into his lung. Dark blood running down his shirt. Charity squeezed her eyes tightly. *Don't think about it.*

Lok chewed on his lower lip, his dark brown eyes looking at her expectantly. As though he wanted to say something, but was too afraid to write the words.

"I'm worried, too," she whispered.

Lok averted his eyes. He wrote, *"Ask Arnyn why he doesn't like the woods at night. I'm curious."*

Anything to keep her mind off negative thoughts. "Master Teleran, why don't you like these woods during the night?"

"That's when the Ullmhir like to come out. They have a fondness for long abandoned places."

"I thought the Ullmhir were just a children's story." Charity remembered her father telling her and her sisters about the Ullmhir, shadow creatures who haunted the woods at night, looking for children to steal. A cautionary tale invented to keep children out of the woods after nightfall, the real dangers being wolves and wildcats.

"They're featured in many children's stories, I imagine. Joined by Howlers and the Seltachai. But that doesn't mean they ain't real. And trust me, they are some creepy bastards."

"You've actually seen them?" she asked, raising an eyebrow.

"Unfortunately." Arnyn shivered. "Please ask me another question that has nothing to do with those creatures."

"Very well. You mentioned abandoned places. Did this settlement use to be a town?"

"About a thousand years ago. No one's really sure. Did those letters reveal anything useful about your attackers?"

"Only that the king hired them to find Serena."

"Then this Serena must be a very important or infamous person. What exactly did she do?"

"Stole the king's horse." Nothing about Serena seemed very important or dangerous. She was just an orphan, down on her luck with nowhere to turn.

"That's it?"

"I imagine the king values his horses."

"Did they ever find the horse?"

"Yes. Why?" What was Arnyn getting at?

"That's odd. That's very odd." He rubbed his chin.

"Care to explain?"

"The king's horse is stolen, and the horse is recovered. Who cares if the thief is caught?"

"Isn't there a punishment for horse theft?" The pathway dipped down, positioning them between two small hills. Charity adjusted her stride accordingly.

"Of course. Three months in jail is the minimum, and I've heard of some thieves getting two or three years under contract. But this is King Logan we're talking about. The man likely has hundreds of servants. Why would he take on another contract, specially one that's a thief?"

Charity shrugged. "Maybe he wants Serena to serve her punishment under someone else."

"Now that's interesting! Send a thief to someone else. Perhaps to steal something? No, the king can just demand it. Unless it's another noble or a Thane. Hmm." Arnyn rubbed his chin. "You've given me something very interesting to think about, Miss Loy."

Did the king wish to use Serena as a spy? Spying was a form of theft, odd as it sounded. But why were Kanton and Callum fighting? Why did Realta look so frightened? Stars above, she hated not knowing!

"Master Teleran, how much longer until we reach the settlement?"

"Won't be long now. Do you hear that?"

Charity listened. Laughter. Human voices in the distance. Tears pricked her eyes, an invisible weight lifting off her shoulders.

"Now," said Arnyn, "walk behind me, and let me do the talking."

9

Rangar Keep

Three hooded men armed with bows and arrows emerged from the forest. Lok positioned himself next to Charity. She did not appear to be afraid. In fact, she seemed happy. Lok preferred not to meet strangers in the middle of the woods. He wished Arnyn had led them back to the main road. Then he could have found his bearings, gone back home.

Home. Only one person was waiting for him there. Only one person who wanted him. Going to the Academy sounded like a good idea. A chance for him to escape the mocking eyes and quiet laughter that always followed him. Being attacked by the people escorting them had never been taken into account. Seeing these three, he feared Arnyn was no different.

"Hey there, Arnyn," said one of the men, pulling down his hood. His brown hair contained hints of red. "Pick up some strays?"

"Two children bound for the Academy with no safe passage," he said in a dramatic voice, like a narrator in a bad play.

"I hear you." He nodded to his two companions. They split up and headed deeper into the forest. Lok's eyes followed them until they disappeared into the foliage.

"I take it there's room at the Keep?" Arnyn asked.

"Not as much as usual, but enough for two more." The man turned and walked along a semi-hidden path. The vegetation in this part of the forest was denser, obscuring most of the sunlight.

Arnyn motioned for Lok and Charity to follow. Charity did so, holding onto the horse's reins. Lok thought over Arnyn's words. There must have been a secondary message within them, one that only he and their new guide knew. Lok held onto the horse's saddle, eyes and ears open for any possible surprises.

"Don't worry," Charity whispered. "Arnyn will make sure we're okay." Lok heard the smile in her voice.

Lok had his doubts. Charity had a bad habit of being too trusting. He'd seen her speaking with the madman, Darran Zall, numerous times and not even batting an eye to the fact that he might hurt her. Anybody with an ounce of sense went to Esme Haar for medicine. Lok could not walk past the healer's house without trembling.

Human voices rang throughout the forest. The path grew wider and cleared of debris. Lok spied a vine-covered stone slab sticking out of the underbrush, like the foundation of a long-abandoned building.

"Does this place have a name, Master Teleran?" Charity asked. How could her voice be so calm and level?

"Rangar Keep, located within the forest of the same name," the shady man replied.

Lok didn't know if he ought to trust the man. He claimed Lok was a Thane, that he had light coming out of his skin. But that was impossible. Thanes were born into noble families. Everyone knew that. And Lok had never seen any light streaming from his skin. But hadn't he always felt different? That something other than being a mute caused him to be an outcast?

"And this place was a city a thousand years ago?"

"That girl asks a lot of questions," said the reddish-brown haired man.

"What do you expect, Danior? She wants to be a Scholar," Arnyn laughed.

"A healer, actually."

"Oh, and why is that?" asked Danior.

"Well," Charity hesitated. "Our village has a healer and a midwife, but the healer is getting older and isn't able to help everyone. If I study medicine, more people can be helped."

That was a very nice way of putting it. Lok wondered how she would describe his inability to speak. *Oh, Lok's a great listener. Never interrupts.*

"Sounds like a noble cause," Danior replied. "And I see the boy is going there for obvious reasons."

Sweat broke out on Lok's forehead. *No, by the Creator, no!*

Arnyn smiled. "See, Young Tolman. You truly are a Thane. And as further proof, which Thane would you say he is, Danior?"

Danior turned around and studied Lok, and he continued to walk. The man was walking backwards! He didn't even trip on a downed branch. Just stepped right over it.

"Now that's a sight. An Elemental! Never seen one of your kind before."

"You're just like Master Teleran," Charity exclaimed. "Did you learn this ability or were you born with it?"

"I've had the ability since childhood."

"Danior's life is equally balanced. You see, being a member of the Hiraeth..."

"Wait, you're Hiraethi?"

"Last time I checked," Danior laughed, his dark brown eyes smiling.

"Do your people wear earrings or give earrings to foreigners?"

Danior raised an eyebrow. "Now, that's an interesting question."

"Like I said," Arnyn chimed in. "Scholar."

"Our Great Mother wears earrings, and some tribes give earrings to their warriors. But never to outsiders. Why do you ask?"

"Well," Charity hesitated, "my friend's uncle is Hiraethi, but he never talks about his early life. And there are so many stories about the Hiraeth. I wanted to know if they were true."

Lok did not know any stories about the Hiraeth, only that they lived in the mountains, tended to keep to themselves, and Mayor Gan's story was a lie. The man was a Thane. Just like Lok. And he had chosen to hide his identity. Why? Was being a Thane a good thing or bad?

Sunlight poured down on Lok's head. He looked up and saw that the forest had given way to a large clearing. People milled about the space. The remnants of stone pillars and foundations were strewn around the area, and most were covered with vines. If Lok focused hard enough, he could imagine buildings instead of ruins. Houses, a town hall, market stalls, a central well or maybe a fountain. What had this place been a thousand years ago? How much more of it was hidden by the forest? Why would anyone abandon it?

"Fire and smoke," Arnyn muttered. He asked Danior, "Are you sure there are empty places for these two?"

"I'm sure there are. There's Rawni. I'll ask." Danior walked off towards a small group of people. He spoke to the sole woman of the group. A woman with coal black hair and dressed in a man's shirt and trousers. Lok blinked, making sure his eyes saw correctly. He had only seen two other women dressed in men's clothes: Serena and that female guard. She had chased Lok into the forest. Why had she stopped?

"This might take a while," said Arnyn. "Feel free to wander around and talk to strangers. Rawni has everyone swear an oath of nonviolence while in the Keep."

"Is Rawni the mayor?" Charity asked, faltering on the word 'mayor'.

"More or less." Someone called out Arnyn's name. He waved to them and said, "Excuse me." He then sauntered off, leaving Lok and Charity alone with Dane Kanton's horse.

"I'll find somewhere to put Tiber," said Charity, "and you can look for some food."

Now that Charity mentioned it, he was very hungry. In fact, they hadn't eaten since the common room in Lothian. The same place they met Arnyn.

Wait a minute.

Lok tapped Charity on the shoulder and quickly wrote, *"Who is Tiber?"* The letters were a mixture of jagged lines and faint squiggles.

"Oh, the horse. I figured he ought to have a name."

Yeah, that made sense. It was far better than 'the horse'.

Charity walked off, heading in Danior and Rawni's direction. Lok wondered how many more people here could see Thanes. He suddenly felt very uncomfortable, as though thousands of eyes were staring at him. Everyone thinking he was an idiot, that he could tolerate. Everyone thinking he was a powerful and important person, that was pure lunacy. More like a cruel trick than a gift to balance out his life.

Lok wandered around the clearing, keeping his distance from other people. What was he even doing here? His mother had planned for the Scholars to test him on Autumntide. Lok had devoted one hour every evening for studies. Mathematics, history, natural sciences. Anything the Scholars might test. It was his best chance to get out of Vala. Then word reached his mother that Callum was taking Charity, Realta, and Gareth to the Academy. Short noticed as it was, the opportunity was too good to pass up.

But what if the Scholars rejected him? Being a Thane was one thing, being wanted another.

The scent of bubbling stew wafted around Lok's nose. His stomach growled. Following the scent, he saw a group of four people, three men and one woman, sitting around a cook fire. A black pot hung over it on a tripod. They sat near the ruins of what Lok assumed was a stone house. Within the former house sat a fifth figure, obscured by heavy, black robes.

"Can we help you?" asked one man in a strange accent.

Lok wrote, *"May I have some food?"* and handed his notebook to the man. He scoffed and handed it to the woman.

"He wants to know if he can have food," the woman informed him. A sinking feeling formed in Lok's gut. Yet another person who could not read. Another person he could not communicate with.

The man called out to the figure, "Westermor, e dag un po ciig."

The robed figure slowly got to his feet and walked forward. Though his hood was down, Lok sensed the figure's eyes on him. The figure approached the fire, picked up a spare bowl, and ladled out a hearty portion.

The woman glared daggers at the man. The other two men snickered. White hot anger flashed through Lok. He had lost count of how many times people mocked him and hated seeing the same treatment inflicted on someone else. Gareth Haar's awkwardness had made him a prime target as well. At least he had the intelligence not to trust Kanton.

The figure handed the bowl to Lok. He nodded in thanks.

"You may sit," said the woman. She had the same accent as the first man.

Lok did so. The figure sat, too, huddled at the woman's side.

"Hey, boy," the second man said in a Teyrnian accent, "didn't your mother and father teach you to speak?"

Lok sheepishly set aside and bowl and wrote. The woman translated, "My father died two months before I was born."

The two men stopped smiling and shifting uncomfortably. The

woman handed back the notebook, her face solemn. The man with the accent continued eating. Lok never liked bringing up his father's death. But it had put an end to the starting and mocking laughter. He could eat in peace.

The small figure perked up and said, "Is mio West."

Lok shook his head. The language was nothing like Lowyrnic or Averillian. He only knew a handful of phrases from each. Yes, no, hello, goodbye, thank you. But the words sounded like neither language. Where were these people from?

"He said that his name is West," replied the woman.

Lok wrote, *"My name is Lok."*

"Is er Lok," the woman translated.

West pulled down his hood and beamed a smile at him. He was not much older than Lok, a year or two at most. His eyes were blue-ish gray, like the sky at the advent of a storm. A long, white scar rested near his hairline.

The accented man scowled and pulled the hood back over West's head. "Cos ti detemas, stolt?!"

West shuddered, huddling closer to the woman. The four adults glared at Lok.

"I think it best if you go. Keep the bowl," said the woman.

Lok, bowl in hand, slowly rose and walked away. He heard the man speaking in his unknown language to the woman, and the woman replying. The only word he understood was 'West'. Why did that man not want West to show his face? Something was off about the group. Not in the same way Healer Zall was off, but very similar. He stole a glance back.

You should stay with West and make sure he is okay.

Ignoring his gut feeling, Lok kept walking.

He saw Charity speaking with Arnyn and another woman, this one wearing a simple, light blue dress. The woman crossed her arms and scowled at Arnyn.

"Cross the Nerin! I just came from there, and you want me to go back without pay?"

"Who said anything about you not getting paid?"

"Oh, so you have money this time?"

"Well, no." Arnyn gave her a sympathetic smile. "But money is a temporary thing. There is no currency in the Realm of Stars."

"But we ain't in the Realm of Stars, are we, Arnyn Teleran?"

"My mother and father have money," Charity chimed in. "Once I write them, I'm sure they will pay your fee."

The woman smirked. "Once you write them, and if the letter ever reaches them, is that correct?"

"I'm sure they'll find a way." Charity's eyes hardened. "Their names are Sardic and Aida Loy, and they live in Vala."

"Best not to give out personal information, young miss," said Arnyn. He turned and saw Lok standing behind him. A wide smile split his face. Lok regretted walking over. "A Thane! Not only will you be transporting future Scholars, but a Thane to boot."

Lok's face grew red and uncomfortably warm. Several people looked his way. He pulled the hood of his cloak over his head. He was pretty sure this fell under the category of personal information.

The woman scoffed. "You expect me to believe you?"

"Ask Danior. He'll confirm it."

"Bloody savage," she muttered. She studied Lok, looking him up and down. "Five days. Give me five days, Teleran, and I'll take the girl and this so-called Thane across the Nerin. Deal?"

"Yes, thank you, Kelia."

The woman rolled her eyes and walked off.

Lok met Charity's eyes and cocked his head in the woman's direction.

"She's a ship captain. She's going to take us the rest of the way to the Academy," Charity explained.

Lok held out the bowl of stew for Charity. He had never met a female ship captain. Or a male ship captain.

"Thank you, Lok." Charity held the bowl and grinned.

Lok raised an eyebrow. What did that grin mean?

"I was just thinking. You can't speak but you communicate very well."

Facial expressions could only say so much. The ability to speak, in Lok's opinion, was infinitely better.

"You two think you can stand five days in this place?" Arnyn asked.

"Yes. The Academy isn't going anywhere. And who knows? It might give our friends a chance to find us."

Lok nodded. He did not like the idea of being in the middle of nowhere, but it was peaceful here. People didn't bother him. Nobody knew he was a mute. And those five days might grant him another opportunity to see West.

There is something wrong with that group, and you know it, Lok Tolman. But what? His gut feeling did not explain.

"*Do people from different kingdoms travel through here?*" Lok wrote and Charity read out loud for Arnyn.

"Most people coming through here are from Teyrnas and other Vogel kingdoms. Why?"

"We're future Scholars," Charity replied. "Curiosity is in our nature."

"Can't argue with that. Where'd that stew come from?"

Lok pointed over his shoulder towards the ruins. Several people had set up cook fires in similar ruins, preparing for the evening meal.

"Well, what are we waiting for?" said Arnyn. He walked over to the nearest group, two women and one man speaking in Teyrnian accents, and asked to join them. They accepted, and Charity and Lok sat down as well. The two women were playing a game of mancala. Charity asked if she could play the winner. The women readily agreed.

Lok glanced over at the ruined house. The fire had been put out. West's group was nowhere in sight.

10

Moonlight

Realta laid perfectly still on the small bed, listening to the footsteps up above. They had spent two days and one night at the healer's house, giving Callum a chance to recover. Healer Tesell had stressed that Callum should not be on his feet for another few days and did not want them to leave until Master Loy's letter had arrived.

Too much time had been lost already. Kanton could be right on their trail, knocking on the Tesells' door at any moment. Callum had instructed her and Serena to wait until the dead of night, when the couple were fast asleep.

The footsteps ceased. Realta strained her ears. No other sounds came from the second story.

The door to Realta's room creaked open. Sitting up, she spied her father's dark silhouette in the doorway. His right shoulder was stiff from fresh bandages. Healer Tesell changed them just before retiring that night. And he had been kind enough to lend Callum a clean shirt and coat.

Realta felt a pang of guilt as she slipped out of bed and laced up her boots. The Tesells had been more than kind to them, fixing them up at no charge and giving them free room and board. They had shared supper with them the last two evenings. They were good, honest people. Leaving without a proper thanks felt wrong.

A second, slimmer figure joined Callum at the door. Standing side by side with Callum, his satchel over her shoulder, Serena looked so much like Kel. All that was needed to complete the effect was a crutch and a tattered cloak.

Realta joined them, mindful to keep her footfalls light.

"Have you got everything?" Callum whispered to her and Serena.

Realta nodded. She had only the clothes on her back.

Serena held up the satchel in confirmation. Inside were Callum's maps, his rite of passage, and what little money they had. The bulk of the funds had been with Kanton.

"Should we take more?" Serena asked.

"You mean steal?" Realta was appalled. How dare she even suggest stealing from these kindhearted people. *Maybe Serena isn't used to kindness*, she considered, remembering the girl's upbringing.

"No," Callum replied. "If everything goes as planned, we won't need to steal."

"What have you planned?"

"For you to follow me to Teyrnas."

"That's not much of a plan," Serena muttered.

"It's all you need to know, girl." Callum paused. Footsteps resumed on the second floor. Four steps one way. Pause. Four steps back. Realta's heart pounded against her ribs, her whole body shaking in tandem. Callum continued, "Just trust me."

"Fine."

"And Master Loy's letter?" Realta asked.

"The mail carrier picked it up yesterday. He will know the truth in a day or two."

Realta did not envy the Loys or Mistress Tolman. They had entrusted Kanton and his team with their children's wellbeing, only for that man to reveal himself as a killer. It was a position nobody wanted to be in. But word of Kanton would spread throughout the Hinterlands like fire. Everyone would know his true character.

"And I left a partial explanation for the Tesells," Callum added. He said to Serena, "Do you remember where the public stables are?"

"Somewhat. Might take a while."

"We have until sunrise."

Callum headed for the back door. The front door had a chime that would alert the whole house, and the back door faced an alleyway. Fewer people to see them. The village guard in Vala had a nightly routine. To think the guards in Narfalk did not was foolish.

Realta and Serena stepped out of the house. Callum silently closed the door. The door clicked. Callum glanced up at the second-story window. The window remained dark. Not enough noise to warrant lighting a candle to investigate. Realta breathed a sigh of relief. Funny, she thought sneaking out would be much harder.

"Which way?" Callum said as they exited the alley and faced the street. The light of the two moons in a cloudless sky bathed the town in an eerie, white glow.

Serena looked down one end and then the other. A pair of guardsmen sauntered down the street, talking and laughing. They entered the tavern on the corner. No one else walked along the silent street.

"This way."

Callum clamped a hand on Serena's shoulder. "How sure are you?"

"Mostly sure." She shrugged off Callum's hand and headed down the street. Realta and her father followed.

The world always appeared so different at night. All colors were washed away by shades of white, blue, and black. Realta never liked being out so late. Childhood stories of the Ullmhir and wildcats made every shadow seem alive, no matter how many times she told herself that the Ullmhir were just a story and wildcats lived on the other side of the Vogel Mountains.

Realta jolted, her heart leaping into her throat. A signpost's shadow had moved, inching away.

Calm down. You moved. That's why it seemed to move, too. Keeping her eyes fixed on Callum, she moved forward.

At the end of the street, Serena turned and paused in front of a large wooden building. She pressed her ear against the door. Realta heard nothing except her heart beating in her ears. Serena pulled open the door. Dim yellow light poured into the street. Callum and Realta entered close behind.

The stables were empty of human life. Half of the thirty odd stalls were occupied, the horses patiently nickering or stamping a hoof. The Tesells, having nowhere to keep the horses, had sent them to the stable for safe keeping.

Realta spied Shadow near the back. The black gelding shook his mane, recognizing her and Callum. The Tolman's horse occupied the stall next to him.

"Just the ones that belong to us," Callum informed Serena. The girl had been insistent on taking a third horse. Callum was more insistent on not stealing. Stealing would give people a reason to follow them. Serena relented, seeing the logic.

Serena opened the two stalls. Taking two saddles from the supply rack, she and Realta placed them on the horses. Realta had watched her father and Master Loy saddle horses hundreds of times. The action was as easy as walking. Callum checked both saddles, making sure each was secure.

"You and Serena on the Tolman horse," Callum said, climbing onto Shadow's saddle. He winced, inhaling sharply. He rubbed his wounded chest. Should he really be riding so soon?

Serena placed her foot in the stirrup.

"No. Realta has the reins."

"Why?"

"Because I don't trust people who lie to me."

"I haven't lied. I told you the truth."

"As much of the truth that you deemed necessary." Callum glared at her.

Serena opened her mouth to protest, but no words form. She turned away.

"You're seventeen. Almost an adult. You need to learn that lies don't befit adults."

"You should tell that to my siblings," Serena muttered.

"Then you understand?" Callum's voice softened.

"Yes, sir." Serena, head hung low, took a step back, allowing Realta to saddle the horse first. Her dress was not made for riding, and she couldn't ride sidesaddle with Serena behind her. The dress came up to her knees. Maybe she should copy Serena and wear trousers instead. Or trousers underneath her dress. That would be more proper.

Serena led the two horses out of the stables, closing the door. The streets remained empty. Not a single candle glowed in the houses. Storefronts were locked tight. Serena climbed into the saddle, placing her hands on Realta's shoulders for support.

"Hey, who's there?" called out a voice.

Realta spun her head around to see the voice's owner. He wore the long coat of a guardsman and carried a short sword at his side. Since when did village guards wear swords? She gripped the reins in her sweating hands.

"Greetings!" said her father in a cordial voice. "We were just traveling through, looking for a place to spend the night."

"Nightfall was five hours ago," the guardsman replied, placing a hand on his sword hilt. "Why aren't you camped for the night?"

"We heard rumors of bandits near Lothian. I feared my children and I would be robbed if we didn't stay in a village."

"Lothian is about six hours from here. Why not stay there?" The guardsman stepped closer to Callum. The moonlight cast eerie shadows on his angular face.

"Do you want to know the truth?" her father asked.

"Obviously. Now—"

Callum swung out his fist and punched the guardsman on the side of the head. The man toppled to the ground without a word, laying in a heap. Realta covered her mouth to keep from crying out. A guardsman! Her father had assaulted a guardsman.

Callum dismounted Shadow and stooped down beside the fallen guard.

"Is he...?"

"Unconscious." He rifled through the guard's coat pockets.

"What are you doing?" Realta whispered, desperate to leave, to run far away from the scene. What if another guard came by? How would they explain this?

"Call it a hunch. Now what's this?" He stood, holding a short stack of papers. "Serena, look in my satchel for some matches."

Serena readily complied and handed one to Callum. He lit it on the stone pavement and held it up to the papers.

"Damn it to the Abyss!"

"What?" Realta asked. How fast could her heart beat before it burst?

Callum read, "Wanted: Serena Molyns for the theft of King Logan's horse, the attack on members of the King's Guard, and the disappearances and possible murders of Miss Charity Loy and Young Master Lok Tolman. Wanted: Callum Haar, escaped slave. Both were last seen in the village of Lothian on the evening of Alet first. Orders for arrest issued by Dane Kanton, Captain of the King's Guard."

"What?!" Realta was too stunned to think. Murder? But Charity and Lok were alive. She saw them run into the forest. She saw them! And Callum an escaped slave? Impossible! He was an indentured servant, not a slave, and he would never do such a thing.

Callum ran to the next street, eyeing every building.

"Where are you going?" Serena called out.

Shut up, you idiot!

Callum ran back and scrambled into the saddle. "Every door. Fire and smoke, the notices are on every door."

Every door. In the morning, the entire village would discover these charges. And who would prove them false? The possible murderer and the escaped slave? As though anyone would believe them!

"He's here," Serena whispered, her face pale in the moonlight. "Kanton's here. How else would they know?"

Callum pulled hard on Shadow's reins, forcing the horse to turn around. "We can't waste any more time. Go!"

Callum dashed off. Realta slapped down the reins, and Jak took off.

"Where do we go?" Serena asked. "He knows which way we're going."

Callum did not respond.

Realta urged the horse to run faster. Leaving Narfalk behind, she had an odd notion of racing against the moons.

11
Informal Lessons

"Now," said Arnyn as he placed a bucket of water in front of Lok, "we have the water. We have earth and fire." He pointed to a small mound of dirt and their morning cook fire. "And of course," he threw his hands upwards, "the air."

Charity observed the display, sitting on a stone and wrapped in a blanket. The morning air had taken a turn for the crisp. Not uncommon during the first week of Alet.

During their morning meal, Arnyn had suggested testing Lok to determine which elements he could control. Charity readily agreed, but Lok needed some convincing. He had been very solemn the past three days, keeping to himself and writing no more than a word or two in response to questions.

"Imagine how impressed the Scholars will be if you already know how to use your ability," Charity had told him, hoping this exercise would improve his mood. "They'll have to accept you."

The young Thane relented.

Lok sat crisscrossed, facing the three, technically four, elements. He stared at them, eyes narrowed and lips nothing more than a thin slit. Nothing happened. He shook his head, a mop of dark brown hair flying in every direction.

"Nobody walks on the first try," Charity assured him. She turned to Arnyn. "How do the Scholars test Thanes?"

"That's a good question. Too bad I ain't got an answer."

Charity frowned, propping up her chin with one hand. There had to be a clear-cut way. How did Kel test her and her sisters? With spelling, he would sound out the word and they did their best to write it. History was a matter of memory, and mathematics was problem solving and logic.

"What if you hold each one in your hand?" Charity suggested.

Lok pointed at the fire and frowned.

"Place your hand close to it, I guess?" She shrugged.

Lok reached for the mound of dirt, grabbing a handful. Taking a deep breath, he closed his eyes. A minute passed. Two minutes. Charity studied the dirt in Lok's hand and then the dirt pile. No change. Not a single gram moved. Wasn't that what Elementals did? Move the elements they could control?

A passerby, an older man with shoulder length, gray hair, called out to Arnyn, motioning for him to follow.

"I'd better see what that's about. Keep practicing, Young Thane." Arnyn caught up with the older man, and they walked off towards a series of half-fallen stone pillars. A handful of other people, Rawni included, waited for them.

Charity had not gotten a clear explanation of what this place used to be. A city, obviously. But which kingdom had it belonged to? When had it been abandoned or destroyed? And why? She should have paid better attention to those history lessons.

She turned back to Lok and found him in a familiar posture. Arms wrapped around his knees and shoulders hunched, looking so much smaller.

"Is something wrong, Lok?"

He responded with a single nod. He tossed the dirt back onto the pile and sighed.

"Try the water."

Lok placed his hand in the bucket. Another minute passed. Nothing. He angrily dried his hand on his shirt.

"You just need more practice."

Lok reached for his notebook and wrote, *"What if he made a mistake?"*

"I seriously doubt that. Master Danior knew you were a Thane the moment he saw you."

"What if they lied to get our trust?"

A shiver ran down Charity's spine, her mind racing back to Kanton. He had promised to take them to the Academy. But that was a lie. She hadn't figured out the man's reason, but she did know this. Callum Haar did not start fights. He ended them. She prayed that he and Realta were safe. That Callum was alive.

"No. If they wanted to lie, they would have said I was a Thane, too. But neither did. So there has to be some truth."

Lok flung his notebook on the ground. The small campfire shot up. Half dead embers burst to life, sending sparks into the air. The log snapped in half, glowing bright orange.

"That's it!" Charity jumped up and pointed at the fire. Lok stared at her like she had grown a second head. "Lok, the fire grew the moment you got angry. Do you see?"

Lok inched closer to the fire. He picked up a nearby stick and placed one end into the flames. He held the burning end to his face. Staring at it, the fire leaped up and consumed the rest of the stick in seconds, leaving nothing but charred wood. Lok yelped as the fire burnt his fingers. Flinging away the stick, he doused his fingers in the water bucket.

"Let me see." Charity crouched down beside him. Burns had several forms of severity, each needing a different form of treatment. Healer Zall had told her about a man whose arm was burned to a blackened crisp, and the limb had to be amputated. Her parents, and even Esme to an extent, would be horrified to learn how much time she had spent with the healer. Yes, the man was mad, but every time he spoke about his profession, he was so clear, so lucid. His madness temporarily forgotten.

Lok's thumb and forefinger were not so bad. Just a little redness. Charity wondered if being an Elemental protected him from burns. She'd have to consult the Scholars.

"That settles it. Lok Tolman, you're a Fire Elemental."

"Fire?"

Charity spun around and saw a figure wearing a heavy, black cloak standing over her and Lok. They shot to their feet. The hood hid the figure's face. But now that she was standing, she realized the figure was only a few inches taller than her. Not quite as threatening.

Lok grabbed his notebook and wrote, *"That's West."*

"I see." Lok had told her about the strange young man and the odd people traveling with him. Lok tried to find him that evening and a good portion of the next day to no avail. Charity assumed his group had moved on. People constantly traveled through the ruins, resting for a few days before leaving. Dozens, if not hundreds. She was shocked she had never heard of this place.

"It's nice to meet you, West," she said, extending her hand. She made sure to pronounce each word carefully. Lok informed her that the boy did not speak Teyrnian.

"Nice to meet you," West mimicked, shaking her hand. He pushed back his hood just enough for her to see his blue-ish gray eyes.

Charity glanced around. "Where are the people you're traveling with?"

"Traveling with?" West tilted his head to one side, his eyes wide and expectant.

Charity exchanged a glance with Lok. He shrugged. She tried a different approach. "What language do you speak?"

"Language?"

She pointed to herself and Lok. "Teyrnian. We speak Teyrnian. And you?"

West's eyes suddenly lit up. "Marish! Mi laro Marish!"

"Great!" Charity had never heard of that language. But it was a start.

"Great!" West mimicked, smiling. "Fire?" he pointed at the flames. They had started to die down again. Much quicker than Charity expected. She glanced at Lok. He seemed calm, at ease now that he found West. *There must be a link between emotion and elemental control.* She filed the idea away for later.

"Yes," she replied. "Fire."

"Fire?" he pointed at Lok.

Lok went pale. He took a tentative step back.

Is he like Arnyn and Danior? What were the odds of that? Over seven hundred people in Vala, and not one knew that Lok was a Thane. But three people they happened to meet in the middle of nowhere? Charity was not a mathematical genius, but even she knew the odds must be astronomically slim.

"Westermor!" called out a woman wearing a plain, woolen dress, a dark blue shawl draped around her shoulders. She rushed over to him, placing her hands on his arm. "Catt ti andamis va?"

West hung his head, pulling the hood over his face. He shook like a leaf caught in a storm.

"Are you his mother?" Charity asked.

"No, his aunt," she replied in an accented voice. "I hope he has not caused too much trouble."

"Not at all, ma'am."

The woman tried to lead West away, but the young man stood his ground and pointed at Lok. "Mida, sparti, sparti!"

"Pay no attention to him, please," the woman apologized. "You see, he injured his head as a little boy and has not been right since."

"It's no problem." A head injury. That would impair his ability to learn foreign languages. Except he did not seem impaired, not to Charity. If he was not learning Teyrnian during their conversation, then she was queen of the Summer Islands.

West pointed at himself and addressed Charity, "Sparti ac ack. Nik tira no arna."

West's aunt slapped him across the face. The young man cowered, cradling the left side of his face. She whispered heated words to him in Marish. West glanced over towards a copse of trees, a stone slab jutting out of the earth. Three men stood there, glaring at him. The other traveling companions. Trembling, West made his way over to the men.

"You didn't have to hit him." Charity's face burned. Had she been a Fire Elemental, that small fire would be a blaze.

"Sometimes words are not enough, young miss."

"Your nephew is a human being, not a dog."

"All children need to learn boundaries. I see you could have benefited from the same methods." The woman sauntered off, joining the others at the stone slab. They exchanged a few words. One of the men cuffed West on the side of the head. The group turned and walked along the path towards Lothian. West stole a glance at her and Lok, his eyes glistening.

Charity darted towards the group, but Lok grabbed her arm.

"You're just going to let them get away with that?" Charity snapped.

Lok looked at her sorrowfully.

"Let who get away with what?" asked Arnyn, walking towards them. He inspected the bucket, the fire, and the mound of dirt. "Any luck with these?"

"That woman." Charity pointed at the trees. "She slapped her nephew because he wandered away and wouldn't listen."

"Well, sometimes small children—"

"He's not a child. He's around mine and Lok's age. And she

claimed he had a head injury."

Arnyn let out a low whistle. "An unfortunate fact of life."

"So we're going to do nothing?" Charity stared at him, aghast.

"Are they still here?"

Charity looked back at the copse and stone slab. No humans. A sense of defeat washed over her. "No. They're gone."

"Then, there's nothing we can do. But don't worry, young miss. The Creator will balance out the boy's life. Just give Him time."

Charity doubted Arnyn's life philosophy. So what if West could see Thanes? How would that stop his aunt and that other man from hitting him? How would that counteract a head injury? Head injury. How much of that was even true?

"You going to answer my second question or just admire the lovely trees?"

"Oh, yeah. Fire," she replied, controlling her anger instead of the other way around. "Lok can control fire."

"Now, that's really useful." Arnyn smiled. Lok sat down on a stone, his head hung low. "Don't tell me you don't like your gift."

Lok shrugged.

"He needs time to process everything," Charity said quickly. Back in Vala, Lok always shied away from attention, both good and bad. She had lost count of how many times she had said hello and Lok ran away in response. All this extra attention from Arnyn was not doing Lok any favors.

"Fair enough," Arnyn replied.

"Master Teleran, do you know when we'll be leaving?"

"Yes. We'll head for the river on the evening of the seventh and ship out at first light."

"You're coming with us?"

Arnyn held up his hands. "Only as far as the shore. You can't pay me to cross the Nerin."

"Why is that?"

He let out a short sigh. "A man is allowed to keep secrets, Miss Loy."

"Very well."

Arnyn wandered off. Yet another person called him away. Charity wondered just how many people the man knew. He even knew Callum. She would have to ask Arnyn how the two of them met. It ought to be an interesting story.

Charity turned around and caught Lok walking away.

"Where are you going?"

Begrudgingly, Lok walked back and wrote, *"I want to be alone for a while."* His eyes were rimmed with red.

"Okay." Charity watched as he headed for the stone pillars. Too much change in too short a time, she assumed. She glanced back at the copse of trees, at the road heading to Lothian. West had looked to her and Lok, pleading. She wished she could do something, anything, to help.

12

Errands

Realta crept through the streets of Tronton, her father's satchel clutched tightly to her chest. Tronton was many times the size of Vala, far larger than any village she had ever seen. People crowded the wide, stone-paved streets, many of them heading to or from West Bridge, the great port city on the Nerin's western bank.

They had arrived at the village early in the morning, the spring air taking a turn for the colder. The first farmhouse they passed had several cloaks and coats hanging on a line. Callum grabbed three.

"I know it's wrong," Callum explained, seeing the wounded look in Realta's eyes. "But those warrants have our descriptions. Kanton's at least a day ahead of us. If he isn't in this town, he'll be in the next one. We can't take risks."

Realta understood and donned the smallest of the cloaks, colored a dull brown. Serena's cloak was far too large for her. She did not say anything, half numb with shock.

As farmhouses gave way to paved roads and brick buildings, Callum signaled for them to halt. Dismounting Shadow, he ran off, creeping along the backs of buildings. Realta stole a glance at Serena. She sat there motionless, but Realta had a sinking feeling that the girl might try to run away again. To get as far away from Kanton as possible. Callum returned before Serena could try anything. Sweat coated his brow and his breaths came out as wheezing gasps.

"Are you all right, Father?" She did not like that wheezing sound.

"Yes. I didn't see any warrants. There might be some in the town center. You two listen carefully to me." Realta and Serena dismounted their horse, waiting for instructions. "Serena, take this money and buy enough food for two days. Realta, take this money and buy everything I write down." He proceeded to write a small list on the back of a map. He tore it off and handed it to her.

"What are they for?" None of the items made any logical sense.

"Go to an apothecary or an herbalist. Tell them it's for your mother. And if anyone asks your name, tell them it's Lily, and your mother's name is Joy. You're traveling from West Bridge to Caman's Pass. And Serena, your name is Mayra. Tell the same story if anyone asks. Repeat it to me."

"My name is Lily. My mother's name is Joy. We're traveling from West Bridge to Caman's Pass." The words felt weird on her tongue.

"Good. Now you."

Serena repeated every word perfectly.

"I will stay here with the horses. Try to be back in two hours. We can't risk staying here any longer than necessary."

Two fears dominated Realta's mind as she and Serena headed into Tronton. That Kanton would find them, and that Serena would take this as an opportunity to run away. No one was watching. No one would stop her. And the way Callum was breathing bothered her. The healer wanted him to wait for at least four days. What if he was doing too much too soon?

On the other hand, if they had stayed, they'd likely be under arrest, waiting for Kanton to arrive while locked behind bars. Helpless. That was the last thing she wanted. But was it worth risking her father's health?

She and Serena parted ways at an intersection in the town's business district. In Vala, the business district was a single road. Here, it covered multiple square blocks and contained dozens of shops. How was she supposed to find the right one?

A guardsman dressed in a long coat loitered on a street corner. He leaned against a shop with a tailor's sign over the door. He appeared to be half asleep.

Realta wondered if she should ask him. It would be a lot quicker than wandering up and down every street. Then again, he was a guardsman and a stranger. Speaking to him could end in a dozen different ways, only a few of them good.

Only one way to find out. Clutching Callum's satchel closer, Realta approached the guard.

"Excuse me?" Realta asked, her voice trembling.

"What's that?" The guardsman stood straighter, pulled out of his stupor.

"I'm looking for the herbalist or the... The..." Blast, what was the other one? Apothecary? Yes, that was it. "Or the apothecary. I'm on an errand for my mother..." *For my mother.* The words felt so bizarre, leaving her lips. She had never known her mother. Had never had the opportunity to say the words 'for my mother'.

"An errand?" The guardsman rubbed his bloodshot eyes.

"Yes, sir. We're traveling from West Bridge to—"

"Oh, I see, I see. New in town. Um..." He scratched his head. "Go down this street. The third shop on the left is the apothecary. Nice fellow. Won't give you any problems."

"Thank you, sir." *Well, that wasn't too difficult.* She had worried over nothing.

"You be careful now, young miss. We've had a rash of bandits here in the Hinterlands."

"Bandits?" Realta's mind screamed for her to move along, keep walking, complete her task, and return to Callum without incident. But she needed to know. Knowing might be the difference between safety and falling back into Kanton's hands.

"Yeah. From what I hear, they robbed several traveling groups. One even killed a young lady about your age." The guardsman shook his head, his expression a mixture of sorrow and disgust. "Are you and your mother traveling with anyone?" He furrowed his brow.

"Yes. My older sister Mayra and my father Cal—" Realta stopped herself. Callum never gave himself a false name. She hoped it was distinct enough.

"Good. Safety in numbers is a fact of life these days. Sometimes, I don't know what Teyrnas is coming to. You be safe, Miss..."

"Lily. Lily Zall." Really? Of all the names she just had to pick the healer's!

"Be safe, Miss Zall." The man was so genuine. Realta felt a pang of guilt for lying to him.

She thanked him and turned down the indicated street. The guardsman called out to her.

"Miss Zall, one moment. I forgot I was supposed to show you this."

Realta's heart dropped. She knew that had been too easy. Steeling herself, she faced the man.

"Can you read?" he asked, unfolding a piece of paper.

"Yes," she whispered. Oh, Creator and the Eight Gadyeni, no! Don't let Dane Kanton be here in Tronton. Don't let that murderer be one step ahead of them!

The guardsman handed her the paper. Realta watched as her hand grabbed it. The words were unmistakable. Wanted. Callum Haar, escaped slave. Serena Molyns, horse thief and suspected murderer. The descriptions were as accurate as a charcoal drawing.

"Have you seen anyone matching either description? The Captain of the King's Guard has posted a handsome reward for their arrest."

She shook her head and handed back the warrant. The guardsman took it, folded it up, and returned it to his pocket.

"I thought so. The King's Guard gave us these warrants at sunrise. The way I see it, they ain't even here."

"Oh?" A small weight fell from her shoulders. Though not enough for her to feel completely safe.

"Yeah. These bandits would have to be pretty stupid to continue on the River Road. Way I see it, they fled into Rangar Forest. Now, that's a place you don't want to visit."

"I'm glad to hear it."

"Good day to you, Miss Zall."

Realta replied in kind and headed towards the apothecary. So, Kanton arrived here around sunrise. Mere hours ahead of them. Could he still be in Tronton? If they quickened their pace and crossed the Nerin before him, they might be able to lose him. She had no idea how big Teyrnas was. Many times larger than Tronton, she guessed. It was the capital, after all. If she moved quickly, they might have a chance.

A sign displaying a mortar and pestle painted in blue hung above the apothecary's door. A bell chimed as Realta entered the shop. Shelves filled with bottles and jars lined the walls. A handful of people milled about, paying no attention to her. At the back of the shop, a man with dark brown hair and fine lines around his bespectacled eyes stood behind a counter. He carefully measured a paper container filled with finely ground powder. Satisfied with the weight, he poured the powder into a glass jar.

Realta walked up to the counter, her steps a bit surer. She fumbled around inside the satchel. Where was that list?

"May I help you, young lady?" asked the apothecary, a wide smile on his face.

"Yes." Found it! She placed the list on the counter. "I um... I need these for my mother." Saying it a second time did not make it any less weird.

The apothecary examined the list, adjusting his glasses. "Let's see. Ground lily root, dried cranberries, flaxseed oil, a small mixing bowl, and one application brush. Not a problem." The apothecary went from shelf to shelf, gathering the items. Realta still could not fathom Callum's intentions for these things. Cranberries and flaxseed oil could be used for cooking. But what of the other three?

"Here you are, miss." He placed the items on the counter. "That will be two silver marks."

Realta pulled the coins out of her pocket. Two silver marks and three coppers. Thank the Creator for small miracles. She handed over the two silvers.

"And would you like these in a bag? No charge."

"Yes, please."

The apothecary placed each item in a paper bag with care. "Now, you be careful, young miss," he said, handing the bag to Realta. "There are rumors of bandits not far from here."

"I've heard. Thank you."

Realta quickly ducked out of the shop and retraced her steps down the street. The guardsman was no longer there. Turning a corner, she spied Serena with a small burlap sack. She wore the cloak over her head. What little Realta could see of her face was ashen.

"We need to go," Serena said, holding up a crumpled arrest warrant.

"I know." She was relieved and honestly a bit surprised Serena hadn't run away.

They walked down the street at a quick trot, as fast as they could walk without running. A trio of guards spoke with a group of locals. The locals shook their heads. They hadn't seen those bandits. Serena pulled the hood down further, covering her face and short hair. The effect made her look more like a boy than a girl. She and Realta quickened their pace. The guards had not noticed them.

Out of the town proper, Realta breathed a little easier. Part of the danger had passed. She glanced over at Serena. The girl stared straight ahead, clear blue eyes fixed on nothing in particular.

"Did you see him?" Realta was half afraid to ask. But their safety, and possibly their lives, depended on it.

"No. I thought I did. But no."

"Psst."

Realta nearly jumped out of her skin. Callum stood next to a dilapidated barn, the two horses tied to a fence post and eating grass as though nothing was wrong in the world. He motioned them closer.

"You have everything?"

Realta opened the bag. Callum crouched down and spilled the contents on the ground. She and Serena crouched beside him.

"And you?"

Serena opened the sack, revealing a loaf of bread, slices of cured beef, and an assembly of dried fruits.

"You two eat. We leave the moment I'm done."

"Dane Kanton is here," Serena said, her voice hollow.

Callum paused. He ran a hand through his black hair. "All the more reason to hurry."

As Callum inspected the items Realta bought, she made herself a farmer's lunch. Strips of meat between two pieces of bread. A simple meal that could easily be carried without making a mess. Serena copied her, a ghost of a smile creeping onto her face. They watched Callum while they ate.

Callum dumped most of the ground lily root, a white powder, into the mixing bowl. He then mixed in the oil until it was a white paste. He grounded up the dried cranberries, two or three at a time, and added them to the paste. The paste soon turned a dull pink, almost the same color as Callum's skin. He added more oil to the mixture. Using the application brush, he covered his servant's tattoo with the reddish-pink paste.

"They're searching for an escaped slave," Callum explained.

"These marks are the first thing they'll look for. It ain't perfect, but it will be enough to fool most."

"How long will that last?" asked Serena.

"A few days, hopefully. Long enough to get us past East Bridge."

"When do we cross the Nerin?" Anxiety rose in Serena's voice. Realta noticed Serena had only taken a few bites of food. Looking at her own food, she realized that she had not eaten much either. Too focused on Callum.

Callum was quiet for a moment. "One town lies between Tronton and West Bridge. Traveling at a trot, we'll reach it by evening. Leaving in the morning, we can be in West Bridge in a few hours. We'll cross at the first available passing. Do you remember the cost?" he asked Serena.

"Going on the slow boat, it's free. They charge for horses, though."

"We will have to leave them behind." Callum touched the paste on his arm. Small flecks of it came off. "One more hour. Feel free to rest. We should be safe here." He picked up a piece of dried fruit and ate it.

He used his left hand. Realta's father was right-handed. Now that she thought about it, his right hand had been shaking while he applied the paste. She glanced up at his chest, where Kanton had stabbed him. No blood. The stitches had not ruptured. He just needs time to heal, she reminded herself.

But time was not a luxury they had.

13

The Nerin

The morning sun was high in the sky by the time Realta, Serena, and Callum arrived in West Bridge. Their short rest had lasted long into the night, the three of them falling asleep in the abandoned barn. Realta had not realized the effect of losing two nights of sleep. By the time they awoke, the two moons were halfway finished with their nightly race. They quickly gathered their supplies and joined the River Road's early morning traffic.

The large city sprawled for miles along the River Nerin's western bank. Thousands of people crowded the board streets, just as many riding in carriages and on horseback as those walking. And Realta thought Tronton was a big town. This town, the first proper city she had ever visited, could easily hold every person living in the Hinterlands.

"Which way to the docks?" Callum asked, holding the reins with only his left hand. A slight grimace was the sole indicator that he was in pain. Her father had a very bad habit of hiding injuries. Years ago, Callum had fallen and sprained his ankle. He did not admit it until Esme noticed the limp. Four days after the fact.

They really ought to go to a healer, just to make sure Callum's wound was healing properly. But resting had allowed Kanton to get ahead again. Running into the man, or someone who had seen an arrest warrant, was only a matter of time.

"A couple of blocks this way." Serena pointed down a street lined with shops. Dark bruises circled her bony wrists.

Callum flicked the reins, and Shadow continued in that direction. The people passing by did not pay much attention to them. The month of Alet saw many travelers. Too many to take note of each one.

Safety in numbers, Realta thought. How long had it been since Kanton and his people attacked them? Six days? It felt like a lifetime. And what about Charity and Lok? Had they managed to get back to the main road and return to Vala? Would she ever see them again?

They turned a corner, edging closer to the docks. Cobblestone streets gave way to wooden boardwalks. The air grew both fresher and staler, the scents of water and recently caught fish mingling together.

Realta's eyes grew wide as the Nerin came into view. A wide expanse of blue stretching towards the horizon, the land on the other side invisible. Myriad boats, their sails every color and pattern imaginable, crossed the river, a constant flow of back and forth. Many of those boats were as big as houses, some larger. How in the world did structures that massive stay afloat? It was incredible!

Serena dismounted.

"What are you doing?" questioned Callum.

"We can't afford to take the horses across. We should sell them. Use the money to get to Teyrnas."

Sell the horses? It made logical sense. They desperately needed the money. They barely had enough to equal a silver mark. But neither horse truly belonged to them. And Shadow could be so finicky. What if his new master was not as kind as Master Loy?

Realta heard herself say, "No."

"What?" Serena turned clear blue eyes on her, her expression a mixture of annoyance and curiosity.

"What if..." How to put her thoughts into words? "What if Master Loy comes looking for us? He might see Shadow with someone else and..."

"I see," said Callum. He asked Serena, "Where is the nearest stable?"

"I don't know. Probably close by."

"Follow me." Callum steered Shadow towards the row of buildings opposite the docks. One building housed several horses. Some of the stalls were empty.

Callum dismounted and led Shadow into a stall. Realta also dismounted and led Jak into the neighboring one. She found it odd that no one was present. No one to question their reason for being there, or why they were leaving the horses.

Callum motioned for Serena to hand him the satchel. Rifling through it, he took out his notebook and a charcoal pencil. He wrote a brief note and tied it around Shadow's reins.

It read: "This horse and the one to its left belong to Master Sardic Loy of Vala in the Hinterlands of Teyrnas. See that both horses are returned promptly. Apologies."

"Do we have everything?" Callum asked, handing the satchel back to Serena, again using his left hand. Realta did not like that. His pain could be minimal or excruciating, and he would never admit it.

On a better note, the paste over his servant's tattoo remained. It looked like a scar from a burn wound. She hoped the people working the docks drew the same conclusion.

"Wait." Realta walked over to Shadow and placed a hand on the horse's nose. He had always been a good horse, and she hated leaving him behind. "Be good now, Shadow. You'll be home soon enough." She wished she could say the same for herself. The horse shook his glossy mane once. Realta turned to her father. "Okay."

Following Serena's direction, Callum led the way. He walked side by side with the girl, always keeping one eye on her. Callum had not said a word about Serena's appearance. How the girl looked just like Kel. Realta hadn't had the courage to bring it up, fearing how her father and Serena would react. Teyrnas was over a week away. She hoped she could find the courage by then.

"Those are the free boats," said Serena. Judging by the other boats, these were of medium size with a large central sail. Thirty some odd people, barefoot dock workers wearing leather vests and travelers dressed in a variety of clothes, milled about. "They don't ask a lot of questions."

"Good."

They approached the nearest boat. A cool breeze drifted in from the river, coating them in a fine mist. Realta pulled her cloak tighter and walked closer to Callum. Strange white birds circled the air, cawing to one another. Two swooped down and tried to grab a fish. A fisherman chased them off. A blue draig, longer and slimmer than its green counterpart, used the distraction to jump onto the barrel and steal a fish.

"Looking to cross?" asked a man about her father's height with gray in his short beard. He wore well-tailored clothing and a black, wide-brimmed hat.

"Yes, sir," replied Callum.

"Just you three?"

Callum nodded.

"Very well," he said, inspecting her and Serena. The girl looked nothing like her or Callum, but the man did not seem to care. "Head on board that ship. We take off in half an hour."

"Thank you, sir." Callum led them down the dock. The wooden platform undulated in the water. Realta grabbed hold of Callum's good arm for support, her stomach lurching and thankful she hadn't eaten breakfast. This part of the dock was connected by a series of poles. Circles had been cut into the wood so it could move up and down in the water.

They climbed up a rope ladder, Callum forcing Serena to go first, followed by Realta. The climb wasn't so bad. It was no higher than the hay loft back home, and she did not want to spend another minute on that strange dock. Callum struggled to climb up, relying on only his left hand. His right shoulder and arm were completely stiff. Realta rushed to help him on board.

"I'm fine," Callum said, his voice coming out as a raspy breath.

"But your shoulder—"

"Just needs time to heal." Callum stood straight and waved to the approaching men. Again using his left arm.

"Heading to East Bridge the cheap way, huh?" asked one man with a smile.

"Yes, sir."

"Sir?" The man laughed. "Hear that, Garr? I'm a sir!"

"Good for you," Garr replied sarcastically. He addressed Callum, "There are a few empty cabins down below, but you'll have to share. Lots of travelers today."

A spike of panic coursed through her. Was Dane Kanton here? Had he been waiting for them this whole time? No. He was a captain in the King's Guard. He could afford to ride on an expensive boat. They would be safe. For the moment.

"Thank you. Come along, Mayra and Lily."

False names. Message received.

They followed Callum below deck, the steps creaking underfoot. Realta had never been on a boat before, never had the chance to see one up close. How did they float? It must contain the same amount of wood as Tolman's Inn. Maybe she could ask one of the Scholars at the Academy.

What makes you think you'll ever get there? Callum stated they were going to Teyrnas. He only mentioned the Academy as a means of finding Charity and Lok. Realta touched Kel's raven necklace, making sure it was still there.

Callum selected an empty cabin. This one was flanked by two occupied ones. Realta heard women talking in one. In the other, a man and a woman laughed, accompanied by the laughter of small children. A family. Nothing to fear.

Their cabin, a six-foot by five-foot space, contained two long benches attached to each wall. A circular window had been carved into the side, giving them a nice view of the river. Endless blue.

Realta sat down and was overwhelmed by exhaustion. Yesterday's sleep had not been enough to make up for those long nights of running. Serena sat next to her, stiff and uneasy.

Callum closed the cabin door and sat down, closing his eyes and leaning his head against the wall.

"Father, are you sure you're all right?"

"Just need some rest. You should rest, too. This ride takes a couple hours, doesn't it?"

"About three," Serena replied.

"And we'll spend the night in East Bridge?" Realta hoped. Callum was one of the strongest men she knew, but he was no longer young. He was rapidly approaching middle age. Wounds did not heal as fast at thirty-nine as they did at nineteen.

"If it's safe," Callum replied, his breathing labored and eyes closed. "Just rest for now."

Realta turned to Serena. The girl had lapsed into silence again. She clung to Callum's satchel but made no move to open it. Good. It was none of her business what was in the bag, even if she did wear Kel's face.

Up above, a man shouted orders, and feet ran across the deck. The boat lurched, drifting away from the harbor. Realta relaxed some. It was impossible for Serena to run away now.

Placing the satchel between them, Serena leaned her head

against the wall and slept. Realta waited a few moments. The girl's breathing grew slow and even. Fast asleep.

Realta found herself relaxing as the waves gently rocked the boat. Slow and rhythmic. And her eyelids were so heavy, as if weights had been tied to the lashes. Gazing out the window, her eyes drifted shut.

Realta's eyes opened. The small cabin had disappeared, replaced by a green, open space. The space was hedged in by a stone wall about ten feet high, but the structure was more decorative than imposing. Trees of a dozen varieties dotted the landscape. Apple trees, sprawling oaks, cherry trees with a few remaining blossoms. Her back rested against the wall. A warm summer sun shone on her. Another dream. Peaceful.

Her eyes fell on a young man, no older than eighteen, leaning against an oak tree, a faded blue cloak draped over his shoulders. The weather was far too warm for a cloak, and judging by the sun, it was only midmorning. Realta stood and walked closer.

The young man's hair was sandy brown and long enough to cover his ears and touch his shirt collar. Tufts of hair stuck out at odd angles. His skin was deathly pale and dark circles framed his eyes. He opened them, pale blue like the sky, and sat up a little straighter.

Realta followed his line of sight and saw two people approaching, a young woman the same age as this young man and another man about ten years older. The young woman wore a matching blue cloak while the man wore a white one.

Where am I? Realta wondered, noting the newcomers' complexions. The woman had the typically Hinterlander look with ruddy skin and dark hair and eyes. The man shared the same hair and eyes, but his skin was a deep tan.

She glanced behind them. The green space was flanked by a large building, one that reminded her of palaces in stories. Its central tower stood at five stories tall. The building's two wings, each at three stories, stretched from east to west, and connected to smaller structures.

Well, it was a dream. Not every dream had to make sense. Perhaps this dream world bordered multiple kingdoms, the peoples mixing together. And wearing cloaks in the middle of summer.

"Have you been here this whole time, Kel?" the young woman asked.

Realta's breath caught in her throat. Kel. The face was free of scars and twenty years younger, but it was undeniably her uncle. And the young woman. She didn't just look like a Hinterlander. She was one. Her Aunt Esme. That building must be the Academy. She never imagined it would be so beautiful.

Kel sat up a little straighter and smiled. "Where else would I be, Lovely?"

"In the infirmary." Lovely. Kel's nickname for Esme. There was no denying it now. These people were the younger versions of her aunt and uncle.

"Healer Wik is half out of his mind looking for you," said the man in the white cloak.

"When isn't he half out of his mind?" Kel smirked.

The white cloaked man rolled his eyes. "Can you talk some sense into him?" he asked Esme.

She sat down beside Kel and wrapped her arm around his. Realta had not noticed how thin Kel's arms were. Nothing more than flesh stretched over bones. No wonder his leg never healed properly. Esme lifted Kel to his feet without any trouble. A warm breeze rushed past them. A bell sounded in the distance.

"Drat," said the cloaked man. "I'm going to be late."

"You have a perfectly reasonable excuse, historian," replied Esme, a playful inflection on the word 'historian'.

The cloaked man walked over and supported Kel's other arm. They took a few steps forward when the man turned and saw Realta. His eyes widened, shocked.

"Realta!" he called out.

She jumped, shocked that the cloaked man had noticed her. In a flash, his black hair faded to gray. His skin paled, turning deathly white, and the white cloak darkened to black.

"Realta!"

His voice sounded different. Familiar.

She blinked and was back on the boat. Her father stood over her, nudging her shoulder. She blinked a few more times, making sure this was the real world and not another dream. She glanced out the window. The sun was lower in the sky.

"Is everything all right?" she asked.

"Yes," Callum smiled. "Welcome to East Bridge."

Realta stood, her legs and back protesting. A wooden bench did not make a comfortable bed. But the tired feeling had fled. Callum looked well, most of the ruddy color having returned to his skin. Something, however, was wrong.

"Where's Serena?" Realta's eyes darted around the small cabin. The girl was nowhere in sight.

"She wanted to stretch her legs. Don't worry. We aren't fully docked yet. That girl isn't going anywhere."

Should she ask him now? Mistress Loy claimed every dream had a meaning. If dreaming about Kel and Esme wasn't a clear-cut sign, she didn't know what was. "Father, do you think—"

Serena peered into the doorway, damp hair clinging to her forehead.

"We're docking now," she said. "The captain wants everyone on deck."

"How does the city look?" asked Callum.

The girl shrugged. "Like a city." She paused. "Are we staying the night?"

"If the coast is clear." Callum addressed Realta, "Shouldn't keep the captain waiting."

Realta followed her father and Serena up the steps to the deck. People moved every which way, carrying supplies, pulling or casting ropes, and waiting to disembark. Those waiting numbered twelve. Most appeared to be Teyrnian, though one woman had fiery red hair, the ringlets going all the way down to the small of her back. She was speaking with another woman, one with a typical Hinterlander complexion. Judging by the conversation, they appeared to be friends.

"Stand in line! Everybody, stand in line," the captain bellowed. The three of them obeyed, Realta standing close to her father. Glancing over the railing, she spied numerous people along the harbor. And she thought the crowds at Springtide were large! There had to be hundreds of people in this area alone. What was the rest of the city like?

Realta felt a strange form of comfort. Even if Kanton was in East Bridge, it would take a large effort to run into him. *Safety in numbers.*

Once all the ropes were tied off, the captain called for the gang-plank, a wide piece of wood that reached all the way to the dock, to be lowered. Why did they have to climb a ladder when that was an option? Perhaps they had arrived just in time.

"Single file and stay in line!" the captain ordered. Nobody seemed panicked. This was normal procedure.

"Fire and smoke," Callum swore under his breath.

"What's wrong?" Okay, maybe this wasn't normal procedure.

"Passenger inspection. Why didn't you tell me?" He glared at Serena.

"I didn't know," the girl said, shrinking back. "They didn't do anything like this in West Bridge. Kanton..." Serena's eyes widened. "Kanton must be here. He must—"

"Don't panic," said Callum, keeping his voice low and even. "They see you panicking, and they will know something's up. Stick close to me."

Serena complied, chewing on her lip, fighting back tears.

Realta forced herself to look forward, to keep the panic down. Callum was right there. He would not allow anything bad to happen. Right?

The captain was the first to walk down the gangplank. He spoke with three men on the docks. Two were dressed in the same dark blue coats as Kanton. The third struck Realta as utterly bizarre. He stood barefoot in ragged clothes with manacles on his hands and a rope tied around his neck. A tattoo of a circle with eight lines, like compass points, was on the left side of his face. A prisoner? Someone Serena had run into during her flight from Teyrnas? She glanced over at her. The girl was deathly pale.

All the passengers stood on the dock. The two guardsmen led the chained man along the line, inspecting each person. The red-haired woman whispered to her companion. The Teyrnian woman shook her head in disgust. Nobody else seemed bothered, except two small children. Their parents assured them that everything was fine, nothing to fear.

"What is he?" Callum asked.

"I don't know."

"Why do I get the sense you're lying to me, girl?"

"I'm not lying."

"Father..."

The chained man stood right in front of them. His dark eyes glared at Serena, boring into her. The girl stood her ground, not flinching. The man made his way over to Callum. Same neutral response. The man looked at Realta. His eyes grew wide.

"Her! Her!" he screamed. One of the guardsmen pulled him away, telling him that was enough. He'd done his job.

"What's going on?" Realta asked, her heart thumping against her ribs, beating in her throat. She held onto Callum's arm, fearing that if she let go, then she'd start falling and falling until she landed in the Abyss. The other guardsman was approaching. Oh Creator, preserve them!

"What's this about? Who's that man?" Callum questioned.

"If you and your daughter will come with us, sir." The guardsman held out his hand.

"You tell me what this is about."

"In due time, sir," he replied, his voice level. "Please, young miss, come with us."

"Run!" Serena yelled. She dashed into the crowd, the other passengers staring in varying degrees of shock. Callum cursed and ran after her. Realta had no choice but to follow.

"Hey, wait!" The guardsman waved his hands in the air. "It's not what you think!"

He isn't running after us. Shouldn't he be running after us?

She had no time to think. Serena was quick on her feet, and she and Callum struggled to keep pace.

The docks of East Bridge faded from view as Serena led them deeper into the city. People glanced their way, curious but not hostile. Realta looked for more man in dark blue uniforms. More chained men. She saw none. A stitch formed in her side, and her legs ached. It wasn't exactly easy to run in a dress. Serena, mercifully, came to a stop in a marketplace.

Callum grabbed Serena by the shirt and flung her against a building. Her head contacted brick with an audible thud.

"Now," Callum said through his teeth, "you're gonna tell me exactly what happened back there. Lie and you're dead."

"Father!" Had he really just threatened to kill a girl? A girl who looked just like his brother-in-law? Realta could understand anger and frustration, but death threats? That was not like Callum at all.

"Cuchasi," Serena said, trembling. "That man was a Cuchasi."

"Speak Teyrnian, girl."

Realta glanced over at the marketplace. Unlike the orderly one in Vala, this one was rundown. Many of the banners were ripped or frayed. The wood on some stalls had started to rot and splinter. The food was in a similar state. Half rotten, like someone had thrown it out and someone else had collected it for a quick profit. The people wore ragged clothing. Only a handful paid attention to the man holding a teenager against a wall.

Which part of town did you bring us to, Serena?

"Most people call them Hounds," Serena explained. "They're good at finding things or knowing if a person is hiding something." She licked her dry lips. "A few can find people based on their scent."

"Kanton. He..." Realta trailed off. A few more people had grown interested. Two men stood uncomfortably close, staring at her the same way Kanton had.

"Speak up, girl." Callum relaxed his grip on Serena's shirt. A button had been torn loose, exposing her thin collarbone.

Realta collected her thoughts. "Kanton gave people yours and Serena's descriptions, but not mine. Maybe he thought to use a different method to find us and gave the Hound my scent." But where would he have gotten that? Clothing. They had been forced to leave their extra clothes behind. Kanton could have easily taken an article belonging to each of them.

"Damn it," Callum sighed. "That means Kanton is here."

"Then we have to keep moving," Serena replied, her voice shaking. She glanced over at Realta and quickly averted her eyes.

I'm sorry, Serena. Father isn't normally like this. Oh, wasn't he? Whenever there was fighting or an argument getting out of hand, who did people call for help? Callum Haar. Her father never started fights, but he was very good at ending them.

"Don't have much of a choice. Let's walk a little ways," said Callum, eyeing the growing crowd. A handful dispersed as his glare fell on them.

They walked a few blocks away from the rundown market. Realta kept her eyes open for guardsman and strange men in chains. She'd never heard of Hounds. People who could locate others based on their scents? It was so bizarre.

They stopped at a series of benches near a tavern. A handful of people talked nearby but paid them no attention. Callum reached into his satchel and pulled out a map. "Next village is Alhyrst, about twenty miles from East Bridge." He glanced up at the sky. The sun was midway to the horizon. "It will be nightfall before we reach it."

"Better than risking the night here," said Serena. "What if they post more Cuchasi at the city gate? We will never get out."

"Think it's a good plan?" Callum asked Realta.

Realta was silent for a moment, processing the question. Callum was relying on her opinion? He was the experience mountain guide, not her. She said, "Yes, but I think you should see a healer first." A dark red stain had formed on his shirt. Running had caused the stitches to rip.

Callum studied his shirt. "It can wait another day." He covered the blood stain with his cloak. "Where are the gates?"

"This way," replied Serena. She walked at an even pace. The sun had sunk low in the sky, dyeing it a deep orange by the time they reached the city's edge.

14

Seltachai

The common room of the Red Eagle was quiet during the mid-morning lull between meals. Gareth and his father were the only ones present, save for the innkeeper and the head maid who was enjoying a break by the fireplace.

They had arrived in Lothian the night before, leaving Vala the moment Kel read Callum's letter. Gareth knew that Kanton man was a liar. He knew it! If only he had been able to convince Realta and the others. Words had never been his strong suit. All he could convey was the desire to go home.

"I'll go with you," Master Loy had said as Kel and Esme saddled Dust. Gareth's mother had not been keen on Kel tracking them down, but his father was adamant, explaining that this was his fault.

"No. The fewer people, the faster we can catch up to them. Gareth, are you packed?"

Gareth had nodded. He didn't understand why Kel wanted him to tag along. Esme couldn't go because that guardsman still needed care, and nobody could predict when Healer Zall would enter another 'mood'. His mother preferred that term over 'too crazy to function'.

Using his good leg, Kel climbed into the saddle, his crutch lying across his lap. Gareth followed suit, climbing into the saddle of a borrowed horse. Half the people in Vala had heard the news, and all of them wanted to help.

"Write to us the second you can," said Mistress Loy, her eyes rimmed red.

"I promise." Kel leaned over and gave Esme a kiss. "I'll bring them back," he promised her.

"You'd better." She smiled. She then gave Gareth's hand a small squeeze. "Listen to your father."

Gareth promised he would, wishing he was the younger sibling. Even at age twelve, Estrid was better suited for this.

The two of them took off, not stopping until they reached Lothian.

Pulling the hood of his cloak over his face, Kel stood and ambled over to the innkeeper, his left leg more stiff than usual thanks to a day of riding. Gareth trailed behind him. He was thankful his father was the one asking questions. The idea of talking to a stranger made Gareth feel like he was going to be sick.

The innkeeper, a board shouldered man with dark brown hair, stiffened as Kel approached. The maid realized she had work to do and hurried off.

"Good morning, Master Kel," he said with rehearsed kindness.

"Hello, Master Flynn. I wanted to thank you for letting my son and I spend the night here."

"It's no trouble. So long as your money's good," he laughed.

"I was wondering if I might ask a few questions."

The laughter left the innkeeper's face. "About?"

"My brother-in-law and niece were traveling through here about a week ago with a company of guardsmen. King's Guard. We lost contact with them. Did they happen to stay here?"

"We get a lot of travelers this time of year, Master Kel. It's difficult to remember."

"Perhaps this will jog your memory." Kel reached into his pocket and pulled out seven gold marks. Master Flynn's eyes narrowed.

"Sir, I am an honest man. I don't accept bribes."

Kel smiled. "It's not a bribe. It's a reward."

Gareth stiffened, swallowing a lump in his throat. Kel, knowing that Gareth had no love for surprises, had prepared him for this part. Because the truth was, Gareth's father was a Seltachai, a creature with gold and silver wisps of light mixed with red sparks coming out of his skin. Lights that only Gareth could see.

The coins floated above Kel's hand, spinning and gliding between his fingers. Master Flynn's jaw dropped. Going to one knee, he bowed and said, "Forgive me, sir. I didn't realize—"

"An honest mistake," Kel replied. The coins floated gently back to his palm. "There was no way for you to know. Now, about those guardsmen."

"I do remember them now, good sir," he replied, standing and plastering on a smile. "There were four of them. One was a woman. I thought that odd. Your brother-in-law was one of them?"

"No. He was traveling with them. A tall man, black hair, dark eyes."

Master Flynn's face fell. "Callum Haar?"

"Yes."

"So, you've heard about that business, then?"

"It's why I'm here."

Gareth inched closer to his father. The air in the common room had grown heavier, darker.

"You know he killed one of those guardsmen, right?"

Kel paled. "What? How?"

"Should I get the healer and the head guard?"

"Yes. I have questions for them. And if they refuse, tell them exactly what I am."

Master Flynn exited the inn, almost running.

"Damn it," Kel swore under his breath.

"Uncle Callum killed a man?" Gareth asked, not believing it. Callum was the man who played with him when Gareth was little, who taught him and Realta all about plants and animals and let them ride on his shoulders. He couldn't kill someone. It was impossible.

"Excuse me?" asked a timid voice. Gareth turned and saw a girl about his age with wavy brown hair and wearing an apron. "I remember those people. The ones with the guards."

"What is your name?" Kel asked, facing her. The girl flinched. Kel pulled his hood down lower. His scars had never bothered Gareth. He didn't understand why other people were so frightened by them.

"Lea. They were traveling with a prisoner."

"That's right. A young woman. How much do you remember?"

"It was a big group. Too big to board everyone, so Master Flynn let them eat in the common room before they moved on. The leader, the guardsman with red earrings, he kept yelling at them. The other guards sat a little ways off. I think they were afraid of him, too."

"Was the leader named Kanton?"

Lea shrugged. "He didn't say."

"Can you describe the people he was with?"

Lea nodded and accurately described Callum, Realta, Charity, and Lok Tolman, as well as the prisoner. Serena.

"The guards came back in the middle of the night, two of them badly injured," Lea continued. "They said the prisoner got loose and the leader's servant helped her escape."

"Servant?"

"The tall man with black hair. The leader said he was his serving man."

"Lea, what in the world are you doing?" demanded Master Flynn, entering the common room with two other people, a healer dressed in white and a guardsman with a signature dark blue coat. The innkeeper did not look pleased.

"I had a few questions for her, that's all," replied Kel. He placed one of the gold coins in Lea's hand, her eyes widening. "Thank you." Pocketing the coin, the girl scurried off.

"Are you Master Kel?" asked the guardsman.

His father nodded.

"You're related to the man responsible for attacking the King's Guard?" His voice grew more hostile with every word.

Again, Kel nodded.

"Do you have any idea what that man did?"

"I will once you tell me," Kel replied, pulled back his hood. The three men gasped, eyeing the latticework of white scars covering the left half of his face and the jagged flesh along both ears. "And I am not a man who likes be to kept waiting."

The guardsman whispered something to the innkeeper, too softly for Gareth to hear. The innkeeper replied curtly, "Of course! I saw him move those coins with my own eyes!"

"Would you like to see with your own eyes, sir?" Kel caused one of the coins to float over to the guardsman. He caught the coin and studied it.

"Would you care to sit while we talk, sir?" the guard asked.

Kel smiled. "Very much, yes."

Seated at the nearest table, the guard told them about that night. Captain Kanton, badly injured and bleeding, rode back into Lothian. He and the two conscious guards told the same story. Callum Haar helped their prisoner, a horse thief, escape. The two of them and the three teenagers with them disappeared without a trace.

"Did you question them individually or all together?" Kel asked.

"Together, sir."

Kel frowned. "What about the third guard?"

It was the healer's turn to speak. The third guard, Aleyn Tock, was covered in severe burns and succumbed to his injuries a few hours later. The guards all claimed that Callum shoved Tock and Kanton into the campfire. Two of the teenagers fled into the woods. The female guard followed on foot, but she was shot in the leg with an arrow.

"That proves the attack was premeditated," said the guardsman. "Haar was seen speaking with a local thief right here in the Red Eagle. Obviously, he enlisted his help."

"Obviously," Kel repeated. "Where is this thief now?"

"Disappeared into the forest. Hasn't resurfaced yet."

Kel drummed his fingers on the table, deep in thought.

Gareth tried and failed to picture the scene. Everything these men had said felt wrong. Callum would never plot against guardsmen, and Realta and Charity would never help a prisoner escape. It simply was not in their nature.

"What did the guards do next?"

"They rode to the next village, hoping to find word of them there. Haar was injured. He likely sought medical treatment—"

"He was injured?! Why didn't you tell me before?"

The guardsman turned as white as fresh linen. "It slipped my mind. Please, forgive me, sir."

Kel sighed. "When did the guards leave?"

"The morning of Alet third."

Kel stood, wincing. "Thank you all for your help. If you hear anything else, pass the news on to Master Sardic Loy and Mistress Vera Tolman of Vala. Come along, Gareth."

Gareth stood, casting a nervous glance at the men.

"Master Flynn, see that our horses are saddled. We're leaving within the hour."

Without waiting for the innkeeper's reply, Kel headed for the stairs. Gareth stayed one step behind, in case his father lost his balance. The shock of him being a Seltachai would immediately disappear if these men saw him fall down the stairs.

"It's a lie, right?" Gareth asked once they were in their room, a sparsely furnished space with a small desk and two narrow beds. Kel sat down at the desk and began writing a letter to Esme. "Uncle Callum didn't do what they said."

"A man is dead, no doubt about that," Kel replied as he wrote. "How do you feel about going to Teyrnas, son?"

"Why?"

Kel smiled. "I love that you're so direct. The King's Guard is stationed in Teyrnas. If they find Callum and Realta, they'll take them to the capital to stand trial."

"But they're innocent."

Kel's pen fell silent. He looked up at Gareth, his blue eyes tired. "Son, we don't know what happened that night. I want your uncle to be innocence. The man is the closest thing I have to a brother. But I also know what he's capable of. Finding Kanton means finding Callum and Realta and Charity, and finding the truth. Will you go to Teyrnas with me?"

Gareth hesitated. He had never been this far from home, from everything that was comforting and familiar. But home would never be the same without his uncle and cousin.

"Yes. I'll go."

Kel breathed a sigh of relief and continued writing.

Gareth glanced out of the room's sole window. In the yard below, the stable hands were saddling Dust.

15

Questions of Balance

The run rising over the River Nerin was more beautiful than Charity ever imagined. The warm light shimmered on the blue-green expanse. Calm water lapped the banks. Rangar Forest grew to the very edge, some of the trees stretching out their roots to meet the water. A cool breeze tussled her hair.

Oh Realta, if only we could have seen this together.

There was still no sign of her best friend. Arnyn has asked a group of hunters if they saw anyone on the main road that met Realta or Callum's descriptions. No such luck. Before leaving, he had asked Rawni to keep an eye out for them. The unofficial mayor of Rangar Keep agreed. Their best bet now was to head for the Academy and hope their friends were traveling in the same direction.

"You're up early," said Kelia, the ship captain who had agreed to take her and Lok across the Nerin. She wore tight-fitting trousers underneath her plain blue dress. Charity assumed that was normal attire for female ship captains. Though, until recently, she believed female captains only existed in adventure stories set in far-off lands, like the Cayuga Islands.

"We always get up at sunrise back home," Charity replied. She stood, brushing the dirt off her dress. Little good that did. She hadn't had a chance to wash it in days.

"Good practice. The Scholars will appreciate that."

"Did you attend the Academy?"

Kelia laughed. "I'd no desire to stay cooped up in a dusty library. The open water is where I belong."

Lok stirred in his sleeping roll. He opened one eye, blinking against the bright light.

"Time to get going," said Kelia. She walked over to Arnyn, fast asleep near a tree, and kicked his leg.

"What?" Arnyn sat upright and observed the surrounding forest and river. "Ah, daylight. That makes sense."

"Time to move."

The four of them gathered up their meager supplies and followed Kelia a short distance up the river. Her ship was docked not far from there.

"How long does the crossing take?" Charity asked. She held onto Tiber's reins, and the horse was happy to follow. He had become much easier to manage over the days, getting use to Charity's presence. In his saddlebags were some supplies and all of Kanton's letters and notebooks. Deciphering the Old Eltrian texts would grant much needed insight into the guardsman's motives.

"A couple hours if the waters are calm," replied Kelia. "Worried about missing a deadline?"

"No. Just wondering."

"Don't worry, Miss Loy," said Arnyn, sauntering up to her side. "Everything in the world is balanced. You'll get to your destination soon. It will make up for the detour."

Charity sighed. Everything with that man was balance. She was not so sure about that, not after her encounter with West and his abusive aunt. Yes, the ability to identify Thanes was beneficial, but how did it benefit someone with mental impairments who lived in fear of his own relatives?

She and Lok had tried to find him again, Charity hoping to take him with them to the Academy. The Scholars might be able to help him with his ability. But the young man had disappeared like a puff of smoke.

"Speaking of balance," Kelia chimed in, "what about the money you owe me for this job? Running a ship ain't cheap."

"All things have their time."

"Meaning he'll get someone else to pay for him," Kelia whispered to Charity. She laughed under her breath.

"I hear laughter. That's always a good sign."

As their trek led them farther upriver, Charity glanced back at Lok. He had been uncommunicative the last few days, refusing to write or respond with facial expressions. He was a Fire Elemental Thane, someone of great importance. In his shoes, Charity would have been ecstatic. Perhaps that was just it. Lok had lived his whole life being looked down on. He never expected people to look up to him.

"There she is," said Kelia, beaming with pride. Before them stood a large riverboat, easily as big as Tolman's Inn, docked on the bank. The words "Storm Chaser" were painted on the side in blue trimmed with white. Several people moved about the deck. One of them spied Kelia and waved to her before alerting the others.

"How does it work?" Charity asked. Of course she knew ships floated on water and moved either by oars or sails. But she'd never seen one so big. It was a wonder it was able to float at all!

"You'll see." Kelia then called to one of the men, instructing him to lower the net. He and another man tied a large fishing net to the deck and draped it over the side. The end hung less than an inch above the sandy riverbank.

"And this is where I leave you," said Arnyn.

"Thank you for all your help. I don't know what Lok and I would have done if you hadn't found us."

"The Creator led me to you. All things are in balance, Miss Loy. Remember that."

Lok extended his hand, and Arnyn shook it. Lok did not meet the man's face, his eyes focused on his scuffed boots.

"Same with you, Young Master Tolman. Your life is being brought into balance. And sometimes that is a very painful process. But you will survive it, and be stronger for it."

Lok gave him a quick nod and headed for the boat, his small pack slung over his shoulder.

"Wait," said Charity. "What about Tiber? How will he get on board?"

"Are you adamant about bringing that horse?" asked Kelia, raising an eyebrow.

"Well, yes." Kelia never said she couldn't bring Tiber.

Kelia let out a pained sigh. "Sylas, lower the gangplank!" A stocky man with a mass of black hair readily obeyed, pulling a crank that lowered part of the boat's siding. Two other men then lowered a long plank of wood, wide enough for a cart.

"This will cost you extra, Teleran."

"So be it," he said with a smile. Charity doubted the man would ever repay her.

She followed Kelia towards the boat. Lok was already on

board, gazing over the water. It seemed calm. Hopefully, that meant an easy trip.

A thought popped into Charity's head. "Master Teleran, I have a question."

"Ask away."

"You say that everything is in balance. If that's true, then why are there eight Gadyeni and only one Midnight King?"

Arnyn gave her a pained look. "My dear, eight Gadyeni and one Midnight King is balanced."

Charity felt a pit form in her gut. She was sorry she had asked that stupid question. And where had it come from? Some weird desire to prove him wrong? That wasn't like her at all. This entire ordeal, Kanton attacking them, being separated from her friend, and finally the encounter with West, had unsettled her more than she'd been willing to admit.

"Have a good trip, Miss Loy," Arnyn said with a bright smile. "May you arrive safely."

"Thank you, Arnyn. And sorry I asked that question."

"Why? Without questions, we never learn." He waved a final goodbye and disappeared into the forest.

Wait. How did he meet Callum? She had meant to ask but always forgot or something interrupted her line of thought. She would ask Callum. When she was reunited with Callum and Realta, she'd ask. Yes, that was a good plan. A hopeful plan.

She walked up the wooden gangplank, leading Tiber. The horse did not protest and boarded the boat as easily as climbing a small hill.

On the deck, seven people moved every which way. One man led the horse off to the side. Charity kept an eye on the saddlebags. A part of her worried the men would steal more than a glance inside. Not all of them seemed trustworthy.

"If you like, miss," said the man called Sylas, "you and your friend can rest in the spare cabin below deck."

"I'd rather stay here. If that's all right." This was her first time crossing the river, and she did not want to miss a single moment.

"No problem. It's there if you change your mind." Sylas walked off towards Kelia.

A few minutes later, the ship left dry land and began its slow journey.

Charity walked over to Lok. The young Thane stared out over the water, his face downcast.

"What's on your mind?"

Lok shrugged.

"I promise to keep it just between us."

Lok relented and wrote in his notebook, *"Don't tell the Scholars that I'm a Thane. If this is real, then they will know."*

"Lok, you already know it's real." He had manipulated fire twice since discovering the ability. Nothing big, just causing the flames of their cook fires to rise and fall. But only when nobody except Charity was watching.

"Promise you won't tell."

"I promise, Lok. But if they ask—"

Lok shot her a pained look. He underlined the word Promise.

"I promise, so long as you agree to tell them yourself."

Lok sighed. He wrote, *"Fine."*

"Did you ever think you'd be traveling on a boat?" Charity asked, hoping to lighten their conversation. The forest grew smaller in the distance, the eastern bank a thin line of green and brown.

"I want to be alone for a while," Lok wrote.

"Okay." Charity was not surprised. Lok hadn't been the same since encountering West and his aunt, seeing the way she treated him. Mistress Tolman had always been king to Lok, giving him small encouragements and allowing him to help at the inn. Everyone else, not so much. The incident must have brought back a painful memory. "Let me know if you need anything."

Lok stared at the water.

Charity spied Kelia talking and laughing with her crew members. She walked over to join them. Perhaps the men were trustworthy, after all.

16

Academy Bound

Lok did not notice the amount of time it took to cross the Nerin. A single thought dominated his mind, that this was a mistake. He had come to terms with being a Thane. You can't escape a fundamental part of yourself. But did anyone have to know? He could leave the second they arrived on the other side, find a way back to Vala. He could continue living life as normal.

Life as normal. People staring at him, whispering behind his back. Thinking he was an idiot. Did he really want that?

His thoughts drifted to West. In that regard, he truly had been an idiot. The boy needed help. If he had let Charity go after him or alerted Arnyn, West could be with them right now. Safe. That slap to the face had sent Lok reeling, making him relive all the snide remarks and mocking eyes. But never from his mother. Never.

Lok grabbed onto the railing as the boat jolted. Pulled back into the present, he realized they had reached the eastern bank. Few trees dotted the flat landscape, completely devoid of hills. The land stretched unbroken towards the horizon.

Leaving the railing, Lok walked over to Charity. She beamed a smile that lit up her entire face. Dane Kanton's horse stood docilely next to her. Lok found it odd that the horse had been saddled that night outside of Lothian. He could have sworn he saw Kanton and the other guards unsaddle each one. His memories of that night were kind of a blur.

"We're finally here!"

"Not quite," replied Captain Kelia, striding over. "The Academy is a good ten miles from here."

"No problem. Thank you so much for help us."

Kelia gave her a half-smile, half-smirk. "Just doing my job. You and your friend be safe. And stay away from the capital."

"Why is that?" Charity's smile faded, her face darkening. Lok raised an eyebrow.

"A good number of gangs operate in the city's Western Quarter. It's not the safest place in the world. Anyway, I doubt the Scholars would let you wander that far. Good luck."

Charity again thanked her. Lok gave her a nod and a smile.

They exited the boat, walking down the narrow gangplank. The wood creaked underneath the horse's weight. Lok forced himself to keep steady and focus on the ground, not on thoughts of the wood breaking and ending up in the water. A lot of good it would do him to drown before reaching the Academy.

Once on solid ground, Kelia pointed them in the right direction. Due east until they reached the city of Norgard. The Academy was on the outskirts and was very hard to miss.

Even someone like you can follow that, Lok, Reder Yorath's mocking voice echoed. Lok pushed the unwanted thought away. Reder was far away in Vala. His words could not hurt him anymore.

"What do you want to study? I don't remember asking," Charity said once the boat was nothing more than a dot on the horizon. Lok was amazed he could still see it. The land was nothing like the Hinterlands. No hills, no valleys. Hard to believe both lands belonged to the same kingdom.

Lok took out his notebook and pencil. *"I'm not sure. Maybe history."* He had no talent for mathematics, and natural science bored him. But history was something different. It was stories that actually happened, people who really lived. And with his nose in a book, nobody would expect him to speak.

"That sounds wonderful. I bet you'll make a great historian."

Lok could not help but smile. Yes, Charity's words were always positive, even a little heavy-handed at times, but they did manage to make people smile.

Is that why you spend so much time with Healer Zall? Are you trying to make him smile, too?

The ten miles to the Academy were the easiest ten miles of Lok's life. No hills to climb up or down. No trees or crowds to maneuver around. And oddly no people. They were not even walking on a road. Just a wide field of ankle high grass. Charity had to steer the horse away from the grass multiple times. Lok found himself relaxing. No one to bother him or stare or mock. It was an odd feeling, and he welcomed it.

"I suppose that's it," said Charity, pulling Lok away from his thoughts. In the distance stood a large stone wall, easily twice as tall as him. Within the wall stood a trio of towers, all composed of the same gray stone. The central tower rose a hundred feet in the air with a flag waving in the breeze.

Walking closer, the sounds of human voices rose from behind the wall.

Lok's palms began to sweat. The Academy. They were finally here, and Lok was terrified. What if they didn't accept him? Sorry, young man, being a Thane is not enough. You have to speak to attend this academy. His mother said she would not be disappointed. But Lok felt deep in his gut that she'd consider him a failure. Just like everyone else in Vala.

"Come on, Lok." Charity smiled, grabbing hold of his hand and leading the horse with the other.

Well, maybe not everyone in Vala.

They circled around the wall until they reached the road. A road paved with stone and worn down until it was completely smooth. A large wooden gate framed with iron rested within the wall. At the top flew the flag of Teyrnas, a dark blue banner divided diagonally by a silver stripe with two ravens, one on each half.

Charity approached the gate and knocked.

"Yes?"

Lok looked around. Where had that voice come from? He looked up. A man was stationed on top of the wall. He wore a dark blue overcoat, just like Kanton.

"Hello," replied Charity. "We've come to study at the Academy of Teyrnas. This is it, right?"

"Yeah. One moment." The man disappeared. Lok heard metal clanking against metal. The gate divided in two, slowly opening inwards. The man, who stood a head shorter than Lok, looked them up and down. "So where in Teyrnas are you from?"

"Vala. In the Hinterlands."

The man thought it over. "Yeah, sounds familiar. What are your intentions?"

"To study."

"Yeah, but study what? All prospective Students need to have a written letter of intent before being admitted."

"Oh." Neither she nor Lok had written a letter. Kanton had never mentioned it. Lok had a sinking feeling that the man was never taking them to the Academy. "Well, can we tell you and then write the letters?"

The man rolled his eyes. "Sure, kid."

"I want to study healing, and my friend wants to study history."

"All right. Either of you Thanes or related to Thanes?"

Don't tell him, Charity. You promised.

"We don't know."

"That's fine. Most kids don't know. We'll get that sorted out. Hey, Syd," he called out to someone behind the wall, "contact Scholar Lucan. Tell him we got two hopefuls."

"Yes, Baltyn." The reply had an odd, raspy intonation. A large hawk soared into the air, heading for the central tower.

"Come in," said Baltyn. Once they were inside, Baltyn released a mechanism next to the wall, a series of metal gears and oiled ropes, and the gates closed smoothly. A central mechanism then locked the doors into place.

"Where's Syd?" asked Charity. No one else was stationed at the gate.

"He just flew off. Didn't you see him?"

"You mean the hawk?" Charity asked, shocked.

"Haven't you kids ever heard of Deirow Hawks?" Baltyn raised an eyebrow.

They shook their heads. What this some sort of joke?

"Caman's staff! Vala must really be out in the Hinterlands. Don't worry. You'll acclimate soon enough. This horse belongs to you?"

"Yes. His name is Tiber."

"We will find a place for him in the stables."

"Is there always a guard posted at the gate?" Charity asked as Lok studied the Academy. A large, green expanse covered the front half of the complex. Various fruit trees grew in small clusters, and flower beds lined the wall. The Academy itself was divided into multiple buildings connected by covered walkways. The smaller buildings were two or three stories tall, while the central building rose six stories into the air, the largest structure

Lok had ever seen.

Numerous people moved from building to building, all wearing blue, gray, or white cloaks. Those in blue appeared to be his age, while those in gray several years older, and those in white were around his mother's age and older.

Those must denote different levels. Students in blue or gray and Scholars in white. Did they have to wear those cloaks all the time? Lok would hate having to wear one during the summer.

"Always," Baltyn replied. "We switch off every four hours."

The hawk returned and landed on Baltyn's shoulder. Slightly larger than a regular hawk, it had black and brown feathers, the tips of its wings and tail pure white. Its eyes were tinted a deep gold.

"Scholar Lucan will arrive momentarily," said the hawk.

Lok and Charity jumped back. A talking hawk? He thought Baltyn was just pulling their legs. What in the world...

"Thanks, Syd," replied Baltyn, completely unfazed by a talking bird. What other oddities were at the Academy?

An older man dressed in a pristine white cloak and well-tailored shirt and trousers walked up to the gate. He stood slightly shorter than Lok, his back perfectly straight. His hair was completely white save for bushy black eyebrows framing his dark eyes.

"Are you Scholar Lucan?" asked Charity.

"Yes," he replied in a deep, authoritative voice. "And who are you, young lady?"

"Charity Loy. And this is Lok Tolman."

Overhead, thunder rumbled. Lok glanced up and saw dark gray clouds forming in the west. He hadn't noticed clouds on the way here. Granted, his mind was on other matters.

"Let's continue this meeting inside." Scholar Lucan addressed Baltyn, "Good work, guardsman. If you will take their horse to the stables."

"Not a problem." He took the reins from Charity.

"What about our bags?" asked Charity, a hint of anxiety in her voice. Lok had no idea how the Scholars would react if they discovered Kanton's belongings. He feared it would be worse than a mere rejection.

"You can collect them later," the Scholar replied as Baltyn, with Syd the hawk on his shoulder, led the horse away. "No one will disturb them. Come." He turned on his heels and headed for the looming stone building. Students and Scholars alike sought shelter in one building or another. Thunder rumbled again.

Alet's showers bring spring flowers, his mother's voice echoed. A kind, pleasant voice that knew nothing but love. Lok felt a great sense of longing tug at his heart. How was she managing by herself? The serving girls helped during the day, but what about at night, when everything was quiet? Perhaps leaving was a mistake. He did not belong here.

But neither did he belong there.

Two large wooden doors, about eight feet tall, guarded the entrance to the Academy's central building. The wood had been carved to mimic vines of ivy climbing towards the sky. Scholar Lucan opened the door with easy. It slowly closed behind them, making only the slightest sound.

The front hall was as wide as the marketplace in Vala. Two giant staircases, wide enough for two carts and branching off at each story, flanked the hall. Beyond them were narrower hallways lined with doors on one side and windows on the other. Cloaked individuals, the majority in light blue, moved every which way.

"Charity and Lok," Scholar Lucan tested their names. "Where in Teyrnas are you from?"

Charity informed him.

"Ah, yes. Hinterlanders give their children such quaint names."

The scholar's tone made Lok frown. It was jovial, but a mocking quality lied underneath. Charity, still smiling, had not seemed to notice.

The Scholar led them up the stairs to the second floor and down a hall to a spacious room. Windows lined one wall, sunlight pouring in. The other wall contained a bookshelf, the volumes organized by the color of their spines. In the center of the room sat a long table with enough chairs for twenty people. An engraving of a compass rose was set into the table's center.

Scholar Lucan took a seat at the end of the table. Charity sat on his right while Lok sat next to her. He could see right over Charity's head. Why did he have to be so tall? His height made it next to impossible to blend in.

Two other Scholars, each wearing white cloaks of their own,

entered the room and sat at the table. The one who sat opposite from Charity was a woman in her late thirties with wavy brown hair and sharp blue eyes, and her cloak was trimmed with gold thread. She had a pair of gold earrings to match. The Scholar opposite Lok appeared to be in his late forties or early fifties with black hair peppered with gray and dark eyes. His skin tone was a deep tan.

"Scholars Maryn and Kuno will assist me in your acceptance hearing. After the hearing, you will take the entrance exam. You will know the outcome by midday tomorrow. Let's start with your letters of intent."

"Well, we don't have any," Charity replied sheepishly. Scholars Maryn and Kuno shared a glance. Lok shrank down as best he could. "Nobody told us we needed a letter."

"Write them now," replied Scholar Maryn. "Kuno can take diction. If that's approved?" She looked to Scholar Lucan.

The older man nodded. Scholar Kuno stood and retrieved papers, pen, and ink from a nearby shelf. Retaking his seat, he nodded for Charity to begin.

"State your name and why you wish to study at the Academy," Lucan prompted her.

"I, Charity Loy, wish to study healing and medicine at the Academy because my village needs a new healer. The one we have is unable to properly care for everyone." Charity hesitated. "He isn't right in the head. The midwife tries to help him, but sometimes it isn't enough. Most people are afraid to speak to him. And a few have died because they're too afraid to seek medical attention. I want to fix this, and the best way I can is by studying here at the Academy."

Scholar Kuno finished writing and handed the paper off to Scholar Lucan. The older man nodded and placed the paper off to the side.

"Begin when you are ready," he said to Lok.

Lok stared at the blank paper, at the pen in Scholar Kuno's hand, and finally at the Scholar's expectant face. His dark eyes were filled with patience. Dark brown. The same color as Vera Tolman's. The other Scholars waited. Charity held her tongue. She promised not to reveal that he was a Thane. But you cannot hide being a mute.

Lok reached for the paper and slid it over to himself. He gestured for the pen. Scholar Kuno, perplexed, handed it over. Lok began to write.

I, Lok Tolman, wish to study history at the Academy because I have always had an interest in the subject, nothing more. I don't know if that is a good enough reason for you to accept me. I will understand if you don't.

He signed the bottom of the page and handed it to Scholar Lucan.

The room was silent while the Scholar read. Even the thunder had stopped.

"Can't you speak?" Lucan asked him.

Lok shook his head.

"He hasn't said a word in his life," Charity explained.

Lucan thought quietly for a moment, his fingers steepled. "Well, that is something to take into consideration. Maryn, check to see if Rune has arrived."

"Yes, Master Scholar." Scholar Maryn stood and walked into the hallway, casting a quick glance at Lok. He shrank down in his seat.

Scholar Kuno clapped his hands together, the sharp sound echoing off the walls. Lok jolted, nearly jumping out of the chair. What on Eltriar...?

"There's nothing wrong with his hearing," Kuno addressed Lucan. "And his handwriting is legible. Perhaps—"

"It will be taken into consideration. Keep in mind, there's still the entrance exam."

Scholar Maryn reentered the room, trailed by a man dressed in simple work clothes. He had bright green eyes and his black hair was gray at the temples.

"Who is he?" Charity asked Scholar Lucan.

"Rune if one of the Cuchasi. He's here to determine if you are Thanes."

"Really?" Charity brightened, the sun peering from behind the clouds. "How will he do that?"

Lok's heart sank. Was this man like Arnyn?

"He just knows."

Fire and smoke, he was like Arnyn!

Rune calmly walked over and inspected them. "The girl is a normal human. And the boy..." Rune's eyes grew wide, his jaw dropping. "Elemental. The boy is an Elemental Thane!"

No!

Lok buried his face in his hands and sobbed. He hadn't cried since he was twelve, the time Reder Yorath and Lon Millar beat him until he could not move. His leg as well as his collarbone and several ribs had been broken. He'd been too terrified to name his attackers, unable to cry for help as they landed blow after blow.

Ander, Lon's older brother, had figured it out a few weeks later. Lon had a big mouth, never could keep his accomplishments quiet. Ander ended up breaking Lon's jaw. Master and Mistress Millar sent the two boys to work at the Loy farm as a way to keep them out of trouble. That had stopped the beatings, but not the insults and stares. Lok promised himself he would never cry again, that he would be strong and face his fears. Yet here he was, sobbing his eyes out.

"An Elemental?" he heard Lucan ask. "Are you sure?"

"I think so. He has a green Aura. That signifies an Elemental, right?"

"But an Elemental hasn't been recorded in Teyrnas in over three hundred years!" Kuno exclaimed.

"I'll inform the Premier." Scholar Maryn took off running.

"I can't believe it! I can't believe it," Scholar Kuno repeated in a quiet voice.

"So, he's accepted?" Charity asked.

"We will have to verify Rune's findings with the other Cuchasi and the records. And the exam. But yes. He's accepted." Scholar Lucan's words were filled with awe.

"Did you hear that, Lok? Lok?" Charity placed a gentle hand on his shoulder. "It's all right, Lok. You're going to be a Scholar. Everything will be okay. I promise."

Okay? How could anything in life ever be okay again? All Lok wanted was a chance at a normal life. Now that normal life was impossible.

17

A Matter of Time

"Realta."

Realta stirred as the morning sunlight peered through low tree branches. Leaving East Bridge had proven difficult. The city gates were heavily guarded at night. News of bandits was more prevalent on this side of the Nerin, with many gangs operating in the capital. From what they could glean, several gangs had moved their bases of operation to East Bridge to avoid competition. But there was no news concerning them. Horse thieves and escaped slaves were a mere drop in the bucket.

They had to spend the night and most of the following day in the city, waiting until the guards changed posts. They slipped out and camped in a small copse of trees a few miles away. The Teyrnas Highway, a direct line to the capital itself, was just visible, giving them ample warning if anyone came looking.

"Realta." Someone nudged her shoulder.

"I'm awake." She sat up, wrapping her cloak around her shoulders. She half expected to find Charity or her little cousin Estrid by her side. Instead, she found Serena. She was genuinely surprised the girl hadn't tried running away again. Blinking away the sleep, Realta noticed that Serena's eyes were wide, her face pale.

"What's wrong?"

"Your father won't wake up. He's still breathing, but—"

Realta rushed to Callum's side, her heart sinking and racing all at once. His face was deathly pale, and his breaths came out in shallow gasps. The right side of his shirt was stained dark red. Realta, fingers shaking so badly they barely functioned, unbuttoned Callum's shirt. The wound on his chest had ripped open. Dark blood crusted the wound's edges, while the inside contained a reddish yellow fluid.

"It's infected." Why hadn't Callum thought to buy medicine?

They had money. Well, actually, they had a mere handful of coppers. Barely enough to buy food for the day, let alone last them all the way to Teyrnas.

"There's a village a few miles from here," Serena said. "We should go and bring back the healer." She hesitated. "If they have one."

"Who will stay with Father?" She didn't dare leave Callum alone, not in this condition.

"I will."

Realta shot her a glare.

"I won't run, I swear. And Kanton's looking for me. Not you."

"What about those Hounds?"

"They only operate in big cities." Serena quickly added, "Little villages don't need them. I promise I will be here when you get back."

Realta stood on shaking legs. She did not trust Serena, not completely. One look at Callum told her that did not matter. This was a risk she had to take. She glanced through the trees. The highway was clear with the sun just above the horizon. Traffic would pick up in an hour or so.

"I'll bring help, Father. Don't worry." *And don't die. Please, don't die.*

Realta stepped out of the copse, glancing back every few seconds. Serena was still there. This was the perfect opportunity for her to run away. She wanted to believe her, but every other word was a lie or a half-truth. Even if she ran, Callum still needed help.

The road stretched towards the horizon. No trees or hills interrupted it. In fact, there were no hills in this part of the kingdom. Realta did not mind. A smooth, straightforward path meant reaching her destination quicker.

But how far? Serena did not specify. A few miles could be two or four or six. Realta kept her eyes on the road. It did not matter as long as she took one step after another. And another and another.

Small dots appeared on the horizon. Houses, farms, shops. A small village, around the size of Vala. She had made it. But where to go now?

People milled about the streets, chatting with friends and neighbors and going about their daily business. The chapel's

wind chimes sang in the cool breeze. This village could have easily been Vala, except for one difference. Most people here had blue
eyes. The majority in Vala had dark brown.

"Do you need help, little girl?" a woman asked her. She had
black hair and bright blue eyes, and she wore a red shawl over her
shoulders. Those bright blue eyes were filled with concern.

"Yes." Realta's legs felt like they were going to collapse from lack
of movement. How far had she walked? "Where is the healer?"

"He lives up this road. I'll take you to him."

Realta felt like crying. The last people who had shown them
any kindness were Healer and Mistress Tesell. And they had re-
paid them by sneaking out in the middle of the night.

The woman knocked on the door of a well maintained,
two-story house. The sign on the door read "Caradek". Various
herbs were painted along the sign's edges. A man who was no
older than thirty answered.

"Good morning, Milly." He smiled.

"Healer Jestin, this young girl needs your help."

"I see." He studied Realta. Self-consciousness flooded her. She
hadn't bathed since leaving home, and her dress was coated in
dirt. "Come in, please."

The woman, Milly, gave her a reassuring nod and headed back
down the road. Realta entered the house. It smelled clean.

"Now, what do you need, young miss?" asked Healer Jestin,
leading her into a large room filled with medical supplies, each
item in its proper place. In the corner stood a large mirror. Realta hardly recognized the girl in the reflection. Wild hair, a dirty
face, ragged clothes and boots caked with dirt. Haunted eyes. No
wonder Milly knew something was wrong.

"We..." Realta's throat was terribly dry. She tried again. "My father, and sister, and I." She hated referring to the girl as her sister.
Hated lying. "We were attacked by bandits a few days back. One of
them hurt my father. And now he won't wake up. I..." Large tears
fell down her face, creating tracks in the dirt. "Help. Please..."

"Oh, my dear." Healer Jestin placed a gentle hand on her shoulder. "They didn't hurt you or your sister, too, did they?"

"No. Please help my father." *Please don't leave me lost and alone.*

"Where is he?"

Realta wiped the tears away, but they kept coming. She did her best to describe the copse along the highway.

Healer Jestin grabbed a black bag and ushered her out the back door. Behind the house was a small stable with a horse and cart. The healer quickly and calmly hitched the horse to the cart, each motion made with precision. He instructed Realta to ride next to him in the driver's seat. With a flick of the reins, the healer's house disappeared down the road.

"Bloody bandits," Healer Jestin muttered. "Lost count of how many times I've seen their handiwork. Were you traveling alone? Just the three of you?"

"Yes."

The healer let out a frustrated breath. "Not safe to do that anymore. Need to travel in a group. May I ask where you're traveling to?"

"Teyrnas. We have family there." Such a simple lie. She always hated lying, felt so guilty afterwards. She felt no guilt now.

"I see."

"There!" Realta pointed at the small copse. "Right there." At least, she thought so.

Healer Jestin pulled the horse to a stop and jumped off the cart, making a beeline for the trees. Realta followed. She breathed a sigh of relief at seeing Serena poke out her head. She had kept her word for once.

"How is your father's condition?" the healer asked.

"He still won't wake up."

The healer knelt beside Callum's unconscious body. Opening his black bag, he removed a short tube made out of thick paper. He placed one end on Callum's chest and his ear on the other.

"Breathing sounds obstructed." The healer placed two fingers on Callum's neck. "Heart rate elevated."

Realta ran her hands through her hair. Why couldn't he speak clearly, like Esme? Did those things mean Callum was dying?

He examined the wound on Callum's chest. A deep frown creased his face. "When did this occur?"

"About a week ago. We don't really remember," Serena replied.

"Help me get him on the cart." The healer lifted Callum by the shoulders while Serena lifted his feet. They gently placed him in the cart. Realta climbed in next to him, holding his hand. The skin was cold and clammy. The healer got into the driver's seat.

"Wait!" Serena ran back into the copse. She returned with Callum's satchel. The satchel! Realta had completely forgotten. Thank the Creator and the Gadyeni that Serena remembered.

Once Serena was in the driver's seat, the healer drove back to the village. The ride seemed twice as long. Callum's breathing grew more labored. Small drops of blood fell out of his nostrils and the sides of his mouth.

"What's wrong with him?" Realta cried.

"Punctured lung, most likely. Might require surgery."

Surgery? He was going to cut Callum open? *It's to save his life. He would not do surgery if it wasn't necessary.*

Back at the healer's house, they carried Callum into a small room on the first floor. It contained a single bed and a long counter on the far wall with shelves overhead. Medicines and herbs. Bandages.

Knives.

A young woman, who closely resembled the healer, appeared in the doorway. "Why didn't you tell me you were leaving?"

"Didn't have time, Jera. Take these two to the waiting room. Wash up for surgery," he said as he removed Callum's shirt. The yellow fluid had seeped out of the wound.

Muttering a curse, Jera led Realta and Serena into a room down the hall. The room was set up like a parlor with tables, chairs by the windows, a few books. Even a fireplace. A room designed to put people at ease.

"Don't worry. My brother and I will fix him up good as new. Is there anything you need?" Realta and Serena shook their heads. The only thing she needed was Callum alive and well. Jera exited the room, closing the door softly.

Realta sat down in one of the chairs, her entire body trembling. Her legs felt like they were boneless, ready to collapse in an instant. Callum's wound dominated her mind. She had never heard of a punctured lung, did not understand what it meant. If it could be fixed. What would happen if Callum died? Would they return home or continue on to Teyrnas? Would she be able to continue at all?

Serena sat in the chair next to her. "My nephew had surgery once," she whispered. "He came out of it all right."

"You never mentioned a nephew," Realta replied. She was grateful that Serena spoke up. She needed the distraction.

Serena bit down on her lip. "Well, half-nephew."

"Oh." Right, she was a bastard. "How many half-siblings do you have?"

"Three. Two brothers and one sister. They're all a good fifteen, twenty years older than me. My sister has always been nice to me, but my oldest brother can't decide whether to love me or hate me. And Mal acts like I don't exist." Tears glistened in her eyes. "Morgan and Mannix, my oldest brother's sons, they don't know what to make of me. Morgan is old enough to understand the truth, but Mannix only knows me as Aunt Serena."

"Do you think he'll care when he's old enough?"

"I hope not."

The wall clock ticked, filling the silence.

"What kind of surgery did your nephew need?" Realta wanted to keep the conversation going. The more Serena talked, the more she learned, and the less she thought about the healers cutting open her father.

"Morgan's appendix got infected. The surgeons had to remove it."

"What's an appendix?" Charity and Esme would know. Its function, its location in the body, everything. Both of them would have the right words to say to make her feel better.

"It's a small organ near the hip. Can't tell you what it does, though. Don't know anything about medicine."

"That makes two of us." Realta gave her a weak smile. She returned in kind.

Serena stood and went to the door. She listened for a moment and then resumed her seat. "I've been wondering if I should say this. I might be wrong."

"What?"

"You've really never heard of a Cuchasi, right?"

"Yes."

"Well, that part about them finding people based on scent? I lied. They see certain kinds of people." A pause. "Thanes."

Realta frowned. "A Thane? You honestly think I'm a Thane?" Thanes were powerful individuals born to noble families. They were not the daughters of indentured servants. It was more absurd than her original lie.

"I know it's a lot to take in, especially with all that's happened recently. But if we can get another Cuchasi to verify it, maybe we can use it as leverage against Kanton."

"How?"

"Thanes take an oath to protect one another. If word gets out that he attacked a young Thane, he'll be a disgrace."

Realta mulled over Serena's words. "How do I know any of this is true? For all I know, you've lied about everything. Why should I trust you?"

"Why should I trust you? You hit me on the head with a bucket."

She glared at Serena. "You hit Ander on the head with a shovel and injured a guardsman."

"That was self-defense. And what's-his-name would have alerted the village guard."

"You don't know that. Master and Mistress Loy would have heard you out."

"And would they have let a stranger stay in their house?"

"Yes."

"Really?" She scoffed. "A complete stranger?"

"The bedroom doors lock from the inside. They're kindhearted, not stupid."

Serena smiled. "You sound like him. Your father."

The reply caught her off guard. "Is that a good thing?" she asked hesitantly.

"Yeah. It's a good thing."

"Do you sound like your father?"

"No. Also a good thing."

Realta peered out of the window. A handful of people walked along the quiet street, waving to one another and exchanging a few words as they passed. So similar to the people back home. A guardsman dressed in the signature blue coat nailed a noticed to a wall. The word "Wanted" was written in bold. The rest of the words were too small to read.

"How long did your nephew's surgery take?"

"About an hour. But Morgan was bedridden for a full week. Why...?" The question died in Serena's mouth. She saw the notice, too. "Damn it to the Abyss."

"We can't run. Not with Father in this condition." She refused to risk Callum's health again, even if it risked Kanton finding them.

"It might not be for us." Serena stood and headed for the door.

"What are you doing?"

"I'm going to see what it says."

"No, someone might recognize you." She could not believe she was saying this. "Let me read it."

Serena, chewing on her lower lip, gazed out the window. "Okay."

Realta walked into the hallway, forcing one trembling foot in front of the other. Muffled voices came from the surgical room. A plop as heavy object fell into water. Footsteps, but none coming near her. Carefully placing each step, she opened the front door a crack. Waiting until no one was in sight, she crossed the street.

The notice was much larger than it had first appeared. Over a dozen names were written on it, categorized by where the wanted individuals lived. Most were affiliated with gangs in Teyrnas, and one was a murdered from West Bridge. At the bottom were the names Callum Haar and Serena Molyns. Both were wanted by Dane Kanton, Captain of the King's Guard, for murder, theft, and... Realta's heart skipped a beat. Had she read that correctly? The final charge was for plotting to assassinate King Logan.

Was that why Kanton wanted them found so badly? Yes, Serena stole the king's horse. But that was it. Unless stealing the horse was a test. Entering and exiting the palace grounds without getting caught, the guards' focus on the stables instead of the palace itself.

Realta glanced over her shoulder at the healer's house. Serena stood in the window, watching her with Kel's clear blue eyes. Yet another mystery.

Making sure no one was watching, she crossed the street and returned to the healer's house.

"Well?"

"Your and Father's names are on the list."

Serena cursed under her breath.

"It stated that you—"

The door opened. Jestin and Jera stepped inside. Their shirt-sleeves and smocks were stained bright red.

"How is he?" Realta asked.

"We got the blood out of his lung and cleared away the pus," the healer replied.

"Can I see him?" Realta would not believe he was all right until she saw him with her own eyes.

"Not right now. He's still unconscious."

"How long before we can leave?" asked Serena.

"Hard to say," replied Jera. "These things are a matter of time. Could be a few days, could be a few weeks."

"Do you want us to contact your family in Teyrnas and tell them what happened?" asked Jestin.

"Yes," Serena replied. Realta felt uneasy. She didn't know anyone in Teyrnas. Serena was from the capital, but her family wanted nothing to do with her. Was that plot against the king even true, or just another one of Kanton's lies? Or Serena's lies?

"Our uncle. Master Gregor Pym. He's the stable master at the royal palace."

Her heart sank. The stable master. In other words, the person in charge of the place Serena stole that horse from. Who did she believe, the man who attacked her and her friends, or the girl who wore her uncle's face?

"Very well. Feel free to wash up and rest. We will tell you when your father wakes."

Realta prayed he woke soon.

18

Confirmation

Serena stared into empty space, her back against the wall. The accusations of her plotting against the king had shaken her to her core. Realta had waited until after Callum regained consciousness before telling her. Those accusations were against him, too.

"Your brothers are noblemen," said Callum, that painful, wheezing sound no longer in his throat. The surgery had been successful, though he was still weak and pale from blood loss. "Are you sure you've never heard of a plot against King Logan? Not even a rumor?"

"There are always rumors," Serena replied, her voice barely audible. "Always someone plotting against someone else. It's a bloody game to them."

"Do nobles get assassinated often?" asked Realta. She did not feel like talking this evening. Too many thoughts clouded her mind. But if she didn't steer the conversation, Serena might bring up Thanes and the possibility that Realta was one of them. She pushed the thought away. It was too ridiculous.

"Maybe one every couple of years. A lot of what they plan is speculation. Weird contests to see who can create the best plots." She shook her head in disgust.

"Kanton knows all about this?" Callum asked.

"Yeah. The man lives in Teyrnas. It's impossible for him not to know."

"So it's just another ploy. The man's growing desperate."
Serena nodded.

"For a horse thief. Kid, there's something you ain't telling us. Is King Logan that vindictive, or does Kanton have something over your family?"

"I don't know!" Serena buried her head in her heads. "Why won't they just let me leave?"

"Someone's coming," Realta whispered, hearing footsteps echo in the hall.

The door opened, admitting both Jestin and Jera. Jestin held Callum's satchel in his hand. Neither he nor his sister looked pleased.

"Well, the rite of passage is legitimate," Jestin said, returning the satchel to Callum. "But so is that notice across the street." Jera had seen it while visiting another patient and had swiftly informed her brother.

"We want to believe you, but the village guard is involved. We need proof," added Jera.

"Master Sardic Loy will verify our account," said Callum. "He met Captain Kanton and can vouch for everything the man said."

"So can our Uncle Gregor," added Serena.

"How exactly are you related?" asked Jestin, folding his arms. Realta inched closer to Callum.

"My father's cousin," Callum explained. "Thought he could make his fortune in the capital. Life taught him a different lesson." How could he lie so easily?

"We charged a messenger to take your letter to Teyrnas," said Jestin. "It should arrive in a half week. The one to Vala won't be here for a week or more. We won't inform the guard, not until we have enough evidence either way."

"In the meantime, you need to focus on recovery," said Jera.

"Thank you for hearing us out."

"Think nothing of it. Our..." Jera and Jestin exchanged pained looked. "Our father was in a similar situation. It didn't end well for him."

Realta bit down on her lip, fighting back tears. Every person they had met on this ill-fated journey had been more than kind to them, more than they deserved. With one exception. Dane Kanton. Putting a single grain of trust in him had been a mistake. One that almost cost them their lives. What if that dream hadn't woken her? Would they all be dead? She shivered, not wanting to think about it.

"Let us know if you need anything." With that, Jestin and Jera exited the recovery room, closing the door softly.

"We can't wait a half week," said Serena.

"Maybe we can."

"What?"

"Shut up and listen." Callum paused, steadying his breathing. "Kanton has been traveling at the same rate as us, only a day ahead or behind. If we wait, he will move on. Those wanted posters only stay up for a few days. Our names will soon be replaced by others. If Gregor Pym makes good on that letter, we will have a means of transportation straight to Teyrnas. All we have to do it wait."

Her father made a good point. "I agree."

Serena muttered under her breath.

"Is that a yes or no, girl?"

"Yes. Don't have much of a choice, do I?"

"Then it's settled." Callum leaned against the pillow propping him up. "Get some rest. We all need it."

✳✳✳

Realta could not sleep. She had laid in bed for hours, watching the moons race across the sky from the bedroom window. Her entire body was tired, drained of energy. But sleep refused to come. It was like walking home after a long journey, only to realize you had lost the key.

She heard a small plink. Sitting up, she glanced over at Serena in the other bed. The girl seemed to be asleep. It was hard to tell with her. The plink came again. Muffled voiced rose from the street.

Realta glanced out the window. Two men in dark uniforms stood in the street. One of them called up, asking for Jestin Caradek. A door slamming open and pounding footsteps sent a shudder down her spine, every inch of her trembling. The front door opened. The two men spoke with the healer, too softly for Realta to hear.

Her heart pounded in her throat. What had happened? Jestin and Jera had promised to keep them safe. Had someone discovered what they were doing?

You don't even know if this is about you. They might want something else. They were the village healers. Someone must have taken ill or been severely injured.

Her gut told her otherwise.

Slipping on her boots, Realta crept out of the room and slowly walked down the stairs, pausing after each step. The two men did not sound happy.

"Do you want to end up like your father?" asked one, a dark silhouette in the door frame.

"Tell me what this is about," Jestin demanded.

"You know damn well why we're here. Those documents you brought the alderman belong to an escaped slave."

"That document proves he's traveling with his master's permission, you idiot."

"We have our orders."

"From who?"

"Does it matter? Hand him over and whoever he's traveling with."

"He is my patient. I can't just—" Jestin finally noticed Realta standing off to the side. Eyes growing wide, he swallowed a lump in his throat. "Go back upstairs, dear. There's nothing to fear."

"Is that the slave's kid?"

"Yes," Realta replied. She trembled from head to foot, a leaf in a storm. She felt herself take a step forward.

"Are you a slave as well, child?" asked the second guard, who stood a head shorter than his colleague.

"No." Realta rolled up her left sleeve, revealing no marks on her skin. "Do you know why my father's master gave him permission to travel?" Where were these words coming from? They were out of her mouth before she had time to think.

"The way we hear, your father forged those documents."

"He's taking me to the Academy. The Cuchasi in our village..." What if Serena was lying? She lied about the Cuchasi's abilities before. What would stop her from lying a second time? Her gaze wandered to the swords on the guardsmen's belts. Steeling herself, she said, "He said that I'm a Thane."

The two guardsmen looked at each other, dumbstruck. They turned away, whispering. Jestin pulled Realta into the parlor, his expression deadly serious.

"Why did you say that?"

Realta could not think of a good reply.

"Is it true?" The healer furrowed his brow. "Are you really—"

"Hey!" called the taller of the two guards. "Stay right where you are." He turned to his colleague. "Go get Donna." The shorter man went running down the darkened street. The guard stepped inside the healer's house. "Girl, you best not be lying to us."

"It's the truth," she stammered. *It better be, for your sake, Serena Molyns.*

"Would you care to sit?" Jestin asked the guard, pointing to a chair. The guard did so. Jestin lit two oil lamps, bathing the room in a soft, yellow light. "You'd better sit, too," he whispered to Realta. The healer raced upstairs, calling for Jera to wake.

Sitting down, Realta kept her eyes on the guardsman, her body shaking. She wished she had on more than a borrowed nightgown. She could see why this man joined the guard. He was easily a head taller than her father and was as board as Master Loy, except this man appeared to be all muscle.

She sat completely still, not wanting to attract any more attention. The guard glared at her, dark eyes like fire. She assumed the punishment for lying about being a Thane was very stiff.

Jestin and Jera returned down the stairs, propping Callum up, one on each side. Callum's breathing was labored by the time they reached the bottom step. Jestin led him to an unoccupied chair next to Realta. Serena followed them, her face as white as a sheet. She screamed, seeing the guard, and turned to flee back up the stairs. Jera caught her by the shirt collar, the fabric ripping. Serena stumbled, landing on her knees and elbows.

"There's nothing to fear," Jera assured her.

Serena eyed the burly guardsman. She sat down on the steps, her arms wrapped around the railing.

"What brings you here this evening, guardsman?" Callum asked.

"You."

Callum glanced over at Realta. She gave him a weak smile. How would he react if she really was a Thane? She would still be his daughter, and he would still be her father. Nothing could ever change that. Right?

After a time, each minute passing as slowly as an hour, the second guardsman returned, ushering an older woman with gray hair in a tight bun into the house. She wore eyeglasses and carried a black, leather-bound book under her arm.

"This is the child?" she asked, pointing to Realta. She shrank down in her seat, wishing she could take back every word.

"Yes, Mistress Donna," replied the guardsman.

"Who are you?" asked Callum. "Who is she?" he asked Jestin and Jera.

"She's a Cuchasi."

Realta frowned. She was nothing like the man in East Bridge. No chains, no strange facial tattoos. She was so calm, so ordinary.

Mistress Donna walked up to Realta, studying her. She nodded and made a note in her book. "Fascinating."

"What's fascinating?" Callum asked, leaning forward.

Serena groaned.

"How long have you been aware that your daughter is a Thane?"

"A Thane?" He glanced at Realta. She gave him a quick nod. "Just over a week. It's why I'm taking her to the Academy. My master insisted."

Jestin let out a sigh of relief. Serena buried her face in her elbow. Why was she acting like this? She was the one who told Realta this information in the first place. Did she expect her not to use it?

"What's his name?" asked the larger guardsman.

"Pardon?"

"The Cuchasi. What's his name?" He stood, one hand on his sword hilt.

"Arnyn Teleran."

Realta raised an eyebrow. The man they had met in Lothian? Why? *May the Gadyeni guide your paths*, Arnyn's words echoed. He had said that to her and Lok, but not to Charity or Serena. Did that mean he really was a Cuchasi? Had Callum known this whole time?

"What about your other daughter?" asked Jera.

Mistress Donna studied the girl and shook her head. "Ordinary human. But this is quite common in non-noble families."

"Which type of Thane is she?" asked Callum.

"That is a matter for the Scholars. I've never been able to tell. Color blind," she explained, making another note.

"Color blind?" asked Callum. It was his turn to raise an eyebrow.

"I see the world in various shades of gray. Whenever someone mentions a red flower or a blue sky, I cannot fully understand what they mean. But rest assured, my good man. Your daughter is a Thane."

"You said you're going to Teyrnas?" asked the shorter guard. "We can arrange transportation for you."

"At whose expense, Tormod? Yours?" his colleague questioned.

"I will help make arrangements," replied Jestin.

"Thank you, but…" Callum paused, his mind working. Perhaps he had not believed Arnyn or was not expecting the information to be confirmed so soon. But this made three. Three people who had never met each other saying the same thing. "But this is too much. I can write my master to send funds."

"We appreciate it," said Jera. "But we would be honored to help you and your daughters. The only Thanes in Alhyrst are the mayor and two of his children. We never expected to meet more. Please, it would be an honor."

"Very well."

The two guardsmen left, the burly one stomping out and the second one escorting Mistress Donna down the steps. He and the Caradeks treated her with such regard. Why was the one in East Bridge chained up like an animal? A question to ask Serena later. Realta was grateful that she told the truth for once.

"Why didn't you tell us your daughter was a Thane?" asked Jera. She had put on a pot of tea. Ilana had set below the horizon, her sister not far behind. There was no use going back to sleep.

"We didn't wish to advertise," replied Callum. He looked at Realta, his eyes filled with awe. She wished he would not do that. She was still his daughter. Still the little girl who used to ride on his shoulders.

"Well, this changes everything," said Jestin, taking the empty seat across from them. Serena remained on the steps, motionless. "Once you feel up to it, we'll have you on the road to Teyrnas."

Callum thanked him again.

Realta wanted to be thankful, too, but the way Jestin and Jera looked at her made her want to curl up into a little ball and disappear. Being a Thane did not make her a different person than the girl they met yesterday morning.

Did it?

19

Elementals

Charity walked through the halls of the Academy, shoulders slumped and head hung low. She and Lok had been accepted without question. Her entrance exam scores were excellent, save for history and languages. Other than that, she was a perfect candidate. And Lok was an Elemental Thane, the first in centuries. News had spread through the Academy like wildfire. Everyone wanted to meet him, much to Lok's dismay. But no one mocked him for being mute. That had to be a plus.

Once their acceptance had been finalized, they were shown to their rooms, given their light blue Student cloaks, and introduced to their mentors. They, like most Students, were housed on the third floor. The rooms were small and rectangular with a sole window on the back wall. Charity had a roommate named Maggi, a third-year student who was less than thrilled to be sharing her living space. Lok had a room to himself, much to his liking.

Lok was paired with Scholar Kuno, a historian with in-depth knowledge of antiquity, and Charity was paired with Scholar Roseen, a surgeon specializing in the functions of muscles. She was nice, but Scholar Kuno seemed more personable, able to hold a conversation on anything from current events to obscure folklore.

Once introductions were done, they were allowed to rest.

The next morning, they were given their class schedules, determined by their interests and academic weaknesses. The day was divided into five class periods, three in the morning and two in the afternoon. Most Students took four classes per semester. Charity had been overjoyed to see that she'd been placed in Old Eltrian and Basic Medicine. The former would help her decipher Kanton's notes, and the latter would help her achieve her goals. Not to mention that Old Eltrian was Scholar Kuno's class. Sadly, Lok had been given a completely different set of courses. They would be separated for most of the day.

Her first two classes had been in the central building, called the Academy Proper. Easy to find. The classroom for Basic Medicine, however, was in a different building. She got turned around several times, even going to the wrong building. Twice.

"Excuse me," she asked two Students, identical twin brothers, as they walked past her. "Do you know where to find the medical classes?"

The two boys shared a mocking look.

"You new here?" one asked. They appeared to be two or three years older than Charity.

"Course she's new. Her cloak ain't even dirty yet."

"Yes. I'm Charity Loy," she replied, thumbing the soft fabric. She had been ecstatic to receive her cloak, to be officially recognized as a Student. Students had to wear their blue cloaks at all times, while Journeymen, the level between Student and Scholar, wore gray. Scholars wore white cloaks trimmed with colors according to ability if they were Thanes. One day, Lok would wear one trimmed with green. "Who are you?"

"I'm Edrick."

"I'm Yedrick."

"It's nice to meet you both."

Edrick and Yedrick shared that mocking look again. A pit formed in her gut. Maybe she should have asked a Scholar for directions instead.

"Which class is it?" asked Yedrick.

"Basic Medicine. Scholar Alia's class."

The boys smiled. "No. That's Scholar Wik's class."

Charity removed the schedule from her dress pocket and checked the name. Scholar Roseen had perfect handwriting. "No. It says Scholar Alia."

"Well," said Edrick, "it's a two Scholar class."

"Oh, that sounds interesting." How did a two Scholar class work? They must alternate days.

"Yeah. Interesting."

"It's in the Dwyryn," said Yedrick. "The building near the East Wall. Second floor."

"Thank you very much." Charity smiled. The two boys snickered and walked away. Charity put them out of her mind and headed in that direction. The late bell had already rung, and she did not want to waste any more time.

Scholar Alia, a primly dressed woman in her fifties with gray at her temples, let out a small sigh of frustration as Charity arrived. She apologized and slipped into an empty seat in the second row. There were over twenty Students in the class.

It was so odd being surrounding by other Students. Back home, it was just her, her sisters, Realta, and her two cousins, and rarely all at once. Her mother and Kel took turns teaching them based on age and subject, with Kel focusing on math and history and Mistress Loy on grammar and basic trades. Learning in a large group was a challenge she readily accepted.

"Good day, class," said Scholar Alia, opening a large book that rested on the desk at the front of the room. "Let us continue from yesterday."

The Student next to Charity groaned.

"What is it?" she asked her.

"She's going to take out Scholar Wik."

Take out? What on Eltriar...

Scholar Alia walked to the wardrobe in the corner. She removed a tall, thin object covered in a sheet and wheeled it to the center so all could see. More than a few students groaned, others exchanging furtive whispers. The scholar removed the sheet, revealing a human skeleton suspended by wires.

A skeleton! A complete human skeleton! Charity had seen illustrations of skeletons in Esme's anatomy textbook, but never dreamed of seeing one in real life.

Charity stood and walked over to 'Scholar Wik', inspecting the bones. Each one had been bleached white, and the wiring was loose enough to allow a degree of movement. She recalled the annotations from the book. Collarbone, humerus, ulna, radius...

"Student Charity, is it?" asked Scholar Alia, arms crossed.

"Yes, ma'am."

"No one gave you permission to leave your seat, and no one gave you permission to touch that skeleton."

Several Students snickered. The same mocking noise as Edrick and Yedrick. Charity's face flushed bright red. She scurried back to her seat. The girl seated next to her moved her chair farther away, whispering to the other two students at the table.

Scholar Alia called the class back to attention. Charity bit down on her lip, fighting back tears, and paid zero attention to the lecture. She felt every eye staring at her. Every whisper spoken in her direction. Scholar Alia glanced at her several times, waiting for her to break another rule. Why had she acted like such an idiot?

The bell rang, and Charity ran out of the room, away from the other students. She had not meant to do anything wrong. She was just curious. And a real human skeleton? How many people got the opportunity to study one up close?

Most people don't want to look at skeletons.

Her family had always encouraged her interests. But there was also a look of concern in her parents' eyes whenever she talked about bones and organs. The way Bridget rolled her eyes in disgust and Nina excused herself from the room. Especially if Esme got involved and the conversation grew more detailed. But that made sense. Their interests didn't lie in medicine. And they still loved her. Still accepted her.

Is this how Lok feels? Everybody laughing and pointing?

No wonder he wanted to get out of Vala.

She skipped the midday meal and spent her free hour wandering. She did not want to be around people right now. Circling the Academy's perimeter, one hand brushing against the cool, gray stone, she arrived at the courtyards on the campus' north side.

The yard had been sectioned off into five equally spaced rectangles. Three of them were occupied by different classes. One Scholar had students run from one end of the field and back. Another had Students throwing balls, seeing who could throw the farthest. The third taught students how to spar with quarterstaffs.

Lok belonged to the third group. He stood off to the side, patiently waiting his turn while Scholar Kuno spoke with him. Charity was glad the Scholar had been chosen as Lok's mentor. He petitioned for Lok's acceptance before learning that he was a Thane. Lok nodded to something the Scholar said.

Another Student caught Charity's eye. He was a few years her senior with slightly long, dark brown hair and dark blue eyes, like deep pools of water. He wore a blue earring in his right ear and was shirtless. She had seen many men shirtless growing up, but never one this... defined.

He sparred with another boy, each with a quarterstaff. The second boy moved to hit him, but the first dodged the blow. Another attempted hit. Another dodge. The first boy spun out of the way and hit his opponent on the shoulder. The Scholar overseeing the group called for them to stop, naming the first boy the winner. The two Students shook hands and walked off to the sidelines, handing their quarterstaffs to the Scholar.

"Hi," he said, noticing Charity standing off to the side.

"Um, hi." She stood straighter, composed.

"Let me guess. You're a first year."

"Yes. I'm Charity Loy." How quickly did news spread between students? The incident with the skeleton happened an hour ago. If he knew someone in her class, it was possible. Her palms began to sweat.

"I'm Zandon Jons," the boy replied. "Come here to watch?"

How did he know?!

Charity calmed herself. He did not ask if she watched him specifically. "Sort of. My friend is in this class."

"Which one?" asked Zandon.

"Lok Tolman. The lanky one with hair in his eyes." As she spoke, the Scholar handed Lok a quarterstaff, instructing him to feel the weight.

"The Elemental!" Zandon exclaimed, eyes brightening. "You're friends with him?"

She nodded.

"Stars above. We all were taught they were goners. That kid changes everything." Zandon looked at Lok with awe. Not mocking laughter or annoyance. Pure awe. Charity's heart soared, embarrassment disappearing.

The feeling did not last long. "Wait. What do you mean by goners?"

"You know. Extinct. There used to be eight types of Thanes, but now there are only five."

"What happened to the other three?"

"They just stopped being born, I guess. All the Scholars and Thanes are losing their minds over that kid."

The pieces fell into place. Zandon wore an earring in his right ear. Just like Mayor Gan. "You're a Thane, too."

"Yeah. A Farsight. But not a very good one."

"What do you mean?"

"I can only see things a few seconds before they happen. It's useful in fights, but not much else."

"Isn't that kind of like cheating? You knew where your opponent was going to hit beforehand, so that's how you won."

"Not really. It's like this. There are two people. One is near-sighted, and the other has perfect vision. Is the person with good eyesight cheating at life?"

"I suppose not."

Scholar Kuno stepped in to help Lok. Quarterstaff in hand, the Scholar positioned himself in a fighting stance, his feet evenly apart with one slightly back and standing straight. He placed both hands two-thirds of the way down the staff. Stepping forward, he swung the quarterstaff in the air, stopping inches from Lok's face. Lok flinched, shielding his head with his arms.

"Don't worry. I won't actually hit you," the Scholar said with a smile.

Lok relaxed some and motioned for the Scholar to continue.

"The best way to win is to study your opponent. Does he favor his right hand or his left? Does he have any weaknesses you can exploit? Small details like these will help you—"

"Scholar Kuno," the Scholar in charge of the class yelled, his arms crossed. Kuno turned and locked eyes with his colleague. "Whose class is this, yours or mine?"

"Apologies, Scholar Tell. I was only trying to help."

"Help your own students. You, boy," he pointed at Lok. "Come here."

Kuno handed the quarterstaff back to Lok. He sheepishly walked towards Scholar Tell. The Scholar instructed Lok to spar with another Student, a slender girl with coal black hair tied in a braid.

"Scholar Kuno is a weird one," said Zandon, smiling.

"Oh." Charity did not think he was weird. He was just being helpful.

"I mean, weird in a good way. We all like him because of it."

"So, people can be weird in good ways?"

"Yeah."

She shifted from one foot to the other. "What about weird as in wanting to study a human skeleton up close?"

Zandon nodded. "Yeah, that's weird. But not if you want to be a healer."

Charity breathed a sigh of relief. Someone here other than Lok would accept her for being herself.

"Hey, do you and your friend want to eat supper with me this evening?" asked Zandon. "I can introduce you to my friends, give you some tips to survive your first semester here."

"I'd love that," Charity beamed. "I'll have to talk Lok into it, though. He's kinda shy."

"Great. See you then." Zandon walked off to talk with his sparring partner.

Charity breathed deeply, the sadness she had felt melting away. She had made a friend! She could not wait to tell Realta when she arrived.

When. Always when.

Glancing over to the field, she watched Lok attempt to spar. The girl lunged at him. He flinched and dropped the quarterstaff. Scholar Tell yelled at him to pick up the staff. He would not pass if he didn't spar. Charity watched as Scholar Kuno shook his head, pacing back and forth as though physically restraining himself from intervening.

Come on, Lok. You can do it.

Lok picked up the quarterstaff and tired again.

20

Preparations

Lok placed a small stack of books on the table in the Academy's Grand Library. Scholar Kuno sat opposite him, reviewing the selections. The student-mentor relationship was created to ensure a smooth transition into formal education and that Students were on the right academic track. Usually, Thane Scholars mentored Thane Students with the same abilities. But Lok was the only Elemental. So Scholar Kuno, with his knowledge of ancient Thanes, volunteered to help him as much as possible.

"Let's see," said Kuno, selecting the first book in the pile. Lok hoped they were the right ones. He had never been inside an actual library, and research was the key to academic success. The sooner he learned these skills, the better.

"Excellent. You found these remarkably quick."

Lok nodded in thanks.

"Are you sure there isn't a library in Vala?"

He nodded again.

"Could have fooled me," Kuno said, studying the book titles and smiling.

Lok opened his notebook to an empty page and wrote, *"How many students have come from Vala?"*

"Very few, as far as I know." The smile faded away. "Though there was this one girl. She was a Student when I was a Journeyman. She was raised in Vala."

"Really? What was her name?"

Kuno hesitated. "Esme. Her name was Esme Haar."

Esme Haar? As in the village midwife and Gareth Haar's mother? She had always been kind to Lok and helped reset his leg after it was broken. Lok had been too terrified to go to Healer Zall, and Esme readily agreed to help.

"Can you tell me about her?" he wrote, wanting to verify that

she was the same person.

Kuno gave him a weak smile. "She was a very intelligent young woman. Always asking questions and reading at all hours of the night. She even hung around us Journeymen, wanting to know more than her teachers taught. I believe she wanted to study medicine."

The scholar fell silent, absentmindedly leafing through one of the books. Lok waited for him to continue. A minute passed. He then wrote, *"I know her. She still lives in Vala."*

Kuno's eyes widened. "She's alive?! That's... After the accident, I thought..." He shook his head, clearing his thoughts. "How is she?"

"Very well, I guess. She's a midwife, and I used to play with her son when we were younger." At first, Lok believed Gareth was just like him, unable to speak. But it was something different. Gareth had the ability to speak, but only with certain people and in certain locations. Otherwise, he was mute.

"Her son? I heard she lost the child after..." The Scholar again fell silent.

"Did something bad happen?"

"Well, after graduating as a Student, she remained at the Academy to study medicine as a Journeyman. About a year later, she got engaged to another Journeyman, a young man studying natural science. She then started an internship at Teyrnas' Royal Hospital." A smile formed on his face. "She absolutely loved it, and it gave her and Kel some extra space. Of course, they still had their studies. The Scholars would visit them once a month to make sure both were keeping up.

"But one month, neither of them showed up to their appointment. The Scholars waited for three days and then contacted the city guard. No one had seen them. It wasn't like them to run off without telling anyone."

"Did they find them?"

Kuno faltered. "Yes. Kel had been badly beaten. His face was almost unrecognizable, and his leg was mangled. It would have been amputated if he'd lived. They found Esme shortly after that. She was so distraught, she couldn't continue her studies. I didn't know where she had gone until you told me. I'm glad she found a good life."

"What do you mean if he'd lived? Kel is still alive."

The scholar's jaw dropped. "He lived?! But everyone said... How is he?"

"He has a lot of scars on his face and walks with a crutch and leg brace. Do you know who hurt him?" Kel and Esme never talked about the incident that left her husband crippled, claiming it was an accident.

"No. It happened in a bad part of the city. Any number of bandits or gang members could have been responsible. There weren't any witnesses. None that came forward, anyway. But Lok, that's amazing. Thank you so much for telling me. You don't know how much this means." He smiled. "And they have a son. Incredible."

"And a daughter."

Kuno's smile widened. "Perhaps I'll write to them one day. Wouldn't that be something? Now," he changed the subject, "there is a matter we have to discuss. The Thane Ceremony."

"What is that?" Lok had a dozen more questions to ask about Kel and Esme, but they could wait.

"It's the ceremony in which a young Thane is formally accepted into the Academy and recognized by other Thanes. Every Thane in the Academy will be present, along with the Premier Scholar and the Council. It's a relatively short ceremony. No longer than ten minutes."

The Scholar locked eyes with him. "Lok, there's a catch. You have to speak."

"But I can't speak!" A spike of panic rose in him.

"I know. That's what has me concerned."

"Can I write the words instead?"

"No. You're not allowed to bring any worldly possessions."

Great. He had been accepted to the Academy despite his inability to speak, thanks to him being a Thane, a very rare type of Thane. But now that inability prevented him from undergoing the Thane Ceremony. What was the bloody point?

"The Council is aware of your disability, Lok. Perhaps they will make an exception."

A thought popped into his head. *"What if someone speaks the words for me?"*

"I don't know," he shrugged. "The Council might go for it..."

"Can Charity Loy speak for me?" Charity would say yes in a heartbeat. She'd do anything to help a friend.

Kuno frowned. "Charity is not a Thane. Ordinary humans aren't even allowed to witness the ceremony. I only learned about the details in books."

"But I've known her my entire life. If it's a secret, she will keep it. Please."

"Okay," he relented. "I will make a proposal to the Council and the Premier. No promises that they will agree. Your ceremony is scheduled for the twentieth. We have until then to find someone to be your voice."

The wall clock struck six. Time for the evening meal to begin. Charity had invited him to eat with some of her new friends. Lok was hesitant. What if these people were just like the ones back home? What if they only invited him to mock him?

Kuno stood, gathering up the books. He gave Lok a curious look. "Aren't you going to get some supper?"

Lok shrugged.

"Listen to me, Lok. Most Students spend four or five years at the Academy. For many, those years are filled with exploration and enjoyment. They can also be very lonely years if you don't make an effort to meet new people. I know the first week is terrifying. I've been in your shoes. Please trust me with this."

Lok had to disagree. While the Scholar had once been a new Student, he had never truly walked in Lok's shoes. Shoes that belonged to a kid who could not speak, who could never fully express himself or join in a normal conversation.

But I want to trust him. The scholar had been nothing but kind towards Lok. A form of kindness he'd only known from his mother. He had always liked to think that his father would have treated him the same way.

Placing his notebook and charcoal pencil in his pocket, Lok slowly made his way to his feet. He gripped the back of the chair, mulling over Kuno's words. He had spent his entire life being lonely and afraid. Attending to the Academy was supposed to change that. He looked up at the scholar and gave him his best smile.

"Atta boy, Lok. I'll see you tomorrow." Kuno wandered off to another part of the library.

Steeling himself, Lok headed for the dining hall.

***

Charity sat at a small, round table with five other students. Zandon Jons sat on her left and had introduced her to his friends. Evelyn and Coryn were sisters who were both studying history, specifically the history of kingdoms surrounding the Vogel Mountains. And Coryn was a Learner Thane with a red earring in her right ear. At least Dane Kanton had been truthful in that regard.

Jaim was also a Thane, a low-level Manipulator who always had coins floating around his hand. He, like Zandon, planned on joining the Garrison after graduation. Last at the table was Ivar, a young man with black hair, dark brown eyes, and deeply tanned skin who was from the northern lands of Madan Och. He didn't talk much, and the silver ring in his right ear signified that he was a Minder Thane.

"How long have you been at the Academy?" Charity asked, taking a bite of food. The evening meal consisted of potatoes and vegetables with strips of cured beef.

"Coryn started on Autumntide," replied Evelyn. "This is my third year."

"So how come you arrived late?" asked Jaim, three gold talons, a small fortune in the Hinterlands, swirling in between the fingers of his left hand.

"Lok and I ran into some trouble. We were separated from our friends."

"Why didn't you hire guards?"

"Not everyone comes from a wealthy family, Jaim O'Siarlwyn," said Zandon. Jaim replied with a dirty hand gesture. The two sisters laughed, and Ivar rolled his eyes.

"So, a wealthy family. What's that like?" asked Charity. She did not want to talk, or even think, about the journey here. Kanton attacking Callum. The uncertainty that he and Realta were even alive.

She had sent letters to her parents, letting them know that she and Lok had arrived safely. She had also sent one to the postmaster in Teyrnas, just in case Realta and her father had decided to continue that way instead of returning to Vala. She prayed every night for their safety.

"Oh, it's not so bad," replied Jaim, the coins spinning in his open palm. "House Siarlwyn is pretty minor as far as noble houses go. But my old man still gets invited to King Logan's yearly summer party. So we have that going for us."

"You've met the king?"

"Stars no! That privilege was reserved for my older brother and oldest sister. Not for little Jaim."

Charity smiled. "I'm the youngest, too."

"It's a fun lot, isn't it?" he asked sarcastically.

"So, what do you want to study, Charity?" asked Evelyn.

"And when do we get to meet your friend?" Coryn added.

"He should be here soon." *I hope.* Lok did not seem very happy when she invited him to supper with a bunch of strangers. The Creator knew not all Students were as welcoming as Zandon and his friends. She kept a wary eye out for those twins, Edrick and Yedrick. She had no desire to run into them again anytime soon.

"Isn't that him over there?" asked Zandon, pointing to a lanky boy standing by the door.

Charity waved at Lok, smiling broadly. Lok slowly made his way over, careful to avoid running into anyone. She never realized how tall he was. Lok stood a head taller than most of the students, towering over those who were seated. He had seemed much smaller back home.

"Sit right here, Lok." She pointed to the empty seat on her right. Lok sat, warily studying each new face. She introduced him, and everyone replied with a warm greeting.

"So you're the Elemental the Scholars won't shut up about, eh?" asked Jaim.

Lok shrank in his seat, lowering his head.

"What did I say?" Jaim raised an eyebrow.

"He's kind of shy," Charity explained.

"What can Elementals do?" asked Evelyn. She and Coryn leaned forward.

Lok took out his notebook and pencil and wrote, *"I can control fire."*

"Why write instead of speak?" asked Ivar in a heavily accented voice.

"Because he can't speak," she explained. Lok sat lower in his seat, attempting to make himself appear smaller.

"You're a mind reader, man. Why ask?" asked Jaim.

"Because everyone was thinking it."

"One second," said Zandon as he rose from the table. Taking a furtive glance around the dining hall, he walked over to the wall and removed a small lantern. He moved the plates out of the way and placed the lantern in the table's center. He removed the top of the lantern, leaving the flame exposed. "Can you give us a demonstration?"

Lok glanced at Charity, worried.

"It's all right. They're just curious."

Lok concentration on the fire. The flames dimmed, reduced to a hint of red on the wick. Exhaling, the flames shot up, burning bright orange. A handful of sparks escaped through the opened top. Lok grabbed a napkin and quickly extinguished the sparks. A scattering of small, dark dots remained on the wood.

"That's amazing!" exclaimed Zandon.

"Can you also create fire?" asked Coryn.

Lok shrugged. He wrote, *"Charity, can I ask you a question? It's about the Thane Ceremony."*

"Of course, Lok."

"The Ceremony?" Jaim chimed in, leaning over to read the notebook. "Why ask her? No offense, but it's Thane only."

"Yeah. Not even family members are allowed to know the details," said Evelyn, giving her younger sister a questioning look. Coryn just smiled.

"The ceremony involves speaking. Can you be my voice?"

"Yes, of course I'll be your voice. Whatever that means," she asked, looking to the others for guidance.

"Well," said Zandon, making sure none of the other students could overhear, "the ceremony is an exchange. The Premier Scholar asks a question and the Thane answers. It's the same questions and answers every time."

"So, I just have to memorize some lines?"

Lok nudged her shoulder. He had written, *"Scholar Kuno will speak with the other Scholars. He isn't sure if they will approve."*

"I see."

"Tell you what," said Zandon, reading over the words, "if they don't let Charity do it, I'll volunteer to be your voice."

Lok's eyes widened in shock.

"You'd really do that for him?" Charity asked, pleasantly surprised.

"Sure. Why not?"

"Very altruistic," said Jaim. "Are you sure you want to join the Garrison?"

"Shut up," Zandon replied, smiling.

Lok quickly wrote, *"Thank you!"*

"No problem. Hey, you don't have any food yet. Better get some before the kitchens close."

He and Lok left the table, heading for the kitchens at the far end of the room. By the time they returned, the conversation had drifted twice. First to the basic rules of the Academy and which Scholars would allow you to bend them. Scholar Kuno, for example, was very lax about Students spending time in the library after curfew, so long as they were behaving. And Scholar Jonas always offered to escort Students into Norgard on holidays. They then asked about Charity's own interests. She quietly explained that she wanted to study medicine.

"Hold up," said Jaim. "Are you the girl who touched that bloody skeleton?"

Charity's face grew warm. "Um... Yes."

Jaim burst out laughing. "Oh, Creator and the Eight Gadyeni, I wish I could have seen old Scholar Alia's face! You're a bloody legend, you know that?"

"Is that a good thing?" She looked around the table questionably.

"Yes. Yes, it definitely is." Evelyn and Coryn also nodded, though Coryn seemed a bit creeped out by the skeleton. She thought Scholar Wik was only a rumor.

Charity smiled, and that smiled broaden when she saw Lok smiling too. His posture was far more relaxed, though a slight edge remained. Wounds did not heal in a single day.

The conversation switched topics again, this time to the city of Norgard and the best place to visit. They talked until long after the meal ended.

21

Hygate

The journey from Alhyrst to Hygate passed remarkably fast. Once the villagers learned that a young Thane was involved, they pulled together their resources to hire a professional coachman from East Bridge. He promised to take them to the capital with minimal stops, traveling from the first light of dawn to well past sunset.

At first, Realta was leery about traveling after dark. A single coach riding alone did not seem safe. But the first day passed without incident. As did the second and the third. Realta was able to rest comfortably, the coach's interior so lush that at times it felt like they were not even moving.

Many other coaches and merchants, she quickly realized, traveled along the road, heading in both directions. Safety in numbers. And Jestin and Jera had given them a small medical kit so they would not have to worry about Callum's stitches becoming infected, as well as instructions on applying the medicine. They also promised to pass along any letters they received from Sardic Loy.

Realta wondered if her actions had been foolish. Callum had wanted to wait, put a few days between them and Kanton. Realta, or rather Serena, had ruined that by revealing that she was a Thane. The girl had known why the Cuchasi had singled her out, and she'd lied to Callum's face. Why hide the truth from him, but not from her? What was her game? The girl had lapsed into silence the moment everyone learned the truth. No number of questions or comments were able to draw a single word from her.

"I'm worried about that girl," Callum whispered to Realta as they entered Hygate, the last city on the highway before reaching the capital. Serena was fast asleep on the bench opposite them. "All of her words are half-truths, and she's barely eaten this whole time."

Realta had not seen her eat at all. A half week without food. Dark circles had formed underneath her eyes, and she slept more often. Serena might need a healer by the time they reached Teyrnas.

"Maybe this was a mistake," Realta replied. "Maybe we shouldn't be taking her back to her half-brothers."

"Perhaps." Callum glanced out of the coach's window. The city was a bustling hive filled with people and shops. Many shops had their products out front, giving passersby a chance to buy something quickly. Banners and flags flew over storefronts. On the corners stood people with burlap sacks full of rolled up papers. They yelled out about events in the city. A handful of townsfolk bought the papers, reading as they walked.

They turned a corner onto a thoroughfare that was wide enough for four carriages. Traffic poured in from other side streets. Some intersections required a guardsman to direct the flow of traffic. If this was just a city, then what was the capital like?

"Realta, we need to talk," Callum said, locking eyes with her. "I know we've skirted around this conversation ever since that girl came into our lives. I don't want to avoid it any longer. It isn't right for you to be in the dark."

Realta stiffened. The question lingering in the back of her mind for weeks. The reason Serena resembled her uncle so strongly. All of the sudden, she did not want to know.

"Your aunt and uncle fell in love when they were very young. And they only loved one another. Physically loved. When they came back to Vala, they talked about their time at the Academy, some of their friends. But never about Kel's life before the Academy. Nothing about his parents, siblings, anything. One thing I do know: Kel is not that girl's father. No matter how much they resemble each other, it's not possible."

Tears welled in Realta's eyes. That had been the hidden fear, one that did not have words until Callum had said them aloud. That Kel had been unfaithful. Now the fear was gone, banished by Callum's honesty.

"Thank you for telling me." Realta wiped a stray tear from her face. Callum gave her a warm hug. His strength was returning. "But who is she then? She is part Hiraethi, too?"

"That's what I hope to find out."

"She never said her half-brother's name," Realta realized. What was the point of traveling all this way when they did not know who to find?

"We'll pry the names out of her. We already know Gregor Pym."

"If that's a real name."

Callum sighed. "Good point."

The coach came to a stop on a side street. The smell of roasted meat wafted into the carriage. A line of stores, all of them selling different types of food, stood side by side on the street.

Callum opened the door and asked the coachman, "Why are we stopping here?"

"I need to rest the horses. Feel free to get something to eat." The coachman wandered off a short distance, stopping at a food stand.

Realta stole a glance at Serena. She was still sleeping. She hoped she was not getting sick. Being near the Cuchasi, or rather the Cuchasi telling everyone the truth, had really unnerved her.

Well, if you wanted to keep it a secret, why tell me, Serena Molyns? She directed the thought at her. No reply, obviously.

Callum climbed out of the carriage, studying the city street. Everyone was well dressed and in good spirits. No guardsmen in sight.

You don't have to worry about that now, she reminded herself. Mistress Donna had signed a formal document stating that Realta was a Thane, type unknown, and ought to be given free passage to the Academy. The town's mayor and the alderman had countersigned it. Guardsmen could not arrest her without witnessing her commit a crime. Thanes were powerful people, but they were not above the law.

Realta joined her father in the street. The nearest food vendor was selling rolls of flat bread filled with roasted meat and vegetables.

A flash of movement caught Realta's attention. Spinning on her heels, she saw Serena running from the carriage and into the crowd.

"Fire and smoke!" Callum cursed.

Realta ran after Serena, leaving Callum behind. Was she serious? All this time traveling with them only to run away again! If she was so afraid of facing her family, why lead them on this trail? Why agree to go all the way to Teyrnas?

A horrible thought crept into Realta's mind as she chased Serena, dodging people in the busy streets. The charge of conspiracy against King Logan was real. Why would the king care so much about finding a horse thief? Serena had left the animal where it could be found and returned. And surely the king could afford to buy an entire village's worth of horses.

Not to mention Gregor Pym, the master of stables at the palace. An inside man? Someone who informed Serena of when and where to enter to palace grounds undetected. The first person she chose to contact. Not her half-brothers, nor her half-sister. A man who worked in the king's stables. If this was true, then Kanton's determination to find Serena made a lot more sense. A thief was one thing. A would-be assassin, another.

But why bring me and Charity into this? She couldn't help wondering. *Why allow two young girls to travel with a possible assassin?*

It made no sense. Nothing in her life since Springtide had made any sense.

Serena dashed into an alleyway, Realta right on her heels. Her decision to eat very little had backfired on her. Growing up, Realta was one of the slowest kids in Vala. She struggled to keep pace with Charity and Gareth, even her little cousin Estrid. Now she and Serena were neck and neck.

Emerging at the other end of the alleyway, Serena froze. Realta ran into her, grabbing her by the shoulders and pinning her against a wall. She glared at Serena, catching her breath.

"What do you think you're going?" she questioned. The girl stared at her with wide, fearful eyes. Her breathing came out in ragged gasps. Realta peered out of the alleyway. On the other side of the street stood a large, white building with the flag of Teyrnas flying above it. Several men in dark blue uniforms stood on the front steps. Studying them, Realta realized one was a woman, her short hair in a braid. Another had an ugly burn scar covering the left side of his face. He gave Realta a predatory grin.

"Kanton..."

Serena grabbed hold of her hand and ran down the street.

How was he here? The city had thousands, no tens of thousands of people. As big as all the villages in the Hinterlands combined. And Serena had managed to run into the one person they had been desperately trying to avoid. Realta wanted to scream.

"We have to go back," she called out.

"What?"

"To my father. We have to go back to my father. To the coachman."

Serena did not slow down. She kept running into alleyways and down side streets with no discernible pattern. The sounds of boots on cobblestones haunted them, growing closer. Panic forced Realta's legs to run faster and faster, her heart racing.

Turning a corner, she saw it. The coach! Callum stood next to the vehicle, waving for them to hurry, hurry!

Men shouting behind them. People moved out of the way, watching from the safety of store windows. No one dared interfere.

Callum ran towards them, meeting them at the same time as a hand grabbed Realta, yanking her backward.

"Father!"

"Let go of her—" Callum's words died. He froze, eyes wide in disbelief. "You."

Dane Kanton handed Realta off to Wills while a third guard quickly tied Serena's hands behind her back. Realta kicked Wills in the leg, just below the knee. The guard yelped but maintained his vise-like grip. No, they did not come so close to be capture now. She kicked again, but Wills anticipated it, moving his legs out of the way as he tied her hands together.

Kanton sauntered over to Callum.

"You proved a very difficult man to find, slave Callum." He spoke loud enough for everyone on the street to hear. He motioned to the left side of his face. "You gave me quite the souvenir. I never got the chance to thank you for it."

Kanton raised his hand to strike Callum. He blocked the blow and landed one of his own, jabbing Kanton in the ribs. The man grunted, stumbling. Marsh and another guard seized Callum in an instant. They struggled to hold his arms while a third bound his wrists.

"What crime have I committed?" he asked the guardsmen.

"Conspiracy to assassinate the king," replied Kanton.

"Where's your proof?"

The crowded muttered, all eyes watching.

"We've never been to Teyrnas!" Realta yelled, surprised by how loudly she spoke.

"Be quiet!" Kanton bellowed. Realta shrank back, fearing he would hit her. Kanton turned his attention to Serena. "Do they even know who you are?"

"Don't—"

"Serena of House Kelwyn, bastard half-sister of King Logan!"

Serena hung her head, tears spilling down her face. Several people in the crowd broke away, spreading the news to others.

Realta stared at the girl. She had claimed to be the bastard of a nobleman, an important but not too important man. Another lie. But this explained how she stole the horse. She had already been inside the palace. No need to sneak in.

Would you have believed her if she had told you the truth? Realta doubted it. Claiming to be the king's sister was so outlandish. No wonder she lied.

Kanton addressed the crowd, "I, Dane Kanton, Captain of the King's Guard, arrest Serena O'Kelwyn on the charges of conspiracy against the throne and the murders of Charity Loy and Lok Tolman. And I arrest Callum Haar and Realta Haar on the charges of being escaped slaves and aiding Princess Serena in her escape. They are to stand trial in the city of Teyrnas."

"Lok and Charity aren't dead!" Realta cried, frustrated tears stinging her eyes. "They ran away from you!"

Kanton loomed over her. "And where are they now? Did you really see them enter the forest, or was it just your mind playing tricks on you?"

Realta shrank back. No, she had seen Callum place Charity on a horse, and that horse ran into the forest. Lok ran after her. And after that? Everything had happened so fast. Once they were riding away, she'd been too afraid to look back. Oh Creator, had Kanton gone into the forest and killed them? Was her best friend dead?

Tears ran down her face as Wills led her towards the carriage. The coachman, very confused by the situation, asked the guards what was going on. Wills handed him a small purse bulging with coins. The coachman accepted the money without further question.

"My daughter is a Thane," Callum said. "You can't do this is her."

Kanton raised an eyebrow. "Is she?"

"Yes. We have the papers to prove it."

"Let me see."

"They're in my satchel." Marsh fished out the satchel from the carriage and found the paper along with Callum's rite of passage.

Kanton inspected both papers, frowning. He shot a glare at Callum and Realta, eyes like icy daggers. He snapped his fingers at one of the guards.

"Do you have a match?"

"Yes, sir. But—"

"Give me one."

The guard obeyed.

Kanton lit the match and set both papers on fire.

"No!" Callum screamed.

The burning pages fell to the ground. Realta felt something die within her as she watched Kanton crush the ashes with his boot.

"What are you doing, sir?" asked the guard, his face aghast. Marsh shot him a warning glance. He ignored it. "Those papers were legitimate. You can't—"

"Excuse me, Guardsman York, but are you questioning a captain of King Logan's Guard?"

York swallowed a lump in his throat. "No, sir." His gaze shifted to the smoldering ashes.

"Then load these prisoners into the carriage. You, as well as Guardsmen Wills and Marsh, will accompany me to Teyrnas and see that these prisoners do not escape. Is this understood?"

"Yes, sir," he replied with a halfhearted salute.

Kanton and Marsh walked towards the front of the carriage, Marsh taking the reins. Kanton exchanged a few words with the coachman, thanking him for his service to the kingdom. York glared at him but did as he was told.

Realta, her legs numb, felt herself being guided back into the carriage, her eyes fixed on the burned papers. The ashes blew away in the breeze.

22

Wardens of the Night

Realta looked all around the carriage, her heart and mind racing. There had to be something they could do. Some way to escape. The carriage rode at a relentless pace. Far too fast for them to jump without severe injury.

She looked at her father. Callum stared straight ahead with a haunted gaze. That rite of passage was the only thing keeping him out of jail. No one would believe that he was traveling with permission.

And what of Serena? King Logan's half-sister. She understood why Serena lied, but those lies were nothing but harmful. Here she thought they would meet with her brother, a nobleman, and learn the missing details from him. Commoners were allowed to speak with nobles as long as the nobles decided to hear them out. Commoners did not just saunter into the palace and demand audience with the king. Serena's lies had made them worse than blind.

The carriage halted in front of a massive gate. The metal gate was built into a wall that towered fifty feet, the parapets seeming to touch the sky. They were here. Teyrnas.

She heard Kanton's muffled voice speaking with the guards. Moments later, the gate opened, and they entered the grand city. No escaping now.

However large she thought East Bridge and Hygate were, they were rural villages compared to Teyrnas. Buildings, ranging from two to four stories tall, lined the busy, paved streets. Merchants called out to the passing crowds. People, dressed in clothing of all styles and colors, walked up and down the streets. Carriages and people on horseback clogged the roads. Guards wearing dark blue uniforms patrolled the area.

Serena let out a soft groan. Callum shot her a glare. The girl wilted under his gaze.

Serves you right.

What would become of them? According to Kanton's claims, Serena conspired against the king, and Realta and Callum helped her escape. Meaning they could be found guilty of the same crime. Would the king even hear them out? He must know they were not from Teyrnas.

The carriage halted in front of yet another gate, this one guarded by a wall that was thirty feet high. Realta racked her brain, trying to remember maps from Mistress Loy's books. The palace was in the exact center of the city. Judging by the fearful look in Serena's eyes as they passed under the gate, she had no doubt this was the place.

The carriage door opened, causing Realta to jump. Kanton smiled wickedly at them.

"Get out."

Realta shuffled out of the carriage, doing her best to climb down with her hands tied behind her back. Callum followed suit. Serena remained in the carriage, motionless. Kanton sneered and grabbed Serena by the shirt, pulling her to the ground. She landed on her knees, the pavement tearing her trousers and skin. Head down, she slowly stood.

"Take the carriage to the stables," Kanton instructed one of the palace guards.

"Aren't we supposed to return this to Hygate?" asked York.

"It will be taken care of. Do as you are told."

Guardsman York muttered under his breath and led the carriage away.

Realta glanced around the open area. To her left was a paved area that led to the other side of the palace, a towering building at five stories tall. To her right were the stables and the edge of the gardens. At the gate stood a guardhouse that was built into the wall. Two men stood guard at each side of the gate. She figured two or more guards were always stationed there. The king's safety was at stake. Either Serena got very lucky in stealing that horse, or she had help.

"This way," said Kanton. He led the way as Marsh and Wills walked behind Realta and Callum, their hands on their swords. Realta noted that Marsh had a slight limp. Serena walked just behind the guards, her head bowed. Neither guard paid her much attention.

They entered the palace through the main doors, walking through the atrium. Blue and white checkered tiles decorated the floor. The space branched off in three directions, one ending at a grand staircase. Kanton led them to the right, a long hallway as wide as a village road. Large windows, each decorated with the symbols of the Eight Gadyeni, bathed the hall with bright, multi-colored light.

A handful of servants passed by, whispering among themselves.

"Is that Serena?" one woman asked her colleagues.

Kanton shot them an icy glare, and they hurried away.

"You," Kanton pointed at a guard, a young man who was no older than twenty with sandy brown hair and blue eyes. The guard stood at attention and saluted, right fist over his heart. "Inform King Logan that his bastard sister and those responsible for helping her escape have been captured."

"Yes, sir. Should I inform the king that you'll meet him in the Audience Chamber?"

"Naturally."

The guard hurried away, walking so fast he might as well have been running.

"We brought her back," said Callum.

"Did you say something, slave?" Kanton asked as they continued down the hall.

"How do you expect—"

"No one gave you permission to speak. You will be silent until King Logan addresses you. If he deems that necessary."

Marsh furiously whispered, "You really need to be quiet," in Callum's ear. He replied with a frustrated sigh.

Realta whispered to Serena, "Your brother will believe us, right? Serena?"

The girl said nothing. She kept her head bowed and shoulders slumped.

"Serena, he has to know that we aren't from Teyrnas. That we convinced you to come back here." Again, no response. Didn't she care?

At the end of the hall stood a large, open chamber, the size of

Vala's marketplace. The vaulted ceiling was painted to look like the sky with ravens flying between the clouds. At the front of the room sat two thrones on a dais. One throne was decorated with two ravens, wings raised as though they were about to fly upward and join their painted cousins. The second throne had no such decorations. Silk tapestries adorned the walls, depicting landscapes and important historical events. Another door was located on the room's opposite side, too far away for them to run. The rest of the space was empty.

Kanton had her, Callum, and Serena stand side by side, facing to two thrones. Marsh and Wills remained at the door. Kanton strode forward, standing tall and proud with one foot resting on the dais. The same young guard walked into the chamber. Kanton removed his foot.

Taking a deep breath, the guard announced, "Her Majesty of the Great Noble Houses Kelwyn and Margents, Queen Isla!"

Realta was taken aback. The queen?

A slight woman dressed in a light green, silk dress with a silver crown over her auburn hair entered the room. At her side stood another woman, wearing a plain blue dress and holding a tablet that contained papers, pens, and ink. The queen's brisk pace slowed as she approached the group.

"Queen Isla," said Kanton, bowing respectfully.

Ignoring him, her eyes fell on Serena. "What are you doing here?" she asked, not unkindly.

Biting down on her lip, Serena managed, "I'm sorry. I…"

The queen placed a gentle hand on Serena's face. "You always had such lovely hair. Why did you cut it off?"

"It was safer that way."

Queen Isla sighed. Her eyes fell on Realta and Callum. Realta noted she wore blue earrings. Did that mean she was also a Thane? Isla screamed.

"The girl! Death and destruction follow in her wake. The Wardens of the Night seek her out. Nothing can stop them now!"

"What did you say?" Callum demanded, stepped closer to the queen. Kanton clamped a hand on his shoulder.

Realta, trembling from head to foot, stared at the queen. Her mind yelled at her to run, but her legs were frozen. The ropes around her wrists bit into her skin.

The queen herself was trembling, too. The woman at her side was calmly writing. Horrified, she said, "Don't write that down!"

"But Your Majesty, you've had a premonition. I must—"

"Una, scratch out what you've written. Forget I said anything."

The woman, terribly confused, did as the queen instructed.

"Now," Queen Isla said to Realta, "my husband will be here presently. You must not speak of word of this. Do you understand, little one?"

Realta nodded.

The young guardsman cleared his throat. Queen Isla composed herself, stepped off to the side. He announced, "His Majesty of the Great Noble House Kelwyn, King Logan, the Raven King!"

A tall, lanky figure with a cloak covering his finely tailored clothes sauntered into the chamber, standing between them and the thrones. His trousers and shirt were both a deep black while the cloak was covered in geometric patterns, all in various shades of blue. A gold crown rested on his messy, light brown hair. In his ears were two sets of earrings. Silver in the lobes and gold half an inch higher.

What type of Thane did Kanton called himself? A Learner. So, if red meant one was a Learner Thane, what did silver and gold mean? And more importantly, what did blue mean? Why had the queen said those bizarre things about her?

Realta's thoughts halted as she met the king's clear blue eyes. Eyes she had seen every day of her life. Kel's eyes. If the king was an unhealthy twenty pounds lighter and had scars crisscrossing half his face, he'd be the spitting image of her uncle. Not quite identical, but similar enough to not be a coincidence. Realta glanced at her father. Callum's shocked expression indicated that he saw the resemblance, too. And was equally baffled.

"What happened to your face?" the king asked Kanton. His voice was calm, almost cold.

Kanton raised a gloved hand to the scars covering the left half of his face. "That man, Callum Haar, attacked us while we were trying to capture your sister, Your Majesty. I—"

"Stop." King Logan raised a hand. Kanton fell silent, averting his eyes.

King Logan walked over to Callum, inspecting him. The king was the same height as her uncle and shared his thin limbs, though his face was not as gaunt. But Realta felt only fear around him, growing around her like an invisible mist. This man was the most powerful person in the kingdom, the farthest thing from a crippled tutor in a farming village. A single word from him had been enough to subdue Dane Kanton.

"Your name is Callum Haar. Correct?"

"Yes, Your Majesty."

"Where do you come from, Master Haar?"

"From Vala, a small village in the Hinterlands. And 'Master Haar' is not my title." Callum gestured to his left wrist.

The king snapped his fingers. The bonds around Callum's wrists unraveled, falling to the floor. Realta nearly jumped out of her skin.

How did he do that? Is it because he's a Thane? Realta had learned about Thanes from chapel and stories Kel told her, but she never understood what their gifts were. What they could or could not do. And she was somehow one of them.

The king inspected the servant's tattoo on Callum's wrist. "I see. And you said Vala. That's near Caman's Pass, correct?"

"Yes, Your Majesty."

The king slowly nodded. He glanced at Realta, and his eyes widened. "And what of this girl?" he asked, a slight tremor in his voice. "Where did she come from?"

"She's my daughter."

Why is he looking at me like that? The look of shock and confusion tinged with anger made Realta's skin crawl. The king quickly turned away. She breathed out a relieved sigh.

The king snapped his fingers again. The bonds around Realta and Serena's wrist fell away. Serena did not look surprised. She kept her eyes on the floor.

"Your Majesty," said Kanton, resting a hand on his sword hilt, "I don't think—"

"Did I ask for your opinion, Captain Kanton?" King Logan shot him a glare.

"No, Your Majesty, but—"

"Shut up." Kanton paled. The king then addressed Callum,

"Where did you first meet my half-sister?"

Callum told him about finding Serena in the barn, the village guard arriving to help, and Kanton's intervention. "He asked that I help escort the girl back to Teyrnas to stand trial," he finished.

The king narrowed his eyes. "Trial for what?"

"For stealing your horse, Your Majesty."

"He mentioned no other crimes?"

"No, Your Majesty."

"And how did Captain Kanton receive those burn scars?"

Kanton shot Callum a glare, daggers in his eyes.

"I awoke in the night and saw him trying to kill the girl. We fought, and he fell onto the campfire."

King Logan took a step back, studying both Callum and Kanton. "And why," he asked, his voice icy, "would he try to kill that girl?"

"I don't know."

"The simple explanation," Kanton stepped forward, "the explanation that this slave failed to see, Your Majesty, was that I was merely checking on the girl. She tried to run away multiple times. The slave saw the knife and assumed the worst. He attacked me before I was able to explain."

"He's lying," Realta said. The words were out of her mouth before she could think. The king directed his gaze at her. Kel's eyes full of anger.

"Tell me, young miss, has your father ever been to Teyrnas before today?"

Okay, that was not the response she expected. She chose her next words carefully. "I don't think so. Well, maybe once or twice when his sister was at the Academy."

"A sister? And what was her name?"

Realta looked at her father. He gave her a reassuring nod. "Esme."

The king studied her for a long moment, his eyes softening. She shifted from foot to foot, wishing he would stop staring at her.

"Your Majesty," Kanton said, "you're ignoring that fact that your sister escaped the palace grounds without raising an alarm. That means a major breech in security. And with those threats sent by the queen of Nowan—"

"Yes, I'm aware," he snapped. "I'm also aware that the Nowani nobility is also fond of Death Charades."

"Death Charades?" Kanton looked at him, aghast. "Your Majesty, your own sister tried to kill you and fled the palace! And these people have been helping her escape justice every step of the way!"

"What?" Callum shot a glare at Serena. The girl maintained her silence, eyes fixed on the ground.

"Oh," said the king, finally taking his gaze off Realta, "the girl neglected to mention that little fact, didn't she? Luckily for me," he pulled down his shirt to reveal a fresh scar just below his left collarbone, where it met the shoulder joint, "she has terrible aim."

Oh Creator, it was true! Serena really had tried to murder the king. Kanton had been truthful. And if he'd been truth in that regard, then... Realta dug her fingernails into her palms. Charity and Lok were not dead. They couldn't be.

"What do you think, my dear?" the king asked the queen, beckoning her to his side. "Think they are telling the truth?"

"I want to believe them," she replied, standing side by side with her husband. "Perhaps they should be questioned again, separately. See if other details match up."

The king smiled. "A wonderful idea." His eyes again fell on Realta. The smile faded. "Where did you get that necklace?"

Realta placed her hand on Kel's necklace, two ravens flying on a white pendant. "I... I got it from—"

"From my sister," Callum finished. "It was a birthday gift."

"And where did your sister get it?" His anger rose with every word.

"I don't know. Traveling merchant probably."

King Logan grabbed the necklace, snapping the leather cord. He studied the necklace, seething. The queen placed a hand on his shoulder. He immediately shrugged it off.

After tying the necklace around his own neck, the king snapped his fingers. The guards stood at attention. "Escort Callum Haar to the holding cells. Take the girl to Mistress Cray. I'll deal with them later. Serena, off to your room."

"You're just going to let her go?" the queen asked, apprehensively.

"Let's call it a test. Off with you, girl."

Serena, never taking her eyes off the floor, hurried out of the Audience Chambers. The guards exchanged wary whispers.

"Serena, wait!" Realta cried. The girl disappeared through the doorway, her footsteps fading. *Don't run away from us again!*

"We've done nothing wrong," said Callum as Wills pulled him away from Realta. "You have no right to imprison us!"

King Logan gave him a wicked smile. "Actually, I do. The law states that a king may imprison those he suspects of treason for a period of ten days. After that, they must stand trial in the magistrate's court. We will get the truth out of you soon enough."

Wills and another guard grabbed Callum's arms. He fought back, sending kicks to their knees and jabbing them in the ribs with his elbows. One guard punched Callum in the lower back. Callum responded with an uppercut to the man's jaw, sending him to the ground. Two more guards ran to him, hands on their daggers. Realta stood frozen, unable to make a decision. She wanted Callum to fight back, to escape. But what if the stitches ripped?

King Logan snapped his fingers. Callum froze, his eyes growing wide with fear. The guards all stepped back, watching their king. Callum's breathing grew labored. Tears leaked from his eyes.

"I don't... How?"

"What are you doing to him?" Realta cried, taking a step towards the king and queen. The queen held up a hand and shook her head, telling her to stay right there. Don't move. The king stared at her father. "Stop it!"

Callum fell to his knees, sobbing uncontrollably. Realta rushed to him, but a guard grabbed her, holding her back.

"Please, stop!"

The king snapped his fingers again, but Callum continued to sob.

"He will be much easier to deal with now."

The guards lifted Callum to his feet and led him out of the Audience Chamber.

Realta glared at the king. She didn't care how powerful he was, didn't care how much he resembled her uncle. He had no right to do that to her father! Whatever he had done. She'd never seen her father so scared. Not even when he fought Kanton in the middle of the night.

The queen averted her eyes. "I must be going," she informed her husband. With Una trailing behind her, the queen exited the Chamber, her silk dress swishing.

"Your Majesty," said Kanton, stepping forward, "I must warn you that the man Callum Haar is prone to lying. He received his slave status by foreclosing on his father's farm. Gambling debts, I was told by his master. Anything he says must not be taken at face value."

King Logan locked eyes with Kanton and smiled. "Captain, your new face suits you."

Kanton's jaw dropped.

"Colm," the king addressed the sole guardsman, the same one who announced him and the queen, as he walked away, "escort the girl to Mistress Cray in the morning. Take her to Master Scannail. Normal procedure."

"Yes, Your Majesty."

"And, Kanton," the king called over his shoulder, "resume your normal duties." With that, the king exited the Audience Chamber. The door closed with a bang, echoing throughout the empty space.

Hand on his sword hilt, Kanton assumed the same haughty air he had before the king and queen arrived. He smiled wickedly at Realta, the same smile he wore on Springtide, and marched out of the room.

Realta glanced up at Colm the guardsman, shaking like a leaf in the wind.

"What did he do to my father?" Realta asked. New tears leaked from her eyes.

"He used an Illusion." He shivered. "Come, we don't want to be late."

"Late for what?" A part of Realta did not want an answer.

Colm never gave her one.

23

Cuchasi

Gareth fidgeted in his seat. The boat ride across the Nerin had been very smooth. In fact, the experience was downright pleasant. Until it ended. All passengers had been required to stand in a single file line before being allowed to officially enter East Bridge. A pair of guards led a chained man down the line. He did not speak a word until he reached Kel.

"Him! Him!" the man shrieked. Gareth ducked behind his father. Kel responded by hitting the man over the head with his crutch. The guards pleaded for him to stop and asked apologetically for him to come with them. They would explain everything.

"It's very curious," said Kel as he took the seat next to Gareth in the guardsmen's office, "that your Cuchasi is from Sykeria instead of someone local."

Gareth glanced at this Cuchasi. The chained man sat in a cell in the far corner. He rubbed his injured head, the facial tattoo contorting with every winch. The man noticed Gareth watching him. Smiling wickedly, he pointed to himself and then to Gareth. Gareth shuddered and turned away.

"We find that Sykerian Cuchasi are more accurate," said Guardsman Mullen. "Would you care for anything to drink, sir?"

"They are also far more terrifying," Kel replied, ignoring the offer. "Not to mention you don't have to pay slaves."

Guardsman Mullen and his colleague, Guardsman O'Tyre, exchanged pale-faced looks.

"I'm Academy educated. I know exactly what that tattoo means," Kel added with a devious smile. "Where did you find him?"

"Well," O'Tyre replied, "it was a bit of an exchange. Too long of a story to go into."

"I'm sure. Tyre. That's a minor noble house, isn't it?"

"Yes, sir, but—"

"It would be such a shame if word of this reached your... Grandfather, correct? Connor of House Tyre is still alive, isn't he?"

"He is." The guardsman's face was as white as fresh snow.

"Wouldn't do him any good to know that one of his grandsons was involved in a scandal. You know have gossip flies in the capital."

"What is it you want, sir?" asked Mullen. "We don't have all day."

"Don't speak to him that way," O'Tyre said through his teeth. Plastering on a smile, he addressed Kel. "Have you spent a lot of time in the capital, Master...?"

"Kel. And yes, when I was younger."

Gareth raised an eyebrow. His father was Hiraethi, born into a tribe of nomads who preferred forests to cities. What game was Kel playing?

"How many other Thanes have passed through this port in the last week?" Kel asked.

Thanes?

"No more than a dozen."

"There was that one girl," said Mullen. "She'd been scared out of her wits. Ran off before we could explain anything."

"Describe her."

"Pretty girl. Middle teens. Black hair, dark eyes."

"Like this?" Kel pointed to an empty corner. Mullen jumped up, his chair crashing to the ground.

"Yes, exactly!" he replied, pointing at the empty wall. Gareth squinted his eyes. There was nothing there.

"And what about these people?"

"They were there, too. How did you...?"

"They're my family," Kel replied, his voice growing grave and dark. "They were attacked on the River Road and have been running ever since. I need to know exactly what happened to them and where I can find them."

O'Tyre bit down on his lower lip, averting his eyes. Mullen, his face downcast, replied, "I'm so sorry, Master Kel. Like I said, they ran away before we could explain that the girl was a Thane. We didn't know they were being chased. I truly am sorry."

Kel let out a heavy sigh. "Could they still be in East Bridge?"

"We've no idea, Master Kel. Odds are, they left the city as soon as possible. We can send word to other guardhouses in the city, if you'd like."

"Yes, please. What type of Thane was the girl?"

"Black as night," the Cuchasi yelled, wrapping his long fingers around the cell's bars. "The girl was black as night!"

Kel raised his crutch over his head. The Cuchasi retreated to the far corner of the cell, cowering.

"We don't know what he means," replied Mullen. "He's never given that description before."

Kel nodded. "Guardsmen, do yourselves a favor and hire a local Cuchasi. Had they looked like my son instead of that lunatic, my niece would not have run and maybe, just maybe, she and her father would be here, safe and sound."

"We apologize, sir," said O'Tyre. "After all, we wouldn't want any bad word getting out."

"Of course not," he replied disdainfully. Standing, Kel said, "Come along, Gareth. Our business here is done."

"How long will you be staying in East Bridge, sir? I can recommend a few inns you can spend the night in."

"I appreciate it."

Guardsman Mullen gave them directions to the nearest inn, and the two of them left, Gareth leading Dust by the reins.

"What's a Thane?" Gareth asked once they were several blocks away from the guardhouse, and that Cuchasi creature. Just thinking about him made Gareth's skin crawl.

Kel was quiet for a moment, quiet in the way that meant he was thinking carefully. "It's another word for Seltachai."

"That makes no sense. Realta is not Hiraethi."

"You don't have to be Hiraethi to be a Thane. It's..." Kel sighed. "It's very complicated. And the closer we get to Teyrnas, the more you are going to see."

"How do we see them?"

"We don't see them. You see them."

Gareth's palms began to sweat. "I don't understand."

Kel gave him a patient smile. "What do you see when you look at me? At my skin?"

"Lights. Silver and gold lights." Gareth gripped the reins. He thought of the purple lights coming from Mayor Gan's skin, almost too faint to see. The blood red lights streaming from Kanton, the man's horrifying presence. No one understood, nobody could see expect for Gareth. His chest tightened, making it harder for him to breathe, to think. "How did you know?" he whispered.

"I've known since you were a baby. Your mother and I chose to keep it a secret. If people knew you were a Cuchasi, then they'd start asking questions. Questions about me, about my past. You see, when I told people I was Hiraethi, the majority stopped asking questions. Everyone's heard stories about them, not all of them pleasant. It was a perfect disguise."

"You're not Hiraethi?" Pain teared at Gareth's heart. His father had lied to him.

"Not completely. My mother had some Hiraethi blood mix with enough noble that nobody cared when my father married her." Kel paused. After walking another block, he said, "Gareth, you need to be very careful when we go to Teyrnas. I have a history there, one I've spent the last seventeen years running from. Don't be shocked if you discover some unpleasant facts about me."

"Like what?"

Kel absentmindedly touched the scars on his face.

Gareth did not press further. Him being a Cuchasi and Realta being a Seltachai were enough unwanted surprises for one day.

24

Servants

The first rays of morning light shone through the narrow window. Realta's eyes, heavy and red from a sleepless night full of crying, wandered to her bandaged wrist. Small droplets of dried blood stained the white cloth.

Colm the guardsman had escorted her to a small room in the palace's lower level to meet Master Gilnyn Scannail. He asked no questions, only instructing Realta to sit perfectly still and make no sudden movements. He then took out a needle and a jar of ink. Scannail clamped one large hand around her wrist and went to work.

No one had told her that tattoos bled! Every pin prick sent new pain up her arm. The ordeal lasted no more than fifteen minutes, but it might as well have been hours. Her left wrist was now marked with two diamonds surrounded by thin bands circling her wrist. The same marks as her father.

His work done, Master Scannail had Colm escort Realta to a small room on the palace's second floor, in the servant's wing. The sun had set by then, the first moon appearing over the horizon. The sole light in her room was a small candle, casting flickering shadows on the walls.

She pleaded to speak with her father, to just see if he was all right. Colm regretfully said that he could not allow it. The king would not approve. He left, closing and locking the door.

Realta extinguished the candle and laid down on the cot, pulling a thin blanket with frayed edges over her shoulders. A sense of helplessness pervaded the room, surrounding her more thoroughly than the darkness. Fresh tears spilled from her eyes. They did not stop until both moons had ended their race.

The door opened on creaking hinges. Realta sat up and saw a small woman standing at the threshold. She was no taller than a ten-year-old girl, though her hair was gray, wrapped in a neat bun. She had fine lines around her eyes and the creases of her mouth. Hands folded in front of her, she studied Realta with sharp, brown eyes.

"Realta Haar?" the woman asked.

"Yes, ma'am?"

"I am Shasta Cray. I am to show you your duties as a member of the palace staff." Mistress Cray narrowed her eyes. "Did you sleep in your clothes, child?"

"I um..." Realta lowered her head. She rubbed her throbbing wrist, each throb shooting through her hand and lower arm. "I'm sorry, ma'am."

"No matter. There's a change of clothes in that closet. And stop picking at your tattoo. You'll risk infection." Mistress Cray moved to close the door. "I will wait until you are ready."

Realta slowly walked over to the closet. Inside were two plain, gray dresses and a white smock. She changed into the new clothes, though the dress was a bit too large for her. As she braided her hair, she studied her new surroundings. The small room contained only a bed, closet, and a simple writing desk. The window gave a decent view of the gardens, the flowers in full bloom. And the walls were made of gray stone, smoothed to the point that she could not feel the edges.

This is familiar. I've seen these walls before. But where? Most buildings in Vala were made of wood, not stone. Yet, this type of wall was familiar. She knew it. The sensation was like visiting a place one hadn't been to in years. Different and familiar all at once.

You're just tired. You can't think straight. You don't even know what happened to Father. And Serena...

Serena had betrayed them. She doubted she meant to, but her actions had led to Callum in a cell and Realta with a servant's mark.

Muffled voices sounded from the hallway. Realta tied the smock around her waist and creaked open the door. Outside stood Mistress Cray, speaking with none other than Queen Isla herself. The queen spied Realta and smiled politely.

"Good morning, Miss Haar," said Isla, wearing a blue silk dress, the same color as her earrings, with silver embroidery in the shape of ivy. "I take it you did not sleep well. No one does on the first night."

"Where is my father?" she asked, voice trembling. She still had no explanation of the queen's cryptic words from yesterday. What if she had another outburst? And why had she been so frightened by the words being written?

"Your father is well. Though that wound on his chest is disconcerting. The palace healers are examining him presently."

"Can I see him?"

The queen mulled it over. "Perhaps this evening, if all goes well." She then addressed Mistress Cray. "Any more news concerning the East?"

"None that I've heard. It would be wise for Logan to plan on meeting with Gallia's messengers in a few days."

The queen grimaced and wrung her hands. "They're that close?"

"According to my sources."

"Very well. Good day, Mistress Cray." She paused, studying Realta. Wavering, she said, "Miss Haar." She walked down the long hallway, the silk dress swishing, and nodded to other servants as they passed one another.

"Come," Mistress Cray instructed Realta.

She followed the woman to the end of the hallway and down a narrow flight of stairs that seemed to have been cut from a single piece of stone. Small windows, as narrow as her forefinger, lighted the way. From this vantage point, she could see the courtyard and the palace's looming walls. The stairs ended at the entrance to a large kitchen. Several servants hurried about, preparing the morning meal.

"Was she telling the truth about my father?" Realta asked Mistress Cray.

"Why would Her Majesty lie, dear?"

"I... I don't trust her. She said some odd things about me. And the king..." The words caught in her throat.

"Ah, the Illusion." Mistress Cray sighed. "Una is quite the gossip. What King Logan did to your father caused him no physical harm. It only made him easier to subdue."

"But how did he do that?"

"The king is a Minder Thane as well as a Manipulator. Quite common for Thanes of noble blood to have two, or even three, abilities. And the queen is a Farsight. After a fashion," she added under her breath.

Two or three Thane abilities in one person. How could she be so ignorant of these things? The chaplains taught about Thanes alongside the Gadyeni, but everything was so vague. So filled with awe that there were very few facts.

"Do you know a lot about Thanes?" Would this woman believe that Realta herself was a Thane? She doubted it.

"What did I say about picking at your tattoo?" she replied sternly.

Realta found her hand scratching at the bandage. She quickly placed it at her side, balling it into a fist.

"Now," Mistress Cray led her to the end of the kitchen, "your first few weeks in the kitchens, if you are assigned to them, will involve serving the royal family and their guests. You might even be allowed to assist with the cooking. Do you have any experience in this area?"

"A little." Mistress Loy had taught all of them, including Gareth, the basics of cooking, but only Nina had been allowed to cook unaided. Charity had nearly burned the house down the sole time she'd cooked unaided. Her nose was buried in a book. Fresh tears stung her eyes. Her friend was alive, she told herself as she fought off the tears. She had to be.

"A little is better than none."

Serving women in white aprons set several plates on the far counter. Cooks scurried to place food on them. An assortment of fried eggs, toast, and various types of jam. Two women picked up the plates, one in each hand, and hurried out the side door.

Realta caught a glimpse of a dining room the size of the farmhouse's dining room, kitchen, and living room combined. Stain glass windows and tapestries hung on the walls, bright light pouring onto a table designed to hold twenty people. The king, queen, and two children sat at the table. But not Serena.

Mistress Cray was staring at her.

"Yes, ma'am?"

"Serving the royal family means you take the food to the table. Is this clear?"

"I'm not a servant," Realta whispered. Even at the Loy farm, she had never been treated like a servant. Her own father, a real indentured servant, had been viewed as a member of the family, as though he were Master Loy's younger brother. And she'd been treated like their fourth daughter. They were her family. The fact that they didn't share the Loys' blood was irrelevant. She and her father were loved. Those people sitting at the lavish table would never view her in the same light.

Mistress Cray motioned for Realta to lean forward. "I do not know the circumstances for your being here, not in full. But from my years at the palace, you have been given far better treatment than most. Logan and Isla are reasonable people, and tattoos can be removed." Mistress Cray rolled up her left sleeve. Small scars crisscrossed the skin, but no ink remained. "I will speak with them on your behalf, but for now, you must act the part. Do you understand, my girl?"

"Yes, ma'am," she replied quietly.

"Very good. Now, take this food out before it gets cold."

Realta grabbed a plate of fried eggs with one hand and a plate containing three bowls of jam with the other. Mistress Cray held the door open for her. The other two serving women were busy arranging the plates. Realta walked over and placed the food on the table. One woman let out an impatient sigh and put the plates in their proper places. Neither she nor her colleague said a word to Realta.

Taking a step back, she studied the royal family. King Logan still wore the same black trousers and shirt, his blue cloak draped over the back of the chair. Kel's necklace hung around his neck. The queen sat to his right. She had put on a silver necklace decorated with sapphires and rubies since speaking to her and Mistress Cray.

The two children at the table eyed Realta warily. The older boy was about twelve years old with auburn hair, the same shade as his mother. The rest of his features, thin and gaunt, were an eerie combination of the king and Kel. He regarded her with piercing, blue eyes. *His father's eyes*, Realta observed. *The same as Kel's.* The younger boy was around five or six years old with reddish brown hair. He sat on a large book so he could reach the table. He waved timidly at Realta.

The motion caught the king's attention. Eyes like blue fire, he demanded, "What in the name of the Abyss is she doing here?" The queen averted her gaze, her features as still as a statue.

"Shasta!" the king yelled. Realta's heart pounded as her face grew uncomfortably warm. Did she do something wrong?

Mistress Cray, visibly confused, walked into the dining room. "Is there something amiss, my king?"

"I gave implicit instructions to lock that girl away until I had time to question her. Why is she serving breakfast?"

"I apologize, Your Majesty. I was not made aware of that." She raised an eyebrow in the queen's direction.

"That's my mistake, dear," said Isla, placing a hand on the king's arm. "I heard you say the girl should be taken to Shasta. I thought you meant for her to train the girl as a servant. It was my mistake," she added.

Logan rubbed his forehead. "I can see where the confusion arose. Well, don't just stand there, girl, do as you're told. Shasta, keep a close eye on her until I have time to question her. I don't want her conferring with her father or my sister in the meantime."

"Yes, Your Majesty," Mistress Cray replied.

Queen Isla released a small, relieved sigh. She gave Realta a quick nod, smiling.

Realta stared at her, confused. She acted to protect her, but why? It did not add up, considering her words from yesterday. What had she said? The Wardens of the Night were looking for her? The title meant nothing to her. And why look for her? There were far more important people in the world.

A solitary figure slipped into the dining room. Serena, still dressed in the same tattered trousers and work shirt, stood several paces behind her brother and sister-in-law. Her clear blue eyes studied the area. Those eyes landed on Realta. She responded with a glare. Serena bowed her head in shame.

"Serena!" cried the younger boy. He climbed off his seat and ran to Serena, embracing her. Serena reached down and hugged the boy. "I knew you'd come back!"

"Mannix," said the queen, with a slight tremor as her eyes grew wide, "come back here and finish your breakfast."

"Listen to your mother, Mannix," added the king.

Mannix. Serena told her that her nephews were named Morgan and Mannix, and that her older sister was the only one who loved her. What had she said about the rest of her family? Morgan was the one who had surgery. And her oldest brother...

My oldest brother can't decide whether to love me or hate me, Serena had told her during Callum's surgery. *And Mal acts like I don't exist.*

The little boy grabbed Serena by the hand and led her to the table, smiling from ear to ear. Serena averted her eyes, not wanting to meet her family's gazes. The queen had attention only for the table in front of her. Morgan studied his aunt with wary eyes. The king cast a sharp glare before shaking his head in contempt.

Mannix resumed his seat, pointing at the empty chair next to him. "Sit down, Serena." The girl wavered, placing a hand on the chair. She looked at her brother.

"Stars above, Serena, why are you looking at me?" the king questioned. "Sit or leave. Make up your damn mind for once!"

The words echoed off the walls. Neither of the other serving women seemed fazed.

"May I eat in my room?" Morgan asked his mother.

"If it's all right with your father."

Logan slammed his fork on the plate, the clatter ringing in Realta's ears. "Why? Give me one good reason why you can't eat with the family?"

Morgan swallowed a lump in his throat. "I'm not hungry anymore, actually. May I be excused?"

"Fine. Leave," the king replied tersely.

Morgan stood and said to his mother, "Tell the tutor I'll be in the solarium, please."

"Of course, dear," she replied quietly.

Morgan cast a wary glance at his father and left the dining room. Mistress Cray pursed her lips, her eyes following the boy as he walked away. Realta wondered if she ought to leave, too. Her being there had put the king in a foul mood, and she didn't want to anger him further. She stepped closer to Mistress Cray.

"Did you sleep well, Serena?" Isla asked.

"Somewhat." Serena looked at the empty seat, biting down on her lip.

No wonder she ran away. There was no love for her here. Realta felt guilty for being angry at her.

"What is she still doing here?" the king asked Mistress Cray, his voice low and cold.

"Apologizes, my king. Come, dear." Mistress Cray led Realta out of the dining room and into the adjacent hallway.

"Goodbye, new girl!" Mannix called out, waving.

Realta glanced back at the little boy, and at Serena. She stared at her blankly with Kel's eyes. The eyes she shared with her brother, as well as his sandy hair and tall, thin frame. That mystery had been solved, but it presented new questions. The king was the healthy version of her Hiraethi uncle who claimed to have no family, leaving his tribe behind in order to attend the Academy. The Haars and the Loys were his family now. So why did not one but two members of the royal family share his features?

"The kitchens might be a bad location for you, dear," said Mistress Cray as they walked down the hallway. They passed other servants and a handful of guardsmen playing a game of dice.

"Can I see my father, please?" Realta asked quietly. She needed to be near someone who loved her, to forget her situation for just a moment.

"Not now. I would not want word of it reaching the king. He is not a person you want as an enemy. Especially not with his half-sister back in the palace and the queen hiding one of her premonitions from him."

"Premonitions?"

Mistress Cray sighed. "Her Farsight is not always reliable, so she hired Una as a personal scribe to write them down. That way, each one is noted and judged to be valid or invalid. It's rare for Farsights have to inaccurate visions. The king is quite interested in the phenomenon, so when word reached him that Isla had one redacted, he was upset, to say the least."

Realta hesitated. "Does he know what it was about?"

"In part. He knows it concerns you. Something about death and destruction. But the queen refuses to confirm anything. I don't know why she's hiding it, but Her Majesty has her reasons." Mistress Cray eyed her. "How much of it do you remember?"

"Very little."

She nodded as though she expected that answer. "It would be wise to tread lightly, in that case. The king's temper has a tendency to flare up this time of year."

"Is that why—"

A woman screamed, dropping a basket of laundry, the clothes spilling onto the floor. Realta spun around, searching for any signs of danger. There was no one else in the hall save for herself and Mistress Cray.

"Amzie, what's the matter, my girl?" asked Mistress Cray, placing a hand on the other woman's arm.

"Her... It's... She..." Amzie wrung her hands, eyes darting back and forth between Realta and Mistress Cray.

"Calm down. You've just had a fright, is all. Oh, this is Realta. She'll be with us for the time being."

"Realta? I..." Amzie let out a deep sigh, placing both hands on her chest to steady herself. "My apologies. I could have sworn you were someone else. But you're just a girl."

"Really?" She was not convinced. The woman acted like she had seen a Shade straight out of the Abyss. Realta glanced at the woman's ears. No rings.

"A dear friend who passed into the Realm of Stars some twenty years ago, my girl," Mistress Cray clarified. She turned to Amzie. "Wouldn't want the king and queen to see all this laundry on the floor, would we?"

Amzie squeaked and quickly piled all the fallen clothes back into the basket. "I must be on my way now," she told Mistress Cray. She glanced at Realta and hurried down the hall.

"Why did she look at me like that?" Realta asked.

"Poor Amzie is prone to nervous fits. Come, there's much work to be done." Mistress Cray continued down the hall.

Realta had no choice but the follow.

***

Allowing Callum Haar to bring her back to Teyrnas was a mistake. Coming into the dining room for breakfast made that fact abundantly clear. She should have run away the first chance she got. Those healers in Narfalk would have taken care of Callum and Realta, seen that they got home safely. The only place for her was beyond Caman's Pass.

But Serena had felt an instant connection to the Haars. They had shone her kindness, even when they were questioning her after discovering her in their barn. And that strange man with the scars covering half his face felt so familiar. Almost a comforting presence. A sensation she could not express in words. Not to mention that Callum and Realta had stuck by her side throughout this whole ordeal. None of the people seated at this table would have done the same.

And she had betrayed them. There was no way this homecoming could have ended well. Not for her, and certainly not for people Logan believed helped her escape custody. She should have been more truthful from the start.

"Are you going to sit?" asked Logan, glaring at her with those cold, blue eyes. Serena's skin bristled. She hated being underneath her brother's gaze.

Serena took a piece of toast and headed out of the dining room. Neither Logan nor Isla made a move to stop her. Logan never forgave her for being born, and Isla refused to openly take sides.

"Where are you going?" asked Mannix.

Serena kept on walking. She saw no point in explaining her place to the boy. In time, Mannix would grow to hate her, too.

Shoving the piece of toast into her mouth, Serena made her way towards the stables. Servants and guards filled the hallways. Several attempted to speak with her as she walked by, and the guards eyed her warily. Why shouldn't they? She was the bastard who had tried to kill their king.

She assumed Dane Kanton was lurking nearby, regaling his tale of how he tracked Serena to the edge of Caman's Pass and back. The vast majority of it lies.

You should have warned them about Kanton. The Haars and the Loys were good people, trusting people. They had no reason to suspect that the man was a pathological liar, albeit a loyal one. Perhaps that was why Logan allowed the man to keep his position.

"I swear on my mother's name," said one of the servants, Amzie Fenn, to two other women. "That girl looked just like..." She trailed off, spying Serena out of the corner of her eye. "Why, Serena, you really are home!"

"For now." Home? No, this place stopped being her home the moment her mother died.

The other servants exchanged goodbyes with Amzie, explaining that they had work to do, and left Amzie by herself. She wrung her hands together, trying and failing to not look Serena's way.

"Did you enjoy your time away?" she asked innocently.

"Parts of it." Half of the time, she was cold and hungry, on the point of starvation by the time she reached the Hinterland's outer villages. Thankfully, there were plenty of merchants who were too busy with crowds to notice a thieving hand. "Who were you talking about?"

"Oh, no one. Just a new servant."

"Do you mean Realta?" A pang of guilt shot through her. She had never meant for the girl to be forced into servitude. *This is all your fault. You shouldn't have— Shut up!*

Amzie paled. "Um... Well..."

"I traveled with her for over a week. I know who she is." Over a week of travel, masquerading as sisters with Callum as their father. For a while, Serena had wished it were true. Sure, she did not look like them, but plenty of families had some children resembling the father and others taking after the mother. Why couldn't that have been the case for them?

"Yes, of course, Serena." She continued wringing her hands. Poor woman. Always walking on eggshells, even around friends. Living underneath Logan's hand did that to people.

"Can I have my evening meal with you and the others tonight?" Serena asked, hoping to put her at ease.

"Yes, of course, Serena!" She smiled, relieved. Funny how the same words could carry different meanings. "I must go now. The queen..."

"I understand. Be well, Amzie."

"Be well, Serena." With that, Amzie Fenn scurried down the hall.

Serena sighed. She continued down the hall, grateful not to be stopped by anyone else wanting to talk, and entered the courtyard. A cool breeze blew past her, ruffling her sandy hair. The sun was high in the sky, and several gray clouds were moving in from the east. Most importantly, it was quiet. A small moment for her to breathe.

She glanced over at the Southern Gate. Two guards stood at their post, eyeing her suspiciously. Her head low, Serena hurried towards the stables. One guard pointed her out. The other shook his head and motioned for his colleague to focus their attentions elsewhere. It was just the king's bastard sister.

The stables, a large, well-ventilated building with room for over fifty horses, stood near the wall, midway between the courtyard and the Southern entrance. Logan's prized horses occupied a dozen of those stalls. Magnificent beasts known throughout the kingdom for their speed and endurance. The precise reason Serena had stolen one.

An older man, his hair thinning on top and graying at the sides, stepped out from one of the stalls. He glanced up, meeting Serena's eyes. He blinked, standing absolutely still as though he was not sure if the girl was real or a Shade. Tears welled in his dark blue eyes.

"Serena?"

"Hi, Gregor."

Gregor Pym rushed forward and embraced Serena with a crushing hug. "Oh Creator! Oh, my girl, what are you doing here?"

"Kanton and his cronies found me. Tricked some people into bringing me back."

"Why didn't you run?" Gregor asked, stepping back so he could get a better look at her.

"I tried." Tears brimmed her eyes. She forced them down.

"Has your brother seen you? You're nothing but skin and bones!"

"It wasn't an easy path."

Gregor grew silent, as though debating his next words carefully.

"What's wrong? What did Logan do to you?" Gregor had been the first one she confided in about running away, explaining why she needed to leave. The man, a close friend of her mother's, helped Serena escaped every step of the way. He picked out the best horse and bribed the guards at the Southern Gate to look the other way while Serena slipped out. Every detail had been timed perfectly, the plan known only to her and Gregor.

"Here's some money," Gregor had said, handing Serena a small pouch, the coins jangling loosely. A single lantern burned in the stables, banishing the darkness around her and the older man. "It's not much, but..."

"It's perfect. Thank you." As long as it got her through Caman's Pass. She placed the money in her trousers pocket and pulled the hood of her cloak over her hair, wavy locks that fell down to the middle of her back.

As she moved to mount the horse, the stable doors burst open, slamming against the walls. Cold air rushed in, causing her skin to breakout in goosebumps. The horse reared up, kicking and screaming. She and Gregor grabbed the reins, bringing the animal under control.

Serena's mind raced. Had that been the wind? No, it was a calm night. A pit forming in her gut, she turned and saw a tall figure in a black cloak standing at the entrance. A shadow come to life. She looked to Gregor for an explanation. No one at the palace wore a black cloak. The older man stared at the figure, his face a mask of fear.

"Your Majesty," Gregor stuttered, giving a quick bow. "What brings you here at this late hour?"

Your Majesty? The figure pushed back his hood, revealing the king's face, blue eyes piercing and full of anger.

"What is the meaning of this?" Logan demanded.

"What does it look like?" Serena spat. Was this man really surprised that she was running away? After he had treated her like dirt all these years?

"You're chasing a fool's dream, girl," Logan said, walking up to her. "There is no one beyond the Pass."

"I don't believe you." Serena had not learned that she was the late king's daughter until she was six years old, believing that her real father had died when she was an infant. But then her mother became sick, too sick for the healers to do anything but make her comfortable. Nell Molyns feared for her daughter's future, so she called for King Yestyn's three children, Logan, Mal, and Sarra, and told them the truth. Serena was their half-sister. Yestyn did not deny the truth, but neither did he claim any responsibility for the child. His children swore they would care for her, regardless, and Nell was able to die peacefully.

As Serena grew, she heard many rumors from servants and nobles alike. That Serena was not the only bastard Yestyn had fathered. Logan vehemently denied all those rumors, forbidding anyone from saying them on the palace grounds. That did little to stop people from talking. One rumor claimed that Yestyn sent those children through Caman's Pass, to the neighboring kingdom of Lowyrn, where they could do no harm. Serena grew more and more determined to find them.

"Yestyn was unfaithful to my mother many times," Logan said, his eyes softening. "But you are his only illegitimate child. Accept it."

"No. I know there are others. I heard Gregor—" Serena cursed herself. She hadn't meant to let anything slip.

"You heard Gregor say what?"

Serena's voice caught in her throat. Did she tell her brother the truth, or did she protect the man who was more family to her than all of Yestyn's legitimate children combined?

"What did you tell her?" Logan rounded on the older man, looming over him.

"Nothing, Your Majesty!" Gregor cowered, squeezing his eyes shut. "I swear on my father's name..."

Anger seized hold of Serena. A deep-seated anger that had been building for a decade, ready to explode.

She grabbed the dagger tied to the saddle and swung the blade at her brother. The knife took Logan in the chest, just below the collarbone. Logan looked at Serena in shock. Time seemed to slow. Had Serena really stabbed him? Was the king dead? Logan stumbling backwards, the blade hilt deep in his chest, and collapsed onto the floor. A crimson stain spread across his shirt and cloak.

"Run, Serena!" Gregor cried, his voice muffled in Serena's ears. The older man rushed to the king's side.

Serena mounted the horse and took off at a gallop. The two bribed guards, ignorant of the king's injury, allowed her to exit without incident. She rode past the gate and into the city proper. Nobody stopped her. No one was fast enough. She did not stop until the city disappeared behind the horizon.

"The king didn't do anything to me," Gregor explained. "After you ran off, I help him to the infirmary. The healers asked him who was responsible. The whole palace was in a panic at that point, thinking an assassin was on the grounds. The king claimed it was an accident. That he was trying to Manipulate the dagger towards himself, and his aim was off. The healers took his word for it." He hesitated. "The King's Guard dragged the truth out of him, once everyone realized you were gone."

"He... He tried to cover for me?" Had Serena heard that correctly? They were talking about King Logan O'Kelwyn, right?

"I swear to you, dear, it's the truth. The king relented and sent Captain Kanton after you. Many in the Guard want you to stand trial for conspiracy, but that's the king's call. Not theirs."

"Why Kanton?" Other guardsmen were far more skilled at tracking.

"Because of his experience in the Guard, and the king prefers to keep a healthy distance between Kanton and the queen."

"Why's that?"

Gregor Pym sighed. "Your father wasn't the only one with a wandering eye."

"Oh." Isla having an affair seemed beneath her. Then again, she could have any man she wanted. Dane Kanton, for obvious reasons, should have been at the bottom of that list. "Does Logan know?"

"Yes, but the affair was a onetime thing. It happened years ago. Long before Mannix was born." Gregor frowned. "I really ought not to be telling you this, dear."

"It's fine. I won't repeat anything you say. Do you know where Callum Haar is being kept?"

"Who?" Gregor gave her a startled look.

"The man Kanton brought in with me. Do you know what happened to him?"

"No, afraid I don't." Some of his tension faded. "You might want to ask Shasta or one of the guards on prisoner detail. Hamish is your best bet, if you give him a pint of ale," Gregor added with a smile in his eyes. At least she could always count on that.

"Thank you, Gregor. Will you be eating with the other servants this evening?"

"Of course. And yourself?"

"If you'll have me."

"Always, Serena. You're our girl, no matter what."

Serena bid Gregor farewell, eyeing the horses as she left. Should she try again, or was it too great a risk? And why had Logan lied? The man had never protected her, never acted like he cared. She shook her head. None of this made sense.

25

Ceremony

Lok's heart pounded in his chest. The Thane Ceremony would begin in a matter of minutes. What if he made a mistake? No. He couldn't make a mistake. It was impossible. All he had to do was stand in front of the Premier Scholar and the Council. An idiot could do this.

Thankfully, after a prolonged meeting and drafting a nondisclosure agreement, they had approved of Charity being his voice. This was a special circumstance in more ways than one.

Lok faced a mirror, steadying himself. He wore nothing but a knee-length, sackcloth tunic over his undershorts. The course fibers itched terribly. He balled his hands into fists to keep himself from scratching. Scholar Kuno had explained that wearing sackcloth was an ancient sign of humility. Every Thane who had passed through the Academy had worn the same.

A small knock came at the door. Scholar Kuno poked his head in.

"Ready?"

Lok nodded. Though the Scholar was not permitted to witness the ceremony, he was allowed to guide him to the Council Chamber. Lok stepped into the hallway and saw Charity wearing a simple white dress. She, like him, was barefoot. Another sign of humility.

That did not quite make sense. Thanes were powerful people, capable of incredible fetes. The last word that came to mind when thinking of them was 'humble'.

Everything will be explained. Just keep calm and breathe.

The Scholar led him and Charity out of the Students' dorms and up the grand, central staircase, wide enough for ten people and carved out of dark wood, so dark it was almost black. The Council Chamber was on the top floor. A number of Students lined the steps, watching the procession. All of them were smiling. Some reached out and patted Lok on the back, causing him to flinch. Strangers touching him out of affection? How odd.

Scholar Kuno paused in front of a massive wooden door with symbols carved into it. A compass with geometric lines and shapes at each of the eight cardinal points. The symbols of the Eight Gadyeni, the ones who granted humans Thane abilities millennia ago.

"Good luck," Scholar Kuno said. He turned and headed back down the staircase.

Another Scholar, an elderly woman with snow white hair and silver earrings, approaching them. She carried a small, white bowl full of ashes. She reached into the bowl and took a handful of ash, sprinkling the ashes into Lok and Charity's hair and rubbing it on their cheeks and foreheads.

"Born in war," she said, "you wear the ashes of war as you strive to live in peace."

An uneasy feeling crept into Lok, like frost forming on a pond. War? No one said anything to him about war.

The elderly Scholar stepped back. The doors opened from the inside, revealing a large, circular room with a glass dome ceiling. Seated in a semicircle near the back were the Premier Scholar and the eight Thane members of the Council, the seats for the eight human members standing empty. Along the walls stood hundreds of people. Scholars, Journeymen, Students. All wearing earrings. All Thanes.

Lok wished his mother were there. He had written to her, stating that he and Charity arrived at the Academy, but he never mentioned that he was a Thane. How could he explain that her idiot son was a person of great importance?

She never thought you were an idiot. Only that you were different.

Different. Yes, he supposed he truly was different.

"Walk forward," instructed the elderly Scholar.

Lok and Charity did so, keeping their heads low. They were not to make eye contact with the Premier until the ceremony was complete.

They stood in the center of the room, on a mosaic of a compass. The symbols were identical to the ones on the door. Except this compass had a star in the center, and each symbol was a different color. The stones were cool under his feet.

"Who stands before the Premier Scholar and her Council of Scholars?" asked Premier Scholar Emera, her voice echoing off the walls and domed ceiling. Shuddering, Lok took a step closer to Charity, stealing a glance at the premier. She was a woman well into her seventies with stark gray hair and gold earrings. The sign of a Manipulator Thane. According to Kuno, she was powerful enough to lift boulders into the air. Lok tried not to dwell on that fact.

"I, Lok Tolman," Charity said in his place as he mouthed the words, "stand before the Premier and the Council, newly humbled by my burden."

"And what is your burden, young Thane?"

"By the Gadyeni, I have been granted the burden of Fire Elemental." Excited murmurs spread through the crowd. "Other burdens may come if I am deemed worthy."

"And how will you use your burden?"

"For the good of the people of Eltriar, in the sight of the Gadyeni and the Creator."

"Rise then, Thane Lok Tolman, and accept your burden."

Lok raised his head and stepped forward as Charity stepped back. One of the Scholars, a Minder and Empath who sat in the chair reserved for Elementals, met Lok midway. In his hand was a green earring.

Will I have to sit in that seat one day? He hoped not.

"Welcome, Thane Lok Tolman, of the Elementals," he said, cupping one hand around Lok's right ear. He felt a slight pinch on his earlobe. The Scholar resumed his seat. Lok placed a hand on his ear, feeling the new earring.

Was that it? He stared expectantly at the Council, one hand still on the earring.

"Welcome, Thane Lok Tolman," said the Premier. The other Council members echoed the statement. Then the crowd, hundreds of voices booming like thunder, welcomed him. Lok shuddered, searching for the exit. Instead, his eyes fell on Zandon, Coryn, Ivar, and Jaim. His friends. He'd never expected to have so many. A tear escaped his eye, leaving a clean trail in the ashes.

The entire crowd erupted in claps and cheers, surging towards the center. Surging towards him! Lok's heart leapt into his throat. Many shook his hands, calling him a miracle. He didn't want to be a miracle. He didn't want all these people around him. Eyes staring. Hands touching. Too much... Everything!

Charity made her way through the crowd and hugged him. He held onto her, a refuge in a storm. His new friends quickly made their way to him as well.

"Come on," said Zandon as the first people left the chamber. Many had formed groups, Students with Students, Journeymen with Journeymen, and Scholars with Scholars, speaking with one another. Everyone smiled excitedly. "They're throwing a party for you in the dining hall."

"Does this happen during every ceremony?" asked Charity.

"Not really. Lok's a special case. Every Thane Scholar in Teyrnas must be here."

Lok's eyes widened.

"Are you serious?" Charity asked.

"Yeah. Everyone thought Elementals were goners, remember? That's why they delayed your ceremony. So as many as possible could witness it."

Lok's knees turned to water. He held onto Charity as the crowd filtered out of the Council Chamber and down the long stairway. He kept his eyes focused forward, thinking only of the next step, and the next, and the next. Every once in a while, someone patted him on the head or the shoulder. He really wished they would stop touching him.

At the base of the stairway stood the rest of the Scholars and Journeymen, crowding every inch of the atrium, a field of gray and white cloaks. All of them cheered. Scholar Kuno stood on a chair and waved, his face beaming.

"You mark a new era of Thanes, young one."

Lok turned to face the voice. Premier Scholar Emera stood at his side. Old age had only made the woman more regal, like the expensive wines his mother kept in the cellar, only to be used on special occasions. He nodded to her in thanks.

"Take care of yourself, young one. We are all eager to see what you accomplish in life." Reaching the last step, the Premier bid Lok farewell and went to converse with the other Scholars.

"Oh, Creator and the Eight Gadyeni," whispered Jaim, barely audible over the crowd. "The Premier herself spoke to you!"

Was that a rare occurrence?

"This way, Lok," said Zandon, leading them through the crowd. Lok kept his eyes on Charity the entire way to the dining room, a constant he could rely on.

The space had been cleared of tables and chairs, all of them stacked precariously against the walls. Hundreds of Students greeted him. Hundreds. Every single one.

Lok did not feel so good. The sackcloth irritated his skin and sweat beaded and fell down his forehead, causing the ashes to sting his eyes. He reached up and touched the new earring. It was cold and metallic to the touch. A solid object he could focus on. He was fine. Charity was by his side. She wouldn't allow anything bad to happen to him here.

"Lords and ladies, boys and girls," said one Student at the front of the room, his voice booming, "I present to you the first Elemental Thane in over three hundred years, Lok Tolman!"

A new round of cheers erupted from the crowd. They swarmed him, reaching out to touch him, slapping him on the back, patting his head, grabbing at his hands. Lok latched onto Charity's arm for support. Too many people. Too much noise. He had to leave. He shouldn't be here. He shouldn't be here!

"Don't worry, Lok," she said. "No one here will hurt you."

No one will hurt him.

Lok took a series of deep breaths, placing a hand on the new earring. Cool, smooth metal lacquered green. He smiled at the crowd, wondering what he should do. Wave? Yes, that seemed like a good idea. He waved his hand in the air. More cheers responded. These people, they... They actually liked him. Not a single one cared that he was mute. They accepted him as he truly was.

He belonged.

***

The celebration lasted long into the afternoon, the setting sun bathing the sky orange and red. The day had taken a turn for the colder, a common occurrence in early spring.

Lok, Charity, and their new friend group sat underneath a

small grove of apple trees in the gardens, near the Eastern Wall. Green leaves and white blossoms budded the branches. People of all three academic ranks walked up to him every once in a while to congratulate him. None stayed for long, sensing his need for privacy.

Lok had been allowed to change into his regular clothes. Both he and Charity wore their light blue Student cloaks. The fabric felt remarkably comfortable and warm.

"You have to tell me what it was like," Evelyn said to Charity.

Charity gave her a sly smile. "I've been sworn to secrecy."

"Give me a hint."

"It involved talking, and Lok getting his earring."

Evelyn rolled her eyes. "Fine. I'm sure there are books that have the details."

"Ask Scholar Kuno," Lok wrote. Getting his notebook back was like finding a light in the middle of a dark forest.

Evelyn furrowed her brow. "I'll pass."

"How come?" asked Charity.

"He's nice and all, but..."

"Weird," Zandon finished. "In a good way," he added.

"Why did the Scholars choose him to help you, do you think?" asked Ivar.

"I think he volunteered."

"Ivar has a point," said Jaim, spinning a few leaves around one another. "Each of us has a mentor with the same ability. Lots of Thane Scholars have several Students under them. Why not pick a Thane for you?"

"Well, you see, Jaim," Zandon began, eyes laughing.

"Yeah, yeah. Bloody Elementals were bloody extinct last month. But aren't Thanes better at training Thanes than normal people?"

"Wow, you actually have a good point," replied Coryn.

"I always have a good point. You just fail to see them."

"You should ask him tomorrow," Charity said to Lok. "I'm sure the Scholars know what they were doing."

"He is a historian, after all," added Coryn.

Lok nodded. That was the explanation he was given. Scholar Kuno focused his studied on ancient history, specifically the time before and during the Thousand Years War, in which the

Nine Thanes rose up and defeated the Midnight King. Very few documents existed from that time, making Kuno's work all the more difficult.

A bell sounded from the main building. Six o'clock. The normal time for supper.

"How much extra work will the Scholars give us tomorrow?" Coryn asked. Today had been an unscheduled free day. No classes and no work.

"I suspect they'll go easy on us," replied Zandon. "I saw the guards bring in over a dozen kegs. Some Scholars might not be much for teaching tomorrow." He grinned.

"There were lots of people, though," said Ivar. He stood, dusting off his trousers and cloak. "I still have research to do. See you in the morning." They waved goodbye as he made his way to the main building.

"We should be going, too," said Evelyn. "Wouldn't want someone developing bad habits." She smiled at her sister.

Coryn acquiesced, and the two left.

"What about you guys?" asked Zandon.

"My first class is a free period," replied Jaim.

"I'm not tired," said Charity.

Lok sheepishly wrote, *I would like some time alone. I appreciate the party, but it's been a lot for one day.*

"No problem," replied Zandon. "Good night, Lok."

Lok stood, and Charity stood as well, giving him a hug. The hug felt warm and good. Not at all like those pats on the back. The gesture was kind and familiar. She released him, smiling.

"Good night, Lok. Everyone in Vala is going to be so proud of you."

Vala. Home. A place he did not want to think about. But his mother was there. She would be proud of him.

He hoped.

26

Dreams

Realta's dream took her to the royal palace. The walls, floors, and tapestries were all the same, but the young boy was a stranger. No older than ten, he wore brown trousers and a plain white shirt, both frayed at the edges. He had the same blue eyes and sandy brown hair as the king, and he was terrified. A bang sounded down the corridor, and the boy ran.

Is that King Logan as a child? Realta wondered as her shadow self drifted along with him, powerless to change her course. The king was the last person she wanted to dream about, even if this was a younger version. A half week at the palace and she had no word of her father's condition. Logan had forbidden the servants from letting her see Callum, or even telling Realta his location. He offered no explanation. What type of person did that?

The child turned a corner and ducked into a workroom, a series of pails, mops, and other cleaning utensils lining the walls. He pulled open a cabinet and crawled inside. In an instant, Realta was in the cramped space beside him. The cabinet door was open just enough for Realta to peer into the room.

A door slammed. A man's voice echoed throughout the hall. The boy clamped his hands over his head, whimpering.

More footsteps, lighter, approached the cabinet. Realta spied work shoes and a woman's skirt. The person crouched down and peered into the small space.

"What are you doing here?" asked a young Shasta Cray, no older than twenty-five. Her gray hair was coal black, and her face was perfectly smooth.

"Please, don't tell him," Logan pleaded, his voice a hoarse whisper.

The footsteps grew louder, pounding like thunder. Logan hugged his knees and bit down on his lip to keep from crying out. Shasta gave him a quick nod and stood up, placing her small frame in front of the cabinet.

The workroom door slammed open. Realta held her breath, heart pounding in her chest.

This isn't real. It's just a dream, she reminded herself. Then why was she so scared?

Steeling herself, she peered out of the crack. A tall man, thin as a whip and wearing well-tailored clothes, stood in the doorway.

"Where is he?" the man demanded, looming over Shasta.

"Where is who, Your Majesty?"

"That good for nothing son of mine," replied King Yestyn, his voice cold and dark. Logan began whispering a catechism, just like the ones Realta had learned in chapel.

"I'm afraid I haven't seen him, Your Majesty. Might I inquire what he has done?" She quickly added, "In case I do see him?"

Yestyn glared at her with cold, blue eyes. The same ones Logan had looked at her and her father with. Finally, the king replied, "I caught him spying on one of my guests. I mean to teach him the proper punishment for spying."

"I understand, Your Majesty. Is there any other way I might be of service until the boy is found?"

"Just do your damn job." King Yestyn turned on his heels and stormed out of the room.

A few tense moments passed. Shasta glanced down the hallway and closed the workroom door. She then said, "You can come out now."

Logan cautiously pushed open the cabinet door and studied the room. As he crawled out of his hiding space, Realta blinked and was standing side by side with Shasta's younger self. The boy stood on shaking legs.

"Thank you."

"Do you have any idea how much trouble I'll be in if Yestyn learns I lied to him?" Shasta demanded, keeping her voice low.

Logan shrank back. "I'm sorry. I don't want you to get in trouble."

Shasta sighed. "Well, what's done is done. And it will do you well to learn that spying is beneath the crown prince. If the rest of the nobility found out—"

"My father will beat me black and blue," the boy finished.

"I know."

In the light, Realta noticed yellow and purple bruises on the boy's arm. Bruises in the shape of fingers.

"I think it's best you run along now," said Shasta. "I suggest somewhere private where—"

"He was sleeping with her," Logan blurted out. "That woman he brought into the palace. I saw him sleeping with her." He paused, biting down on his lip. "I heard them."

Shasta placed a comforting hand on the boy's shoulder. "I'm so sorry you had to learn this way."

"It doesn't matter. I know this isn't the first time." Tears welled in his eyes. "I thought if I had proof," he reached into his pocket and pulled out an onyx bracelet decorated with sapphires and rubies, "then I could tell Mother and she would believe me."

"Your mother already knows."

"What?!"

"Your parents married for politics, not love. This was part of their agreement."

"But... Does Mother..."

"No. Her Majesty has remained faithful to her vows."

"Then why does she allow him to do this?"

"I was not present when the agreement was made, so I can't say." She placed her arm around his thin shoulders. "Run along now. You're too young to trouble yourself with these matters." Shasta opened the door. Looking both ways, Logan dashed down the hallway, running in the opposite direction as his father.

Realta blinked and found herself in bed. Rain pounded against the windows. Lightning flashes illuminated the small room.

She sat up, contemplating the dream. This one felt real, same as the others. And just like the others, she could not interact with the environment. Though it did involve people she knew. People she could question. That woman in Alhyrst confirmed she was a Thane, but not which kind. Did some Thanes have odd dreams? There was only one way to find out.

Pushing back the covers, Realta donned a simple house robe over her nightgown and headed down the hall. Every third lamp was lit for the night, and the lightning flashes helped guide her way. All the servants lived in the same wing on the palace's second floor. Mistress Cray said that Realta could come to her at any time if she needed help. She hoped the middle of the night counted as 'any time'.

Dread seized Realta as heavy footsteps sounded behind her with the same horrible echo as her dream. She spun around and came face to face with Dane Kanton. He gave her a wicked smile.

"Awfully late to be up and about, isn't it?" he asked, looming over her. The lightning highlighted the scarred half of his face. Realta, heart beating in her throat, stumbled backwards.

"Is there something wrong?" Kanton sneered. "Don't like the face your father gave me?" He rounded on her, pining her against the wall. She opened her mouth to cry out, but her throat constricted like a vise. No sound escaped. "You know, it wasn't just my face your father ruined. The scars are on my chest, my back, all the way up my arm." He leaned closer with every word. "I haven't been able to properly hold a sword since that night. The healers claim the fire scarred my muscles, too. Did you know that fire could do that?"

Realta shook her head, too afraid to speak but afraid of what Kanton would do if she didn't respond.

Kanton smiled. "I try not to worry about that, though. Your father will get exactly what he deserves once I find him. Just like your little friend Charity."

"No!" Realta screamed, pushing against him. It was like pushing a wall.

The man laughed. "Oh, does that upset you, you little bitch?"

"What is the meaning of this?"

Realta peered around Kanton, looking for the voice's owner. Shasta Cray stood in the doorway of her rooms, holding a lantern. Several other doors opened, wanting to know the source of the outcry.

"Mistress Cray," said Kanton, turning and folding his hands behind his back. Realta noticed a knife attached to his belt. No doubt the same one he used to stab Callum. Was he going to stab her, too? "A fine evening, isn't it?"

"Hardly. What are you doing here?"

"Making my nightly rounds, that's all."

"Nightly guard duty has never been a job for Guard Captains."

"The king and queen insisted. You can never be too sure these days." A handful of servants muttered to each other. Realta heard one mention Serena's name.

"I'm sure. Is there something you need, Realta?"

Realta's tongue stuck to the roof of her mouth. The words were there, but they refused to form.

"Did the storm wake you?"

"Yes," she managed to say.

"Why don't I make you a cup of tea while Captain Kanton continues his rounds?"

"Yes. Thank you." Realta scurried away from Kanton and entered the safety of Shasta Cray's rooms. Safety in numbers, as always.

"I appreciate your vigilance, Captain Kanton," Shasta said as she closed the door, sliding the bolt lock into place. Realta stood next to the door, muscles tense and ears open. Half a minute passed. Heavy footsteps moved away from the door, fading. The tension rushed out of her.

"Please, take a seat, child." Shasta walked towards the back of the room, a much larger room than the one Realta slept in. It was more akin to a parlor with a fireplace, dining table, and a short bookcase with houseplants on the top.

Realta took a seat at the table, facing the window. Thunder roared outside, shaking the windowpane. Rain streaked the glass. The flashing lightning revealed a mass of black clouds. The storm was far from over.

Shasta placed a kettle on the fire and sat next to Realta, her dark eyes taking in every ounce of information.

"Did he try to force himself onto you?"

"What?" Realta jumped.

Shasta Cray silently waited for an answer.

Realta fidgeted, her face growing uncomfortably warm. "No. Not in that way, I mean."

"In what way, then?"

"He, um..." How could she explain? "He got those scars on his face from fighting my father. He fell into a fire. So, he blames Father. And me, I guess."

"That behavior is not unheard of, not in his case. Why were you out of your room, child?"

"I was looking for you." A piece clicked in her head. That door had been locked every night at curfew. Who had unlocked it? She turned away from Shasta, trembling, her mind racing.

"For what reason?"

"I had a question about the king and his father."

"At this hour?"

Realta shrugged. How could she explain this without sounding insane?

"Very well." She folded her hands patiently. "Ask your question."

"Was the late king mean to King Logan when he was younger? I mean, did he hurt him?"

Shasta was silent for a moment, contemplating the words. "That is a very interesting question, child. What prompted it?"

"King Logan doesn't get along with Serena. Did the king favor her over his legitimate children?"

"Not in any way. In fact, Yestyn denied the girl was his, despite her mother's claims and the fact that she is his spitting image."

"Just like King Logan?"

"All of Yestyn's children resemble him, save for Logan's true sister. She takes after their mother. But you still haven't told me what prompted your first question."

Should she say it now? This was the only way to determine if her dreams were true. "Logan used to spy on Yestyn when he was a boy. He caught his father sleeping with another woman. And you helped him hide."

Shasta leapt to her feet, knocking over the chair. Her eyes were narrow slits. "Who told you that?"

"Logan wanted proof," she forced herself to continue, voice trembling, "so he stole the woman's bracelet. It had rubies and sapphires. He was afraid that his father would beat him if he was caught. And you knew Yestyn would, that's why you lied and said you hadn't seen him."

The tea kettle whistled. Shasta moved to take it off the fire, placing it on a metal cooling plate. A few silent minutes passed, the rain pelting the window and streaking down. Shasta finally asked, "Who told you this? Was it Serena?"

"No one told me." *Say it! You will never know if you keep quiet!* "I saw it in my dream."

That curious look returned to Shasta's eyes. "Would you mind repeating that?"

Realta tried to swallow the lump in her throat, but it was too dry. "I saw it in my dream. The one I had just before I woke up. I..."

"Prove it. How old was he when it happened?"

"Maybe ten. He wasn't dressed like a prince." Realta recalled all the times she had seen Morgan and Mannix. Both boys wore tailored clothing of fine material. And she had never seen them in the same outfit twice.

Shasta sat down at the table, the tea forgotten. "He was twelve, actually. He'd always been small for his age." She shook her head. "But someone must have told you this."

"No, ma'am." Realta lowered her head. "When we were in Al-hyrst, there was a woman who said I was a Thane. But she didn't know which kind. She signed a document stating the fact, but Kanton burned it along with my father's rite of passage."

"Alhyrst," Shasta tested the word. "Where would that be?"

"About a day's journey from East Bridge. The woman's name was Donna."

Shasta went over to the bookshelf and selected a volume. Placing the book on the table, she turned to a very detailed map of Teyrnas. Alhyrst was the first village on the Teyrnas Highway. Another page showed a map of the village itself along with population records.

She returned to the shelf for another book, this one bound in leather with yellowed pages. Thunder continued to roar as Shasta searched for the right page.

Realta suddenly regretted telling her. It was a perfect lie. No one could prove or deny what a person saw in their dreams. Or that she was a Thane. Shasta could deny it and Realta could assert it was the truth all day and neither would get anywhere.

"Apparently," Shasta said slowly, "there was a variant of Thanes who could see the past in their dreams." She locked eyes with Realta. "But the last known Dreamer died two hundred and fifty years ago."

An invisible weight pressed down on Realta, threatening to crush her. "What?"

"That is what the text reads. Now, if you are being truthful, I can send for a Cuchasi to test you. Logan doesn't like having them around the palace, so it will take some time and planning. You are being truthful, aren't you, child?"

"Yes, ma'am. I promise." The dreams were real. Glimpses into the past.

Shasta placed a cup in front of her and poured the tea. Steam rose into the air. The thunder had reduced to a light rumble. Most of the rain had stopped.

"And you are certain that the boy in your dream was King Logan?" she asked, pouring a cup for herself.

"He looked just like him."

"Yes, but all of Yestyn's children save for Lady Sarra resemble him."

"Are you saying it was his brother?" The name Sarra stirred something in Realta's mind, something buried deep in her memory that slowly rose to the surface.

"I remember the incident quite clearly. It wasn't Logan who spied on his father. It was his older brother. Prince Carwyn."

"Older brother? Then shouldn't he be king?"

Shasta let out a pained sigh. "Carwyn would be king, if he had lived."

Phantom screams echoed in Realta's ears. A room with gray stone walls, identical to the ones in the palace. A young woman asking after her sick brother. A man screaming in pain, in an unspeakable sorrow. The young woman's mother calling her, calling Sarra, to stop. Don't go in that room. Carwyn had been badly injured.

"The king beat him to death," Realta whispered.

"Another dream?" Shasta guessed.

Realta nodded, numb. The dream that had awakened her in Lothian, the reason they were still alive. The other woman had been named Shasta. Realta wanted to kick herself for not realizing it sooner.

"Officially, Prince Carwyn died of a wasting disease. A convenient way to avoid an open casket funeral. Carwyn had discovered that Serena was Yestyn's child and went to confront him. To say Yestyn lost his temper is an understatement. The man was a powerful Manipulator, able to move objects far larger than himself and much faster than throwing them. Carwyn never stood a chance. By the time Yestyn was through with him, he no longer looked human. The healers did what they could, but he'd lost too much blood. He died the next day."

"Did anyone tell the guards, or a magistrate?"

"What good would that do? It was the word of the king versus a dead man. Everyone did what was best and kept silent on the matter."

"Is that why Logan hates Serena?"

"Unfortunately, yes. He believes that if Carwyn hadn't confronted Yestyn with the truth, the late king would never have killed him."

Realta stared into her tea, feeling very tired.

"Does your father know of your ability?" Shasta asked, taking a small sip of tea.

"He knows I'm a Thane, but not which kind."

"I will inform him in the morning."

"You will?" Realta sat up straighter. "Where is he? Is he all right?"

"Yes. Logan is a good man, though it takes a trained eye to see it. The prisoners are always well cared for."

"When can I see him?" Hearing that Callum was well wasn't enough. She needed visual proof.

"I will speak with Logan and Isla. Now," Shasta folded her hands on top of the table, "what else did you see in that dream?"

"The dream ended with you telling Logan, I mean Carwyn, to run along and not spy on his father anymore. Was he much older than Logan?"

"They were only thirteen months apart and very close growing up. Carwyn had difficulty breathing at birth. The healers told Yestyn and Owena that he was unlikely to survive infancy and they should make a new heir as soon as possible. Carwyn survived his first year, much to Yestyn's disappointment. He wanted his firstborn to be strong.

"So Yestyn took a greater interest in his second born, instructing Logan in politics and economics, all the things he should have taught Carwyn. It was no surprise that Carwyn's interests leaned towards medicine and natural science, and his mother's heritage."

"She wasn't Teyrnian?" Realta asked.

"Not entirely. Her mother had been Hiraethi. Carwyn always felt closer to that aspect of himself. Even changed his name and claimed to be Hiraethi when he attended the Academy." Shasta shook her head, smiling ruefully. "Yestyn was furious, but Logan behaved himself and that was his main concern.

"The one thing that stood in the way of Yestyn's fantasy was the law. Carwyn was his firstborn and was set to inherit the throne. Yestyn decided the best way to prepare Carwyn was through an arranged marriage to King Nolfri of Byyar's second daughter. Byyar has long been Teyrnas' ally and Princess Isla had been tutored in politics ever since she was old enough to read and write. If need be, she could be the real power behind the throne. One problem stood in the way. Carwyn had fallen in love with a young woman at the Academy, had brought her to the palace to meet the family. And when Yestyn discovered that Carwyn had gotten her pregnant..." Shasta closed her eyes, taking deep, steady breaths. "Confronting Yestyn about Serena was not the only thing that got Carwyn killed."

"What happened to her?" A part of Realta was afraid to ask.

"We got her out of the city. I don't know what became of her after."

"But what about their child? Would it—"

"She lost it when she heard that Carwyn was dead. After the funeral, Isla's engagement was transferred to Logan. Yestyn refused to let a deal that good go to waste. Though he did have the sense to wait a few months. I don't think Logan ever properly grieved his brother. Sarra and Mal were still at the Academy, still had something to keep their minds busy."

"Do you know why Serena stabbed her brother?" Realta ventured to ask.

Shasta grew silent, staring into her tea. Realta wondered if she had asked one question too many. Finally, Shasta said, "Serena was well cared for by Logan and Isla once they learned the truth. But Logan had no room in his heart for the girl. Every time she tried to get close to him, Logan pushed her away. She was too young to understand his pain.

"When she was about thirteen, Serena started asking questions. She heard rumors about Yestyn's extramarital affairs and women claiming he fathered their children. Then she heard a rumor that the old king had sent his bastard children through Caman's Pass, to the kingdom of Lowyrn where they would not be his problem. She grew convinced the rumor was true and planned to find her siblings."

"Was it?"

"Including Serena, Yestyn fathered at least three bastards. I have no doubt there are others. But as for the rumor," Shasta shrugged, "who can say. Serena could not be talked out of it, so we collected some money and helped plan her escape. We genuinely saw no harm in it. The girl had no place in the royal court. Logan had made certain of that. Why not let her find a new life?"

She let out a deep sigh. "Logan discovered the plan. He confronted Serena, tried to reason with her. The two of them fought. Serena stabbed him in the chest. We don't know if she intended on killing him. No one can pry the truth out of her. But the deed was done. Serena ran away. We never expected to see her again."

"But the king and queen sent Kanton after her."

"Yes, they did."

The room lapsed into silence. The outside world was quiet, save for the occasional raindrop falling from the windowsill.

Realta wondered if she should ask more. She decided against it. Shasta looked tired. She ought to be grateful for the information this woman had given her, and for giving her the benefit of the doubt in the first place. This conversation could have easily taken a turn for the worse.

"We still have a few hours before morning," Shasta said. "You should try to get some sleep."

"Yes, ma'am." Realta rose from her seat. "Thank you for the tea. And for believing me," she added.

"Think nothing of it, child. It's been so long since I've talked about Carwyn. He was a good man. But if I were you, I would not go about telling others those dreams. Logan is quite sensitive about his brother," she added.

"I understand." Realta peered out the door. The hallway was clear, no signs of Kanton or any other guards. She quietly slipped out and ran all the way to her room. Just to be safe.

27

The Storm

Charity shoved her head underneath her pillow, trying to deafen the sound of rain pounding against the window. She had always been a light sleeper, and the storm wasn't doing her any favors. The pounding came again, this time sharper and more regular. Knocking. Who in their right mind...?

More knocking.

Letting out an exasperated sigh, Charity threw off the blankets and donned her cloak, noting that her roommate was fast sleep. Some people had all the luck.

The dim light from the hall lanterns revealed Jaim, fully dressed and wearing an oiled cloak.

"Is everything all right?" she asked him.

"Well, it's just that..." His hands reached for his pockets. He quickly clasped both hands behind his back and rocked back and forth on the ball of his feet. "You see, Scholar Maryn is my mentor, and she invited a bunch of us to observe the storm with her. Up on the roof. She's got this new gadget that measures wind speed and all that. I was wondering if you'd like to watch, too?"

The offer took Charity aback. It was close to midnight. And going out on the roof in the pouring rain? She'd be soaked in seconds! It was the type of thing she had always tried getting away with at home.

"I'd love to watch. Give me a moment."

"I'll be here." Jaim reaching into his pocket and took out four coins. Light glittered off the coins as they spun in his open palm.

Charity closed the door and quickly exchanged her nightgown for her dress and boots. Her Student cloak was not oiled like Jaim's, but it would do. Clothing was made to be dried. She slipped into the hallway.

"Are any of the others coming?" she asked as Jaim led her up a narrow staircase.

"Nah. The sisters were both asleep. Ivar's too busy studying. Can you believe that? Here we are at the stroke of midnight and that man is still at the books. Bloody Madani work ethic! Anyway, Zandon said no, and Lok was sleeping. Not that I blame him. This must have been the biggest day of his life."

"So, just you and me?" Charity gave him a coy smile.

Jaim blushed. "And Scholar Maryn and some of her Students and Journeymen. Not like I go about asking pretty girls to spend an evening up on the bloody roof."

"You really think I'm pretty?"

The blush darkened. "Fire and smoke. No, it's just... No, I mean yes. You know what I mean."

"Not really, but I appreciate the complement."

Jaim smiled and held his tongue until they reached a terraced portion of the roof adjacent to the fourth floor. The door was propped open by a brick. Gusts of wind blew in rain, forming a large puddle on the stone floor. She and Jaim stepped outside.

The wind ripped at Charity's cloak, rain swirling all around her. Lightning flashed overhead, creating shadows in the dense clouds. Her heart raced, exhilarating her. She had never been out in a storm this powerful. Neither had she been up this high. How tall was this part of the Academy? Forty feet, at least.

"Over there!" Jaim yelled against the wind. His oiled cloak flapped behind him, leaving his clothes drenched. So much for the added precaution.

Charity glanced to the side and saw several figures standing around a tall metal device. At six feet in height, the device rested on three legs, equally spaced apart. At the top was a small metal bar, spinning wildly in the wind. Underneath that, in an open section, was a gadget that resembled a clock. It ticked off in tandem with the spinning, metal bar.

"Keep an eye on that reading, Sawel," said Scholar Maryn, her figure hidden beneath a rain soaked, white cloak, the gold trim reflected by the lightning. "Accuracy is everything."

"Yes, Scholar." Sawel, who appeared to be a good five years older than Charity, focused his attention on the device. The gray cloak labeled him a Journeyman.

Lightning flashed. A young woman counted off. "One, two, three, four—"

Thunder roared. Another Journeyman, facing away from the wind and rain and protected by oiled cloaks sewn together, wrote the number in a logbook.

"The flashes are growing closer, Scholar Maryn," said the young woman.

"Wonderful, Lona. How are those notes, Eoin?"

"Kinda wet, but legible."

Scholar Maryn turned towards Charity and Jaim. "Is this all, Jaim?"

"Yes, Scholar. Was I supposed to bring more?"

Charity spied half a dozen others, both Journeymen and Students, standing off to the side, talking and observing the storm.

"One is better than none. You're the Elemental's friend, aren't you? Charity Loy?"

"Yes, ma'am. I mean, Scholar."

"Glad to have you here. Wait a moment." She glanced around at the faces. "Jaim, you didn't fetch Shari?"

"She wasn't in her room."

"Oh well. She can look over the notes in the morning. Come along. The best view is over here."

Charity and Jaim followed the Scholar towards the small cluster of people. They stood along the chest-high railing, at the very edge of the rooftop. Charity found a space and stood between Jaim and Scholar Maryn.

"What are you studying?" Charity asked her.

"Weather patterns." Scholar Maryn had to yell. The winds picked up speed, threatening to tear away Charity's cloak. She gripped it with one hand and held onto the railing with the other. It was truly amazing. She could see the whole campus and the trees growing beyond that wall. Small lights flickered in the neighboring city of Norgard and the Garrison. Near the horizon, she could just make out the River Wallach. She felt like she was flying.

"Most storms in Alet," Scholar Maryn explained, "are mild and occur during the day. Typically, we don't see storms of this magnitude until summer."

"What's causing it?" Charity had never questioned what caused storms. They simply were. A force of nature beyond human comprehension.

"We're not sure. See the direction the wind is coming from? Due west, from the other side of the Nerin. Normally, storms from the west are mild. The mountains don't allow them much time to form. Now storms from the east, those can be quite strong."

Lightning flashed again. Lona only got to two before the thunder roared. The booming echo shook Charity's bones. The group cheered save for one Journeyman. Groaning, he reached into his pocket and handed a copper mark to a Student. She smiled and asked if he wanted to bet again. He declined.

"They could move storms," Jaim whispered.

"What?"

Jaim jolted, surprised that Charity had heard him. "Nothing. Just thinking. They say that Manipulators during the Thousand Years War could move storms. Force them to their wills. Just a story, though."

"All stories begin somewhere, Jaim," Scholar Maryn replied.

"What do the stories say about Elementals?" Charity asked her.

"That the four elements truly belonged to them. Rivers diverted at their feet. Storms obeyed them. Fires the size of cities were snuffed out with the snap of a finger. Your friend is descended from greatness."

"And you're a Manipulator, too, right?" She noted the gold trim on the scholar's cloak, as well as her earrings. The same shade as Jaim's sole one.

"Yes. Only a little more powerful than Jaim. I can take apart that device," she pointed to the contraption measuring the wind, "with my mind and move the pieces simultaneously. But I can't move it as a whole. It weights far too much."

"That amazing."

Another bolt of lightning scored the sky. Five seconds passed before the thunder roared. The winds slowed as the rain reduced to a handful of drops. Some Students, Jaim included, complained. They had expected the storm to last all night.

"How much longer, Scholar?" asked Sawel. The bar's speed had reduced dramatically.

Scholar Maryn studied the wind and rain for a moment. "Give

it a few more minutes. Until the rain stops."

The Students and Journeymen not directly involved with the project bid the Scholar goodnight as they exited the rooftop, shaking the water from their cloaks and hair. The Scholar returned the sentiment and looked out at the night sky. Lightning. Ten seconds passed. The thunder was nothing but a rumble.

"Scholar Maryn, you're Jaim's mentor. What exactly does that mean?" Her own mentor, Scholar Roseen, informed her that they only had to meet once a week to review her progress. Nothing more. Nothing like this.

"It means she uses me as a lackey." Jaim smirked.

The Scholar smiled. "In terms of mentors, Jaim has two. Scholar Tell is his academic mentor, since his focus is on martial arts. So long as his interests don't change to, say, nature science."

Jaim rolled his eyes.

"I'm his Thane mentor. As well as Eoin's. He's a Manipulator, too. And I also serve as his, Sawel, Lona, and Shari's academic mentor."

"Then where does that leave Lok?"

"In an unfortunate position, I'm afraid." She sighed. "The Council was wise in selecting Kuno as his mentor. Though he has no Thane abilities, Kuno is the foremost authority on ancient Thanes. He's accomplished so much, despite his youth. Lok is in good hands, Charity."

Youth was not a word Charity would use to describe a man in his late forties. But Kuno always seemed eager and energetic.

"Will my mentor ever allow me to help with projects?"

"It depends. Your mentor is Scholar Roseen, right?"

She nodded.

"Perhaps in your third or fourth year. Roseen is very guarded about her projects. She only allows the best students to help."

"I see." That was disappointing.

"Scholar," said Sawel, "the wind stopped."

Scholar Maryn approached the device. The metal bar was perfectly still. "Excellent. Time to pack up."

"Can I help? Or at least watch?" Charity asked.

"Of course. Jaim, a hand, please?"

Jaim sauntered over to the device. Along with Sawel, he and the Scholar mentally disconnected each piece of the device, moving their hands in tandem. The various parts floated gently onto the rooftop. The metal bar, the clock-like mechanism. The three legs folded into themselves, shortening the device in half. In a matter of seconds, the job was done. Charity watched in awe.

***

Lok tossed and turned on his bed, thunder roaring as wind and rain pounded against the room's sole window. Sleep fled from him. The room was far too hot. His body felt like it was directly underneath the sun.

He sat up in bed, placing a hand on his new earring, the only thing that indicated that today's events had been real instead of some fantastical dream. Feeling the metallic smoothness, Lok also felt something wet.

Pulling his hand away, Lok inspected it in the flashes of light. The liquid was dark and sticky. He touched his ear again. Blood. Spinning around, Lok saw a large, dark stain on his pillow. More blood. How long had he been bleeding?

Lok, heart pounding, rushed out of his room. His knees almost buckled. He steadied himself against the door frame. The hallway spun around and around, the floor and ceiling alternating their positions. He blinked until his vision returned to normal.

It's really hot in the hallway, too.

No. The heat was coming from within him. He was running a fever. He was bleeding and running a high fever.

Help. He had to get help. His mother had always kept herbs in order to avoid going to Healer Zall. The man was truly insane! What about the healers at the Academy? A place this big with so many people had to have an infirmary of some sorts.

But where?

A single name came to mind. Kuno. The Scholar ought to know.

Yes, Scholar Kuno. I have to get to Scholar Kuno.

The Scholars' quarters were on the third floor, in the wing opposite the Students' dorms. Thankfully, he would not have to brave any stairs in his condition.

Bracing himself, Lok headed down the hallway, keeping one hand on the wall and leaning on side tables whenever they were available. He'd have fallen flat on his face a dozen times without those. Lok racked his brain. How had he gotten sick? The bleeding ear was obvious. He had either slept on the piercing or tried to pull it out in his sleep. The fever was another matter.

The last time he was sick, Lok had been fifteen. A wave of summer flu had struck the village, Lok and his mother included. His mother had fared much better. She was only sick for two days. Lok had spent nearly a week in bed. In fact, he had felt the same as he did now. Arms and legs weak. Vision blurry. A fever that threatened to burn him from the inside out.

Remember, Scholar Kuno had said, *if you ever need me, I'll be in my rooms. The door number is twenty-seven.*

By some miracle, Lok found himself standing in front of door number twenty-seven. Thunder and lightning continued to rage around the building. He knocked on the door.

Inside, he heard voices. Someone mentioned the storm.

No! It's not the storm. It's me!

Lok knocked again with both fists, surprised he had the strength to manage the fete. Voices. The sound of a bed creaking. Footsteps walking towards the door. It opened a hair. Scholar Kuno poked his head out, his hair all messy and a confused look on his face.

"Who is it?" asked a female voice.

"Lok Tolman," the Scholar replied. "What is it, Lok? Something..." Kuno's eyes grew wide, filled with horror. Was there really that much blood? "Fire and smoke! One moment, wait!" Kuno slammed the door shut. Yeah, there was probably a lot of blood. Gray clouds swarmed in front of his eyes. He blinked them away.

Where was he? This hallway looked different from the one in the Students' wing. Number twenty-seven on the door. Oh, right.

The door opened once more. Scholar Kuno wore his white cloak over a pair of trousers. Apparently, he could not find a shirt.

"Where are you going?" asked the young woman in the Scholar's bed. She had flowing blonde hair, and the blanket barely covered her naked breasts.

"Sorry, Shari. I'll make it up to you, I swear."

"But what on Eltriar—"

Kuno grabbed Lok by the shoulders and pivoted him so that Shari could see the bloody ear.

"Oh, Creator..."

Without another word, Kuno slammed the door and hurried Lok down the hallway. Funny, that hallway seemed a lot longer than it did a minute ago. As though it went on into eternity.

"When did the bleeding start?" Kuno asked.

Lok reached for his notebook and pencil, but they weren't there. He was clad in only his undershorts and a sleeping shirt.

"I'll find you a pen," Kuno muttered, turning around a corner and down a flight of stairs. Lok had never been in this part of the Academy. The infirmary. That's where they were heading. An infirmary with hopefully sane healers.

The infirmary was not an infirmary. It was a small kitchen adjacent to the real infirmary. Rows of cabinets lined the walls, and there was a sink with a water pump. The larger, neighboring space was dark and silent. Lightning flashes again, but not as intense as earlier. Kuno instructed him to sit in a chair as he lit a candle. Lok did not object. His legs were very weak, as though they no longer contained bones.

"Where is it?" Kuno muttered as he rummaged through a cabinet. "Lok, you'll have to nod and shake your head until I can find some paper. Did the ear start bleeding in your sleep?" The Scholar gave him an odd look. "Lok?" He walked over and placed a hand on Lok's forehead. He muttered a curse and searched through another cabinet.

Lok was surprised at how thin Kuno was. He could count every single one of the scholar's ribs. He bet he could do the same with the scholar's spine if he wasn't wearing a cloak. Why was he just wearing trousers and a cloak? And why was there a naked woman in his bed?

Oh...

"Here, drink this. It will reduce the fever." The Scholar handed him a drink. It looked like cold tea and had a bitter smell. Lok drank it anyway, grimacing.

Kuno pulled up a chair and sat down, pressing a wet cloth to Lok's ear. The fabric was instantly stained red. Lok did not feel any pain. Should he be in pain?

"Sorry about this," Kuno said, exchanging the bloodied cloth for a clean one. "Sometimes new piercings bleed. We should have told you to sleep on your left side. Remember to do that for the next few nights, okay?"

Lok nodded. The gray clouds swam in again but dissipated much quicker this time. The room no longer spun. He took another sip of the bitter tasting medicine.

"You noticed the bleeding when you woke up?"

Lok nodded.

"It's a good thing you did. Blood loss isn't something to take lightly." He inspected the cloth. "There, it's almost stopped. Are you done with that medicine?"

Lok handed him an empty cup.

"Great. Hold this cloth to your ear."

Lok obeyed. The Scholar stepped out of the room. Lok stared at the single candle, the shadows dancing on the walls. He focused, and the flame pulsed in tandem with his heartbeat. Slow and steady. He smiled.

Scholar Kuno returned with a sheet of paper and a pencil. Relief flooded him.

"Now," said Kuno, resuming his seat, "did you see a lot of blood on your pillow?"

"Yes," Lok wrote, struggling to hold the pencil properly. *"A lot of it."*

"I was afraid of that," Kuno sighed, pulling his cloak around himself. Lok spied an odd, white scar on the Scholar's chest, right in the center. "I will inform the head healer in the morning. He'll need to check you out. Did you experience any symptoms other than a fever?"

"Yes. Dizziness and my legs and arms felt weak."

"Probably a mild infection from the piercing. It's rare, but it happens. Sorry you had to be one of those rare cases."

"It's okay. I feel a lot better now."

"Good. Do you want me to help you back to your room?"

"In a moment. I want to rest some more."

Kuno nodded. "No problem. Take your time."

Lok hesitated before writing. *"Who is Shari?"*

A thin smile appeared on the Scholar's face. "Shari is someone who is very special to me. And I'm special to her. If you don't mind, Lok, don't tell anyone we were together. Scholars, the unmarried ones, are expected to be devoted to their work. People will get the wrong idea."

"*Why don't you marry her, then?*"

"It's complicated." The Scholar leaned back in his chair, staring at the blank wall.

Lok listened to the silence. Silence. The rain had stopped. A thought occurred to him.

"*Can Elementals control more than one element?*"

"Supposedly." Kuno's dark eyes brightened, happy for the subject change. "Elementals during the War had complete control over all four elements. Why, Faryna could control the storms as easily as you and I can breathe. She truly was a sight to behold. According to the histories, say," he added, reining himself in.

"*Who was Faryna?*"

"You really don't know?" Kuno raised an eyebrow.

Lok shook his head.

"She was one of the Nine Summit Thanes who ended the War against the Midnight King, handpicked by the Gadyeni themselves. She and the others fought the Midnight King and his armies for ten years before he was defeated. And the Cycle claims she was only nineteen when she was chosen. A spindly, little priestess who would have rather spent her days in a monastery than fight in a war. But the Gadyeni knew what they were doing. They won the War, after all."

"*What cycle?*"

"The Gadyeni Cycle. It's the technical term for the documents written during the Thousand Years War. Many prophesied the arrival of the Nine and the Midnight King's defeat with accurate detail." He smirked. "Well, the accuracy is debatable. It's a large part of my work, the thing that inspired me to be a historian when I was no older than you."

"*Can I read it?*"

Kuno smiled. "Of course you can. Any time you want, the documents will be available. How do you feel now?"

"*Much better.*"

"Enough to return to your room? You wouldn't want to stay up all night."

Lok nodded. Some of the strength had returned to his legs. With the Scholar's help, he made his way back to the dorms.

28

Points on a Compass

The ten-day period in which Logan could keep them prisoner had nearly expired by the time Realta was allowed to see her father. Shasta Cray gave her the good news during her morning chores.

"Can I see him now?" Realta asked, abandoning the stack of fresh laundry. The kitchens turned out to be a bad place for her. Queen Isla always tread lightly around her, and Serena tended to roam around there. She refused to talk to Realta, running away the moment they made eye contact. Realta wanted to the mad at her but found it more difficult the more she saw the way the royal family acted around the girl. Isla's polite avoidance and Logan's indifference. She wondered if Serena planned on running away again.

"Finish that laundry first," Shasta replied.

Realta did as instructed, folding the clothes neatly and forcing herself not to rush. Doing a job poorly meant doing it twice. Mistress Loy had taught her that. How could she have taken such a wonderful and loving person for granted?

The laundry folded, Realta joined Shasta in the hall. Shasta led her up a flight of stairs.

"I thought the dungeons were underground," Realta said. They were always located underneath the palace in stories.

"They are. But the queen requested that your father be moved to a more accommodating suite. She and the king are expecting many guests in the coming days. It would not look good to have a possibly innocent man imprisoned."

"He believes us?" Realta's heart lightened.

"He is leaning in that direction. Perhaps he will pardon your father on the twenty-ninth. He tries to do a good deed on his brother's birthday."

Right, the king's yearly exhibition, held in honor of his late brother Carwyn, was on the twenty-ninth. It would take days to prepare everything. She had to help with the guest rooms this afternoon.

Shasta led her into the guest wing. Dozens of servants moved to and fro, carrying fresh linens and other supplies. They walked towards a door near the end of the hall. Shasta knocked twice. Callum's voice told her to enter.

Tears welled in Realta's eyes. Her father's voice!

Shasta stepped back, allowing Realta to enter first. The room was small, but neat and well kept, containing a bed, writing desk, and a wardrobe. The room's sole window allowed bright morning light to illuminate the space. Callum stood in the middle of the room. His hair needed a trim and stuck out at odd angles, and he had the beginnings of a beard. His eyes were hard and suspicious. That hardness faded the moment he saw Realta. Grinning from ear to ear, he held out his arms. She ran to him, getting caught up in his warm embrace.

"Oh, Realta. I'm so sorry."

"It's nobody's fault," she replied, afraid to let go, that he would dissolve away like one of her dreams.

"I should have fought harder for us. If I had known it was just an Illusion..."

Realta looked up at him. "What did the king make you see?" She knew all about Illusions now. Shasta's books contained tons of information on Thanes, specifically Minders, Manipulators, and Learners, the three most common types. Empaths and Far-sights were becoming rarer, while Elementals, Dreamers, and Healers had disappeared centuries ago. Or so it seemed.

When it came to Minders, they could either read minds or create Illusions. Rarely both, and rarely affecting more than one or two people at a time.

Callum let out a pained sigh. "Your mother. Kiana."

"What? How?"

"I don't know," Callum replied, shaking his head. "He must have gleaned her face from my mind, learned what would throw me off kilter." He sighed. "I thought it was her Shade."

"Is he going to let us go?" Realta changed the subject.

"Possibly. Though, walking around with this tattoo will make things difficult." Callum showed her his left wrist. The two diamonds now had diagonal lines within them.

"What does that mean?"

"It marks me as a runaway twice over."

"They gave me tattoos, too." Realta then showed him her wrist. Two diamonds, empty for now.

Callum's eyes burned. He closed them tight, suppressing the anger. "I never wanted this life for you."

"Tattoos can be removed."

A weak smile appeared on his face. "Yes, they can."

"May I interrupt?" asked Shasta, pulling the door closed and locking it.

"Of course," Callum replied.

"You remember our conversation from earlier?"

"How can I forget?"

"What conversation?" Realta asked.

"I had to verify your claims, child. Though that account you gave was very accurate. Still, I had to be sure. Your father's account was identical to yours. Callum Haar, I have good evidence that your daughter is a Dreamer Thane, one who can see the past."

"I still don't understand how," he replied, placing a gentle hand on Realta's shoulder. "No one in my family was Thane."

"What about your wife's family?"

Callum paused. "I... I never asked. Kiana was a merchant's daughter. No noble blood. She never mentioned being related to any Thanes. Then again, she was Lowyrnic. They aren't as strict with identifying Thanes."

"That's a possible avenue to consider. I have arranged for a Cuchasi to meet with Realta within the next day. He knows full well King Logan's resentment for his kind and wants to take every precaution. I will inform you once he arrives."

"So, he'll just sneak into the palace?" Callum asked, not convinced. Realta also had her doubts. Guards patrolled the palace grounds around the clock, with men stationed on the walls and at each gate.

"People will start arriving at all hours today. It isn't hard to disguise yourself as a servant, especially in a place were few people pay attention to servants."

"The king will let us go if he knows I'm a Thane, right?"

"I have no doubt he will. Mistreating other Thanes violates their oaths. He will ensure you are well compensated. You have my word."

"I want to thank you for all your help," said Callum, walking towards the writing desk. On it sat numerous papers and notes. Many of them drawings. Callum leafed through the pages until he found the right one. He handed it to Shasta. "It's been far too long since I've drawn someone's portrait."

Shasta gasped, placing a hand over her mouth. Realta peered over the shorter woman's shoulder, getting a better look. It was a charcoal drawing of Shasta, face turned in profile. Every detail was perfect. Every hair and line in its proper place. As accurate as a mirror's reflection. Her father had drawn that?

"I don't know what to say," Shasta replied. "When did you have time to draw this? I never posed for a portrait."

"There was no need," Callum explained. "I've a good memory for faces."

Shasta carefully folded the paper and placed it in her pocket. "Thank you, Master Haar."

"I fear that isn't my title," he replied quietly.

"It ought to be."

A knock came at the door.

"Hello? Is anyone in here?" asked a feminine voice.

Shasta unlocked the door. Amzie Fenn stood at the threshold, carrying an armful of clean linens and blankets.

"Oh, Mistress Cray! I hadn't realized this room was occupied. The first guests aren't scheduled to arrive til noon, and..." She froze, her face pale. "Who's this?"

"Amzie Fenn, this is Callum Haar, Realta's father. He's staying at the palace for the time being."

Amzie stared at Callum as though he were a venomous snake, ready to strike.

Placing his left hand behind his back, Callum extended his right. "It's nice to meet you, Mistress Fenn."

"Oh, um..." She quickly shook his hand and drew back. "Amzie is fine. I... Um... I really should be going." With that, she scurried away from the room.

"What's wrong with her?" Callum asked.

"She's prone to nervous fits."

Realta wasn't so sure about that. Amzie only had those 'fits' whenever Realta was around. The woman would be carrying on a conversation or working without incident until her eyes fell on Realta. Stammering and desperately looking for an excuse to leave followed. Every single time.

It's because I look like her dead friend. Surely she knows I'm not a Shade.

"I believe it's time for both of us to return to work, Realta," Shasta announced. "There's much work to be done. I will inform you when the Cuchasi arrives. Be well, Callum Haar. Either I or another will check on you this evening."

"Thank you, Mistress Cray." He placed both of his hands on Realta's shoulders. Hands that could not only break up a fight but also draw beautiful pictures. Why had he hidden that talent?

"You look out for yourself, Realta," he said. "There are a lot of answers I don't have yet. The most important one being when we can return home. Be careful, my dear."

"I will, Father." Realta embraced him, not wanting to let go. How long before she could see him again? Hours? Days?

"Come," said Shasta. "We don't want to keep anyone waiting."

✳✳✳

"Let me look at you!" exclaimed Lady Sarra of House Lyr, the king's younger sister. She and her husband, Lord Darrys O'Lyr, and their two children had arrived at the stroke of noon. Realta immediately recognized her from that first dream, an eerie feeling accompanying it. Their room was on the opposite side of the guest quarters from Callum and was far more lavish, containing a side room and a view of the gardens.

Realta and another servant stood off to the side, having been instructed to wait quietly in case the lord and lady required anything.

King Logan smiled as his sister gave him a quick hug, followed by an inspection.

"Oh, it's good to see you!" he replied. None of the other royal family members were present. Queen Isla was in the Audience

Chamber, ready to receive more guests. Realta had spied a long line of people at the palace gates and courtyard.

"You need to eat," Lady Sarra said, holding him by the chin.

"I'll eat when I'm not busy. Lord Darrys, all is well with you?"

"Yes, Your Majesty." Lord Darrys was of medium height and stood with excellent posture. His dark gray clothing seemed all the more drab compared to the vivid blues and greens in his wife's gown.

"Now, these children can't be Kaden and Shandri. They're much too tall!"

Lady Sarra motioned for her two children to approach the king. "You remember your Uncle Logan, don't you?"

The children, about five and seven years old, nodded and timidly shook the king's hand.

"Remarkable how much Shandri and Lady Sarra resemble the old queen," whispered Imogene, the other servant. Realta noted that both the lady and her daughter had dark brown hair and slightly oval shaped, blue eyes. The boy appeared to be a mixture of the king and Lord Darrys. Light brown hair, but with a sturdy build.

"What of Mal?" asked the king. "Have you heard anything from him?"

"Yeah, I got a letter from him. Three months ago," Lady Sarra added with a huff.

"Well, he does hold the White Seat at the Teyrnas Chapel," Lord Darrys chimed in.

"He's also the brother of two worried siblings."

"I'm sure Malaky will show," replied the king. "Fashionably late as always."

"The king's brother is a chaplain?" Realta whispered.

"He joined the Church shortly after the king's coronation," Imogene explained. "A sign that he did not desire the throne. Lady Sarra's marriage to Lord Darrys was for similar reasons. Lyr is a powerful house, but very loyal. Their decisions show that King Logan's reign cannot be threatened from within House Kelwyn."

That made sense, though Realta could not imagine siblings turning against one another.

A timid knock came at the door.

"Enter," said the king.

A guard poked his head into the room. Seeing the king, he saluted, fist over his heart. He saw the lord and lady and saluted again. He paled, realizing his mistake, and bowed. The guard stood ramrod straight, eyes darting from the king to the lord and lady.

"Yes, Colm?" King Logan prompted him. Colm always acted like a rabbit in a trap.

"Your Majesty," he stammered, "there is a messenger for you in the Audience Chamber."

"Very well. I—"

"He's from Nowan, Your Majesty. Queen Gallia's personal messenger."

The king balled his hands into fists. "Of course that woman would send a messenger today," he muttered. Composing himself, he addressed the guard. "Inform the messenger that I shall meet with him in one hour. I want him to sweat a little."

"Yes, Your Majesty." Colm turned to leave.

"Colm!"

"Yes, Your Majesty?"

"Leave out that last part. Remember what happened last time?"

Colm paled. He about-faced and sprinted down the hall.

"Bloody greenbloods." The king sighed. "I have to go prepare for that. I'll see you for supper?"

"Of course, Your Majesty," replied Lord Darrys.

"Only if you promise to eat double portions."

The king rolled his eyes. "You're worse than Mother."

"Good!" Lady Sarra gave her brother another hug, and the king departed. It was then that her eyes fell on Realta.

Realta's face grew warm as the lady studied her, as though the woman's eyes were miniature suns. The lady furrowed her brow. She turned to her husband, tapping him on the shoulder.

"What?"

Lady Sarra pointed to her forehead. Her husband nodded. The room grew silent save for the two young children exploring the room. Shandri opened the wardrobe and then dashed off to the adjacent room. Kaden jumped on the lavish bed.

"What's going on?" Realta asked.

"Lord and Lady Lyr are Minder Thanes. See the earrings?"

Realta glanced at them. Lord Darrys wore silver earrings while Lady Sarra wore purple and silver. She was an Empath as well. Most Empaths instinctively knew other people's emotions. Even the best card player's face could not fool them.

"Are they using Illusions?"

"No. The king can use Illusions, but the lord and lady use Linking. Speaking with their thoughts."

Illusions. Linking. So much Realta did not understand. And she understood just as much about her own abilities. She hadn't had any dreams since the storm.

Lord Darrys gasped. He shot a glance at Realta.

Lady Sarra, a warm smile on her face, stepped closer to her, maintaining a comfortable distance. "Hello. What's your name?"

"Realta, my lady," she stammered, giving the lady a clumsy curtsy.

"No last name?"

"I was told not to say. It would be improper."

Lady Sarra smirked. "Well, I'm not exactly proper myself."

"Sarra, let the girl be," said her husband.

Lady Sarra looked in his direction. A silent minute passed. Finally, she nodded, "No matter," she said to Realta. "And you, what's your name?"

"Imogene, my lady."

"Very well. Realta, Imogene, would you mind leaving so my husband and I can freshen up?"

"Not at all, my lady," replied Imogene. Realta repeated the phrase. She exited, grateful to be out from under Lady Sarra's studious gaze.

"Interesting," Imogene whispered.

"What's that?"

"Nothing, just thinking aloud." With that, Imogene hurried down the hall, muttering under her breath.

Realta looked back at the closed door. The only ones talking were the two children. Lord and Lady Lyr were likely continuing their silent conversation. A conversation about her.

Okay, think, Realta. Mistress Cray said you resemble a woman who used to work in the palace, but she died twenty years ago. Lady Sarra, obviously, grew up in the palace. She saw the resemblance, just like Amzie. But why discuss the matter in private with her husband? Why had Lord Darrys acted shocked? Mistress Cray said most nobles don't pay attention to servants. What makes a dead woman so special?

She glanced up and found herself outside the Audience Chamber. A servant escorted a lavishly dressed lord and lady, both with gold earrings, down the hall. More servants hurried about, discussing the upcoming exhibition and all the preparations that still needed to be made. In the corner, a pair of guards played rock, paper, scissors. No one looked at her. Being a servant did have that one benefit. No one noticed her.

"Young miss?"

Her assumptions betrayed her. Realta turned and saw a man standing just outside the Chamber. He was in his early thirties with short, black hair and gray eyes, the same color as a storm cloud. He wore simple black trousers with a gray shirt and a short coat.

"Are you a guest?" Realta asked, a slight tremor in her voice.

"Not exactly," he replied. "You see, I'm here to meet someone." His accent was odd. It wasn't Teyrnian. Nor did it have the sharp, guttural tones of Lowyrnic. Instead, it was smooth, almost musical.

"The king and queen?"

The man smiled. "Actually, I think I'm here to meet you."

Realta gasped. The Cuchasi. She motioned for the man to move into an adjacent hallway, one that did not have a lot of traffic.

"I'm Realta Haar."

"Yes, I know." He smiled warmly. "My name is Valentin. You can call me Val."

"So, is it true? Am I really a Thane?"

"Yes, a Dreamer Thane." He paused, studying her. She really wished people would stop doing that. But this man was a Cuchasi. It was part of the job. "A very powerful Dreamer." Val shook his head. "All this time, we thought Dreamers had gone the way of the sky draig, lost to us for all eternity. But fate brought me to you. Just like fate placed me in Queen Gallia's employment."

Realta started. "Queen Gallia?"

Val gave her a curious smile. "Why, yes. Who did you think

I was?"

"I thought..." Oh dear, how big of a mistake did she just make? "I thought..."

"Oh, you thought I was a Cuchasi. No, just a low-level Minder with a knack for finding other Thanes, like you, Realta. But please don't mention my gift to anyone. The Nowani have all but banned Thanes, thinking we wish to conquer normal humans. Such foolishness. You'll keep my secret, won't you, Realta?"

She nodded. A part of her felt sick. Granted, this man never claimed to be a Cuchasi. She had just assumed. And Val was not wearing earrings.

"Thank you, Realta. Now, I must prepare for my meeting with King Logan. The guard said I have an hour. King Logan wants me to sweat a bit." Val laughed. "The poor boy nearly fainted dead away, letting that slip. I'm here at the palace for the next half week. Will I see you again?"

"I guess." Realta felt a sudden urge to run away, to find Shasta and tell her about her mistake. No, that was too rash. She had promised to keep Val's secret. Why wouldn't he keep hers?

"I look forward to it." He shook Realta's hand. His eyes fell on her wrist. He inspected the tattoo, frowning. "You're a slave?"

"Um... Yes, a servant. But it's not permanent. King Logan might free me and my father soon."

Val sighed and let go of Realta's wrist. "And here I thought things were different in the Vogel Kingdoms."

"They have indentured servants in Nowan, too?" As far as Realta knew, the practice was common throughout the Northern Realm, the details varying from kingdom to kingdom.

Val nodded. "You've given me some interesting things to think about, Realta. Remember this, you and I are two points on a compass. Our fates are sealed."

"I don't understand." A compass?

"You will, in time. Farewell, Realta Haar." Val gave her a short bow and entered the Audience Chamber, leaving her with her thoughts.

29

No More Lies

Serena watched as Queen Gallia's messenger entered the Audience Chamber. The man muttered to himself, too faintly for Serena to hear from her hiding place just behind the thrones, a small alcove used by the guards in case an assassin made his or her way in. The chamber was empty, save for Serena and the messenger.

"Two of the Nine in one place," the man said, pacing closer to the thrones. "The time is near. But I never expected it to be so soon. She's just a girl, no older than fifteen."

Who is he talking about? Serena wondered. One of the servants, or maybe a member of some nobleman's entourage? She'd listen in on the servants this evening. News, especially odd news, traveled fast in the palace.

The Audience Chamber doors opened, causing Serena to flinch. Her brother sauntered towards his throne, the Raven Throne, wearing his customary blue cloak over black clothing. None of the guards accompanied him, which Serena found odd. Then again, this man was from Nowan, a nation often at war with Teyrnas. The presence of guards might be misinterpreted as hostile behavior. Logan stood before the throne and addressed the messenger.

"You may speak."

The messenger, standing a safe distance away, gave the king a curt bow. "Greetings, King Logan. I am Valentin Gardyner, personal messenger of Her Majesty, Queen Gallia Toutain, daughter of His Majesty, the late King Cedric of the Caslanic Kingdom of Nowan."

Serena rolled her eyes. Clearly, this man had never met her brother. Logan didn't need to hear titles and basic facts. Just give him the information and leave.

"I know who you are, and I know who she is. What is your

message?" Logan asked, disdain and impatience dripping with every word.

"For centuries, our two kingdoms—"

"Have been in and out of war," Logan interrupted. "The last war ended thirty years ago when the queen was in her cradle. Am I to conclude that she wants a taste of warfare herself?"

"The opposite, in fact."

Finally. The man had learned directness.

"Explain."

"Queen Gallia is currently en route to Teyrnas and plans to arrive on the twenty-ninth."

"The twenty-ninth. The day of the exhibition. Why am I not surprised?"

"Yes." The man shot a quick glare at Logan. The king's sarcasm had struck a nerve. "She wants for peace between our two kingdoms and wishes to discuss the matter with you in person. If you refuse, then she will return to Nowan without immediate consequences for you and yours. But she is not likely to offer peace negotiations again. Do you accept Her Majesty's offer?"

Logan was silent for a moment. Serena did not blame him. Teyrnas and Nowan had fought countless wars and border skirmishes since the kingdom of Caslan split in two. Each wanting what they believed the other had stolen. Every conflict ended in blood. The few times monarchs on either side offered peace, it had been a trick. A clever way for getting an assassin within striking distance. Serena's grandfather, King Tudur, had lost his life because he had been desperate for peace.

"I will hear her out," replied Logan. "But only after the exhibition, and only with a contingency of guards handpicked by me. Is this acceptable?"

"Your Majesty, it is more than I hoped for," Valentin Gardyner beamed a smile, but the light was not reflected in his eyes. "Your terms are accepted."

Serena felt an irritation inside her nose. Before she could fight it, she sneezed, the sound echoing off the walls of the nearly empty chamber.

Logan spun around and rushed toward the hidden alcove. Serena cringed as the king yanked back the false wall. His eyes were molten daggers.

"What in the name of the Abyss are you doing here?" he demanded, grabbing Serena by the shirt collar and dragged her into the Audience Chamber proper. "You think you can just listen in on private conversations now? Answer me!"

Serena struggled to find a suitable explanation, but she had none. She merely wanted to be alone for a few minutes in a place no one would think to look. She shook her head, averting her eyes.

"Is she yours?" asked Valentin.

The king released his hold on Serena and glared at the messenger. "Excuse me?"

"She looks just like you. A bastard, I take it, based on your treatment."

Logan narrowed his eyes. "The girl isn't mine. She's my father's."

The words made Serena wish she could fade away, never to be seen again.

"My apologizes," replied Val. "So, it is common practice to employ both half and full siblings."

"What are you talking about?"

"The young serving girl, Realta Haar. You have employed both her and her brother." Val turned his attention to Serena. "Young miss, don't you know it's improper to eavesdrop on your betters?"

"Realta Haar doesn't have a brother," Logan replied, confused.

Val raised an eyebrow. "Are you certain? I saw a young man in the stables who looks just like her. They must be siblings."

"Get out," Logan said to Serena in a cold, emotionless voice. It took a lot to get the king that angry, and Serena knew better than to stick around.

She hurried for the main exit at the same time two guards appeared.

"What now?" Logan demanded.

"Your Majesty, the Jemayrti ambassador and Scholars from the Jemayrt Academy have arrived."

"Good. Have them escorted to their rooms. I will meet with them this evening. And have this man," he pointed at the Nowani messenger, "taken to his rooms as well. Make sure he doesn't wander around anymore. Understood?"

"Yes, Your Majesty," they answered in unison.

As the guards turned to leave, Serena slipped out with them.

***

It's now or never, Serena thought, standing outside of Callum Haar's room. She had avoided this man since that terrible day Kanton had dragged them back to the palace. He was no doubt furious, blaming Serena for his imprisonment. And why shouldn't he? Serena had lied to him and Realta the entire time.

Steeling herself, Serena knocked on the door.

Footsteps approached the door. Serena's instincts told her to run. *No! Running only made your problems worse!*

You need to learn that lies don't befit adults, Callum's words echoed in her mind. Fine. No more lies. Only the painful truth.

Callum Haar opened the door and frowned. "What do you want?"

"Can I speak with you?"

Callum stared at her with those dark brown eyes. "Does your brother know you're here?"

"No."

"Well, be quick about it then."

"Can we speak in private?"

Callum, still frowning, opened the door for Serena. She stepped inside and was surprised at how nice the room was. A bed with clean linens, a window with a decent view, and a desk filled with books and papers. Accommodations befitting a guest more so than a prisoner.

"We're in private. Talk."

"At your house, there was a man covered in scars. Who was he?" Serena asked, glancing over at the papers. Most of them were charcoal drawings of people and buildings. A board-shouldered man with a beard standing next to a simply dressed woman, both smiling. A small chapel, the wind chimes blowing in the invisible breeze. The view from the window into the courtyard. Every detail perfect.

"That's an odd question." Callum folded his arms. "What prompted it?"

"For a second, I thought he was my brother. That he'd followed me."

Callum's frown softened. "That man is my brother-in-law. He and my sister met at the Academy and married shortly after graduating. They returned to the Hinterlands after Kel's accident."

"What happened to him?"

"He was beaten within an inch of his life."

Serena bit down on her lip, choosing her next words carefully. "Logan isn't my oldest brother. There was another, a year older than him. He died when I was a baby."

"I'm sorry for your loss," he said genuinely.

"Logan never talks about him, unless he has to."

"He's throwing that exhibition in his brother's memory, isn't he?"

"That was Isla's idea. Carwyn always liked science and learning how machines worked. She's told me a little about him, when Logan wasn't there."

"How did your brother die?" Callum sat down on the bed, his hands clasped in front of him.

"Everyone claims it was a wasting disease. Carwyn had been born sickly. No one was surprised when he died young."

"Is that the truth?"

"King Yestyn killed him. The story varies, but everyone who was here knows that Carwyn and Yestyn got in a fight, and Yestyn beat him to death." Her eyes widened. "Don't tell Logan I said any of this. He's gets so angry when people talk about Carwyn."

"Like I said, we're in private." Callum rose and went to the desk. He removed a page from the pile of drawings and handed it to Serena. It was a portrait of King Logan, but his eyes were lighter, happier. His smile was warm and gentle. Serena had never seen her brother smile like that, not even around his wife and children.

He placed a heavy hand on Serena's shoulder. She shuddered, but the touch did not hurt. They looked each other in the eyes. "Why are you telling me about your brother?"

No more lies.

"When I was thirteen, I got really sick. I was bedridden for days. I remember my brothers standing over me, talking. Mal was asking Logan questions about Carwyn. Mal had been away at the Academy when he died.

"He asked what time of day Carwyn had died. Logan said it

was at night, just after sunset. Mal claimed he arrived at the palace early the next morning. Sarra had sent him a letter, telling him to come home immediately. He saw Carwyn's friend standing over his body, talking. But then he talked back to her." A shiver ran down her spine. "Mal just stood there and listened. When she finally noticed him, she told Mal to forget everything. It was just his grief causing him to see things."

"What was the friend's name?"

"I don't remember. I think it started with an E. They had the funeral that afternoon. Closed casket. Mal looked for Carwyn's friend, but she was gone. So were two of the guards. He tried to open the casket, but Logan and Yestyn stopped him and forced him to leave. They thought he was mad with grief."

Serena forced herself to keep talking. She would never have the courage to continue if she stopped now. "After that, Mal went looking for rumors. The two guards who left before the funeral were never seen again. Neither was Carwyn's friend. Some say Yestyn sent her across the Vogel Mountains, so she would no longer be a problem. Mal believed Carwyn was sent away with them. Yestyn had done the same with his bastard children, so they wouldn't cause trouble. At least, the ones he knew about. Logan told Mal that it was nonsense. I was the king's only bastard, and their brother was dead.

"When I got better, I asked Logan if it was true. He said he didn't know what I was talking about, that the fever had played tricks with my mind. Even Mal denied it. But he's a chaplain. He doesn't have much practice with lying. I made plans to leave when I was old enough, to cross the mountains. I wanted to know if it was true."

"And that's why you were in Vala during Springtide," Callum said. "You wanted to cross the Pass to find Carwyn's friend. And maybe Carwyn, too."

Serena nodded. It felt good to tell Callum the truth, as though a heavy pack had been lifted from her shoulders.

"Do you know who this man is?" Callum asked, pointing at the drawing in Serena's hands.

"My brother?"

Callum smiled. "He's my brother-in-law without the scars. His name is Kel."

***

The corner at the back of the stables was peaceful, quiet. Not at all like the entrance. People had been coming in and out for hours now. Too many people at once for Gareth to handle. Master Pym had been kind enough to let Gareth take a break. He methodically brushes the tangles out of Dust's mane until the chestnut hair shone. He was grateful to be near something familiar.

When Kel had told Gareth to go to the palace without him, he had been terrified, more terrified than riding into Vala with those guards. Kel told him it was necessary. The things he had to do were dangerous, and he refused to risk Gareth's wellbeing. He instructed Gareth to ask for Gregor Pym, stating that he was an orphan looking for honest work, and he was told to give his full name. After pointing him in the right direction, Kel and Gareth parted ways. But only for a few days. They would be together again soon. Kel promised.

Master Pym turned out to be a kindhearted man, just like Master Loy. He immediately hired Gareth to work in the stables, no questions asked once he heard Gareth's name. The first two days passed within incident. But at noon, all those people started to arrive. Strangers. So many unfamiliar faces and voices it made Gareth's head spin.

He still heard new voices, but he was far away from their prying eyes. Taking slow, steady breaths, the way his mother taught him, he continued brushing Dust's mane.

"Good afternoon, Your Majesty," said Gregor Pym. "How may I assist you?"

"Have you had any recent hires?" asked a new voice. Gareth paused. Where had he heard that voice before?

"Just one in the last week. An orphan boy. A bit simple, but a good lad," Master Pym added in a lower voice. Gareth didn't mind people believing that he was simple. People tended to leave you alone when they thought you were dumb.

"Where did he come from?" The new voice sounded angry. Gareth forced himself to breathe.

"A village out in the Hinterlands. He didn't know which."

"Show me him."

"Gareth!"

Gareth flinched, dropping the brush. Dust, sensing his agitation, nuzzled his shoulder. Master Pym appeared around the corner. Heavy footsteps followed.

"Gareth, lad, the king wishes to see you."

"You said I could be alone," he stammered, burying his face in the horse's soft mane. His father never mentioned the possibility of seeing the king, let alone speaking to him.

"It's only for a minute, lad." Master Pym placed a gentle hand on Gareth's shoulder. Every muscle in his body tensed. Gareth forced himself to look at the master of stables. "Gareth, this is His Majesty, King Logan. Your Majesty, this young man is Gareth Haar."

The other man stepped forward. Gareth froze. The man was the same, but different. Too different. A complete face, and cold, unfeeling eyes.

"Where did you come from?" the king asked. Even his lights were the same, except for the red sparks. Those were absent.

"Hinterlands," he managed.

"Who are your parents?"

"Dead." Gareth hating saying that. It gave him a terrible feeling, as though speaking the lie would cause it to come true. He really wished his father was there.

The king's eyes widened. "Master Pym, where did this horse come from?" He pointed at Dust.

"The lad brought it with him."

"This is a Madani painted horse. How did you get it?"

"She's my father's. Was! Was my father's," he stammered, breaking away from the king's icy gaze.

"What was your father's name?"

"He's not here. He's gone, he's gone!" Gareth cried. He wanted to be alone, wanted this man who wore half of his father's face to leave and never see him again.

"The boy really is simple," the king said quietly.

"But very good with the horses, Your Majesty," Master Pym added.

"Good day, Master Pym. If the boy gives you trouble, don't feel bad about sending him away."

"Of course, Your Majesty."

The two men walked away, leaving Gareth alone.

***

King Logan removed his cloak and flung it onto the back of a nearby chair. His meeting with the Jemayrti ambassador had gone exceedingly well. Ambassador Chinasa Ekene was a man of great intelligence, able to carry on conversations ranging from politics to history to recent scientific achievements. The Scholars from the Academy of Jemayrt shed light on each topic, filling in the gaps. He hadn't had such a fascinating evening since he was a Student at the Academy. It was a blessing after having to suffer Gallia's messenger and facing his bastard sister. Perhaps there was something to the Philosophy of Balances.

Logan untied his shirt and carelessly threw it on top of the cloak. Both moons were high in the sky, and he wanted to get some semblance of sleep tonight.

"As much as I enjoy watching a good striping," his sister's voice rang loud and clear, "I don't want to watch one performed by my own brother!"

Logan spun around and faced Sarra who sat in his reading chair. A small lamp hung in the corner, casting playful shadows on her smiling face.

"Who let you in here?"

Sarra laughed. "All those brains and you don't even bother to lock your doors."

"My brains," Logan replied, standing straight, "have been very busy lately. You know Queen Gallia's messenger is here, right?"

"Yes, and I also heard you talking to the Jemayrti ambassador all throughout the evening meal. Did you even touch your food?"

Logan rolled his eyes. Isla, thankfully, never bothered him about his eating habits, or lack thereof. As long as his mind was sound, who cared if his body was bone thin? He took a seat next to his full sister, not bothering to put on another shirt.

"Why are you really here, Sarra?"

"Serena really did try to kill you, didn't she?" she asked in a low voice, eyes focused on the scar.

Logan touched the pinkish-white scar on his collarbone. Blind luck had saved him that night. Had the girl aimed lowed, the knife would have landing in his heart. "No, I don't think that was her intention."

"Then what happened? And don't give me that cock and bull story about Manipulation gone wrong."

Logan smiled. Growing up in the palace and being married to one of the most powerful lords in the kingdom hadn't dulled Sarra's tongue. If anything, they made it sharper.

"Serena tried to run away. I caught her, tried to stop her. Something in that girl must have snapped. She had that dagger in my chest before I had time to react."

"What prompted her to run away?" Her voice took on a new edge. She had always had a fondness for their half sibling.

"She wanted to find the other bastards beyond Caman's Pass. And Carwyn," he added, his brother's name like a knife in his heart.

Sarra grew silent as a heaviness descended upon the room. The only sounds were the occasional footsteps of servants in the hallway. Servants who knew better than to walk in unannounced.

"Mal's theory?" she finally asked.

Logan nodded.

Sarra stood, pacing around the room with her arms folded across her chest. "Why would Mal tell her such a thing?"

"I don't think he did. Remember a few years back, we all took turns watching over her sickbed?"

"How could I forget?"

For a while, they feared Serena wouldn't survive. Logan pushed those thoughts away. "Mal told me his theory then. Serena must have overheard." He shook his head. "Wishful thinking. Nothing more."

"That part about Car's time of death always bothered me. Are you sure Esme wasn't in the palace when he died?"

"Yes."

"Could she have found a way back in? You and Car always played in the tunnels. Could he have shone her—"

"Sarra, Carwyn died at night. We both saw his body. And the old king had sent Esme away with an escort of guards. It's possible she got away long enough to see Carwyn, to speak with Mal, but it's madness."

Sarra locked eyes with him. "So you think the theory has no merit?"

"I don't know." Logan struggled against his wandering thoughts, leading him back to that horrible night. Their father had always favored Logan over his firstborn, and Carwyn knew it. But that never affected his and Logan's relationship. They had been very close as children, always playing together, creating adventures. Their relationship didn't change until Carwyn met Esme and their feelings grew from teenaged crush to genuine love.

Yestyn never approved of the relationship. Though he had groomed Logan for the throne, it was Carwyn's to inherit. And some girl from a backwater village would never do for a queen. So Yestyn arranged a marriage between Carwyn and Princess Isla at the same time Carwyn and Esme learned they were having a baby. Carwyn swore his siblings to secrecy. He feared Yestyn would kill Esme if he learned the truth.

And then Nell Molyns, one of Queen Owena's handmaids, had a daughter. A little girl with sandy colored hair and blue eyes, the opposite of Nell's dark eyes and black hair. Carwyn confronted their father, and the truth about Esme's condition slipped out. The next time Logan saw Carwyn, his brother was broken mess of shattered bones and blood. In the end, Yestyn had gotten what he had wanted, his favorite son as first in line to inherit the throne.

Seeing Carwyn in that state caused Logan's mind to shatter into fragments as his entire world crashed around him. His brother and closest friend was dead, and he was trapped in an engagement he never wanted. It had taken him years to restore his mind, all in private, of course. House Kelwyn could not allow the other noble houses to know about Logan's weakened mind, making them doubt his ability to inherit. He suspected more than a few knew the truth.

Marrying Isla had been more helpful that he assumed. She, too, was grieving. After the old king's death, she proposed celebrating Carwyn's birthday with yearly exhibitions in which Scholars showcased their latest discoveries. He objected at first, but slowly opened to the idea with each exhibition. Carwyn would have loved it.

"Lo," Sarra said, her voice low, "where did that serving girl come from? The one named Realta?"

Logan sighed, touching the raven necklace, identical to the one Esme had given Carwyn. He had the girl attend on Sarra and Darrys to see if the resemblance was genuine, not just some trick of the eye. "What about her?"

"She looks exactly like Esme."

"I know."

"Well, are they related?" Her eyes fell on the necklace. "Logan, is that—"

"Carwyn's necklace? The girl was wearing it."

"Stars above, is she Carwyn and Esme's child?" Rumor stated that Esme had lost the child when she learned of Carwyn's death, but no one had ever been able to confirm it. And Realta Haar was about the right age.

Logan drummed his fingers on the armrest. "I plan to find out soon. Her father, or rather the man claiming to be her father, is also at the palace. I'm going to question him once the exhibition is over."

"What if he runs?"

"He won't." Logan regretted adding to the man's servant tattoo, but he refused to take chances. He didn't know how Serena had found these people, and he hated not knowing.

"What will you do if the girl is Esme's daughter?"

"I don't know." He saw no point in finding Esme after Yestyn sent her away. The palace was no place for her. The kindhearted did not fare well in court politics. He assumed she made her way back home to the Hinterlands. Logan's mind drifted to the new stable hand, the simple-minded boy who claimed to be from the Hinterlands. He shared the same features as Realta, and they are around the same age. Twins? A sickening feeling formed in his gut.

"Lo."

He looked up. Sarra was tapping her forehead, the signal that she wished to speak via Linking. She was too weak a Minder to simply enter a person's mind. She needed permission.

Logan pictured himself opening a door and nodded.

I'm glad you killed Yestyn. It had been years since she had referred to the old king as 'father'. Logan did not blame her.

So am I.

Nell Molyns had asked Logan to protect her daughter. In that sense, he had.

30

A Chance

Charity settled into her seat in the first row of Basic Medicine. The incident with the skeleton was mostly forgotten, though a handful of snide whispers made their way from the back of the class. Lok's ceremony had dominated every conversation. The Students no longer cared about some girl who touched a skeleton, much to her relief.

She opened her notebook to a fresh page as Scholar Alia walked into the room. A few groans ensued as she once again removed the tarp covering 'Scholar Wik' and placed the remains at the front of the room.

"We will now discuss the major organs of the upper torso and their functions," the Scholar announced, using a wooden pointer to direct their attention.

Charity smiled. An easy lesson for today. She enjoyed the Old Eltrian class, but every now and then Scholar Kuno moved too quickly and would often lapse into the dead language, sometimes to test them and sometimes on accident. Today's lapse had been accidental, and he had spoken for ten minutes before another Student brought the problem to his attention.

"First off," Scholar Alia pointed at the ribs, "the lungs. The right lung has three lobes while the left has only two. Anyone want to guess why?"

A darkness edged at the back of Charity's mind. That pointer looked quite sharp at the end. It hovered over the rib cage, sending a coldness down her spine.

Too many late nights. That was the explanation. She, Zandon, and Jaim had talked in the common area until midnight last night. They had to sneak back to their rooms to avoid being caught outside after curfew. She really ought to take greater consideration into her sleeping habits. Her mother certainly would not approve.

"Correct," said Scholar Alia.

Drat. What had she said? Charity sat up straighter, focusing.

"The heart, located to the left, just off center, contains four chambers and an artery heading into the lungs."

Wood skidded against bone. The pointer slipped between two ribs.

Nightmare memories flashed in her mind. A dark forest clearing, the fire burning bright. Callum and Dane Kanton fighting, Kanton getting the upper hand. The two men falling to the ground. Kanton's knife piercing Callum's ribs, buried to the hilt. Callum screaming. So much blood. Realta, Serena, and Lok running. Horses stomping.

Charity, frozen. Powerless to stop the bleeding. Powerless to help.

She screamed, leaping to her feet and knocking over her chair. All eyes turned to her. Scholar Alia, mouth agape, stared at her with wide eyes. No one said a word. They just looked at her, staring.

Charity bolted from the room, tears streaming down her face. The memories of the horrible night haunted her, playing over and over again in an infinite loop. Callum and Kanton fighting. Falling to the ground. The knife stabbing Callum between the ribs, into the lungs.

Blood.

Too much blood.

"Charity?"

Heart leaping into her throat, she spun around and discovered that she was outside a large meeting room. Half a dozen Scholars were packing equipment into boxes. Overnight bags lined the far wall. Scholar Maryn stood closest to the door. She gave Charity a curious look.

"I wasn't aware this was your free hour."

Wiping away a few remaining tears, Charity replied, "Well, not exactly. I just needed a break."

The Scholar, unconvinced, motioned for Charity to follow her to the back of the room, out of earshot from the others.

"Charity, what's wrong?"

"Nothing, Scholar." As soon as the words left her mouth, Charity felt two tears slide down her cheeks. No, she already made a fool of herself in front of Scholar Alia. She was not going to cry in front of Maryn. Tears were for small children. She could handle her emotions.

Callum's scream echoed in her ears.

"Charity, did something happen?" she asked, placing a hand on her arm. "Scholar Alia told us about the incident last week. Is that it?"

Charity shook her head, more tears falling. Though a handful of Students bothered her about the incident, far more commended her for it. Not everyone had the guts to touch a skeleton. So why couldn't she have the guts to face reality?

"It's just, I was traveling here with my friend. And we got separated. Lok and I got here okay. I thought she'd get here soon. But I haven't heard anything. I don't even know if she's still alive!"

"Oh dear, why didn't you tell us?" The other Scholars murmured to one another. Maryn shot them a glance to be quiet.

"I thought she would be here by now. It's been two full weeks. I thought..."

"Calm down." Scholar Maryn hurried over to her colleagues, speaking in a hushed tone. Two of the Scholars exited the room, a sense of urgency to their steps. The rest moved to the far corner. Their faces were masks of concern. Maryn took two chairs from the meeting table and moved them to the back. Sitting down, she motioned for Charity to take a seat.

"Start from the beginning."

Charity began her account on the morning they found Serena in her father's barn. How Dane Kanton, claiming to be a member of the King's Guard, promised to take her, Realta and Gareth to the Academy as a reward for Serena's capture. How Lok joined the group, and Kanton's short temper, causing Gareth to run away. And how they had to camp outside of Lothian, since the inn was full. That had struck her as odd, considering how easily Serena could escape. It would have been far better to hire out a farmer's barn.

Waking up to yelling, seeing Kanton and Callum fight, the dagger stabbing Callum in the chest. A man on fire. Her and Lok fleeing into the forest. Everything regarding Realta, Callum, and

Serena after that was a mystery. She thought they rode away, leaving the guards behind, but didn't know which direction.

"I figured, they either went back home or continued this way. Going to Vala would be more logical. It's closer, and nobody would accuse them of lying. But I don't know."

Charity looked into the Scholar's eyes. They were kind and soft. Not a trace of accusation or thinking that Charity was lying. Why had she taken so long to tell this story?

"What day did this happen?"

"Alet first."

Maryn nodding, contemplating. "Did you send a letter to your parents as soon as you arrived here?"

"Yes," Charity perked up. "Did they respond?"

"Nothing has arrived yet."

She frowned. "Oh."

"You say this man claimed to be in the King's Guard. My husband has a friend who works in the Garrison. Perhaps he can check the record and see if there really is a Dane Kanton."

"He can do that?"

Maryn nodded.

"Thank you. I didn't know you were married."

The scholar smiled. "Happily. And you've already met him. Rune, the Cuchasi who tested you and Lok."

Interesting.

"If you had to guess," Scholar Maryn continued, "what are the odds that your friend and her father headed for Teyrnas?"

"I don't know." Charity frowned. "Let me think." Vala was the obvious place to go. They had the advantage there. Home, friends, witnesses. If it had been up to Callum, they would have returned home. But Serena, from the short time Charity had interacted with her, had a habit of running away. If she had run toward Teyrnas, Callum and Realta would have followed. And they hadn't run into the forest. Charity was certain of that. Only two ways they could have fled. "Fifty percent chance."

"And this occurred twenty-six days ago. Ample time to reach the capital. I have an idea. You see all those traveling bags?"

Charity nodded.

"Tomorrow, we're heading to Teyrnas for the king's annual exhibition. We can speak with the city guard and post notices in all the major inns. See if anyone has seen them."

"You'd really do that?"

"Of course. And if you want, you can come with us."

Charity's eyes widened. "I can?"

"This way, your friends will know it's not a trick, and you'll get to meet the king. Not to mention a change of pace."

"Thank you! Thank you so much!" Finally, a chance to find Realta and Callum, to put her fears to rest. And meeting the king? That didn't happen every day. Or every lifetime. It seemed almost too good to be true. "Wait, what about my studies?"

"Take the books with you. You'll only be gone for three days, so you won't miss too much."

Charity thanked her again. "When do we leave?"

"Early tomorrow morning." Scholar Maryn stood. "I'll inform your teachers and the other scholars that you'll be joining us." She walked over to her colleagues. They nodded in agreement.

Charity could not believe it. A real chance to reunite with her best friend. She felt like such a fool for not telling someone sooner. What if they were already in the city? They could be going from inn to inn, looking for any traces of her and Lok.

She hurried out of the room to pack her things and tell Lok the good news.

***

Lok sat sequestered in a small alcove, a corner of the library next to a bookshelf collecting dust. He was supposed to be in his martial arts class, but he had no desire to learn how to fight. He didn't see the point. Yes, those skills would have been useful back in Vala. Very few people were stupid enough to fight someone who knew how to handle himself. But he wasn't in Vala. Had no desire to ever step foot in that village again.

So he collected all of Dane Kanton's notes and papers and a few Old Eltrian textbooks and made his way to this empty corner. Only a handful of Students and Journeymen were present. And none of the Scholars bothered him. Students cycled through free hours throughout the day, and most spent them at the library.

Arranging the books, Lok opened his notebook to a fresh page and attempted to translate. Since Charity had a roommate, they had hidden Kanton's things in Lok's room. He did not know the punishment for having notes that belonged to a guardsman. He assumed it was very steep. The sooner these books were translated, the sooner they could get rid of them.

And learn why Dane Kanton had attacked them.

Lok removed the letter written in Old Eltrian and copied the first sentence onto a piece of paper. He circled all the nouns and underlined the verbs. Or what he thought were nouns and verbs. Scholar Kuno had given him a few lessons, but not nearly enough.

Flipping through the dictionary, he slowly found the meaning of each word. Some were easy. Others had four or five possible translations depending on the context. He sighed. This was going to be much harder than he thought.

A quarter of an hour passed. The first sentence was complete.

Captain Kanton, forget about the warnings from the king.

That was an odd way to start a letter. Lok buckled down. Ten minutes later, the next two sentences were done.

The girl is a threat. It is your job to remove threats.

An uneasy feeling formed in Lok's gut. He had been wary of that Serena girl from the moment they met. He could not describe the sensation in words. And her desperation to run away from Kanton was disturbing.

Lok removed the letter written in Teyrnian from the notebook. It was from King Logan himself, and it stated that Serena was to be returned to the capital unharmed. "You are aware of the situation," the king wrote. "I ask that you act accordingly, as though everything were legitimate."

Legitimate? Odd choice of words.

"Lok, there you are," said Scholar Kuno, peering around the corner.

Panic seizing him, Lok shoved the notes back into the notebook and hid it under the Old Eltrian textbooks. Not that it did any good. Scholar Kuno had seen everything.

"You didn't turn up for martial arts today. Scholar Tell sent me to look for you. Is everything all right?"

Lok nodded, trembling from head to foot. He trusted Scholar Kuno, knew that the man had his best interest at heart. But how would he react to seeing those letters? Would he be mad?

"Old Eltrian?" Kuno said, picking up one of the books and smiling. "Maybe we should have placed you in that class instead of martial arts. I'll make a note for next semester."

Lok shrugged.

Kuno returned the book to the pile and sat down, his face serious. "You don't like martial arts that much. Or is it Scholar Tell you don't like?"

Lok wrote, *"A bit of both."*

Kuno nodded. "Yeah, Scholar Tell is an acquired taste. But there's nothing wrong with learning how to defend yourself. It's a dangerous world out there."

"Are you going to take me there?"

"To your class? No. I'll say I couldn't find you. Missing a single class isn't the end of the world." He glanced over at the books. "I can give you more Old Eltrian lessons. Would you like that?"

Lok smiled weakly.

Kuno returned the gesture. "Is something else bothering you, Lok?"

"Have you ever met a Learner Thane named Dane Kanton?" Lok had thought about this since the ceremony. Every Thane had to complete it in order to receive the first earring and graduate from the Academy to receive the second. Either Kanton had stolen the rings, or he had attended the Academy.

Kuno frowned. "Unfortunately. Thank the Creator he left for the Garrison after graduating as a Student. Why do you ask?"

"I met him on the way here." Not the truth, but not a complete lie. He really did not feel like relating the entire ordeal to Kuno. *"Is he really a Learner?"*

"Yes, but middling. I only taught him in one class. One Eltrian. He claimed to have no knowledge of the subject on the first day, loud enough for all his classmates to hear. The next day, he walks in and converses with me in Old Eltrian. For half the class period. All the Students were stunned, believing his ability was far greater than it actually is. In reality, he had been studying the language in private for months."

"So, he lies all the time?"

"I wouldn't say all the time. But he knows what he wants and is clever enough to get it. How did you meet him exactly?"

"He was passing through my village, looking for a thief."

"That task seems beneath him. But it has been twenty years. I'm sure he's matured since then. The Garrison doesn't tolerate haughty attitudes."

Well, that settled it. Kanton had a habit of lying. Lok wondered how much, if anything, that man told his mother was true. What were his real plans? And what had led to him and Callum fighting? A shiver ran down his spine.

"You know," said Kuno, "there's still ten minutes left in this period. You could go to the courtyard and explain to Scholar Tell that you weren't feeling well. Infections don't heal in a day."

Lok's ear hadn't bled since that night six days ago. And he hadn't felt feverish in a half week. He shrugged. The explanation sounded too weak.

"Yeah, probably not best to lie. I'll tell you what. Promise me you will attend all your classes from now on, and I'll give you Old Eltrian lessons in the evenings. Deal?"

He nodded, smiling.

"Very good." Kuno stood. "See you this evening. And remember, I don't take broken promises lightly."

Lok nodded again. The last thing he wanted was Kuno to be disappointed by him.

The scholar walked away, leaving Lok with the books and notes. None of Kanton's papers had been discovered. Lok breathed a sigh of relief.

31

The Lateness of the Hour

Lok strolled along the perimeter of the Academy, side by side with Scholar Kuno. The sun had just set below the horizon, bathing the sky with shades of orange fading into deep blue. The first moon, Ilana, peered above the wall.

Yesterday afternoon, Charity told him that she had the opportunity to travel with the Scholars to Teyrnas for the king's exhibition. They also promised to help look for Realta and Callum, in the event they had arrived at the capital.

That horrible night in the woods felt like a lifetime ago. It might as well have been. Lok was a very different person from that timid boy. Now, he was a slightly less timid Elemental Thane, an entire category unto himself. Though some Scholars theorized that more Elementals existed but were harder to find for an obscure reason.

Before leaving, she asked about his progress in translating Dane Kanton's letters. She was equality perplexed by the little he was able to decipher. He hoped these informal lessons with Scholar Kuno would help.

"Okay, time for a test," said Scholar Kuno. "How do you say, good morning?"

Lok wrote down the letters. Lamps had been hung along the wall every one hundred feet. Plenty of light to read and write by. *"Bo'matn."*

"Excellent. How do you say, my friend?"

"Mae zani."

"Count from one to five."

"Onn, det, twan, katt, senn."

"You're a fast learner." The Scholar smiled, the lamplight shining off his dark eyes.

Lok nodded in thanks.

"Do you want to learn some more?"

Lok nodded rapidly. Of course he wanted to learn more. That notebook was not going to translate itself.

"Wonderful. Let's do some more vocabulary."

Lok positioned his pencil on the paper, ready to write.

"The word for sky is 'slyl'. Sun is 'soll', moon is 'laln', and star is 'zkai'."

"What about 'moons'? Or the names of the moons?"

"The plural form of moon is 'lalinni'. As for the names, they're the same and have their own meanings. Ilana means 'runner' and Nalani means 'hunter'."

Lok made a quick note.

"Now, Lok, I'm going to ask you a question," Kuno said, his voice taking on a serious tone. "You don't have to answer right away, but I would like an answer in a day or so."

Lok's chest tightened.

"That paper you were looking at in the library yesterday had an insignia on it. Two flying ravens imprinted in dark blue wax. That's King Logan's personal seal. I don't know why you have it. Your business before arriving at the Academy is your own. But as your mentor, your wellbeing is my responsibility. Take the next day or two to think about where you found that paper. I won't judge. I just want to make sure you aren't in any trouble. Okay?"

Lok responded with a weak nod. He did not want to discuss the journey here, but Scholar Kuno had proven to be on his side time and again. He guessed he could trust this man with the truth.

A blur of movement caught Lok's eye. The Scholar saw it, too, stopping in his tracks and looking upward. Lok squinted in the low light. The dark object flapped its wings and flew closer to them, slowing its approach. The Scholar held out his arm and the object, a large bird, landed on his forearm. The white tips on the wings have the bird away as a Deirow Hawk, the Academy's go-to messengers.

"Your name is Syd, correct?" the Scholar asked.

"Yes, Scholar Kuno," the hawk replied in his oddly human voice, the product of a millennium of breeding. Lok had yet to grow comfortable with the idea of talking animals. "I was told to find the nearest Scholar and bring them to the front gate. You are the nearest Scholar."

"What's wrong? Did something happen?"

Behind Lok, one of the lamps began to burn brighter. Lok forced his own anxiety down, and the flames lowed with it. That had been happening more frequently, even since his fever. When his mood was light, the flames seemed to dance. When he was anxious, the flames increased in size, burning out of control. Anxiety over his first exam left a charred mark on the corner of his writing desk. The old texts stated that this was normal for Elementals, but it still concerned him.

"There is a man at the gate," Syd replied. "A chaplain. He is very worried. Baltyn is very worried." Syd ruffled his feathers. Deirow Hawks shared a strong emotional bond with their human partners. Everything Baltyn felt, Syd felt.

"Let's not keep them waiting. Come on, Lok." Kuno started for the gate. The hawk launched himself into the sky, soaring high and circling downward as he approached the gate.

Hurrying along the curved walls and mindful to stay one step behind Kuno, Lok spied the hawk resting on the stocky guardsman's shoulder.

Next to Baltyn stood a man in his late thirties with very short, light brown hair and blue eyes framed by glasses. He wore the brown robe of a chaplain with a white cord tied around his waist. Odd. The white cord symbolized that he belonged to the highest order of chaplains. How did one so young achieve that rank? In his ears were two sets of earrings, red and purple. A Learner and an Empath Thane.

The chaplain rung his hands and looked every which way. He jumped as his eyes fell on Scholar Kuno.

"Good evening, Holy Brother," the Scholar said with a short bow. Lok imitated the bow. None of the chaplains in Vala required people to bow. Things must be different on this side of the Nerin. "How can we assist you?"

"What do you know of..." The chaplain glanced over at Baltyn, a look of worry cast over his already pale face.

"I should return to my post," Baltyn said, taking the hint. "Good evening, Brother, Scholar, Lok." He and the Deirow Hawk disappeared into the gatehouse.

The chaplain let out a nervous laugh. "The guards here have

always been so good. The ones at the palace are so damn nosy." The chaplain clamped one hand over his mouth. "Apologies. I forget myself."

"No worries, Brother. What is your name?" Kuno asked, smiling warmly.

"Mal. I mean, Brother Malaky. Please, hear me out."

"Of course."

"What do you know about Thanes receiving new burdens? What age are they?"

"Well, most Thanes receive their first burden at a young age. Usually between fourteen and seventeen. Sometimes as young as twelve. New burdens tend to manifest either around the same time or in their early twenties."

"What about at thirty-seven years old?"

Kuno raised an eyebrow. "I've never heard of a burden manifesting that far into adulthood. Why do you...?"

"Look at my rings," Brother Malaky said, stepping closer to the lamp. "What colors are they?"

"Red and purple. An excellent combination of abilities, in my opinion. Though not true opposites, they are both located in the southern half of the Great Compass—"

"I know about theology, Scholar," Brother Malaky snapped. Squeezing his eyes shut, he took a slow, deep breath. "Trust me. I know everything about theology. And I know that of the last twenty-two years, I have been a Learner and an Empath. Until Springtide." Brother Malaky buried his face in his hands.

"What happened on Springtide?" Scholar Kuno asked, a new edge entering his voice. A hard tone that Lok had never heard until now.

"I saw them!" he cried. "The Nine walk the world once more! The souls and the bodies are new, but the essence is there. Scattered across the world but drawn to one another. Like moths to the candle, they move towards the Eternal City. The Wardens of the Night know of their movements. They seek only to destroy. Nothing can stop them now!" The chaplain screamed at the top of his lungs. Lok cowered behind the Scholar.

"Okay, calm down." Kuno placed a hand on the chaplain's shoulder.

Brother Malaky shrieked and swatted the hand away. "I'm not insane!"

"I believe you." Kuno held up his hands nonthreateningly. "But I want to understand. Why don't you come inside and speak with the other Scholars as well? I'm sure someone has an explanation."

"An explanation for spontaneous Farsight," the chaplain scoffed. He then shook his head. "I'm sorry. That's why I'm here. It's just..." He let out a heavy sigh. "It's been a very long month."

The chaplain allowed Scholar Kuno to escort him to the Academy proper. Lok walked two steps behind, mulling over the chaplain's words.

The phrase "Wardens of the Night" was completely foreign to him, but the words "The Nine" and "Eternal City" rang a bell. Both were prominently featured in the Gadyeni Cycle, Scholar Kuno's area of expertise. Lok hadn't had much time to study it. Only the parts pertaining to the last days of the Thousand Years War.

The Nine were nine Thanes chosen by the Eight Gadyeni, with the ninth, Balthazar, chosen by the Creator. Having all eight abilities, or burdens as they were sometimes called, Balthazar became their leader, commanding armies to fight against the Midnight King and his forces. The War ended with Balthazar fighting one-on-one with the Midnight King, an act that resulted in the Midnight King being banished from reality and Balthazar's death. Humans did not fight powerful entities and live to talk about it.

The Eternal City was said to be the location of their battle. Its true location had been lost to time. Many Scholars debated the accuracy of the term and whether it was a physical location or a symbolic one.

Scholar Kuno led the way into the Academy, the large doors opening without a sound. Few people moved about the atrium. Curfew for Students began in half an hour. Kuno stopped a passing Scholar and asked her to gather the Premier and the Council. An unusual situation required their immediate attention.

"Do you have any idea what time it is?" she questioned, shifting her gaze from Kuno to Brother Malaky who was furiously wiping silent tears from his eyes.

"I don't think the matter can wait. Please, Scholar Cybil."

"I will see what I can do. No promises." As she climbed the

central stairway, Scholar Cybil added, "I'll tell them this was your idea."

"Yes, please do," Scholar Kuno muttered under his breath. He turned to Lok. "You might as well run off, Lok. I don't know how long this will be."

Lok nodded. But he didn't want to run off. He wanted to learn more about this chaplain and his strange visions.

Brother Malaky turned and saw Lok for the first time. "How long have you been standing there, Student?"

"Lok was with me when I met you at the gate, Brother," Kuno explained.

The chaplain's brow furrowed. "What color is your earring?"

Lok felt at the ring in his right ear. It had only bled one other time, but only a few drops of blood. He pulled his hand away. No blood.

"Green?" the chaplain questioned. "He's wearing a green one?"

"Yes, Brother." Kuno smiled like a proud parent. "Lok Tolman is the first Elemental Thane at the Academy in three hundred years. I thought the Council already sent word to the Church?"

Brother Malaky shook his head. "Green. Elemental." His eyes widened. "The Raven that sits in Alberik's left hand! Oh, my head!" The chaplain fell to his knees, clutching his head. Kuno knelt beside him. "Don't touch me!"

"Scholar Kuno," said Scholar Cybil, walking briskly towards the atrium, "the Council is seated. What— Oh Creator, what happened?" She rushed to the chaplain's side.

"He just collapsed. Help me get him to the infirmary." Kuno grabbed the chaplain by one arm and Scholar Cybil by the other. Lok wanted to help but felt he would just get in the way.

"No. No, I must see the Council immediately," Brother Malaky protested.

Cybil shrugged, as though saying 'might as well'. Kuno nodded in agreement. Together, they helped Brother Malaky to his feet, waiting to make sure he was steady. They then walked up the stairs to the Council Chamber. Lok followed close behind, curiosity overriding fear.

Funny, back home, he would have run and hid the moment he felt afraid. Would his mother be proud of the man Lok was becoming, or would she be afraid, too?

The ornately carved doors of the Council Chamber stood open. All the Council Members, both ordinary human and Thane, save for one, were seated along with the Premier. Lok recognized Scholar Lucan seated behind the Manipulator's chair. The circular room with its vaulted ceiling seemed much larger without a crowd.

"I prefer to speak with them alone," said Brother Malaky.

Kuno and Cybil replied with short bows. The chaplain entered the Chamber, the doors closing behind him. Cybil bid Lok and Kuno good night and retreated down the stairs. Kuno motioned for Lok to follow him.

Turning a corner, he led Lok into a small antechamber. The room, about four feet square, was empty save for a door. Behind it was a spiral staircase, wide enough for one person at a time. Kuno climbed the steps, and Lok followed. The door automatically closed behind him without a sound. The stairway ended in a small room, partitioned off from the Council Chamber by a wooden barrier, about four feet high, and thick curtains.

Kuno crouched down and removed a small part of the barrier. Crouching beside the Scholar, Lok could see the entire Chamber. The domed ceiling caused each voice to be heard loud and clear.

"Something is definitely wrong with that chaplain," Kuno whispered. "Did you catch the last thing he said?"

Lok shook his head, unsure which part the scholar was referring to.

"The part about a raven sitting in someone's left hand?"

Alberik? Was that the name? Lok wrote the first two letters when Kuno swatted the pencil and paper out of his hands.

"Don't even write it, Lok." The Scholar's dark eyes bore into his skull. "That name is the true name of the Midnight King."

Lok's body went cold, as though drenched in ice water. The Midnight King, the creature that tormented humanity for a thousand years, had a name?

"That name is forbidden. Nobody is allowed to speak it, not even in private. I happened upon the name in a book that was more dust than paper. An accident I regret. We aren't even allowed to write it. And to hear it spoken by a chaplain." Kuno shivered. "Something is very wrong here."

Kuno turned his attention to Brother Malaky. Lok moved closer to the opening, getting a better view.

"Holy Brother Malaky, formerly of the noble House Kelwyn," said Premier Scholar Emera, her voice ringing throughout the room like a bell, "you are registered as a Learner and an Empath Thane, both burdens of middling ability. Why do you come to us at this late hour claiming to also be a Farsight?"

"Because I have no other explanation, Premier," he said with a bow. "The first vision arrived at midnight of Springtide—"

"And have the Cuchasi confirmed this?"

Brother Malaky paled. "No, Premier. I feared they would confirm—"

"So you chose to live in ignorance?"

"No, Premier. That was not my intention at all."

The Premier turned to Scholar Osian, the one sitting in the seat reserved for Elemental Thanes. "Send for one of the Cuchasi. I want the truth, nothing less."

"Yes, Premier." With a quick bow, Scholar Osian exited the chamber.

All eyes returned to the chaplain. Lok was thankful not to be in his position.

"And what did you see in this vision?" asked the Premier.

Brother Malaky took a deep breath. "Eight human figures shrouded in light. I couldn't see what they looked like, only that they were human. They were walking from all directions, from every corner of the world, towards a glowing city that was many times larger than Teyrnas. Perhaps the size of every world capital combined. The ninth figure was already in the city, at the very center. The other figures met him in the center, standing in a perfect circle."

"How do you know the central figure was male?" asked Scholar Ealee, seated in the space for nonexistent Healers. A small smile form in the corners of her mouth.

"I don't know, Scholar. That was merely the impression I received."

"Continue," said the Premier.

"Once all Nine figures were in the center, hundreds of other figures dressed in the night sky, black with points of light covering their bodies, attacked them. The Nine tried to fight back, but the night figures grabbed hold of them, turning the Nine into night figures as well. The vision ended there. I've had one each night since then. Each one a little different."

"Different how?" asked Scholar Adhran, his bushy, white eyebrows knitted together.

"Sometimes the Nine are able to escape, sometimes it's only a few. Other times, the center figure was a night figure in disguise." Removing his glasses, Brother Malaky rubbed his temples. "I'm sorry. It's too much to comprehend all at once."

"Your summary of the first vision is sufficient," said the Premier Scholar. "For now."

The chamber doors opened and closed. Scholar Osian returned to his seat, trailed by a young woman with reddish brown hair. She wore a gray Journeyman's cloak along with men's trousers and a work shirt. Lok recognized her only in passing. She stopped in front of the Premier and bowed.

"Mirela," the Premier addressed her, "this man claims to be three types of Thane. Please verify this for us."

Mirela faced Brother Malaky and studied him. "He's an Empath and a Learner. Middling in both abilities." She paused, frowning. "There are faint traces of blue in his Aura. Yes, he's also a Farsight, but the ability is very weak." She faced the Premier. "Are those the abilities he claimed to have?"

"Yes, Mirela. You've done well. Thank you."

Mirela gave a short bow and turned to leave.

"If you'll stay. Your services might still be needed."

"Yes, Premier." Mirela walked towards the seats and stood beside Scholar Osian. Lok noticed a few similarities between the Scholar and the Cuchasi. Both had dark brown, oval-shaped eyes and sharp, straight noses. Their mouths were the same shapes as well. Each had prominent cheekbones. Now that he was looking, Lok noted hints of red in the scholar's brown hair.

"Uncle and niece," Kuno whispered.

Lok blinked in surprise. Had his observation been that obvious?

"It's very interesting," Kuno continued. "Brother Malaky mentioned the Wardens of the Night to us, but not to the Premier.

Withholding information will only hurt him."

Lok reached for his paper and pencil. He wrote, *"What are the Wardens of the Night?"*

"During the War, they were the Midnight King's human spies. They would infiltrate various governments and groups, turning members to the Midnight King one by one. A few of them even tried to turn Balthazar." Kuno smiled, amused. "The man was smart enough not to fall for their tricks."

"Balthazar was a Minder, too. He probably read their minds."

Kuno sighed. "The Wardens converted a lot of Thanes to their side, too."

The Premier began speaking again. Lok and Kuno fell silent, their attention on her.

"It appears you are truthful, after all, Holy Brother. I am glad you did not break your oaths."

"I would never do such a thing," Brother Malaky replied in disgust.

"Then why not seek the truth immediately?"

"There is no excuse other than my own fears, Premier Scholar. The advent of these visions, and at my age, terrified me."

"Tell me, do Farsights run strong in your family?"

"Not at all, Premier. My family contains every variety of Thane except Farsights. The only one is my sister-in-law, and her family originates in the Kingdom of Byyar."

"I see. Have you written down these visions?"

Brother Malaky wrung his hands. "I have not, Premier. I feared what my fellow Brothers and Sisters would think if they read the words."

"Do chaplains nowadays allow themselves to be ruled by fear?" asked Scholar Koranic, titling his head to one side.

"Of course not! I—"

"Brother Malaky," said the Premier. "Your situation is unique. I request you remain at the Academy for a minimum of one full week and record every vision you receive in that time, as well as record your visions from earlier. One week from tonight, the full Council will convene again to analyze your findings and see if they carry any significance. Scholar Osian and Cuchasi Mirela will escort you to the visitor's wing. Is this understood?"

"A full week? Ten days?" Brother Malaky turned a shade paler.

"Is this request unreasonable?" The Premier raised an eyebrow.

"No, Premier. May I write to the Church and my biological family, stating that I'm staying at the Academy? I don't want them to worry."

"Yes, but do not include your visions. This is a phenomenon that requires great scrutiny before being made public. You are dismissed, Holy Brother Malaky."

"Thank you, Premier Scholar and Council," he replied with a bow. Scholar Osian and his niece led the chaplain out of the room. The other Scholars whispered among themselves for a few minutes, none of the words loud enough for Lok or Kuno to hear. They then left, trailing the Premier and extinguishing the lamps as they exited the chamber.

Lok peered into the empty space. The pale light of the moons shone through the skylight, bathing the seats in eerie, black and white shadows.

Scholar Kuno replaced the small piece of wood, hiding the peephole. He motioned for Lok to follow him down the dark stairway. Lok kept one hand on the wall as he carefully felt for each step. All exterior lamps had been extinguished as well. The nearest lights were from candles at the top of the stairs.

Kuno walked down the short hall towards the stairs, hands folded behind his back and head hung low in thought. Lok walked after him.

"An interesting night, wouldn't you say, Lok?"

He nodded and wrote, *"An interesting nwit."*

Kuno smiled again. Good. The man looked much better when he smiled. "Kii. Y nwit etensans." *Yes, an interesting night.*

The clocks struck eleven.

"And a very late night," Kuno added. "Busy day for you tomorrow, right?"

Lok groaned. He had a short exam in chemistry tomorrow morning. He absolutely hated that class. It was worse than mathematics! At least he had history for the first hour. Scholar Nycal was nice and a good friend of Kuno's.

"Get some sleep, kid." Kuno headed down the stairs.

Lok tried to follow the Scholar's advice, but his dreams were plagued by shadow creatures hunting down figures made of light. No matter how fast they ran or how far away they hid, the shadows found them. One light figure was cornered, the shadow figures grabbing hold of her and draining her of light. The little figure screamed as her light faded away.

32

Little Dreamer

The dream took Realta to a village a little larger than Vala. Most of the buildings were smoldering ruins, black smoke rising from the ashes. Shattered glass littered the cobblestone streets. Here and there rested pieces left behind: a blackened boot, a child's hoop toy, a scrap of clothing. Very few people dared venture out of the remaining structures.

Okay, according to Shasta's books, my dreams reflect past events. All I have to do is find out where and when I am.

The task was easier said than done. She'd never been able to interact with the people in her dreams, and the event that caused this fire had come and gone. Nothing she did could alter the past.

Realta walked down the ruined street, looking for any signs or landmarks. The land was too flat to be the Hinterlands. Perhaps a village closer to Teyrnas? The kingdom had fought numerous wars with its neighbor, Nowan. This was likely the aftermath of a battle.

A tall, bearded man dressed in ragged clothing lit a lantern as he hurried past Realta. The sun was just beginning to set. He paused at a corner building, its front completely burned away, and furtively glanced up and down the street. No one save Realta was watching. The man stepped inside. Realta followed.

In the corner of a backroom was a small bundle of clothing, the outer layer coated in char. The man carefully removed the clothes, wincing as he grabbed an article that was still hot. Realta positioned herself closer. The man removed more clothes, revealing a small child, no older than three or four. He was coated in ashes and had a large gash on his forehead, the blood matting his brown hair. The boy opened his blue-ish gray eyes. He cringed, trying to move farther into the corner.

The man picked up the child, cradling him, and hurried out

of the building. The child did not protest. Realta followed him down the empty street. No, following was the wrong word. The dream moved her along, showing her what it wanted her to see. She did not complain. So long as it led to answers.

The dream halted in front of a store with various farming supplies arranged in the window. She glanced at the sign.

That's not Teyrnian. The letters were the same, but the words were incomprehensible. So, this fire was not the result of a Teyrnian-Nowani war. Then where was she?

The man knocked on the door. He anxiously looked at the sleeping child in his arms. That gash looked deep. Aunt Esme knew all about gashes and injuries, knowledge that she readily passed on to Charity. Her friend could not be dead. Realta refused to believe it until Kanton showed her the body.

The door creaked open. A stout woman wearing an apron over her dress jumped when she saw the man.

"Moteo, what are you doing here?" she asked in Teyrnian. Or maybe the dream was interpreting for her. "Whose child is that?"

"Please let me in. I have to speak with you." The man, Moteo, glanced down the street. At the end were three men dressed in red and white uniforms. Each was armed with a short sword and a cudgel. Village guards, no doubt.

The woman noticed the three men and motioned for Moteo to enter, closing and locking the door behind him. In the blink of an eye, Realta stood in the center of the shop.

"Okay, you're in. Now answer my question."

"My sister is dead."

The woman wrung her hands, averting her eyes. "A lot of people are dead."

"You know about her dealings with Etragian?"

The woman glared daggers at him. "Everyone knows. She's the reason that monster wasn't destroyed years ago. She's the reason this," she pointed out the window to the half-charred street, "happened."

Moteo sighed, looking at the child. "This is her son. Westermor."

"That monster fathered a child?!" The woman paled. "Ilysa allowed that monster to..." She shivered.

"Etragian was only a man. All men are capable of evil."

"Not that kind of evil."

Moteo took a deep breath. "Someone needs to care for the child, Mida."

The woman scoffed. "And you think I—"

"Please. Ilysa always spoke highly of you."

"She was your sister," she replied, her voice harsh. "You care for it."

Flashes of red caught Realta's eye. The three men in red coats passed the shop. One of them, a grizzled, older man, looked through the window. He nodded at Mida. She nodded back. The man and his colleagues kept walking. Realta let out a relieved sigh.

"See," said Moteo. "Even the Watch respects you. If anyone can raise this child well, it's you."

Mida studied both Moteo and the child. The gash still bled. How much blood could a young child lose before succumbing to the injury? Mida took the child in her arms.

"And what am I to tell everyone?"

"That someone left a foundling at your doorstep." Moteo went to the door.

"Where are you going?"

"I'm the brother of the woman who loved Etragian Calbi. This village isn't a good place for me."

"No. I don't suppose it is."

Moteo let out a heavy sigh and disappeared into the darkened street.

Realta blinked, and the dark shop was replaced by her small bedroom, the morning light pouring in through the narrow window.

Getting out of bed, she went to the closet and pulled out the notebook Shasta had given her. She had instructed Realta to write every detail of her dreams. A Dreamer's level of ability affected how accurately they saw the past. Low-leveled ones caught only glimpses and impressions, while high-leveled ones saw every detail perfectly. The notebook allowed her to cross reference people and place names, gauging her own level of ability.

The name of the burned down village was never stated, but the words on the shop door were clear in her mind. "Fortur Colgri". One of Shasta's books might provide a translation. Or a book in the place library. Of course, she'd need permission to enter the library as well as a believable explanation. She still hadn't figured out how to tell the king that she was a Thane. She had trouble believing it herself.

A knock came at the door.

"Just a minute."

Realta quickly finished writing and exchanged her nightgown for work clothes. She placed the notebook back in its hiding spot and opened the door.

"Father!" Realta smiled. Five days had passed since she had seen him. Not a terribly long time, but each day here felt like a year. The tattoo on her left wrist itched.

"Hello, my dear." Callum hadn't shaved. The dark beard looked odd on him. "I've brought a visitor for you." He stepped to the side, revealing a young man with coal black hair and eyes so dark they were almost black.

"Gareth?"

Realta's cousin rushed into the room, catching her in an awkward embrace. His entire body trembled.

"Gareth, how did you get here?"

"Traveled. With my father."

Callum ushered them into the room, closing the door. "Your cousin has had quite an adventure. Sit down, Gareth. Tell Realta how you got here."

The three of them sat on the bed with Gareth in the middle. She waited for him to begin.

"Got your letter. Father and Master Loy, everyone really, were very upset. Father was furious, thought it was all his fault. The two of us when looking for you. The guards in Lothian said Callum killed a man. Is it really true?" He looked at Callum expectantly.

Callum sighed. "What I did was in self-defense. If it were up to me, no one would have died."

Gareth relaxed a little. "My father explained some things to me. He said that I'm a Cuchasi, that I can see Seltachai. The healer was right, you know. My father is a Seltachai, but not the blood drinking kind. He can move stuff without touching it and make people see things that aren't there. But he's still my father," Gareth added defensively. "I still love him."

"We know, Gareth," Callum said.

"Wait, do you mean Uncle Kel is a Thane?"

Gareth nodded. "That's another word for Seltachai."

"What do you see when you look at me?" Realta asked, her heart racing. *Shasta's Cuchasi has failed to get into the palace. This was her chance.*

"Black lights," he replied, hovering his hand over hers. "And little gold sparks. Is that right? The guards in East Bridge told us you were a Thane, but you ran away. I don't blame you. Their Cuchasi scared me, too."

"Running was Serena's idea," Realta said quietly.

"Who is she?" Gareth asked. "I've seen her around the palace. Why would the king let a thief walk around his house?"

"Because she's his half-sister," Realta replied.

Gareth was quiet for a moment, absorbing the words.

"Gareth," said Callum, "have you seen the king?"

The boy nodded. He wrapped his arms around himself, as though an icy wind had blown through the room. "His face... His face..."

Realta placed a comforting hand on her cousin's shoulder. "I know. I saw his face, too." The king's face was nearly identical to Kel's. The eyes a perfect match. Shasta's words echoed in her mind. *Yestyn fathered at least three bastards. I have no doubt there are others.* A pit formed in Realta's gut. Kel had always been secretive about his past. Was this the reason?

"Gareth, I'm going to ask you some questions. Can you do your best to answer them?" Callum asked.

He nodded.

"Your father is a very quiet man, but get him alone and he can talk for hours. Years ago, he explained to me that he was a Thane, with the same abilities that you just described, but he made me swear to keep it a secret. People would talk if they knew their neighbor was a Thane."

"Like how Mayor Gan hid his ability?" asked Realta.

"Precisely. Do you know what Kel did after graduating from the Academy? Before coming to Vala with your mother?"

Gareth shook his head.

"Esme was offered a work study at Teyrnas' hospital. She could tend to patients while continuing her education. While in the city, she lived with Kel and his family."

"He didn't have any family," Gareth said, shooting an accusing glare at Callum. "That's why he lives in Vala. He didn't lie to me!" Fresh tears sprang into his eyes.

"Gareth, every lie your father told has been to protect you and your mother and sister. He never meant to hurt you."

"Where is Kel now?" Realta asked. "Didn't he come with you?"

"He had other work to do. Said it was dangerous."

"I'm sure he'll join us soon. But your father does have family in Teyrnas. They're right here in the palace."

Realta's heart skipped a beat. "Is he a bastard, too?"

"I believe he's Yestyn's legitimate son. Serena unknowingly confirmed it for me."

Pieces fell into place. Amzie Fenn claimed Realta resembled a woman who used to live in the palace. Not a woman who worked in the palace. A woman who lived here. Many of the older servants, Shasta included, claimed the same thing. "They all think I look like Esme."

Callum nodded. "Esme and Kel lived in the palace for three years. They were happy, but life wasn't easy for them. The king had certain expectations for his son. Expectations that Kel could not meet no matter how hard he tried. In the end, Kel gave up trying to please his father and eloped with Esme. Then the king arranged a marriage contract between Kel and a princess from Byyar."

Realta gasped. "Shasta said that's what happened to Prince Carwyn. But he was killed. The old king..."

"The old king killed his eldest son in a fit of rage," Callum finished. "That's what rumor says, though official records state it was a wasting disease. But the three of us know better, don't we?"

"He should have been king," Gareth said, a mixture of confusion and awe. "My father should have been king."

"And you the crown prince," Callum added.

Gareth shuddered. "I wouldn't have liked that."

"Should we tell King Logan?" Realta asked. "Gareth and I are his nephew and niece, and you're his brother-in-law. If he knows we're related—"

"I don't advise telling Logan any of this. Remember, the king believes that his brother is dead. Best thing to do is wait until Kel gets here. Hopefully, Logan will have released us by then, but if not, we'll think of something."

Realta gave an absentminded nod. Her brain struggled to process this information. To think, her aunt and uncle could be ruling the kingdom had things been a little different.

"I guess," said Callum, rising from the bed, "you two have work today?"

"I don't want to work for him," Gareth replied.

"Come," Callum held out his hand. "Stay in my room for the day. I'll tell Master Pym you aren't feeling well. What about you, Realta?"

"Can I stay with you, too?"

Her father smiled. "Of course."

Realta took her father's hand, Gareth opting to walk by his side. She held on tight, not letting go until they were safely in the guest quarters.

✳ ✳ ✳

Father and daughter? thought Valentin Gardyner as he watched the tall man with wild, black hair lead Realta and the stable boy away. The man and the girl both had the stripes and diamonds, the mark of indentured servants, on their wrists. A nicer term for slaves. Curiously, the boy (Realta's cousin, not her brother) did not. *Well, at least they're together.* Val could not say the same about his own family. They had abandoned him the moment they discovered he was cursed.

What a difference a culture could make! The kingdoms along the Vogel Mountains revered Thanes. Many had them as kings and queens. Nobles and scholars. Not so in the lands east of the Caslan Valley. Once, they had been ruled by Thanes, too. But then, the normal people turned the tables on them, claiming they had usurped their abilities from the Creator, that the histories had gotten it wrong.

History, after all, was written by the victors.

For centuries, his kind had been feared, hated. No one wanted anything to do with Thanes. But most Thanes just wanted normal lives. And they would have had those normal lives if it wasn't for the Cuchasi, the Great Equalizers as they were known in Nowan. Thanes could not hide their identities from them. Except for Valentin Gardyner.

He lied about his ability to Realta, but it was a necessity. People always became so frightened when they discovered his true strength. Strong enough to trick the Cuchasi into seeing a normal human. Nothing to fear. And he was a messenger for the queen herself. Not an easy position to achieve.

Certain that Realta, her father, and her Cuchasi cousin were gone, Val snuck into the room. A small space, but clean and well lit. The king did not allow his servants to live in squalor. That was commendable.

The king places his own kind in servitude. Don't forget that!

Impossible to forget. The Vogel monarchs all claimed to support each other and all Thanes living in their kingdoms. Either Logan O'Kelwyn went back on his word, or... Or he simply did not know Realta was a Thane. How was that possible?

A question for another time. Val found his query. A simple notebook. There were only four entries. All of them dated.

"Excellent work, Little Dreamer," Val mused as he scanned the pages. He knew very little about Dreamers, the last one dying two centuries before his birth. But how had she known to record her dreams in the exact same manner as her predecessors? This was surely a sign of genius.

From what he could tell, all of them took place around Teyrnas. One even featured King Logan's brother as a little boy. Val reprimanded himself for being such a fool. He had mistaken Logan for an arrogant prick who had allowed supernatural abilities to go to his head. In reality, he was the product of an abusive home, unable to move past his childhood trauma. Fascinating!

"Now what is this?" Val read the fourth and latest entry. The phrase on the shop door caught his attention. "Fortur Colgri," Val sounded out the words. Definitely not Teyrnian. Tirshic perhaps? No. In the Tirshic language, "Fortur" meant soldier, or referred to an army battalion, but the shop sold farming supplies.

"That's it!" Val snapped his fingers. In Marish, "Fortur" could be translated as "supplies". Now, what would prompt a dream about a burned down village in Bran Maro?

An odd sense of warmth formed inside Val's chest. A warmth that first formed the moment he crossed the border into Teyrnas and grew in intensity as he entered the palace, culminating when he saw Realta standing off to the side, unseen by the world. The fools! Didn't they know greatness when they saw it?

No matter. They would see. See very soon. There were Nine of them. He and Realta were two, and he had his suspicions regarding the Jemayrti ambassador. That would make three.

Wonderful. Absolutely wonderful!

A sharp knock sounded at the door. Val returned the notebook to its rightful location. Standing, he searched the mind of the person on the other side of the door. Another servant. A woman around forty years old with zero amount of patience. Creating a simple Illusion in her mind, Val made her think that he was Realta.

"Yes?" he called out, the woman hearing the girl's voice.

The woman opened the door, hands on her hips. "Where have you been?"

"Sorry. I overslept."

"Overslept?! Today of all days? Get down to the kitchens immediately. Those Scholars will arrive any minute, and we need everyone doing their part. Is that understood?"

"Yes, ma'am." He gave a short bow.

With a huff, the woman marched down the hallway.

Val laughed under his breath. Oh, this was too easy! He sauntered out of the room and made his way to the guest quarters. Queen Gallia would be arriving soon, but not too soon. That woman certainly knew how to make an entrance.

I hope you don't get in too much trouble, Realta, Val thought. But her being in trouble would make her more willing to accept his help.

33

Exhibition

"What do you make of him?" asked Scholar Jori as he and Scholar Aedan reentered the common room. Charity sat at a table by herself, finishing breakfast. The journey from the Academy to Teyrnas had been uneventful, albeit equal parts exciting and stressful. To think, being reunited with her friend! But where to begin? The capital was massive. Scholar Maryn helped her post notices at the major inns, but no one had seen people matching Realta and Callum's descriptions.

"I think he's faking," replied Aedan.

"Are you sure? That limp seems legitimate."

"But did you see his crutch? That's a custom-made elbow crutch. You don't just pick those up off the street."

"Who are you talking about?" asked Charity.

The two scholars exchanged looks. Aedan replied, "Nobody. Just a man pretending to be a beggar. You see it all the time in the city."

"If he's pretending," Jori added.

"Well, if you think he's truly a beggar, why didn't you give him some money?"

"Because it's in a case in my room," Jori replied tartly.

"Is he still there?" Charity asked. The elbow crutch made her think of Kel. She wondered how her old tutor was getting along, and if word ever reached him and her family.

"Yes, at the corner," said Jori. He headed up the stairs. Scholar Aedan, rolling his eyes, walked over to the other side of the common room to join the rest of his colleagues.

Charity, curiosity taking over, rose and ventured into the street. At the corner stood the possible beggar. A tall, thin man, he wore a ragged, gray cloak over stained clothing, trousers torn at the knees. With his left arm, he held an elbow crutch, and he had a brace wrapped around his left leg, metal poles jointed at the knee and tied with a series of belts. Identical to Kel's. Charity stepped closer.

"Spare coin," the man asked passersby, holding out his hand. "Spare coin, young miss?" he asked her.

"I'm sorry, I don't have any." She peered at his hood face. "Kel?"

The beggar raised his hood high enough to give her a wink with his sharp blue eyes.

Charity embraced Kel, arms encircling his slight frame. Kel had to brace himself against the wall to keep from falling.

"It's good to see you, too, Charity," Kel said, laughing. "And I see you made it to the Academy."

"Are Realta and Callum with you?"

The laughter faded away. "I'm afraid not. Callum wrote to us, telling us you were attacked and separated. I should have warned you not to trust Kanton."

"But how could you have known?"

"I had the misfortune of meeting him. What are you doing in the city?"

"I'm here for the king's exhibition. How did you get here?"

"The safe way. Now, listen to me very closely, Charity," he whispered. "The city has grown far more dangerous than the last time I visited. Don't stay here a moment longer than necessary. The Scholars will ensure you're safe at the Academy. Is Lok Tolman with you?"

"Yes. He's at the Academy. And Kel, he's—"

"We'll talk later. After Realta and Callum are safe." He hugged her tightly. "Promise me you'll be safe at the palace. And whatever you do, don't ask too many questions. Chances are you will see things you cannot explain. But that's okay. You don't need all the answers."

"I don't understand."

"Promise me."

"I promise, Kel," she said, looking him in the eye. Those eyes seemed so tired. Had he traveled this far on his own? "Why don't you come with us? I'm sure the Scholars won't mind."

Kel grimaced. "That exhibition is by invitation only. And a person of my standing wouldn't be welcomed among nobles."

"What are you going to do?"

"Keep looking for my family. I have a good idea of where they are. Just need to ask a few more questions from the wrong sort of people."

"Can I come with you, then?"

Kel smiled. "Absolutely not. Your place is with the Scholars. It always has been." He hugged her one more time. "It's so good to see you."

"You, too, Kel." They broke away from each other. "Write me the second you find them."

"It's a deal." Kel turned away from her and called out, "Spare coin? Spare coin, ma'am?"

Charity took that as her cue and went back to the inn.

* * *

The palace rested at the very center of Teyrnas, like a mountain carved from marble. The outer walls alone towered above any building in the Hinterlands and easily stood twice as high as the ones encircling the Academy. Four gates stood at the four cardinal points. A marvelous sight.

But Charity's awe fought for center stage with her conversation with Kel. Everything he told her had been vague, no clear details. Where Realta and Callum in the city or not? And what did Kel gain by posing as a beggar? Too many questions for her already crowded mind.

The guards at the palace gates, all wearing knee-length black coats, motioned for the small caravan to enter. Charity, seated on the driver's bench next to the coachman, sat up straighter and smoothed down her dress. Everything would work out in the end. That was one of her mother's sayings. Her mother. Had she responded to Charity's letter yet? Hearing from her would do Charity a world of good.

One of the guards moved away from the carriage, stepping into the morning sunlight. The way the light hit his uniform revealed that the fabric was not black, but dark blue. The same shade of dark blue as Dane Kanton's coat. Academy records showed that a man named Kanton had graduated as a Learner Thane, but the Garrison had yet to confirm the man's position in the King's Guard.

Charity's throat tightened. Callum holding onto Kanton's wrists, trying to push him back. The flames casting dark shadows. Realta running towards Serena. Callum and Kanton falling. Kanton sinking his knife into Callum's chest. Between the ribs, into the lungs. Callum's horrifying scream. A punctured lung. How many healers between there and Teyrnas knew how to properly treat a punctured lung? How many had ever seen one?

The city has grown far more dangerous than the last time I visited.

"Charity?"

She jumped, heart leaping into her throat. Glancing down, she saw Scholar Maryn standing beside the carriage. They were inside the palace grounds, next to a large stable, two stories high and wide enough for dozens of horses. An older man with graying hair helped unload the equipment. Charity wasn't exactly sure what the equipment did. It was different from the machine that measured wind speeds. The Scholar wanted it to be a surprise.

"Are you all right?" Maryn asked.

"Yes, Scholar." Charity climbed down from the driver's bench. The walk between the stables and the palace was paved with smooth, gray stone cut in equally sized squares. Trees in full bloom, vivid reds and pinks, lined the wall. To her left, Charity spied an expansive garden. Bright flowers, shades of alternating blue and yellow. A bench rested beneath a shady oak tree.

"Is this everything?" asked the older man.

"Yes, thank you, Master Pym," replied Maryn.

Turning away from the garden, Charity spied a young woman, a little older than herself, helping unload the other carriages. She had short, sandy brown hair, and she wore trousers and a work shirt. On her wrists were faint scars, as though they had been bound too tightly.

"Serena?"

The young woman turned. Her blue eyes widened with recognition and fear. She took a timid step back.

Charity rushed over and grabbed her by the wrist so she couldn't run. "Serena, what are you doing here? Where's Realta?"

"I work here," Serena replied, her voice trembling. She glanced over at the older man, but he was busy talking to the Scholars.

A piece of equipment had made him suspicious and Maryn was explaining its function.

"But how did you get here?"

"Traveled. With Realta and Callum."

Charity's heart soared, beating faster and faster. "Are they here? What happened to Kanton?"

Serena flinched, but Charity maintained her grip. This girl wasn't going anywhere until she had her answers.

"They're here. Alive. So is Kanton."

She fought down a spike of fear. Kanton was the last person she wanted to run into. The last person she wanted to think about. But her friend was alive! She wished Kel had come with her. "Can you take me to her? Please?"

Serena glanced over to the palace's north entrance. A handful of guards stood at attention. None of them were Dane Kanton, thank the Creator. Serena shook her head. "Not now. Later."

"I'm only in the city for a day. It has to be soon."

"Okay." Serena licked her dry lips. "After the exhibition. I promise."

"You'd better." Charity released Serena's wrist, and the girl sprinted towards the stables.

"Come along, Charity," called out Scholar Maryn. She followed the group into the palace.

She paid no mind to the interior as they walked down a spacious hallway. Her mind was solely on Realta and Serena. Her friend was here, but she'd been in the palace instead of an inn. A reward for bringing Serena to justice? No. Serena would be in a prison for stealing a horse, not working in a stable full of them. Unless the king was very lenient.

But that did not explain Dane Kanton's actions. Why spend so much time tracking down Serena if the king wasn't going to punish her?

Maybe working for him is a form of punishment. She must have been sentenced to indentured servitude. Arnyn said the normal punishment was two to five years. Picturing Serena, Charity didn't recall seeing a servant's mark on her wrist.

Charity noticed that they were now in a large chamber, the far wall lined with intricate stained-glass windows. Beneath the windows sat two thrones. The larger of the two was adorned with two ravens, their wings spread and ready to take flight. The smaller one was adorned with gold and silver inlays. Both rested on a raised dais.

"When will the king and queen be here?" Charity asked.

"A quarter hour. Just enough time to set up," replied Scholar Maryn. She Manipulated the pieces one by one, putting them in their proper positions. The strange machine was comprised of a small wooden table with a glass sphere placed in the center. A metal rod going through the sphere allowed it to spin forwards or backwards. The top of the sphere just barely touched a metal chain which was coiled around a wooden beam placed above the table. The chain's other end was in a jar of water.

"What does it do?" she asked.

"It's a surprise." Maryn smiled.

Just as the Scholars finished their setups, the chamber began to fill with people. Several of them were servants, making last-minute preparations and inspecting the devices. Others were nobles dressed in fine clothing. Lords wore dark-colored suits with straight trousers and jackets that ended at their hips, as well as dark-colored, button-down shirts. Ladies wore colorful dresses that went down to their ankles while the sleeves only went to their elbows. The majority wore shades of blue, green, and gray.

One noblewoman wore a low cut, dark red dress with slits in the sides, designed more for riding than attending a formal event. A single rose in a garden of bluebells. She wrapped her arms around the arm of a nobleman who had a rigid posture and a serious face.

"Who is she?" Charity whispered to Maryn.

"Lady Sarra O'Lyr. The king's sister."

The king's sister. No wonder she wished to stand out in a crowd.

More people arrived. One group had very dark skin and wore clothing that was either white or light gray. Two of them wore white Scholar's cloaks. The man at the group's center caught Charity's eye. He was older, perhaps fifty-five or sixty, with tightly curled, gray hair. The same shade of gray as a sword blade. His eyes were the same shade of dark brown as his skin. He wore a suit after the same cut as the other noblemen, but it was pure white. The only color in his wardrobe was a necklace made of red stones and matching bracelets. She wondered there the group was from.

A guard dressed in that dark blue coat entered the room. Everyone fell silent.

"His Majesty King Logan of the Noble House Kelwyn, the Raven King, and Her Majesty Queen Isla of the Noble Byyarian House Margents!"

From the far door emerged the king and queen of Teyrnas. The queen was a regal woman with auburn hair, and she wore a dark blue dress with slits revealing silver fabric underneath. The king was quite tall, though not as tall as Master Loy, and he was thin with his facial bones easily visible. He wore black trousers and a black shirt with a dark blue cloak. His demeanor was vaguely familiar, like a word on the tip of Charity's tongue. The royal couple glided across the room and sat in their respective thrones.

"I thank you all for attending this exhibition in the memory of my dear brother Carwyn," the king announced. The audience gave a round of respectful clapping.

"How did his brother died?" she whispered to Maryn.

"Prince Carwyn was sickly. He passed away after a long illness."

"Scholars," the king said once the applause ended, "present your findings."

The first Scholar to do so was Scholar Jori, introduced as a Council member who specialized in archaeology. He had a proposal that Luroradi, the capital of Balthazar's ancient empire, was located off the coast of Port Lystad in Lowyrn. Many fishermen and divers had discovered remains of what appeared to be an ancient city that had sunk into the ocean.

Though the subject was interesting, Scholar Jori was quite long winded. Charity glanced over to the side and saw the dark-skinned man with the red necklace whispering to the other members of his group. He spoke at the same speed as the scholar, pausing every now and then to catch his breath.

He must be the translator.

Two more Scholars spoke after Jori. Both of them were scientists. Scholar Leila of the Jemayrt Academy (That's where the group was from!) had a device that allowed one to see stars and other objects up close. She presented it to the king as a gift once she finished speaking. The other, Scholar Aedan, spoke of his experiments with plants and ways to predict how many flowers would be of a certain color. The experiment had only run for two years, but the results were very promising. The king agreed.

"Can the same be done for human traits?" King Logan asked.

"I believe so, Your Majesty," replied Scholar Aedan. "A colleague of mine at the Lowyrn Academy is doing a similar study with eye color."

"What are the results?"

"Well, they're a bit odd, Your Majesty. She stated that two parents, one with blue eyes and one with brown, either have half the children blue-eyed and half brown, or they have only brown-eyed children."

"Fascinating."

Charity agreed. She had hazel eyes like her father, while her sister had brown eyes like her mother.

Scholar Aedan beamed a smile. "Thank you for your interest, Your Majesty."

The king then turned his attention to Scholar Maryn. "And what of you, Scholar?"

Maryn cleared her throat. "I have created a device that harnesses the power of lightning."

The crowd murmured. The other Scholars exchanged knowing looks and smiles. Charity was the sole member of their group in the dark. The Scholar continued.

"This is a prototype of a much larger device that I wish to create. The end goal will be along the lines of a candle that does not require fire to burn."

"That sounds promising," said the king, leaning forward. "How does it work?"

"I'll demonstrate. Charity, if you will stand here, please." She motioned for Charity to stand next to the glass jar filled with water. Scholar Maryn walked over to the glass sphere and began pushing it forwards, spinning it faster and faster. The metal chain above it spun in an elliptical shape, rocking the wooden beam. Maryn stopped spinning the glass.

"Charity, touch the metal chain, just above the water."

Charity did so. A small jolt shot through her finger, traveling up her arm. She let out a yelp, jumping and shaking her hand.

She examined her trembling finger. There was no sign of a burn or other kind of damage. The strange jolt quickly faded away. It truly had felt like lightning.

The crowd murmured, growing anxious. The king stood and stepped down from the dais. The queen opened her mouth to protest, but the king was already midway to the device. A pair of guards, hands on their swords, rushed through the crowd and followed on the king's heels. They eyed Scholar Maryn warily.

"How exactly does this work?" he asked Maryn, studying each part of the device. Charity moved a little closer. Never in her life had she thought she'd stand this close to a king. *Realta has lived in the palace for days. Being among royalty is nothing new for her.* How much longer was this bloody exhibition?

"By spinning this glass sphere," Maryn explained, "I am able to generate a small amount of electricity. The power within lightning bolts. The electrical current is transferred to the metal chain, which then travels along the chain's surface into that jar of water."

"Why water?"

"I've found that it's one of the best ways to conduct this current."

"Does this device have a name?"

Hints of red formed on Scholar Maryn's cheeks. "I call it a Nyss Generator."

"Incredible. You, Student, how much did that hurt?"

Charity froze. Had the king really spoken to her? Both he and Scholar Maryn were staring at her. Thinking fast, she replied, "It was kind of like touching a hot kettle, but without getting burned."

The king nodded and addressed Maryn. "I want to try."

"Your Majesty," said one of the guards, "I don't advise—"

The king held out his hand. A dagger from the guard's belt floated a short distance in the air, which he caught with ease. Charity positioned herself behind Scholar Maryn, her eyes fixed on the weapon. The same type of weapon Kanton had used. She broke out in a cold sweat. *What is he going to do with that? Oh, Creator, don't let him hurt us!*

"A precaution," the king smiled. A true smile that reached his eyes. Of course he wouldn't hurt them. That would be ridiculous. Besides, Scholar Maryn was also a Thane, and Thanes didn't hurt each other. So everyone claimed.

Scholar Maryn spun the glass sphere again. The king stood beside the jar. The crowd murmured, half approving and half disapproving of the king's decision. Charity spotted the woman in the red dress, the king's sister, smiling and whispering into her companion's ear. The man turned to her, his face in an expression of utter shock. The king's sister laughed and whispered in his ear again. The man relaxed some.

"Now, Your Majesty."

The king touched the chain and yelled, the sound echoing throughout the chamber. The crowd fell silent. The guards reached for their weapons. The king studied his finger and touched the chain again.

"I'm afraid it only works once per change, Your Majesty."

"Is there any way to make it last longer?"

"That's the next step in the project."

The king smiled. "Perhaps you can show me next year." He then walked back to his throne, returning the dagger to the guard. The guard grabbed hold of the blade and screamed, dropping the weapon. It clattered against the tile floor.

"It bit me!" the guard cried.

The crowd, King Logan included, erupted in laughter. Red-faced, the guard picked up the dagger and stalked back to his original position. Charity breathed a sigh of relief. The dagger was in its proper place. No need to worry.

The final Scholar presented her findings, but Charity paid her no attention. She scanned the crowd, looking for any signs of Realta or Serena. Shouldn't Realta be here? She and Callum were the king's guests. They ought to have been invited.

There she is! Charity spotted Serena's slight frame lingering at the back of the crowd. She looked at the king and queen uneasily. So odd that she'd be required to work at the palace, the very place where she had committed theft.

What about her family? She didn't recall Serena ever mentioning them. She and Realta had assumed she was an orphan. Working to repay her debt likely was her best option.

The Scholar finished her presentation. The king stood and addressed the crowd.

"Thank you all for attention today's exhibition, not only to honor my brother's memory but also to witness the wonderful achievements being made in our kingdom."

Charity tried to slip away, but Scholar Maryn's keen eye caught her.

"Where are you going, Charity?"

"I need to freshen up." That was always the excuse she gave her mother.

Maryn replied with a small smile. "Very well. We will be in the Reception Hall. Try not to get lost."

"Yes, Scholar." Charity threaded her way through the crowd towards Serena. "Okay, where's Realta?"

"This way," she whispered.

The doors at the end of the Audience Chamber burst open, interrupting the king's speech. A pale-faced guard, a young man no older than twenty, rushed over to the king, whispering a few words in his ear. The king paled. He nodded to the guard and resumed his seat. The queen whispered to him, but the king brushed her off, rubbing his temples. The crowd murmured in discontent.

The guard stood in front of the crowd and announced, "Her Royal Majesty, Monarch of the Great Caslanic Nation of Nowan, Queen Gallia Toutain!"

"Damn, we need to go," said Serena, grabbing Charity by the wrist.

"Wait, I didn't know another queen was invited."

"She wasn't. Come on."

Charity allowed Serena to lead the way. She only caught a glimpse of a woman with glossy, black hair spilling over her shoulders and wearing a silk purple gown slashed with white. No matter. Scholar Maryn would fill her in.

Serena led her up a series of stairs to the second level. Several people dressed in plain clothes moved about the spacious hall. Some were in a hurry, while others walked at a leisurely pace. A few of them had servants' tattoos, the same as Callum's. Serena walked over to a short woman whose head did not reach Charity's shoulders.

"Do you know where Realta is, Shasta?" Serena asked.

"With her father, last I heard. I believe they went to the guest quarters. And who might this young lady be?"

"This is Charity. Realta's friend."

"Oh? And what brings you to the palace?"

"I'm with the Scholars. I'm a Student at the Academy. Realta and I were traveling together when we got separated. I've been trying to find her."

"Then fate has brought you to the right place." Shasta eyed Serena suspiciously. "How much have you told her?"

"What was necessary," she replied quietly.

Shasta pursed her lips. "I see. I must be going. Queen Gallia has arrived ahead of schedule. Good day, Miss Charity."

"Good day, Mistress Shasta."

The short woman walked down the hall, stopping for a moment to speak with one of the servants.

"What did she mean?" She had the distinct feeling that Serena was hiding something.

"Realta will explain. This way."

The guest quarters were on the third floor, which had a rich, dark blue carpet and white walls decorated with paintings and tapestries. The images were either events of Teyrnas' history or depictions of the Gadyeni. Charity took note of the one for Abhainna, creator of the Elementals. Bright blue eyes framed by dark hair and bronze skin. She, too, wore a blue cloak.

Serena knocked on a door at the end of the hall. No one answered. She opened the door. The small room was empty save for a desk with a few books and papers.

She shook her head and retraced her steps down the hallway. A peel of laughter came from inside one room. Breaking away from Serena, Charity went to investigate. Serena groaned. She had waited nearly a month to find her friend. Serena could wait five minutes.

Opening the door, she saw three small children, two boys and a girl, playing in a lavish room. All three were finely dressed in blues and grays. One of the little boys spied Serena and ran to her, giving her an embrace.

"Serena, come play with us!" The little boy grabbed Serena by the hand and led her into the room. The other two children studied her and Charity with curious eyes.

"Not now, Mannix. I'm busy."

"But you never play with me anymore."

"Are you our cousin, too?" the other boy asked Serena. He was no older than five.

"She's not our cousin," replied the girl who was a few years older. "She's Mother's half-sister. At least, that's what Father calls her. And then Mother always yells at him that Serena is her true sister, no matter who her real mother was. Isn't that right, Serena?"

Tears brimmed Serena's eyes. She blinked them away. "Yeah."

"Who are your mother and father?" Charity asked the girl.

"Lord and Lady Lyr. Mother is the king's sister, just like Serena."

Another jolt passed through Charity, this one much stronger than the generated lightning. She stared at Serena. "Your brother is the king?"

Serena hung her head, hair obscuring her face.

"Yes!" replied Mannix.

"Why didn't you tell us?"

"Would you have believed me?" she asked in a low, sad voice.

No. Charity supposed she would not have believed her.

"Okay, um... Let's discuss this after we find Realta."

"She already knows."

"Who's Realta?" asked the girl.

"She's my friend. She's a little taller than me with black hair and brown eyes. And she usually wears her hair in a braid."

"Oh yes, we've seen her," the girl replied. "Mother and Father got into a silent argument about her, then started whispering. Mother is angriest when she does whisper arguments. She says the girl looks like this other lady, that they're identical. But Father doesn't see a resemblance."

"Do you know where she is, Shandri?" Serena asked, glancing at the open door.

"Yes. I saw her and that tall man with crazy hair go into the room across the hall, because that room will be empty until this evening when Queen Gallia arrives."

"Mother says she's full of bad words," added the boy, smiling.

"What man with crazy hair?" Charity asked, heart beating faster.

"You know. Kind of long and sticking out in places. Like the boy they were with."

"A boy?"

"The one from the stables."

Charity turned to Serena. "Do you know who she's talking about?"

"No. Thanks, Shandri." She walked out of the room towards the one her niece had indicated.

"Serena, wait," cried Mannix. The little boy stood at the threshold, his blue eyes glistening. "Why do you keep going away? Why can't you play with me like normal?"

Serena crouched down, meeting the boy at eye level. "It's complicated, Mannix. You wouldn't understand."

"Yes, I would. I'm six years old. I understand a lot."

"Then understand that I love you, but I can't play with you like we used to. Maybe later when things are better."

"Is it because of what Father said yesterday? Because he didn't mean it. He was just angry."

"Logan is angry a lot these days. I think he just misses his brother. Go play with Shandri and Kaden. I'll be back soon."

"You mean it?" Mannix's face lit up.

"Yes."

The boy gave Serena another hug and rushed into the room to resume playing.

"Your nephew really loves you," Charity said as they walked towards the other guest room.

"He's the only one."

"Why didn't you stay for him?"

Serena stopped in her tracks, pain and sorrow plain on her face. Biting down on her lip, she fought back the emotions. Her face became a neutral blank. Hadn't Charity seen that reaction before? A snide comment causing unspoken pain, only for Kel to fight it back. Now that she got a good look at Serena's face, she noticed the similarities between her and the king. Blue eyes and light hair. Angular faces with thin frames. Features Kel had as well. Why...?

Don't ask too many questions. Chances are you will see things you cannot explain.

Charity followed her tutor's advice and left the question unsaid.

The room Shandri had indicated was near the main stairway.

Voices floated up from the lower levels. Serena led her inside. The room was as spacious as a lecture hall at the Academy with furniture gilded in gold and silver and lush carpets covering tiled floors. Additional rooms adjoined both sides. It was like a miniature palace.

Three large, floor to ceiling windows stood along the far wall. At one window stood a small figure in a plain dress, looking at the world below.

"Realta?" Charity asked, taking a wary step closer.

"Charity?"

Charity and Realta ran to one another, embracing in the center of the room. It was her! Her best friend in the whole world was alive and well! She didn't want to let go. Didn't want the joyous moment to end. Images of Kanton stabbing Callum flashed in her mind, but only for a moment. She did not want anything to interrupt them. Not even the night that had forced them down different paths.

"He told me you were dead!" Realta cried, trembling. Large tear drops fell onto Charity's cloak.

"Who did?"

"Kanton. He found us in Hygate and told me that he killed you and Lok."

"What?" Charity eased the embrace so she could look her friend in the eye.

Realta wiped away the tears with her sleeve. "We were heading to Teyrnas, to find Serena's family, when Kanton found us. He told the city guard that we tried to kill the king, that my father was an escaped slave. He brought us here." Realta shot a glare at Serena. "Guess we found Serena's family, anyway."

"Lok and I escaped into the forest. Arnyn, your father's friend, helped us get to the Academy. And Realta, Lok's a Thane."

Sadness and anger dissipated, replaced by confusion. "Lok, too?"

"Yeah. An Elemental. He can control fire. How amazing is that?"

"Almost too amazing to believe."

A tall figure entered from the side room. A man dressed in nice clothes with a beard and in need of a haircut. A smaller figure, a teenaged boy, stood behind him. Gareth. She rushed to Callum and wrapped her arms around him.

"You're alive!"

"So are you."

"I saw Kanton stab you. The knife went into your chest, and..." Screaming. Blood pouring from the wound, darkening his clothes. No!

"A punctured lung." She knew it. "All healed now." He rested a gentle hand on Charity's shoulder. "Don't you leave, girl," Callum called out. "There are some facts we need to get straight."

Serena, her head low, walked closer to her, Callum, Realta, and Gareth.

"Father," Realta whispered, "Charity says Lok Tolman is a Thane, too."

Callum let out a long breath. "I'd have never guessed that either."

"What's going on?"

"I'm a Thane," Realta said, whispering. "A Dreamer. They think I inherited the ability from my mother's family. And Gareth is a Cuchasi."

"That's..." Charity could not find the words to describe how she felt. Not only was her best friend alive, but she was a Thane. And a Dreamer. The Scholars thought Dreamers were goners, too. This news would whip them into a frenzy. "You have to come to the Academy. They can teach you all about Dreamers, and there's a ceremony, and..."

"Charity."

"Yes?"

Realta held out her left wrist. A servant's tattoo, identical to Callum's, marked her skin.

"I don't understand."

"Kanton lied to the king. Father and I can't leave the palace until he pardons us."

"I can vouch for you. He has to believe me, right?"

"Maybe," Serena replied. "He said he'd try them after the meeting with Queen Gallia. He might keep his word."

"He'd better," Callum murmured.

"Oh, and what is this?" asked a feminine voice with a faint accent.

Charity turned and saw the woman with the purple dress. She was shorter than Charity assumed. No taller than herself. Behind the woman stood King Logan and several dozen others. Guards and servants, judging by the fact that a third of them were armed. All of them wore the same symbol embroidered on their clothing, a hawk with a silver key in its talons. A handsome man with short black hair and gray eyes moved closer to the queen.

"Servants, Your Majesty. I met them a few days ago. You remember me, don't you, Realta?"

She nodded.

"You see?"

Queen Gallia smirked and turned to King Logan. "Waiting until the last minute to prepare my rooms, I see?"

"Your letter stated you would not arrive until this evening." The king glared at her, eyes like blue ice.

"So I arrived early. Don't you plan for the unexpected in this kingdom?" she scoffed.

"We've just finished, Your Majesty," said Callum, standing upright with arms folded behind his back. "In fact, the room was ready an hour ago. We merely wanted to see that everything was in order."

"I see, Callum. Thank you," replied the king, raising an eyebrow. Charity tried to understand Callum's action. This man was holding them against their will for crimes they did not commit. He should be furious. But that wasn't Callum Haar's way. Her father always said he was a good man, albeit one who made a few mistakes too many.

"The king is very good to his servants," the handsome man continued. "See, he even employed Callum's children." He pointed at Realta and Gareth. "Isn't that generous?"

"Your messenger is mistaken," Logan replied, growing pale. "Only the girl is his. The boy is an orphan who is supposed to be working in the stables." He met Gareth with a level stare. Gareth averted his eyes and moved closer to Callum.

"I don't need to know this information, Logan," Gallia replied. "Are these girls servants as well?" She pointed at Charity and Serena. Her face burned red as every eye turned towards her.

"No. That one is my bastard sister. The other accompanied the Scholars. What are you doing here, child?"

Callum placed a protective hand on Charity's shoulder. "Your

Majesty, this is Miss Charity Loy, originally from Vala. With your permission, I'd like to escort her back to the Scholars. And, if it's not too much trouble, could you personally inform Captain Kanton of her safe arrival in the capital?"

The king's icy blue eyes regarded her for a moment. Her own eyes widened, seeing Kel's double staring back at her. *Don't ask questions! Kel said not to ask questions.* "It's no trouble at all, Master Haar. We have much to discuss once my dealings with Queen Gallia are over."

"Come, Charity. Gareth."

"Wait!" She rushed over to Realta, hugging her again. It wasn't fair. They had just found each other. Why did they have to be separated again so soon? How long would they have to wait to be truly reunited?

Charity and Realta slowly let go of one another. Fresh tears fell from Realta's eyes. Charity realized that she was crying, too. She nodded to Callum. The group from Nowan parted to allow them space. A hundred other people, all with the hawk and key on their clothes, crowded the hallway. Gareth muttered the word "silver" under his breath.

"Serena, don't you dare move!" King Logan yelled. The girl flinched, freezing in place. "I want to have words with you." He turned to Gallia. "I assume you want a chance to freshen up?"

"Of course." The messenger whispered in Gallia's ear. "And I want this girl to be in my attendance for as long as I am here." She pointed at Realta.

Realta froze, looking to Callum for help. Charity could only stare, shocked. What could this woman want with Realta?

"The girl is new. Perhaps I can—"

"She's just a servant, Logan. Why do you care? Besides, she strikes me as being intelligent. She will learn."

King Logan acquiesced.

Callum led Charity and Gareth away from the room. She looked back, meeting Realta's eyes one last time.

34
Coalition

Realta struggled to believe this was real. Charity was here in the palace. She was alive! All the horrible doubts and fears Kanton had planted in her mind withered away. But their reunion had been so brief. She had to find a way to see Charity again, learn her side of the story.

And she said Lok Tolman was a Thane, too. She'd have never guessed that in a thousand years. She was grateful that the innkeeper's son was safe at the Academy, that Charity hadn't had to make the journey alone.

Once Charity, Callum, and Gareth disappeared from view, Realta focused her attention on Serena. The girl remained frozen in place, not looking up to meet anyone in the eye for a second. How much trouble would she get in for bringing Charity here? The angry part of Realta did not care. Serena had avoided her this entire time, not even attempting a half-hearted apology. But that anger was slowly being replaced by pity. She was, after all, Kel's half-sister.

Realta did not know how to feel about that fact.

"Do you require anything else, Queen Gallia?" asked King Logan. The man knew that Charity was alive. She hadn't been murdered in the woods by Serena as Dane Kanton claimed. *When is he going to let us go?*

"Not from you," the queen replied. Her entourage dispersed throughout the room. Servants carried in luggage and adjusted furniture. Guards checked every corner and searched adjoining rooms. Dozens of people. The amount seemed excessive, even for a queen. Val remained at her side, smiling at Realta.

King Logan replied with a bow and walked towards Serena. He grabbed his sister by the shirt collar as though grabbing a dog by the scruff of its neck and led her out of the room. Pity overpowered anger, erasing it. Nobody deserved that level of treatment.

"Close and lock that door," Gallia said to one of her guards, a short man with blond hair and gray eyes. "Shilo," she addressed a lithe woman dressed in a blue silk gown. "Check the girl."

A pit formed in Realta's gut. What did that mean? She glanced over at Val. The man winked at her. The bad feeling worsened.

Shilo sauntered over to her, looking her up and down. "The girl's normal." She then walked to the windows, inspecting the view and exchanging words with a handful of guards.

Queen Gallia smiled. "And here I thought Logan had an ounce of cleverness in him. You girl, stand over there and wait for instructions."

Realta quietly walked over to the indicated corner, her legs trembling. What did the queen want with her? She wished Callum was still there.

Val went to Realta's side and whispered, "That Shilo is a good one. As illuminating as a wickless candle." He smiled. "She's the only Cuchasi among us. Very easily fooled by the simplest of Illusions."

"You hid me? How? Why?"

"Where I come from, Realta, Thanes protect one another. Most Minders who are gifted with Illusion can mask an Aura. In fact, it's one of the first tricks I learned."

"I thought you were low-leveled." Shasta's books had described the levels of power certain Thanes could possess. In the case of Minders, low-leveled individuals, such as Lady Sarra, needed permission to read minds. High-leveled ones could read multiple minds at once, or create Illusions seen by an entire crowd.

"In some areas. But rest assured, I can both find and hide Thanes. Your secret will always be safe with me, Little Dreamer."

"What did you call me?" Realta bit her tongue. None of the servants or guards acted like they heard her. Queen Gallia was absorbed in a conversation with the head guard, the two of them walking towards an adjoining room.

Val blushed. "Pardon me. Perhaps nicknames referring to your skill set are inappropriate in this setting. Is there another name you prefer?"

"Yes," she replied, keeping her voice low. "My own."

"Very well, Realta. You know, your thoughts seem much lighter today. Did seeing your friend help?"

You have no idea. "Yes, it did."

"That Dane Kanton is a nasty fellow, isn't he?"

Realta started. "How do you know about him?"

"He was on both your minds, and your father's and cousin's. You see, when several people think about the same person or thing, it's very easy for me to sense it. What did he do to you?"

Images flashed in Realta's mind. Kanton attacking her father, finding them in Hygate and burning Callum's rite of passage. Cornering her in the hallway late at night. A knife in his belt. Would he have used that knife on her if Shasta hadn't intervened? A shiver ran down her spine.

"I'd rather not say."

A grim expression crossed Val's face. "I will warn the queen regarding him. She is very protective of her female servants."

Realta appreciated that. Except she wasn't one of Gallia's servants.

The queen sauntered into the main room, the makeup on her lips and around her eyes refreshed. She nodded to each servant as she made her way towards Realta. She turned to Val and kissed him on the lips.

Realta's eyes widened. Kissing in front of all these people? She had only seen Master and Mistress Loy kiss once, and only because the couple thought they were alone. She and Charity had spied on them from behind a partially opened door. Charity's idea. They had expected to overhear plans for Bridget's birthday, not interlope on a private moment. They vowed never to mention it.

"I don't believe," the queen said, facing Realta, "that I caught your name."

"Realta Haar," she stammered. The queen was no taller than her. Actually, she was a few inches shorter. But her presence loomed over Realta, making her feel like a mouse cornered by a cat.

"What a lovely name. Now, that other man, the one who escorted the Student, he's your father. Correct?"

"Yes, Your Majesty."

"Oh, how interesting! You look just like him. I take after my father in face and my mother in temperament. Is it the same with you?"

"I don't know. Your Majesty," she quickly added. "I never knew my mother."

"What a shame. And that boy. He's the mirror image of your father, but Logan claims he's an orphan. Do you have an explanation?"

"He's my cousin. My father and his mother are siblings."

"I see. So your aunt and uncle passed away?"

"No, they... Um..." Realta's throat turned into a vise. How could she explain that Gareth was the son of King Logan's supposedly dead brother? No one would believe her. And King Logan, most likely, would be furious. Any hope of them being freed would vanish.

"I believe," said Val, "that Realta has had a long day and is too tired to think properly."

"Is this true, Realta?"

She nodded, silently thanking Val.

"I see." Queen Gallia gave Val a light squeeze on the arm. She turned to another servant. "Lucia, have a dress made for Realta."

"House colors, Your Majesty?" Lucia, a woman in her mid-fifties with touches of gray in her straight, brown hair, asked.

"Yes," Gallia smiled. "I want nothing more than to see Logan's reaction. Come, Valentin. I have matters I wish to discuss with you."

"Of course, Your Majesty." He gave Realta a quick nod and retreated into an adjoining room.

"Now," said Lucia, pining Realta into the tight corner, "let's take your measurements."

***

Val reclined in a plush chair, his feet resting on a small table covered with books and documents. He took a sip of wine, the bittersweet liquid coursing through him. Queen Gallia stood on the opposite side of the table, arranging the documents just so. He had hoped that they would have a little fun before getting down to business. But Gallia had an unbreakable work first, play later mindset.

"You've done wonderfully, Val!" Gallia exclaimed, surveying

the documents he had borrowed from the royal library. Stealing was too strong a term. Stealing implied the items would be missed. Each document had two or three copies. They expected one to go missing. He was merely fulfilling that expectation.

Val finished his wine. An excellent vintage. Logan had one thing going for him. He stood and walked over to Gallia, peering at one document from over her shoulder.

The document was a marriage contract signed by King Yestyn of Teyrnas and King Nolfri of Byyar, arranging an engagement between Prince Carwyn and Princess Isla. It read, "In keeping with the customs and longstanding peace between our kingdoms, we hereby arrange the marriage of Crown Prince Carwyn to Princess Isla, second born daughter of Nolfri, to be wed at noon on the Summer Solstice in the Year 1264 of the Academic Era." The document rambled on a bit. More legal terms meant to sugarcoat forcing two strangers to marry for political reasons. The end of the page was signed by both monarchs and their children.

"Is old Nolfri still alive?" Val asked.

"Yes, and he's even more thickheaded than his son-in-law."

"Bloody Thanes." King Nolfri was a Minder of the mind reading variety. Strong, but not nearly as strong as Val. Even he wasn't sure what his limit was, if one existed.

Gallia smiled and ruffled Val's black hair. Oh, how he had missed her! Let the woman have her prejudices so long as Val could have his fun.

"It's a shame he died," Gallia said, surveying the revised marriage contract, this one between Prince Logan and Princess Isla. "I heard he was quite amiable."

"Everyone wants to believe their leaders are benevolent. His early death likely led to everyone thinking he was better than he truly was."

Gallia studied Carwyn's death certificate. "Officially, he died from a wasting disease, but the specific type is never stated."

"There's more than one?"

"Yes. And I've heard rumors that he vehemently opposed the arranged marriage. That he slept with other women to get back at King Yestyn. Some rumors claim he got one pregnant."

"Anything's possible." Even the Nine returning. He, Realta, and

Ambassador Ekene made three. Minder, Dreamer, and Learner. A good start. But where were the other six?

"What's that?" Gallia asked. Val hadn't realized he was muttering. Such a bad habit.

"You don't seem surprised that Yestyn's bastard is here. Alive."

Gallia flung down the documents and shook her head in disgust. "That was Eskandar's plan. I told him it was foolish. I mean, why would the man be more compliant knowing that his bastard sister was dead?"

Eskandar, king of Tarod, the little kingdom due south of Nowan. The man had a ruthless streak. Likely compensation for his kingdom's small size and even smaller importance.

"He doesn't seem to care much about the girl anyway," said Val, though he had gleaned a sense of caring from Logan's mind.

"Doesn't matter. It's the principle I care about."

Val smiled. Yes, even with all her prejudice regarding Thanes, Gallia could not bring herself to hurt one. Val peered into her mind. Of course that memory was in the forefront. The queen's mother and father losing an infant child, the queen's little sister. Her only sibling. Gallia had only been twelve at the time, but she understood her parents' struggle to have another child, felt the same searing pain they felt at the little girl's death. Five weeks. Such a short time.

Logan had already lost one sibling. She would not cause him to experience that pain again.

Did that fool of a man even know about the Eastern Coalition? Probably not. Vogel Kingdoms tended to focus on themselves and their precious trade routes. They only cared about the east when they wanted to go to war.

"But you must admit," Val add, "that King Syleck involving his niece was a stroke of genius."

Gallia shivered. King Syleck of Tirshay had the misfortune of mixed blood in his family tree. Every once in a while, one of them would be born a Thane. Eltzabet was a good kid, and a very powerful Minder. Though not as powerful as Val. Not even close.

Syleck often used Eltzabet to plant thoughts in people's heads. Problem was, they needed to be close by for her to be successful. So old Syleck had sent the girl to Teyrnas to work as a clerk in the local garrison. She had close access to many important people. Dane Kanton among them.

It was a good plan. Misguided in certain areas, but good. The fact that Syleck and Eskandar could be in the same room without coming to blows was good enough for the other monarchs. But Gallia had her doubts.

"You know Captain Kanton is in the palace, right, my dear?" Val asked.

Gallia sighed. "That is unfortunate. We should have vetted him better."

"Realta is terrified of him."

Gallia went back to the documents. Blueprints for the city walls. "Why did you insist she help us?"

"I saw it in the clouds."

She gave him a stern look. Val took no stock in cloud reading, but Gallia gave it the benefit of the doubt. Her mother had been a firm believer in the practice.

"Apologies. I thought Logan being on edge would benefit us, and I decided hiring one of his servants would be sufficient."

"But will it be the edge we want?"

"If we truly want peace, yes."

Gallia measured out the distances between the city gates with her finger.

"We do want peace, right?"

"I'm not sure," Gallia replied with a sigh. She looked at another blueprint, this one for the wall surrounding the palace.

Val smiled.

35

Reception

Serena unconsciously put one foot in front of the other as Logan led her down the hall, away from the guest quarters. Her brother rarely laid hands on her, only when his temper was at its boiling point. The man had been on edge the last few days, contributing to his mood. His dealings with the late king of Nowan, though never resulting in war, were unsuccessful. Nothing guaranteed success with the country's new queen.

Entering the servants' stairway, Logan pinned Serena against the wall, glaring at her.

"What were you thinking, bringing that girl to Gallia's rooms?"

"I was just trying to help..." Serena stammered, unable to look her brother in the eyes.

"Don't you realize Gallia could have had you killed? Half the nobility knows you stabbed me. What if Gallia knew? What if she mistook you for an assassin?"

The thought never crossed Serena's mind.

She tensed as Logan wrapped his arms around her. She waited for the blows, pain, harsh words, but they never came. Logan was hugging her. Why?

"I'm sorry for everything, Serena. I'm sorry I put you in a position that made you want to run away. Your mother would never forgive me if she knew."

Her mother. The royal half of her family never mentioned Nell Molyns, ashamed that their father had been unfaithful to their mother, and with a servant no less. Serena's memories of her mother were very few and fading fast. Tears leaked from her eyes.

Logan eased his hold on Serena and locked eyes with her. They were almost the same height.

"I think you did a very good thing today, Serena."

"How so?" she asked, wiping away a stray tear with her sleeve.

"You brought Miss Charity Loy to my attention. I saw her at the exhibition, but never asked her name." Logan paused, a new light shining in his blue eyes. "Come eat at the reception with me."

"I'm sorry?" Had Serena heard that correctly? She had never been allowed to be present at a royal reception, let alone eat at one.

"It starts in a few minutes. We'll arrive together."

"I don't understand."

Logan sighed. "We made a promise to your mother that you would be cared for. That we would love you as our own. From now on, I intend to make good on that promise."

Serena studied her half-brother's face. She knew how Logan worked, how he made deals with other nobles. He always made sure to gain their trust first, or enough of it. What was the man's endgame? *It must have something to do with Queen Gallia. But why involve me?*

"I'm not properly dressed," she replied, glancing down at her trousers and work shirt.

A smirk crossed Logan's face. "Who cares? You're my sister. The sister of the king can dress however she wishes."

"I really ought to change."

"Nonsense. Come." Logan wrapped his arm around Serena's shoulders, leading her down the stairs. How easy would it be to escape? Serena had already stabbed the man. She had proven the great Thane to be mortal. She could fight him, push him down the stairs. Run away for good this time.

Her conscience held her back. Realta and Callum would still be trapped here. Their imprisonment was her fault. She could not live with abandoning them a second time. She allowed the king to lead the way.

The Reception Hall was on the ground floor in the wing opposite the Audience Chamber, its windows providing a view of the courtyard. Hundreds of people could dine at once. Serena heard voices from the other side of the door. Two guards stood watch at the entrance.

"Waltyr," Logan addressed one of them, "send for Captain Dane Kanton, as well as Peydar Wills and Eirica Marsh. Have them come to the Reception Hall immediately."

"Yes, Your Majesty." The guard saluted and hurried off at a quick walk.

What does he want with them? She eyed her brother suspiciously.

"Your Majesty," whispered the other guard, Ector. He had worked in the palace for as long as Serena could remember. "Are you sure you want her here?" He cocked his head towards Serena. "People are liable to talk—"

"Then let them talk."

Ector replied with a sheepish nod.

Logan entered the Reception Hall, Serena half a step behind him. Conversations ceased and all eyes, both noble born and scholarly, turned to them. Serena's face grew warm. Life was so much easier when she was ignored.

Serena locked eyes with Isla. The queen's eyes darted from Serena to Logan, wondering what to make of them standing side by side. Una, the queen's nosy scribe, tapped Isla on the shoulder, pen and paper at the ready. Isla shrugged her off. Morgan, the only child in attendance, stared at the tablecloth, likely wishing he could be excused.

Serena spied Charity Loy and Callum at the end of the table, seated with the Scholars and the ambassador's party from Jemayrt. Charity flashed her a quick smile, and Callum gave her a curt nod. Was Callum telling the truth about his brother-in-law? Prince Carwyn had died from a long illness. Everyone believed that. Everyone except Mal.

"Sorry for the delay," said Logan, his voice echoing off the vaulted ceiling and pulling Serena away from her thoughts. "Her Majesty Queen Gallia, unfortunately, cannot attend at the moment. Please enjoy the reception despite her absence."

The attendants applauded. More than a few nobles laughed and snickered. No doubt they were relieved not to be dining with officials from Nowan.

"This way, little sister."

Serena started. Little sister? Logan never addressed her as 'little sister'. She glanced around the room. Something felt off. The nobles were enjoying themselves, the Scholars were deep in conversation. No one was a threat. So why had Logan summoned those guards?

"Logan, is everything all right?" Isla asked as Logan took the empty seat across the table from her. The seat to his left was also empty. If Serena sat, she would be facing Morgan and Una. Not terrible. And Sarra and Lord Lyr sat nearby. They had always treated her kindly. Serena quietly slipped into the cushioned seat.

"Is there any reason why things shouldn't be all right?"

"No, my dear, it's just..." Isla stole a glance at the nobility.

"Listen, Isla. Next year, Serena will be of age. You can't expect me to introduce her to the noble court without prior knowledge."

The noble court? Stars above, had Logan lost his mind? A month ago, he would have balked at the idea of Serena being a part of noble society. Had she been born a Thane, that would be different. She'd have some value. What had changed?

"Do you really mean that?" Isla's eyes brightened.

"Every word."

Shasta Cray glided towards the table. "Your Majesty," she addressed Isla, "there is an urgent matter that acquires your attention."

"Can't it wait?" questioned Logan.

"I fear not. My Queen?"

"I'd better see what this is about." Isla rose from the table. Una rose as well. "No, Una, stay here and enjoy the reception."

"But what if you have a Farsight? Who will record it?"

"Mistress Cray has an excellent memory." She nodded for Shasta to lead the way. The pair exited the Reception Hall with little notice.

"May I be excused?" Morgan asked his father.

"No."

The Reception Hall doors opened once more, admitting Captain Kanton and Guardsmen Wills and Marsh. Kanton held his head high, while his two colleagues were less than eager to be present.

"Your Majesty called for us?" Kanton asked. Most people tried to hide facial scars. But the fresh haircut and high-necked, uniform collar seemed to highlight Kanton's, forcing one's eyes towards them.

"Indeed I did." Logan stood. Snapping his fingers, his empty wineglass and a knife floated into the air. The knife rapped on the glass. The sharp sound alerted everyone to be silent. Another snap. The objects gently landed back on the table.

Serena shrank underneath Kanton's glare. She had avoided this man since he dragged her back to the palace. He had tried to murder her, and what was his reward? A place of honor in the King's Guard and a medal for his achievement.

She suddenly felt sick. Was that why Logan had dragged her here? To gloat over his would be assassin?

"Captain Kanton, Guardsman Wills, and Guardswoman Marsh," Logan said in a loud voice. "Your achievements this past month have been exemplary. I thank you all for your service to this kingdom."

The crowd applauded.

"Why, thank you, Your Majesty. We were merely doing our best."

"Your best? No, that word is not good enough to describe your deeds. Noblemen and women, these are the guards who chased my bastard sister," he clamped a hand on Serena's shoulder, "to the far reaches of the kingdom. Successfully returning her to me."

Serena groaned. Her worst fears were coming true. All that talk of love and promises was just another one of Logan's tactics.

"Someone had to bring that girl to justice," Kanton replied humbly. Marsh and Wills nodded in agreement.

"And not only her, but the man who aided her, has been brought to justice. What can you tell everyone of that villain?"

Kanton was taken aback. "You want me to tell everyone?" he asked, pride gleaming in his eyes. Marsh and Wills exchanged whispers.

"But of course, Captain."

"Very well." Kanton smiled. The man was so creepy when he smiled. "That wretch was aided by an escaped slave and murderer named Callum Haar. He had everyone fooled, including his master. During our first night traveling to Teyrnas, Haar killed his master's daughter out of revenge and tried to kill us." Kanton motioned to the burn scars on his face. The crowd murmured, concerned. Kanton soaked it in like water on dry earth. "Sadly, our fellow guardsman Aleyn Tock succumbed to his injuries. It is only by the blessing of the Creator and His Gadyeni that the three of us survived."

"And what was the name of the poor girl?"

Kanton let out a dramatic sigh. "She was a lovely girl in her teens named Charity Loy. She wanted nothing more than to study at the Academy."

"What did she look like? Blue eyes, you said?"

"Your Majesty is mistaken. I believe the girl had hazel eyes. Such a rare and lovely color in our land."

Logan nodded and walked towards the end of the table. The end where Charity sat.

Serena's eyes widened. *That's why I'm here!*

"Young Student," he addressed Charity, "would you mind standing up?"

Charity slowly rose to her feet, her entire body trembling. Tears glistened her eyes. Both hands gripped the back of her chair, the knuckles turning white. She seemed so small standing next to the king.

Kanton and Marsh gasped. Wills turned as white as a sheet.

"Now, young lady, please tell us your name."

"Charity Loy," she stammered. Tears fells down her cheeks. The crowd murmured. People stood to get a better look. Sarra faced her husband and tapped her forehead. He nodded.

"You, Scholar Aedan, what's this student's name?"

The Scholar gave him a puzzled look. "Her name is Charity Loy, Your Majesty."

"And Scholar Jori, you're a member of the Council, right? How long have you served in that position?"

"Eight years, Your Majesty."

"And what is this student's name?"

"Charity Loy." He furrowed his brow. "Your Majesty, what are you—"

"Where is she from?"

Jori paused. "Vala. A small village near Caman's Pass."

"And you, Scholar Maryn, what is this student's name?"

"Her name is Charity Loy." The Scholar's bewildered eyes darted from the king to her colleagues and back.

"How long has she been at the Academy?"

"She and her friend arrived on Alet seventh, Your Majesty. She had been traveling with a man claiming to belong to the King's Guard. A man named Kanton." Her eyes rested on Kanton, growing fearful. "She claimed he attacked them..."

Logan gave Kanton a wicked smile, his white teeth gleaming. "Captain Kanton, it appears that Miss Loy is alive and well. But what of Callum Haar? Master Haar, please stand."

Callum stood, his dark eyes fixed on Kanton. A hint of a smile appeared on his face.

"Your Majesty," said Kanton, placing a hand on the hilt of his sword. "This entire show is very unorthodox. Nothing that man says can be trusted."

"All of the Scholars recognize her," said Marsh.

Kanton glared daggers at her.

"I decide what is considered orthodox in my own house, Kanton. Master Haar, do you recognize this girl?"

"Yes, Your Majesty. She is Charity Loy, the youngest daughter of my master, Sardic Loy. I've known her since she was in the cradle."

Logan reached into his pocket and removed a handkerchief, handing it to Charity. "No need for tears, little one. Not right now. Do you recognize this man?"

Charity Loy, wiping her eyes, said, "That's Callum. He works for my father. He'd never hurt me."

"He is a good man. I see that now. But what of that man?" He pointed to Kanton. "Do you recognize him?"

"He stabbed Callum!" Charity sobbed. "I woke up and saw him stab Callum. I thought he was dead!" Her body shook with every cry.

"That's all I need to know." He gave her a brief hug. "You may sit down."

Charity more collapsed than sat in her seat. Scholar Maryn wrapped her arms around her. She and the other Scholars, as well as those from Jemayrt, tried to comfort her. Callum remained standing, waiting.

Logan jabbed a finger at Kanton and his cronies. "Captain Dane Kanton, and guards Peydar Wills and Eirica Marsh, I denounce you as liars and traitors to the Raven Throne. For the attempted murders of Callum Haar and my sister Serena O'Kelwyn, you are hereby stripped of your titles and banished from the capital. If you are seen in the capital again, it will mean your deaths."

"This is an outrage!" Kanton cried.

"Please, Your Majesty," said Wills, rushing towards him. "You can't do this to us. Marsh and I, we were just following orders. You can't punish us for what Kanton did!"

"Damn you, Wills!" said Kanton, seething.

"Well, Master Wills, considering you are no longer a member of the King's Guard, you won't have to worry about following orders again. Ector! Waltyr!" Logan yelled. The two guards ran into the room, hands on their swords. "Escort these individuals out of the palace. They have until nightfall to leave the city."

Marsh, a look of resignation on her face, led a weeping Wills towards the door. The guards grabbed Kanton by the arms, dragging him away from the table. The man fought back every inch of the way.

"You have no proof!"

Lord Darrys rose from his seat. "Pardon, Your Majesty."

"Speak freely and quickly, Lord Lyr."

"I took the liberty of reading Miss Loy's and Captain Kanton's minds. The girl is truthful, and the captain did try to kill your sister. He would have succeeded if not for Callum Haar's intervention."

"You liar!" Kanton spat. Waltyr and Ector struggled to keep hold of him. He glared at the king. "You just want to get rid of me. You never liked me."

"And why would I want to get rid of you?" he asked with mock confusion.

Sarra hid her smile by taking a sip of wine.

Kanton's face reddened. "Let go of me!"

"Let him have the dignity of walking out," Logan instructed the guards. They obeyed, both a bit winded.

Kanton glared at Logan. He opened his mouth to speak but thought better of it and stalked out of the room, his head held high. Marsh and Wills trailed behind him, followed by Waltyr and Ector, their swords partially out of their sheaths. The Reception Hall door closed with a bang.

The crowd murmured, all of them looking from Logan to Charity and Callum to Serena. But none looked at her with disdain. In fact, a few of them were smiling. That wasn't right. Serena was the bastard. Nobody smiled at her.

"Are you all right, little one?" Logan asked Charity. A few tears escaped her eyes, but she nodded. "He will never hurt you again."

"Thank you," she managed, barely audible.

The king then turned to Callum. "I will reevaluate your situation within the half week, Master Haar."

"And my daughter's?"

"You have my word."

Callum nodded and went towards the door.

"Resume your seat, Master Haar. You are a guest here."

Callum thanked him. One of the Scholars switched places with Callum so he and Charity could sit next to each other. She gave him a teary-eyed embrace.

Logan returned to his own seat. The conversations returned to normal volume, most of them discussing Kanton's dismissal. A pair of noblemen commented that the king had referred to Serena as "O'Kelwyn" instead of "Molyns", noting the political implications of officially accepting the old king's bastard. Serena wished she could create an Illusion to make herself disappear.

"I'm surprised you didn't do that years ago, Your Majesty," Una muttered.

"Young men make mistakes. Older men ought to know better."

"Kanton really tried to kill Serena? Why?" asked Morgan, his face pale.

Logan drummed his fingers on the table. "Damn. I never thought to ask why. He likely thought he could get something out of it."

"Either way, we're glad you're safe." Sarra smiled at her.

"Thank you." Of all her half-siblings, Sarra had always been the kindest. People loved using her and her unusual opinions for their rumors, constantly whispering. No one whispered now. Yes, this was definitely odd. Logan had used her as a pawn and used her brilliantly. But the game was over. There was no reason to keep pretending.

"Logan, may I be dismissed?"

"Why? The food hasn't been served yet."

"I just..." The king's face was unreadable. He had no reason to love Serena. She was living proof of Yestyn's unfaithfulness. She had no Thane abilities. No useful attributes. Just an ordinary, human bastard. "I thought you were ashamed of me."

"The only person I'm ashamed of is myself. There are important matters we need to discuss once my dealings with Nowan are through. Matters I should have discussed with you a long time ago."

"Such as?" She was half afraid to ask.

"Later, sister. For now, enjoy yourself."

Enjoy herself? Serena looked at the nobles and Scholars. They all meshed together perfectly, like tiles in a mosaic. A small group even played Death Charades, trying to see who could create the best assassination plot against the other players. Everyone got along, perfectly in place.

So where was her place?

***

Servants bowed to Isla as she and Shasta made their way through the servants' wing, but not out of fear. Isla had grown up seeing servants cowered whenever her father was nearby. She vowed to never inspire any type of fear. When servants bowed to her, it was of their own free will.

"Shasta, what exactly is this urgent matter?" The head of servants had been unusually quiet.

"I will explain presently. I don't want to risk any rumors, especially with half the nobility at the palace."

"Very well," she sighed. She knew firsthand how rapidly, no matter how ridiculous, rumors spread. They stopped in front of a room near the end of the hallway. "Isn't this Realta's room?"

"Yes, Your Majesty," Shasta replied, removing a key from her pocket and locking the door. "If you'll step inside?"

"I would like to know what's going on first." Images from her original Farsight flashed before her eyes. Fire and destruction. Nine people racing to unite with one another. The Wardens of the Night, whoever they were, seeking to destroy them. She pushed the images away. Not all of her visions were accurate, and she hadn't had anymore concerning the girl.

Shasta glanced down the hallway. No one was within earshot.

"It concerns an old friend of yours. One you haven't seen in a very long time."

"Then why not announce it as such?"

"King Logan appeared to be in a good mood. I didn't want to risk upsetting it. Please, my queen." She motioned towards the door.

Adopting a regal posture, Isla entered the small room. On the bed sat the new stable hand, a teenaged boy with the typical Hinterlander appearance who Logan claimed was simple-minded. The boy stared at her with dark eyes. No, stare was the wrong word. Studied. The boy was studying her. Looking into his eyes, she realized he was anything but simple.

"You're blue," the boy said.

"I beg your pardon?" Her dress was dark blue, but the boy was not looking at her clothing. His eyes were fixed on her face.

"My son is a Cuchasi," spoke a male voice.

Startled, Isla's eyes darted to the far corner. Near the small window stood a man dressed in tattered clothes, his face obscuring by a gray cloak. His left leg was supported by a brace, and he held a crutch with his left arm.

"Who are you?" she demanded, doing her best to mask her fear.

"An old friend. Just as Shasta said." The man walked towards her, his left leg stiff and clumsy. Pushing back his hood, he allowed Isla to get a good look at his face. The entire left side was covering in scars, and his ears were little more than ragged tissue. But that messy, light brown hair. Those blue eyes, so light and cheerful...

"Carwyn?" Isla grabbed hold of the writing desk. Queens did not faint, even in the presence of Shades. She looked to Shasta. The smaller woman nodded in confirmation. "How did you get here? How are you even alive?"

"I had a very good healer." He held out his hand to her. Isla took it, holding it tight.

"Esme?"

He smiled.

"Oh, thank the Creator! I heard all these terrible rumors. That she died. That Yestyn sold her to Sykerian slavers." Isla took a deep breath, steadying herself. "How did you get away?"

"Esme knew my injuries were severe, but not life threatening. She asked me if I wanted to continue living in the palace or if I wanted to start a new life in the Hinterlands. I made the better choice. She found some herbs that would simulate death, causing my heart rate and breathing to slow down so they were undetectable. She then found two sympathetic guards, and they helped us get out of the city. We've spent the last seventeen years in a farming village."

"I'm so happy you escaped." She gave him a weak smile. Though she had only known Carwyn for a few months, she had grieved him along with the rest of his family. But she had always known their marriage would never be. She had known from the moment she first laid eyes on him.

"I wish we could have taken all of you with us."

Isla laughed quietly. "I don't think I would have adjusted well to farming."

"Oh, it's not just farmers. I've made a good living being a private tutor, and Esme as a midwife. It hasn't always been easy. But we were together."

"And you said this young man is your son?" She glanced over at the stable hand. The light fled from the boy's eyes. Every muscle in his body tensed.

Carwyn smiled from ear to ear. "Yes. Gareth, can you come closer, please? There's someone I want you to meet."

The boy cautiously got off the bed and went to Carwyn's side. Isla now saw that the boy had Esme's eyes. She held out her hand to him, but he shied away.

"I just wanted to say," Isla told him, "that I was friends with your mother before you were born. I see so much of her in you."

"Thank you," Gareth replied quietly.

"What made you come back?" Isla asked.

Carwyn's expression darkened. "I'm trying to find my brother-in-law and niece, Callum and Realta Haar. I heard rumors of their arrest in the city, and Shasta confirmed they're in the palace. You have to help me get them out. I can't wait any longer."

"Logan is going to free them once Queen Gallia leaves."

"Who?"

"Gallia. The queen of Nowan."

"King Cedric is dead? When?"

"Last year. I guess news doesn't travel that fast in the Hinterlands."

"No, it doesn't." Carwyn fixed her with a level stare. "Regardless, I can't wait that long. The city is growing more dangerous every day. I can't risk waiting."

"What do you mean? I haven't heard any reports out of the usual."

"Tullcrest district is full of mercenaries. My source said more gangs have moved into the area in the last couple months, driving out the less violent competition."

"Carwyn, Tullcrest has always been that way. Besides, we're safe in the palace."

"His name is Kel," Gareth interjected. Carwyn placed a gentle hand on the boy's shoulder.

"I was called Carwyn long before I was Kel. Isla, do you know where Realta and Callum are now? And Serena?"

"Callum and Serena are in the Reception Hall. I have no idea where Realta is. Carwyn, is that girl a Thane?"

Carwyn was taken aback.

"Yes," Gareth replied. "She's a Dreamer. She told me, and I saw black lights coming from her skin, just like the blue lights coming from yours."

"I would have preferred you told me this sooner, Gareth," Carwyn replied gently.

"I didn't know if it was important. Uncle Callum already knows."

"But Logan doesn't," replied Isla. "If the nobility learns he forced a Thane into servitude, his reputation will be ruined."

"Then the matter will stay between us," replied Shasta. The woman was so quiet Isla forgot she was standing there.

"Wait a moment. Carwyn, how do you know about Serena? Her mother didn't tell us the truth until years after you died. Or when we thought you died."

Carwyn let out a painful sigh. "I figure it out almost immediately. When I heard Nell Molyns had a baby girl, I went to go see her. I noticed I was the only man in the room and asked about the girl's father. Nell told me the truth. I confronted Yestyn, told him he should take responsibility for the child. He told me that bastards were commonplace, and that I shouldn't act so righteous, since I was expecting a bastard, too. I let slip that Esme and I had eloped. He didn't take it well."

"That's why he beat you?" Isla paled.

"His anger got the better of him again."

Isla placed a gentle hand on the scarred half of Carwyn's face. The marks were smooth and white with age. Her eyes fell on his ears. "He ripped out your rings, too?"

"He said I didn't deserve them."

"I'm so sorry."

"Why was he angry about your and Mother getting married?" asked Gareth.

"Because he was engaged to me," Isla replied.

The boy stared at her, wide-eyed. "You aren't angry, too?"

She looked into Carwyn's eyes and smiled. "When I first met your father, I had a Farsight of him wearing a white suit in a chapel, ready to be married. But not to me. It was always Esme standing by his side. And when I first saw your mother, I had another Farsight of her in a field, playing with a little boy. When I heard your father died and that your mother was sent away, I thought my visions were flawed."

"Your visions have always been accurate," Carwyn replied, smiling.

A spike of panic seized Isla. "Carwyn, my visions aren't flawed."

"Isn't that a good thing?"

"No. When I saw Realta, she was in danger. These people were searching for her, trying to capture her and others like her."

"What people?"

"I don't know. I never saw any faces. Only that they called themselves the Wardens of the Night."

"Who else heard this?"

"Just Realta, her father, Serena. And Una, my scribe. But I told her to erase it. I didn't want Logan to see."

"And did she?"

Isla racked her mind. "Yes. She scratched it out. Logan was none the wiser."

Carwyn bit down on his lip, thinking. "Shasta, when does the reception end?"

"This evening. But Callum and Realta can't leave with those marks on their wrists."

"What marks?" Carwyn's voice took on a dangerous edge. Isla wondered if he knew how much he looked and sounded like Yestyn.

"Realta was given a servant's mark, and Callum was marked as a runaway twice over."

"Who ordered that?"

"Your brother."

Carwyn cursed under his breath. "No matter. I know someone who can remove them. We'll leave tonight. Isla, can you—"

"Kel," said Shasta. "Realta has been employed by Queen Gallia. She wishes the girl to wait on her for the duration of her stay. If Realta were to suddenly vanish, the blame will fall on Logan. And tension between those two monarchs is the last thing our countries need."

"When does she leave?"

"In a few days. My advice, lie low until then. Gareth, you need to continue working in the stables."

"I don't want to work for him," the boy replied, adopting his father's harsh tone.

"We all must do things we don't want to do. Your Majesty," she addressed Isla, "do not mention this meeting to anyone."

"I wasn't planning on it. I don't know what this news would do to Logan." Logan had mourned his brother for over a year and still had trouble talking about him. If he learned that Carwyn had been alive this whole time, he would feel betrayed.

"I want to take Serena with us when we leave," said Carwyn. "Esme and I should have taken her all those years ago. I don't want to repeat that mistake."

"I think that's a good idea. The girl has no future here, even though Logan seems to have had a change of heart."

"Is there a place I can stay in the meantime?" Carwyn asked.

"There are emergency apartments in the tunnels," Shasta replied. "Your Majesty, I believe you've been absent for long enough."

"I agree." She gave Carwyn a warm embrace. She had never loved him, viewing him as a friend more than anything else, but it was so good to see him, to know that he had lived a good life. "Be safe."

"I promise."

326

36

Fire and Smoke

Lok sat at his small desk, clumsily trying to translate the rest of Kanton's notebook. His short exam in chemistry that morning had been terrible. There was so much information to memorize in such a small amount of time. Dozens of chemicals that had different reactions when combined with another chemical. And he did not care about any of it! He had told the Scholars he wanted to study history. What did chemistry have to do with history? Nothing!

He skipped martial arts today, despite his promise to Scholar Kuno. Translating the notebook was more important. It might hold the answer for Kanton attacking them. He doubted it was spur of the moment. The other guards were in on it. There must be a reason.

A knock came at the door. Lok sighed. People always interrupted him at the worst times. He hid the notebook underneath a small stack of books and papers and went to answer it. Zandon, Ivar, and Jaim stood in the hallway.

Taking out his notebook, Lok wrote, *"What are you doing here?"*

"Looking for you," Zandon replied. "You weren't at fight practice today. Are you feeling all right?"

Lok was taken aback. That was another thing he had not gotten used to. Someone other than his mother actually caring about his wellbeing.

It's only because you're an Elemental Thane. They wouldn't care about you if you were normal.

Lok pushed the thought away. They were his friends no matter what. He hoped.

"I had a lot of studying to do, so I skipped."

"You skipped the entire afternoon?" asked Jaim. The younger boy dug into his pockets and pulled out three coins. Gold pennies. The coins moved in between his fingers.

The entire afternoon? Lok glanced over his shoulder at the window. The sun was approaching the horizon. But he had only translated five pages. Had it really taken him that long?

"Yeah," replied Zandon. "We figured you'd come down for supper, but you never showed."

"Perhaps you are studying too much," said Ivar, peering around Lok towards the desk. Lok hoped Ivar wasn't reading his mind. He was usually very polite about it, always asking permission.

Jaim smirked. "You're one to talk."

"Ivar has a point," said Zandon, rubbing his chin. "When is Charity supposed to get back?"

"Tomorrow evening, I think." Her explanation of attending the king's exhibition had been rushed, to say the least. She had been so excited at the prospect of reuniting with Realta and Callum that she nearly forgot about the translation. The little Lok had deciphered baffled her as well.

"I have an idea," said Zandon, smiling. "You haven't really been to Norgard, have you?"

Lok shook his head. The neighboring city might as well be on the other side of the Nerin. Zandon's smile widened.

"Excellent. How about the four of us go to Caldeira's Pub?"

A pub? Was that similar to a tavern?

"Yes!" Jaim cried, the coins shooting down the hall. Another Student, who almost got hit, yelled at him to be careful. Reining himself in, he Manipulated the coins back to his hand and said, "Best idea you've had all week."

"And if someone comes looking for us?" asked Ivar.

"We'll say we were taking a walk outside," replied Zandon. "It's not a complete lie."

"But it's still a lie."

"No one's forcing you to come," Jaim said, rolling his eyes.

"Oh, I want to come. But I don't want to get in trouble."

"Are we not allowed to go there?" He didn't want to go if it was against the rules. The Academy had very few, the strictest being curfew. The usual punishments involved chores or writing sentences. Nothing too steep. Even so, he'd rather not have extra work on top of everything else.

"We're allowed to go to the city with Scholars," Zandon explained. "Students aren't allowed to wander around."

"But bloody Journeymen can do whatever they want," Jaim grumbled.

Lok thought of Journeyman Shari, how he accidentally saw her in bed with only a blanket covering her. He noticed Ivar raising an eyebrow and shoved the thought away. Scholar Kuno had asked him to keep the relationship a secret. He did not understand why, not completely.

"It's for our safety. But Students sneak out all the time. So, what do you say, Lok?"

He looked back at the desk. No one would take the books. And the only Scholar who might look for him was Kuno, but that was unlikely. The Scholar was still puzzling out Brother Malaky's strange visions and the fact that the man was having visions in the first place. The odds of Kuno seeing him sneak out were slim. Besides, he could always say that he was with friends, in the event the Scholar came looking. It was the truth.

Lok nodded.

"Great. Oh, don't wear your Student's cloak. It's a dead giveaway."

Lok understood. He donned his old, brown cloak, the one that belonged to his father, and followed the others. The evening air was crisp, bringing new life to his tired eyes. The sun was low in the sky, dyeing the sky a deep purple.

"This way," Zandon said, keeping his voice low. He led them towards the eastern side of the wall, about a hundred meters from the gate. A guardsman stood at his post, leaning against the wall and gazing up at the sky. The first stars were appearing. No other guards, or Scholars, stood nearby.

Zandon pushed back a leafy shrub, revealing a crack in the wall. Originating at the base, the crack was three feet high and just wide enough for an adult to squeeze through. Why hadn't someone noticed this? The Academy vowed to keep its Students safe. A giant hole in the wall, in Lok's opinion, was the opposite of safe.

"Jaim," Zandon whispered. "You first."

Jaim, short and wiry, fit through with ease. "All clear," he said once he was on the other side. Ivar went next.

"Now you."

Bending down, Lok maneuvered his way through the hole. He tried crouching, like Jaim and Ivar, but he was too tall. He settled for crawling on his stomach. Once on the other side, Lok stood and brushed the dirt off his clothes. He saw a small copse of trees a hundred feet away and a road leading towards the city proper.

Zandon emerged from the wall and pointed at the trees. The three took off running. Lok raced after them, his long legs enabling him to catch up quickly. Concealed by the trees, they paused and looked at the gate. No movement, no sounding of the alarms.

"Are we good?" asked Jaim.

Zandon nodded. He led the way down the main road, with Jaim and Ivar behind him and Lok trailing.

Lok stole nervous glances over his shoulder. He hadn't left the Academy since his arrival. He had no desire or need to. He occasionally thought of home and visiting his mother to reassure himself that she was doing well. Then he would think of all the reasons why he decided to leave. Adult whispering behind his back, calling him an idiot or moron. Other kids picking on him, throwing sticks or rocks at his head.

The Loys and the Haars were the only ones who had treated him kindly, probably due to Gareth Haar being different, too. And his mother. Lok was sure his father would have loved him, but his father was just a charcoal portrait hanging on the wall.

The road led to a medium-sized town, a few times larger than Vala, with a port on the river and the Garrison looming in the distance. People moved about the streets, heading to shops or taverns even though the first moon was rising. Lamplighters went from corner to corner, lighting streetlamps. In Vala, most people were home by evening. These people didn't seem to notice the late hour.

Zandon stopped in front of a two-story building with a sign hanging from the door. It had a fish jumping out of the water and read "Caldeira's Pub". Lok peered through the windows. Thirty or so people crowded the space, all of them drinking. A knot formed in Lok's stomach. He had never tasted ale or wine. What if it made him sick?

"Are you okay?" asked Ivar. "You look pale."

Lok nodded. Nobody said he had to drink. It would be fine.

Zandon opened the door and led them inside. The wooden floors creaked underfoot, and the scent of ale and cider filled Lok's nose. Simultaneously sweet and pungent. In the back, a musician sang and played a small drum with metal rings tied on the sides.

"How can I help you boys?" asked a young woman wearing a bright red dress.

"Can you get us a table near the back and a round of ale?" asked Zandon.

"No problem." The young woman led them to a table next to the musician. Lok took the seat near the wall. Fewer people to notice him that way. Jaim sat next to him while Zandon and Ivar sat opposite. A moment later, the young woman returned with four mugs of ale. "Let me know if you need anything else," she said with a wink.

Lok studied the ale. Should he taste it? The others were drinking, and Jaim was two years younger than him. The boy seemed fine. Lok took a sip.

It tasted like bread. Plain bread with hints of apples and pears. How odd.

"So," said Zandon, "what do you think? Not too bad, huh?"

Lok placed his notebook in the middle of the table. *The ale tastes good, but it's kind of loud in here.*

"It's a pub," said Jaim, wiping his mouth with his sleeve. "What did you expect?"

Lok shrugged.

Zandon started up a conversation and Jaim and Ivar joined in, talking about various Students and Journeyman at the Academy, even a few Scholars and their projects. They mentioned nothing about Brother Malaky. The Scholars had kept the matter quiet. No one outside the Council, and Kuno and Lok, knew about the chaplain's visions.

"Fire and smoke," Jaim muttered. "It's those damn twins."

Lok glanced over and spied two teenaged boys. It was as though one had looked in a mirror and his reflection came to life. Each had the same brown eyes and the same dark brown hair cut in the same style.

"Just ignore them," said Ivar.

"Who are they?"

"Edrick and Yedrick Regor," replied Zandon, taking a long sip of ale. The words dripped with disdain. Lok shrank in his seat, fearful of the strange tone in his friend's voice.

"They're trouble," said Ivar. "Pay no attention to them."

Lok observed the twins. They sat at the bar and talked to an older man, perhaps in his late fifties. He smiled kindly at the twins. They replied with smirks.

"Any requests?" asked the musician.

"Tavern Beauty!" one patron called out. Two others agreed.

Zandon laughed quietly.

"What is it?"

"You'll see."

The musician beat a quick melody on his strange drum and began singing. The song told of a young man who had fallen madly in love with the most beautiful girl in his village. But he knew being the wife of a simple farmer was not good enough for her, so he left to find his fortune. The young man traveled far and wide and met many women, but none as beautiful as his one true love. Years later, he wandered into an Averillian tavern and discovered his true love singing and dancing topless for all the patrons.

Lok's entire face grew red hot. If his mother had known he'd listened to such a dirty song, she would force him to wash his entire body with lye. He buried his face in his hands. Jaim and Zandon laughed.

"Same thing happened to me first time I heard that song!" Zandon said in between laughs.

Lok slowly lowered his hands, studying the other boys. They weren't laughing at him. No, this was different. They were laughing with him! His experience had been their experience. He smiled. Some of his embarrassment faded away.

"Sneaking out again, Jons?" one of the twins asked Zandon. Lok hadn't noticed them approaching.

"You know the Scholars won't approve," added his brother.

"Then why in the name of the bloody Abyss are you here?" Jaim snapped.

Zandon cleared his throat, glaring at Jaim, signaling for him to shut up. Jaim ignored him.

"We got word that some Students snuck out through the East Wall."

"The Scholars keep meaning to fix it."

"So why not send a guardsman?" asked Zandon, his face a blank.

"They wanted to be discreet."

"Then why send the ugliest Students in the Academy?"

"Jaim!" Zandon said through his teeth.

The twins smiled. "Why do you live under the delusion that you're special, Siarlwyn?"

"Do you really think twirling around coins will win your father's love?"

"Not that there's much love to give. He's too busy kissing King Logan's ass."

"Not that it does him any good. I forget. Was Lord Siarlwyn even invited to this year's exhibition?"

Jaim sunk down in his seat, his face turning dark red.

"I doubt there will even be a House Siarlwyn next year."

"So do I. Not to mention your mother's gambling debts. A nasty habit, especially for a woman of her standing."

"I hear she does more lying than standing these days."

"Isn't that how she and Lord Siarlwyn met?"

Jaim screamed and launched himself at the twins. One ducked out of the way. His brother was not so lucky. Grabbing hold of this one and pinning him against the table, Jaim punching him in the face again and again. Blood splattered as a blow broke the boy's nose. Ivar rushed over, wrapping his arms around Jaim's waist, and pulled him away.

The other twin darted behind Ivar. Zandon grabbed him by the wrist, twisting it. He cried out and swung his free fist. Zandon dodged it effortlessly. He then spun and pinned the twin against the table, pressing his face against the wood. Lok jumped to his feet, knocking his chair to the floor. He wanted to help, do something useful. But what? His mind and body froze.

"Let go of me!" Jaim screamed as Ivar dragged him back to their table. "Let go of me!"

"I told you to ignore them," Ivar replied in a calm voice.

"You heard what he said!" Jaim screamed again. A chair flew across the room and plowed into the twin with a newly broken nose, sending him to the ground. The other patrons ceased talking and drinking. All eyes on the fighting Students.

"*We should go,*" Lok wrote quickly, the words more scribbles than letters. His hand trembled, holding out the notebook.

Zandon read the words and addressed the other twin, "Edrick, you and your brother leave us alone the rest of the night, and I won't tell the Scholars."

Edrick laughed. "And what am I supposed to say? Poor Yedrick broke his nose by walking into a door?"

"I don't care, just— Damn you, Jaim! Calm down."

Jaim continued to struggle against Ivar's grip, screaming and cursing. A pint of ale, followed by a handful of knives and forks, flew across the room, crashing against the wall and nearly hitting the musician. A table-full of patrons scrambled away.

Sweat broke out on Lok's forehead as the man behind the bar moved closer. He helped Yedrick to his feet, glaring at Lok and the others.

"Hey," said Edrick, looking up at Lok, his brown eyes mocking. "You're that Elemental. What are you doing here?"

"You leave Lok out of this," said Zandon.

"Let go of me, and I'll consider it."

Zandon released his grip and backed away. Edrick rubbed his jaw. Everyone in the pub was staring at them.

"Hey," Edrick announced, "did you hear about that Elemental Thane over at the Academy? The first one in three hundred years?"

The crowd, mostly men, muttered to one another and drew closer to Lok. Why were they looking at him like that? This was a mistake. He shouldn't have come here.

"Well, this is him!" Edrick grabbed Lok and shoved him towards the crowd. Lok's stomach lurched. He grabbed hold of a chair, terror crawling over him like a thousand ants.

Zandon grabbed Edrick by the shirt collar and pulled him within inches of his face. "I said leave him out of this."

"His name is Lok Tolman!" Yedrick announced, speech slurred by his broken nose. Blood dripped down his chin and neck.

"What type of Thane is he?" asked the older man, staring at Lok with eyes like ice.

What accent was that? Lok's mind was too addled to think. So many people staring at him, none of them friendly. He had to leave, had to escape. He wanted to go back to the Academy with its friendly faces and kind people. He wanted to go home!

Lok rushed for the door. He tripped, landing on a table. His jaw clicked on his tongue. A copper taste flooded his mouth. The candles on the table burst to life, shooting flames and sparks into the air. The crowd yelled, pointing accusatory fingers at him. No, he didn't mean to do that. It was an accident.

The candles on the adjacent table burned bright, the wax melting in a matter of seconds. He had to stop. Concentrate. There was too much noise. People ran from the pub, yelling at him to get out. They didn't want his kind here.

He nearly leapt out of his skin as a hand fell on his shoulder. The candles, every one of them, burned unnaturally bright and sputtered as they ran out of wicks.

"Let's go," said Ivar.

Movement flashed in the corner of his eye. Zandon, bucket of water in hand, doused the candles on the table. All that remained were melted, metal candle stands and dark burn marks on the wood. The other candles died down, casting the room into near darkness.

"Don't you bloody move!" the man yelled, his voice booming.

Lok and Ivar froze. The only people remaining in the pub were them, the man, and Zandon and Jaim. The Regor twins were nowhere in sight. Outside, someone called for the city guard.

"Master Caldeira," Zandon said, moving between the man and Lok. "Please, we can explain. Lok didn't mean to—"

"That boy almost burnt down my pub!" he yelled in his accented voice. "I've great respect for Thanes, mind you lad, but I don't tolerate his kind!"

"What do you mean?" Zandon asked, confused.

"Them Elementals bring nothing but trouble. Always destroying everything they touch! I don't ever want to see that thing again. Are you understanding me, lad?"

Zandon took a deep breath. "Yes, sir. We're very sorry about the mess."

"You'll be more sorry when those Scholars find out."

"Which one started the fire?"

Lok spun around and saw three guardsmen enter the pub. Each had a hand on his sword. His heart raced, threatening to burst.

"The tall, pale one," Master Caldeira replied.

"Please, Master Caldeira, don't press charges. Lok didn't mean—"

"Take them back to the Academy. I see any of you in here again, it's the city jail for you!"

"We're very sorry, sir." Zandon, his shoulders slumped, turned to his friends. "Let's go."

"Wait," said Jaim. He Manipulated two small objects towards himself and handed them to Lok. His notebook and pencil. Lok nodded in thanks. He'd be lost without these. The guardsmen escorted them back to the Academy. The moons were high in the sky.

Along the way, Lok realized where he had heard that accent before. It was the same as the people traveling through Rangar Forest with West. The accent was Marish.

＊＊＊

"What were you thinking?" questioned Kuno. Word had reached him once Lok and the other wayward Students arrived at the Academy's gates. The others had been escorted away by their own mentors, all wearing the same expression of disapproval. No doubt they were receiving similar lectures. "You could have injured yourself. Or worse, injured someone else. Do you have any idea how lucky you are that Moteo Caldeira sent you back to the Academy and not to a jail cell?"

Lok hung his head, ashamed. The night had been going so well. But then all those people were looking at him, staring, pointing. It was worse than Vala. There, people stared and pointing because he was an idiot. Here, they feared him. He never wanted anyone to fear him again.

Kuno sighed. He sat down in the chair next to Lok. "Perhaps we've been going about this the wrong way."

No, please don't send me away! Tears stung his tired eyes.

"I thought I could teach you about being an Elemental by reading books. That was a mistake. You ought to be learning how to control your abilities. So, for one hour every day, you and I are going to practice."

Lok studied the Scholar's face. All of his anger and disappointment had melted away.

"How are you going to teach me?" Lok was grateful his notebook hadn't been burned. It held his half of every conversation he had since leaving home. Including the ones in Rangar Keep.

Arnyn Teleran had tried to teach him, explaining over and over that the Academy would be able to teach him more effectively. The unorthodox man's lesson had helped him discover his ability to control fire. He gave him that much. But there were no Elementals left to teach him. No one to properly guide him.

"We'll find a way."

* * *

Master Scholar Lucan Kalgan did not like being awakened in the middle of the night. Muttering under his breath, he donned his white Scholar's cloak and glanced out the window. Both of the blasted moons were in the sky. Whoever was knocking at his door had better quit!

Opening it, he saw the Regor twins, Edrick and Yedrick. One of the boys had a broken nose with dried blood caked around his nostrils. The other had a dark purple bruise on his jaw. Both of them looked like they had seen any army of Shades.

"What in the name of Caman's staff happened to you two?" And why come to him? He wasn't their mentor. Judging by their faces, the infirmary was the proper place for them.

"It was that Elemental and his friend," replied Yedrick, voice slurring because of his nose. "They attacked us."

"Pardon?"

"Did you hear what happened at Caldeira's Pub this evening?"

"No. What happened?" A vein in Lucan's forehead began to throb. Who had given these boys permission to leave campus? Somebody better have a bloody good explanation for him in the morning.

"We were just talking to them, when that Manipulator, Jaim O'Siarlwyn, took a swing at my brother," explained Edrick.

I'd say he took more than a swing, the Scholar contemplated, studying the boy's nose. Had scrawny little Jaim really done that? A part of Lucan was impressed.

"And then the Elemental tried to burn us." Edrick showed him the burned fringes of his Student's cloak. "Nearly burnt down the entire building!"

"What?!" The vein in Lucan's neck throbbed in tandem with the one in his forehead. A Thane student had endangered civilian lives, and nobody had informed him!

"Yes, Scholar," replied Yedrick. "I heard other Scholars talking about Tolman. What we should do with him, I mean."

Lucan rubbed his forehead. "Has the Council been convened?"

"No, Scholar, we don't think—"

"Inform the Council that I've called for a meeting first thing in the morning. Where is Lok Tolman now?"

"He's with Scholar Kuno."

Lucan rolled his eyes. He had never liked Kuno. The man was too eccentric, even for a Scholar. And too secretive to boot.

"Very well. Now get yourselves to the infirmary."

"But what are you doing to do about him?"

Lucan exhaled sharply. It was either too late or too early to deal with this mess. "The matter will be discussed in the morning."

He slammed the door before either twin could continue. First Brother Malaky's visions, and now this? That boy was the first Elemental to enter the Academy in centuries. They could not expel him without facing some form of scandal. The Council would convene in the morning and listen to Lok Tolman's testimony, as well as the other Students who were present. They'd learn the truth soon enough.

You shouldn't have listened to Kuno.

Kuno had been the one who advocated for the boy's acceptance before learning he was a Thane. His inability to speak had been an immediate strike against him. And his test scores were so low, he would have been sent home had he been normal. Mute idiot or not, the boy was a Thane. Turning him away without first trying to train him would have cast the Academy in a negative light.

Perhaps they had made a mistake.

37

An Inkling

Realta studied her reflection. The dress Queen Gallia's tailor had made was light purple trimmed with white. A silver key had been embroidered over her heart. The style was akin to the dresses she'd seen noblewomen wear, though not as gaudy, and the fabric was softer than her plain blue dress, almost like silk. It had also been designed for riding. An interesting choice, not at all what she had in mind for a servant's dress.

From the mirror's reflection, Realta saw Val enter from the adjacent room and pause.

"Realta, it fits you beautifully."

She turned to face him. "Why would she have this dress made for me? I thought she just wanted me as a servant."

"That she does, but Gallia's tactics are very subtle. When Logan sees you, his own servant, wearing Gallia's house colors, it will throw him off guard. Give Gallia a small edge during their peace talks tomorrow."

Tomorrow. Charity was leaving tomorrow morning. Would Realta have a chance to say goodbye? They'd only had a few minutes together. A few minutes to know that the other was safe and well. She didn't want to waste the rest of their short time as someone's pawn.

Maybe the king will free us soon. Then I can go to the Academy, too. But what would she do there, other than be close to her friends? She had no clue what she wanted to study, or what she'd do with an education.

Val approached her timidly, hands behind his back. "Realta, how much practice have you had as a Dreamer?"

A spike of fear rose in her. She glanced at the other servants. Most had left to perform their tasks, the rooms feeling oddly empty. The rest weren't paying her or Val any attention. "Practice? None. I don't really remember my dreams."

"But you remember the most important ones. The ones that reveal the past."

Realta bit down on her lip and shrugged.

"Let's you and I practice this evening. In a few minutes, the ambassador of Jemayrt is going to meet with Queen Gallia. He's a Thane like us. A Learner. He grew up in a fishing village not far from the capital city of Kaiphyr. I want you to try dreaming about him. A real dream."

"I don't know if I can. I've never tried."

"First time for everything, Little Dreamer."

Realta really wished he'd stop calling her that. She had never gone by a nickname and felt no need to do so now.

Val turned towards the door and smiled. "He's here. Come along."

Realta hesitantly followed Val into the main sitting room. Queen Gallia sat at a small table with room for four, her back to the windows. She wore a thin, silver crown in her dark hair, along with a matching necklace. No earrings. Her Cuchasi, Shilo, sat on her left, propping up her chin in a bored manner. A sharp knock came at the door. The queen stood.

"Valentin, the door, please."

Val motioned for Realta to stand next to the table and went to the door. Lucia, the queen's head maid, stood off to the side. Her dark eyes studied Val as he answered the door. In the hall stood a tall man with ebony skin and dark brown eyes. He wore pure white clothes with silver embroidery along the sleeves and cuffs, and he wore a necklace made of red beads. At his side stood Serena and a woman with the same dark skin tone. She wore a white Scholar's cloak over a white dress with blue floral embroidery. Serena, for a change, wore a green dress with her short hair tied back.

"Your Majesty," Val addressed the queen, "Ambassador Chinasa Ekene and Scholar Adanna Obyke of the Jemayrt Academy. And King Logan's bastard sister," he added, raising an eyebrow.

"A pleasure to meet you, Ambassador, Scholar." She gave each a short bow, and they replied in kind. She then motioned for them to sit. Shilo stood and moved off to the side to make room. "It's fortunate you both arrived here safely."

"I don't quite understand what you mean," replied Ambassador Ekene. He and the Scholar took a seat, studying the room. Scholar Adanna took out a small, leather-bound book from her dress pocket and began writing notes.

"You were escorted here by Logan's bastard sister. The girl has a reputation for stabbing people. Haven't you heard?"

The ambassador glanced at Serena, eyeing her up and down. The girl's face reddened. "She does not possess any weapons, and King Logan has no reason to threaten emissaries from another Vogel kingdom."

"Odd that you would label Jemayrt as such. It shares no border with the mountains."

"But all of our allies do, hence our association."

"Understandable. You girl, are you going to stand there all day?"

Serena looked the queen in the eye and replied, "I was told to wait until the meeting was over, so I can escort the ambassador and scholar back to their rooms."

She doesn't seem as afraid, Realta observed. Though she was blushing, Serena did not seem as nervous as the last time Realta saw her. Instead of cowering, she stood at her full height, hands clasped behind her back. She was nearly as tall as her brother.

"Fine. What is it, Shilo?" Gallia asked as the Cuchasi leaned closer.

"That man is a Thane. The woman is not."

Gallia shooed Shilo away. She smiled at the ambassador. "Would you mind telling me which type of Thane you are?"

"I am a Learner. I pose no threat to you," he answered with a patient smile.

"He's truthful," Shilo chimed in.

"Wonderful. You are excused, Shilo." The woman exited the sitting room. The ambassador and the Scholar spoke to each other in Jemayrti. Neither of them sounded pleased. The queen turned her attention to Realta. "Realta, Lucia, bring in some tea for my guests. You as well, girl. Make yourself useful."

Lucia gave the queen a small curtsy and went to the servants' room without hesitation. Realta curtsied as well and followed, Serena a step behind her. She noticed Val taking the empty seat on the queen's left. He gave her a wink.

Don't worry, Realta, Val's voice sounded in her head. *All is well. You'll see.*

Realta shivered, her skin crawling. He... He had spoken to her with his mind. The action felt so... Wrong. Impersonal.

"Realta," Serena whispered as Lucia laid out cups and plates onto a rolling cart. "Dane Kanton was expelled."

"What do you mean?"

"My brother discovered he lied about me and Callum killing Charity, considering she's right here in the palace. He kicked Kanton out of the guard and banished him from the city. He's going to release you and your father soon."

A heavy weight lifted from Realta's heart. "When?"

"As soon as Queen Gallia leaves."

Realta wrapped her arms around Serena and hugged her, catching the other girl off guard. "Thank you. You don't know how much I needed to hear that!" Dane Kanton was banished. She'd never have to fear him again. She and Callum were one step closer to being free. "But what about you?"

Serena shrugged. "Logan wants to make amends. I don't know if we'll ever love each other the way siblings should, but it's a start, I guess."

"Serena, I'm sure your brother loves you. He just has a hard time showing it," she replied, remembering her late-night conversation with Shasta.

"What makes you say that?" Serena frowned.

"I'll explain later." She didn't want to reveal too much about the royal family's history in front of Lucia.

She and Serena followed Lucia back to the sitting room and placed cups of warm tea on the table. The ambassador and the Scholar nodded to Realta in thanks. Queen Gallia and Val acted as though she and Lucia were invisible.

"It's so rare that Nowan is able to have negotiations with Jemayrt," the queen was saying.

"But not unheard of," replied Ambassador Ekene. Scholar Adanna continued writing in her notebook, pausing now and then to study some aspect of the room. She even stole glances at Realta and Serena.

"Of course, there is the obvious different between our people."

Ekene gave her a patient smile. "If you are referring to the rule of Thanes, you are partially mistaken, Your Majesty."

"How's that?"

Realta peered over the Scholar's shoulder to glance at the notebook. It was written in Jemayrti.

"In your kingdom, Thanes are prohibited from holding any form of power, be it political or religious. In my kingdom, the right to rule belongs to anyone regardless of ability, so long as they prove themselves to be capable."

"By what method?"

"Why, the Jemayrt Academy, of course. In order to be crowned king or queen, or to be included in the line of succession, members of the royal family must obtain the level of Scholar. And whether or not one is Thane doesn't come into consideration. Of the last five monarchs, three have been Thanes and two normal humans."

"But what of King Ryzem? Which is he?" Gallia took a sip of tea, studying the ambassador from over the rim.

"A Learner Thane, such as myself. My ability to comprehend foreign languages granted me the position of ambassador."

"Fascinating. But Learners tend to be quite bookish. What of the more dangerous Thanes? Minders and Manipulators, for example."

Val smirked. Scholar Adanna caught the expression and made a quick note.

Ekene smiled. "What makes a person dangerous, Your Majesty?" Realta edged closer to the ambassador. She felt safe near him, an instinctual feeling she couldn't explain. Similar to the way she felt around Callum.

"When they threaten the lives and safety of those around them."

"Is not an ordinary man holding a knife against someone's throat dangerous?"

"Of course."

"But he is ordinary," Ekene continued, folding his hands on the table. "He is no different from a Manipulator using his ability to hold the knife to someone. The method is different, but the result is the same. I fear many in the Eastern Coalition have overlooked this fact."

Queen Gallia started, nearly spilling her tea. "What did you say?"

"The Eastern Coalition. Don't act surprised. I'm a Learner Thane traveling with Scholars. Very little escapes us."

"Does Logan know?" Gallia asked, composing herself.

"I cannot speak for him, but I have not informed him."

"Why not? It would give you an edge over me."

"I don't want an edge over you, Your Majesty. The Eastern Coalition is your business. Therefore, it's your decision whether or not to tell him."

"That's very diplomatic of you." Gallia took a sip of tea, not taking her eyes off the ambassador.

"Is it?" Val interjected. "Because Logan's bastard sister is right there."

The cup slipped from Gallia's hands and clatter onto the table. She shot a glance at Serena, and then glared at the ambassador. Chinasa Ekene's face was calm, unreadable. Scholar Adanna only had attention for her notes.

"Tell me, young lady," Ekene addressed Serena. "What are the odds of you informing your brother of this meeting's events?"

Serena shifted from foot to foot. "I didn't plan on telling him anything," she stammered. "I'm more of a servant than a sibling."

"Teyrnian servants have loose lips," Val added, his tone hostile. Realta edged closer to the ambassador, standing directly behind him. The way Val glared at Serena made her nervous.

Ekene scowled at him. "And what about you, messenger? What is your role here?"

"Excuse me?"

"Last I heard of Nowan, messengers are valued, but they are still a type of servant. Why does Queen Gallia keep you close by? What makes you special?"

Val adjusted himself in his seat. "I believe we've gotten off topic."

"That we have. And the hour is growing late. With your permission, Queen Gallia, may we retire for the evening and continue our discussion tomorrow?"

"I think that is an excellent idea," said Gallia. She rose from her seat. The ambassador and Scholar followed suit. "I appreciate you meeting with me," she said, shaking their hands.

"It was a pleasure, Your Majesty."

Ambassador Ekene nodded to Serena. She opened the door for him and Scholar Adanna, who was still taking notes. Serena flashed a quick smile at Realta before escorting them down the hallway. She returned the gesture, wishing she could go with them. That comforting feeling left with the ambassador.

"The nerve of that man," Val muttered, putting his feet on the table and crossing his arms.

"He made a few interesting points," replied Gallia, walking towards a large, stand mirror.

"He insinuated that there was a relationship between us!"

"There is a relationship between us, dear." Gallia removed her necklace and crown, handing them over to Lucia for safe keeping.

"But how did he know?"

"He's a Learner Thane. It's likely part of his training."

Val drummed his fingers on the armrests. Looking at Realta, he addressed the queen. "If only there was a way for Nowan to utilize Thanes in that way. They could be very useful."

You don't see it now, Realta, but your abilities are so much more than mere dreams. I only had an inkling of my capabilities at your age.

Realta bit down on her lip, forcing herself to remain composed. Lady Sarra needed permission to read someone's mind. But Val could just do it whenever he wanted. Probably without her knowledge. The thought sent a shiver down her spine. Somehow, that seemed just as bad as Val seeing her naked.

Gallia cast a sideways glance at Val. "No. Humanity got along just fine without any Thanes for millennia. We can do so in modern times."

"Well, until the Midnight King arrived."

Gallia rolled her eyes. "Are you coming to bed, dear?"

"Yes. Give me a moment."

Val walked over to Realta as Gallia retired to the bedroom. Lucia and the handful of servants present followed her. "Do you remember what I said?"

She nodded.

"I don't know if meeting the man helped. Focus on him as you go to sleep. Tell me everything you see in the morning, okay?"

"Okay," Realta whispered. She did not feel comfortable with

this. Maybe she ought to tell Callum or Shasta first. Should she ask the ambassador for permission?

"Good night, Little Dreamer."

***

Realta opened her eyes in the dream. She sat on a large boulder along a rocky beach, the waves crashing on the shore. Out in the water, a wide expanse that blended seamlessly with the horizon, she saw three boats casting nets over their sides.

Never in her wildest imagination had she pictured herself on the shore of the Tharys Ocean. The River Nerin paled in comparison to this endless blue. The breeze pushed back her unbraided hair, leaving traces of salt water on her face. Salt water. She tasted a small drop. Yes, the water was salty, far too salty to drink. How had she known that? And the wind playing with her hair. That was new. In the other dreams, she'd been nothing but a Shade.

Standing up, Realta walked along the beach. Warm sand shifted between her toes. Had she always been barefoot in dreams? She studied her clothing. A simple, pink dress made of light fabric. It was neither wool nor silk. Something in between.

Heading away from the beach, she saw a small village comprised of wooden buildings painted in various colors, reds, blues, and yellows being the most prominent. The structures were one or two stories tall and were raised on a series of wooden poles. None of the windows had glass. Instead, they had wooden shutters, opened to allow cool air to enter.

Instead of packed dirt or stone, the streets were sand, bright white and free of rocks or twigs. And the trees were very odd. They had long trunks with giant leaves coming out of the top. They swayed precariously in the gentle breeze.

I guess this is Jemayrt. Realta knew nothing about the kingdom other than its location on the map. The westernmost country in the Northern Realm.

She continued down the road. She passed several people, all of them dark-skinned like Chinasa Ekene and Adanna Obyke. They wore brightly colored clothing, save for a trio wearing white Scholars' cloaks. None of them noticed her presence. So that aspect hadn't changed.

At the end of the road stood a rectangular building with a sign Realta could not read. She felt something pulling her towards the building, beckoning her to go inside. She complied. The interior held multiple rooms, each with half a dozen or so children sitting at tables or desks. A schoolhouse. But this one had a room for each age instead of one large room like the one in Vala. Mistress Loy hadn't cared for that method, opting for Kel to teach her daughters and Realta, as well as his own children. She and Esme also taught lessons, at times only teaching a subject to one or two of them.

The feeling pulled Realta towards a room with a dozen children who were about ten years old. The teacher, a woman with a blue shawl wrapped around her shoulders and wearing red and blue necklaces and bracelets, wrote a series of mathematics problems on a slate blackboard.

Realta's jaw dropped. The problems were far more complicated than anything she had learned. They contained both numbers and letters. Why on Eltriar would you need to put letters in mathematics?

"Who would like to solve problem number one?" the teacher asked, the dream automatically translating her words.

A few hands shot up. The teacher pointed to a little girl. "Yes, Thabisa." The girl went to the board and began solving the problem.

The invisible tugging drew Realta's attention to the final row of desks, leading her to a little boy. On the desk rested his mathematics textbooks, but in his lap was another book. Realta studied the words. Lowyrnic?

The boy silently sounded out the words, moving his finger along the page. Realta tried to decipher the words. Callum had taught her some Lowyrnic, but not enough for her to be fluent. A history book? The text described the coronation of King Ealdredd who had been crowned two hundred years ago, following the unexpected death of his older brother.

"Chinasa," the teacher called out. The boy's head shot up, his dark brown eyes wide. "You've been quiet today. Would you like to solve this next problem?"

"Um, no, Teacher Kalilah."

347

She gave him a patient smile. "We never learn unless we try."

Chinasa sighed. He placed the Lowyrnic book underneath his chair and went to the board.

Realta blinked and found herself in a darkened room. Eyes adjusting, she recognized it as the room reserved for female servants within Queen Gallia's quarters. She could not believe it. She had gone to bed thinking about the ambassador and dreamed of him a as little boy. Val was right! It had actually worked!

Heart pounding as though she had won a race, she wondered who else she could dream of.

***

Dane Kanton sat at the bar of a tavern in Tullcrest district, the crime filled slum near Teyrnas' western gate. The one place in the capital where no one would dare come looking for him. The tavern itself was nice, for Tullcrest, and was owned by a woman named Aska Liddyn, a former thief who came into a sum of money years earlier. A dead aunt or grandmother. Some cock and bull story along those lines. Dane didn't really care so long as the ale kept coming.

The king had wanted him out of the city by nightfall. The sun had set hours ago, and no one had slipped a blade between his ribs yet. Nobody gave a damn about a disgraced member of the King's Guard.

Former member.

Dane slammed his empty mug on the bar.

"Don't you dare break my bar!" yelled Aska, glaring at him, eyes flashing like fiery emeralds. She nodded for her nephew, a tall, muscular lad of eighteen, to refill Dane's mug. That boy would make a great guardsman or soldier. Had he ever considered joining the Garrison?

Who bloody cares? The Guard hadn't done him any favors. A career of following orders to the letter. Even on the night he almost killed Yestyn's bastard, he'd been following orders. Orders from Queen Isla herself. Logan had stupidly charged the girl with theft, not attempted murder, the proper charge. The entire Guard would have hunted down the girl had Logan labeled her as an assassin.

But no one cared about a horse thief. So what if he stretched the truth about Serena killing that girl? No one listened to Dane until he upped the charges. Was that such a bad thing?

Dane took a long swig of ale, draining half the mug.

A slender form concealed by a dark cloak sat at the bar next to him.

"You're only half right, you know," said the form. Bleary-eyed, Dane glanced under the form's hood. A man, about thirty or thirty-five, with black hair. His gray eyes danced in the candlelight.

"What in the name of the Abyss do you want?"

"The queen wrote that letter ordering the bastard's death. But someone else was dictating for her."

"What are you talking about?" Dane reached for his sword. His hand brushed empty air. Dane grounded his teeth. Logan had his sword and daggers taken away as he left the palace gates. He was not a member of the Guard anymore. He could not be trusted with those weapons.

The man smiled. "Do you recall a mousy, young woman in the Teyrnas Garrison? One with blonde hair and blue eyes?"

How could Dane forget? Nobody in Teyrnas had blonde hair. It was like spun gold, shining in the light. A foreign girl. Didn't speak much Teyrnian. But friendly, always attempting to make conversation.

"Eltzy? What about her?"

"She's a Minder," he replied nonchalantly.

"Really?" Dane pictured her again. She hadn't worn Thane earrings. Never wore any kind of jewelry. Were they talking about the same woman?

The man nodded. "Yes, she is so beautiful, isn't she? You've thought of doing all kinds of things to her. But you never got further than a kiss on the cheek. No, it wouldn't have done you any favors to be charged with rape."

Dane nearly choked on his drink. "How did you—"

"Call me Val," the man interrupted. "I'm a Minder myself. But don't worry. Your secrets are safe with me, and Eltzabet would have never allowed you to harm her. In fact, those thoughts helped motivate her."

"What do you mean?" Dane glanced around the tavern. No one was listening. No one cared.

"She used her abilities to influence the queen to write you that letter regarding Serena Molyns's fate. In fact, Queen Isla has no recollection of the event. Eltzabet used her like a puppet, pulling the right strings."

"I don't understand." Dane really wished he had a dagger, something to scare this man away. He never liked Minders, the way they shifted through memories, finding secrets. Like that snake Lord Darrys.

"It was King Syleck's idea to use the girl as a spy," Val continued, leaning closer. "And it was my idea to place her in the Teyrnas Garrison." He chuckled. "Well, I let Gallia think that was her idea. She prefers to be in charge."

"But why? That bastard doesn't mean anything."

"Then why did Logan order to you chase after her?"

"Because the girl stabbed him."

"And what punishment did Logan give to his would-be assassin?"

"None." That had baffled Dane to no end. Had it just been a power play? A way for Logan to tell Serena that there was no place she could run? He never understood their relationship. After Yestyn's death, Logan and his siblings publicly accepted the girl as their half-sister, but he had always been lukewarm towards her. One day, showing her nothing but kindness. The next, acting like she didn't exist. The same way he treated Isla. She deserved better. Why did she break off their relationship?

Val laughed.

"What?"

"You and I are in a similar position. Or in your case, were."

"And that is?"

"Royal plaything."

Dane grabbed Val by the shirt collar, pulling the man within inches of his face. He didn't need a dagger to deal with his one. He... Val just smiled. The man was amused!

"Bah!" Dane released Val and signaled for more ale.

"I hope you have some way to pay for this!" Aska yelled.

Damn. How much money did he have left?

"His bill is on me," Val replied.

"I suppose you want something in return," Dane said as Aska's nephew brought another pint. The fifth or the sixth? Whatever.

"How perceptible of you! Since you already fell victim to our schemes, why not join us?"

Dane scoffed. "And why would I do that?"

"What other option do you have?"

Dane could not think of anything.

"Exactly. Your best bet it to work for Queen Gallia. She's had her eyes on you for quite some time. And you can get the revenge you want on Logan."

"What makes you think I want revenge?"

"Come now, Kanton. I'm a mind reader. You can't hide your true desires from me. And maybe I'll arrange it so you can stab Callum Haar again. This time in the heart."

Callum Haar. That bloody slave was the core of his problems. Isla's letter instructed him to find Haar, one of the best guides in the Hinterlands, and frame Serena's death on him. The explanation: Haar was an immediate threat to Teyrnas and should be dealt with discreetly. That letter neglected to mention that the man was under contract.

And that girl, Realta. She was the spitting image of Esme, Carwyn's lover. Dane had only known her briefly, enough to recognize her face after seventeen years. Seeing Esme and what was left of Prince Carwyn in the marketplace had been a shock, Shades come to haunt him. It was only fate that Realta was Haar's child, and Haar was Esme's brother.

Dane took a slow sip of ale. Yes, he'd love to kill Callum.

"You have a deal."

38

Behind Closed Doors

Realta and Charity watched silently as the Scholars loaded the last of the equipment into the carriage. Bright morning sunlight streamed down onto the palace stables, lighting the way to the northern gate. Realta had taken a chance and snuck away from Gallia's quarters at dawn. She did not want to miss saying good-bye to her friend.

"You really think you'll be allowed to go to the Academy?" asked Charity, hope filling her voice.

"I don't see why not," she replied. Queen Gallia's visit with King Logan ended in a few days. Then Logan would decide how to proceed with her and Callum. He already knew Kanton's charges against her father were false. All he had to do was sign a document and have the tattoos removed. Though they still had to wait for an official Cuchasi to verify Realta's ability. Word of Logan accidentally using a Thane as a servant would reflect badly on him, which was why the king was still in the dark.

"I'm sure the Academy will accept you," Charity whispered, smiling. Realta and Callum asked her not to tell any of the Scholars about Realta's ability. Based on how everyone reacted when they discovered Lok's ability, word spreading through the Scholars like wildfire, they did not want to cause a commotion at the palace, especially with Gallia present. Better for everyone if they waited.

"Do you know how often they test children in the capital?"

"No. Why?"

Realta nodded towards Serena who stood within the stables. She had reverted to wearing her old clothes and maintained a healthy distance from the other two girls. When Charity had tried speaking to her, Serena was very awkward and broke off the conversation at the first opportunity. Realta wondered if she felt guilty for not warning them about Kanton. But that business, Charity had assured her, was over and done.

"I'm sure the Scholars will test Serena if she wants to apply. They didn't turn me and Lok away. Not to mention she's the king's sister."

Bastard sister, Realta thought. Serena never said if she had been tested by the Scholars, only that she was not a Thane. Most of the Scholars weren't Thanes either.

"Charity," said Scholar Maryn, walking up to her. "It's time to go."

Realta and Charity exchanged teary-eyed glances, a darkness descending on them despite the sunny day. Neither of them wanted to part, not after it took so long to find one another. They hugged, not wanting to let her surrogate sister go.

It's only temporary, Realta reminded herself. *We'll be together again before we know it.* Or so she hoped. Nothing in her life had gone right since leaving Vala. Not even this fateful encounter.

"I'll write to you the moment I'm back," said Charity, breaking away from the hug.

"You'd better," Realta smiled.

Charity followed Scholar Maryn to their carriage. She climbed onto the driver's seat, the breeze catching her blue Student's cloak. The driver flicked the reins, and the carriage was off. Realta and Charity waved goodbye, the distance between them growing larger and larger until the carriage passed under the arch and the guards lowered the heavy gate.

It was over. Their brief moment of time together was gone.

Her heart heavy, Realta walked over to the stables. Serena stepped into the light.

"Did you mean it? About the Scholars testing me?"

Realta raised an eyebrow. "You heard that?"

"I have good hearing." She shrugged.

"Well, yes. Hasn't your brother had you tested yet?" The Scholars toured the Hinterlands every five years, testing children between fourteen and nineteen years old. Serena was the prime age for testing.

"Nobody ever mentioned me going to the Academy. I... I don't think bastards count in this case."

"They should."

Serena gave her a weak smile. "You're just saying that because we're related."

Another fact Realta struggled to wrap her head around. Uncle Kel had once been the crown prince of Teyrnas, the rightful heir to the throne. And he left it all behind, preferring that the world believed he was dead.

"Come on," said Realta, walking back to the palace proper. "Let's see if my father or Shasta has any news from the king."

Serena agreed and followed, walking side by side with her. Her steps seemed lighter today, a touch more free.

The palace was quieter now. Most of the nobles had gone home. Only Lord and Lady Lyr and a handful of others remained. Queen Gallia's party kept to themselves, refusing to mingle with the other servants. Realta rarely saw more than five or six of the large entourage at any given time. Likely another power play. Impress Logan with a large retinue under her command. Much like the way she forced Realta to help wait on her, dressing her in house colors. She felt strange wearing those colors, but this dress was far more comfortable than her other one.

Passing the kitchens, they saw Amzie Fenn walking by.

"Good morning, Amzie," said Serena.

"Good morning to you, too, Serena and Es— I mean Realta." Amzie blushed and wrung her hands.

"It's okay. Realta knows the truth."

Amzie let out a sigh of relief. "Oh, thank the Creator! I hate lying all the time. Not being allowed to say her name. Or his name..." She quickly composed herself. "Well, I want you to know that your aunt was a wonderful lady, Miss Realta, and a good friend."

"Amzie, can you keep a secret?" Realta asked.

"Well, I don't know. I've never been good with secrets."

"Esme is alive. She's living in the Hinterlands. And the new stable hand is her son Gareth."

Amzie caught Realta in a tight embrace. "Oh, thank you, thank you!" she cried. "You don't know how much that means... Oh my!" She let go of Realta, wringing her hands. "Pardon me. I forgot myself. We knew Yestyn sent her away. But we didn't know where."

"But don't tell the king, please," Realta added.

"You have my word."

"Have you seen Shasta?" Serena asked.

"I believe she's in the guest quarters, supervising the cleaning."

Serena thanked her, and she and Realta headed that way.

The guest quarters were a bustle of activity, people moving from room to room, exchanging dirty linens for clean ones, carrying buckets of warm water and mops. Realta could not believe this much work needed to be done. She always thought of nobles as being very clean. Mistress Loy was only a farmer's wife, and she never allowed dust to collect in her house.

"Shasta?" Serena called out, going from room to room, her pace quickening. Her calm demeanor faded with each empty room. The head of servants was nowhere to be found.

"Maybe she's with Father," Realta suggested. They went to Callum's room, but it was empty as well. A handful of new drawings rested on the desk. Beautiful depictions of the king's reception and the Scholars.

"I don't get it," said Serena. "Where could they be?"

"Your brother might be meeting with them right now," Realta said, hope rising. How soon before they were free?

"I doubt it. My brother is speaking with Queen Gallia now. He wouldn't let Callum or Shasta listen in."

"Should we wait?"

"Yeah, that's the safest bet." They agreed to stay in the guest quarters. They didn't want to risk interrupting the king, and Queen Isla had been acting secretively lately. Always avoiding Serena and Realta, making excuses, abruptly leaving conversations with other nobles. Realta suspected the queen was having more visions. And the one regarding Realta still bothered her. How exactly would a fifteen-year-old girl bring destruction in her wake? And why had she been so adamant that Realta keep it a secret?

She and Serena walked down the hallway, passing Queen Gallia's rooms. Realta spied a cluster of people through the cracked door. They looked vaguely familiar, yet nothing like the people in Gallia's entourage.

She motioned for Serena to stop and be quiet. She pushed the door open another inch. They peered inside, listening.

Three men stood in a small circle, each of a different complexion. The first had brown skin with touches of gray in his black hair. He wore a red jacket with gold embroidery along the cuff. On the right side of his jacket was a golden sun rising over silver waves.

The second was a good ten years older with pale skin, and his hair was so blond it was almost white. Blond hair. Where had she seen blond hair recently? He wore a black jacket trimmed with silver, a silver stag emblazoned on both sleeves.

The third man, the youngest of the three, was very tall, a head taller than Callum, with fair skin and dark brown hair. One of his eyes was dark brown while the other was blue. He wore a white jacket trimmed in black. A series of six-pointed stars danced around the cuffs.

"This was a mistake," said the man with different colored eyes. "Coming here was too great a risk."

The older man with the black jacket scoffed. "Don't be a coward, Ayrdeen. The plans are in place. All we have to do is wait."

Ayrdeen turned to the man in red. "Don't tell me you don't feel it, too, Eskandar. Something is wrong here. And think of your niece, Syleck," he addressed the older man. "What will happen to her when people discover your relation?"

Syleck frowned. "That girl stopped being my niece years ago. And she agreed to this position. Don't put all the blame on me."

Ayrdeen wrung his hands. "I just can't help but think..."

"Come now, Ayrdeen," said Eskandar, smirking. "You aren't getting visions or impressions, are you?"

Ayrdeen rounded on the man. "How dare you, you backwater snake! You're just fishing for an excuse not to listen to me."

"He does have a point," replied Syleck. "You seem overly worried about that girl's wellbeing."

"Well, pardon me for having an ounce of sympathy. But the king is a Thane, as well as his wife and sister. I heard Lord Lyr can read minds from across a room."

"Bah!" said Syleck. "Stories conjured up to keep the common folk in place."

"I don't think so. I..." Ayrdeen paused. He stood straight with his hands clasped behind his back. The other two men followed his gaze. Eskandar adopted Ayrdeen's posture while Syleck crossed his arms and scowled.

"Gentlemen," said a feminine voice, "don't let in-fighting tear us apart." The woman came into view. She was about fifty years old, with brown hair and pale skin. She wore a white dress with red and orange embroidery in the pattern of flames. Her face was so familiar, but Realta could not put a name to it.

"Apologies, Kenda," said Eskandar. "You know how troublesome those from Bran Maro can be."

"Don't put this all on me!" yelled Ayrdeen.

Realta and Serena exchanged weary glances. Bran Maro was the easternmost country in the Northern Realm. Why would someone from that country be with Queen Gallia?

"Enough!" Kenda ordered. The men fell silent. "We have not come this far to fail. Do you know what Gallia is doing as we speak?"

"Meeting with Logan, obviously," replied Syleck.

"No. She is determining the next step. War or peace. The future of six kingdoms is at stake, and you argue like children. Why?"

Six kingdoms? Realta quickly did the math. Each person, including King Logan and Queen Gallia, represented one kingdom. Were these people emissaries sent along with Gallia? If so, why not be announced as such? Why wait around for the outcome of a single meeting?

Realta stole a glance at Serena. The girl's face was bloodless.

"I don't know," replied Ayrdeen. "I just have this bad feeling all of the sudden. I can't explain it."

"And you two?" Kenda asked.

"No bad feelings," replied Syleck. "Just have to be forced to work with these idiots."

"Now you listen here!" Ayrdeen began. Kenda cut him off with a wave of her hand.

"Odd. You never referred to the other members as idiots before. What changed, Syleck?"

The older man shrugged. "I don't have to explain myself to you."

"What of you, Eskandar?" Kenda asked, unfazed by Syleck's retort. "You've been awfully quiet lately."

"I don't have much to say, honestly. My mind..." He frowned. "My mind is a bit cloudy today."

Kenda tapped her chin with her forefinger. "Something, or far more likely someone, has been getting to us lately. Send out scouts to find Lord and Lady Lyr. They're both Minders. Perhaps the king is on to us."

Syleck scoffed. "How could the man be on to us when he doesn't even know we're here?"

"Logan views the world as a game he's determined the win. Don't underestimate him." She turned and addressed people outside of Realta's view. "Huritt, Chayton, find the Thanes and observe them. Do not interfere."

Serena tugged on Realta's sleeve. "We need to go," she whispered, her voice tense.

Realta tore herself away from the door. She wanted to stay and learn more information, but the tone in Serena's voice unnerved her.

"Who were those people? Do you know?" If they were diplomats, Serena might have seen them in the palace before. And they looked so familiar. If Kenda had worn her hair up... No, that was ridiculous.

"That man, Eskandar. He's the king of Tarod."

Realta halted. "He's a king? Then why—"

"And Syleck. I think he's the king of Tirshay."

Two kings. "What of the others?"

"I don't know. But they're working with Gallia. We have to warn my brother."

"I take it they're not our allies," Realta said as she and Serena hurried down the main stairs. A few servants passed them, wanting to know why they were in such a rush. Neither of them replied.

"Tirshay and Tarod sponsored Nowan during the last war. Without the other Vogel kingdoms' help, Teyrnas would have fallen."

A dark cloud formed in Realta's mind. "What about the ambassador from Jemayrt? Do you think he'll help?"

"I don't know," she replied, fear rising in her voice. "We have to find my brother!"

Reaching the ground floor, Serena sprinted down the corridor. Hiking up her skirts, Realta raced to keep up.

39

Reprimand

Two Scholars accompanied by a guardsman stood outside of Lok's door as he prepared to leave for his first class that morning. He knew the Scholars only in passing, and neither of them looked friendly. Tucking his history textbook under his arm, he turned to an empty page in his notebook, wondering why they were there.

"Stop," one of the Scholars said, a woman in her early sixties with slate gray hair. "Lok Tolman, you have been sentenced to an official reprimand for your actions on the night of Alet twenty-ninth. Leave all of your personal possessions behind and come with us immediately."

A knot formed in his gut. He had gotten no sleep that night, his mind racing, blaming himself for being unable to control his abilities and his own fear. Scholar Kuno had assured him everything would be okay, that he would learn in time. He reluctantly placed his things, notebook and charcoal pencil included, on his desk. The Scholars escorted him to the Council Chamber, the guard bringing up the rear.

The handful of Scholars and Students who passed him averted their eyes. No one spoke to him, let alone acknowledged his presence. One Student whispered in a Scholar's ear. The Scholar shook her head, giving the Student a sharp glare. The pair hurried on without another word. How serious was this reprimand?

They halted in front of the Chamber's ornately carved doors. Scholar Kuno stood there with three other scholars, frowning. Lok recognized Scholar Tell, his martial arts instructor and Jaim's mentor. Lok wished he had his notebook.

"Everything will be fine, Lok," said Kuno.

"Don't speak to him," ordered the other Scholar. Kuno shrank back, his head low.

The doors opened. Lok saw every member of the Council save one seated in their raised chairs. Standing before them on the dais were Zandon, Ivar, and Jaim. Zandon's expression was solemn while Ivar's face was unreadable. Jaim constantly put his hands in and out of his pockets. The Scholars must have confiscated his coins.

This is bad. This is very, very bad.

What if they expelled him? How could he return to Vala? If Dane Kanton was being truthful, something similar had happened to Mayor Gan. And he was so ashamed that he lied to everyone he met. Better for the whole village to believe the Hiraethi had kidnapped him than for them to discover he was kicked out of the Academy.

The Scholars led Lok to the dais. He stood next to Zandon, his legs shaky. The four Scholars stood along the left side of the round room. On the right stood a handful of spectators. Guards, Journeymen, Scholars. And Brother Malaky.

Why is he here? Did the reprimand have to be overseen by a chaplain?

The Premier Scholar, her face an unreadable mask, stood and said, "Lok Tolman, Zandon Jons, Ivar son of Taychar of the Austynsud tribe, and Jam of House Siarlwyn, you have been brought before the Council for an official reprimand concerning your actions on the night of Alet twenty-ninth. Do you understand this charge?"

"Yes, Premier Scholar," his three friends replied. Lok nodded. He glanced at Kuno. The Scholar chewed on his lip, arms crossed.

"Stated by the laws of the Academy, all Students are allowed five reprimands before they are expelled. For the destruction of private property within the city of Norgard, you each receive one reprimand. Jaim and Ivar, this marks the first reprimand on your records. Zandon and Lok, this marks the second reprimand on your records."

The second? How did he receive two at once?

"May I have permission to speak, Premier Scholar?" asked Zandon.

"You may."

"What did Lok do to deserve two reprimands in one night?"

"The first was for reckless use of his abilities. The second for injuring normal individuals. Several patrons at that tavern were burned as a direct result of his actions. Some required medical attention."

Lok's heart dropped. People got hurt? He never meant to hurt anyone. There were just so many people, so many eyes staring at him. He had to get away. He didn't mean to start that fire. It was an accident.

"Lok Tolman," the Premier continued, her voice grave, "as Thanes, it is our responsibility to ensure the safety of human-kind. Your actions cast doubt onto the Academy's ability to teach Thanes. Doubt that we cannot afford. In addition to this repri-mand, you are prohibited from entering the city of Norgard for the next three months. If you are caught within the city, a third reprimand will be given. Is this understood?"

Lok nodded. *I'm sorry. I wish I could tell you that.*

"What about me?" Jaim chimed in. The Council members glared at him. "I used my ability to fight those bloody... I mean, the Regor twins." He frowned. "Why in the Abyss where they allowed in the city? Why aren't they being reprimanded, too?"

Jaim, please, please, be quiet! Lok didn't want his friend to get in anymore trouble. Didn't want him to face two reprimands in one day as well.

"Edrick and Yedrick Regor," replied Scholar Lucan, seated be-hind the Manipulator's chair, "had permission to visit the city that night. And if you will be silent, you will learn of your pun-ishment."

Jaim crossed his arms and looked away.

"Jaim O'Siarlwyn," said the Premier, "you also are prohibited from entering Norgard for a period of three months. As for Zan-don Jons and Ivar son of Taychar, since you did not use your abil-ities to cause harm, you are prohibited for a single month. Do you understand these charges?"

"Yes, Premier Scholar."

"Now, for the matter of your scholarship. It seems that Lok Tol-man, being the only Elemental, is at a disadvantage. Your train-ing under Scholar Kuno is lacking. Therefore, we will transfer your training to another Scholar."

No! Lok mouthed the word, wishing desperately to speak. Just this one time. But the only sound he managed was a long sigh.

Scholar Kuno ran to the dais, standing in front of Lok and the others. The Council members glared at him while the onlookers murmured to each other. None of them were pleased.

"Premier Scholar," pleaded Kuno. "I know I have made mistakes, but give me a second chance. Allow for the three months' probation to be a time for extra training. I promise—"

"You promised the first time," replied Scholar Koranic, his voice booming. "In fact, you claimed to be the best fit because of your area of expertise. We have allowed this experiment to go on long enough. From now on, the boy's training will be supervised by a Thane."

Lok shook his head in frustration. He didn't want to be taught by a Thane. A Thane, regardless of their ability or strength, would not know anything about Elementals. Scholar Kuno had spent his entire adult life studying ancient Thanes. True Elementals. Despite not being a Thane himself, he understood them and their lives. Their failures and triumphs. Why wasn't that enough?

"Please," Scholar Kuno addressed the Premier. "Lok is very intelligent. Give us just three months, and I will guarantee improvement."

Scholar Lucan scoffed. "Intelligent? Based on his test scores, I'd say he is nothing more than a low-grade idiot."

The words slashed at Lok like knives flaying his skin. No, he wasn't an idiot. He had studied for months and months before coming to the Academy. Read every book his mother owned twice. 'Idiot' was just an insult the other children in Vala used because they couldn't think of anything more clever.

It wasn't just kids your own age, Lok realized. It had been adults, too. Including those who claimed to be his mother's friends.

"It means nothing," Kuno replied, fixing Lucan with a level gaze.

"Nothing? The entire system by which we accept Students is nothing? Don't be foolish, Kuno."

"Okay, not nothing. But Lok was raised in a small village. Formal schooling was limited."

"Limited?" Lucan questioned. "Did you see his scores? Did you?"

Kuno's gaze faltered. "They were low, I admit, but he can learn."

"He can learn to control his Thane ability and nothing else."

Lok dug his fingernails into his palms. He wasn't an idiot. He wasn't! He suddenly thought of West, of the way his aunt and those other people treated him. Hitting him, yelling at him because he was different. Lok refused to allow these people to treat him that same way.

"It has already been decided," said the Premier. "Scholar Kuno, it is time to stop neglecting the other Student and Journeyman under your tutelage. We have selected Scholar Nestor for his abilities as a Manipulator and Empath and his scholarship in philosophy."

An older man stepped forward from the group of spectators. He had shoulder-length gray hair and a beard. His blue eyes were cold, unreadable. They made Lok's skin crawl. He did not like this man, did not want him as a mentor. He wanted Kuno! He didn't care that Kuno was not a Thane. He was kind to him, cared for him more like a son than a student. Why couldn't the Scholars see that?

Scholar Nestor stood next to Kuno, facing Lok. No, he would not allow this to happen. He would not allow another person to push him around. They wanted him to control his abilities, then fine!

Focusing on the candles behind the Scholars, Lok caused the flames to come alive and expand, blazing like torches. He pulled the flames together into a fiery stream. The river of fire glided over the Scholars, many of them crying out in terror. Lok ignored the screams. The flames, now a whirling vortex, stood between Kuno and Nestor. Lok raised his arms, and the flames rose, creating a seven-foot-tall wall of bright, orange-red fire.

Lok walked around the barrier and stood beside Kuno, glaring at the Council members.

Kuno is my mentor. Don't you dare take him away from me.

The Council members looked to one another, casting furtive glances at Lok. Their faces were a combination of amazement and stark terror. Lok felt a little guilty about scaring them, but they wanted him to control his abilities. And he did exactly that. The fire obeyed his every command, like a true Elemental.

He looked over at his friends and paled. All three of them had moved to the far wall, standing next to their own mentors. They stared at him, too afraid to speak or move. They wore the same terrified expressions as the people in the tavern. Lok's heart sank. How badly did he just screw up?

"Premier Scholar," said Sorcha, sitting in the seat for nonexistent Dreamers, "he used his ability against another Scholar. That is grounds for immediate expulsion."

Expulsion? No!

"Explain yourself, Lok Tolman," the Premier glared at him.

I can't, Lok lamented.

"You know damn well the boy can't speak," Kuno snapped. "I think his actions speak just as clearly as words."

"You will be silent, Kuno Surylin, unless you want your tenure at this Academy to be forfeited."

Kuno's face turned ashen. He replied with a single nod.

"Lok Tolman, to the best of your ability, explain yourself."

Lok allowed the wall of flame to die down, leaving a dark scorch mark on the beautiful mosaic floor. He pointed at Scholar Nestor and shook his head. He pointed at Kuno and nodded. He didn't know how to make his wishes any clearer.

"Do you understand what the term expulsion means?"

Lok nodded. *It means you're sending me away.*

"Did you know that attacking, or even threatening, another person with your Thane ability can cause one to be expelled?"

Lok shook his head.

"Of course he didn't know," said Brother Malaky, stepping away from the spectators. "This boy is terrified of losing someone he cares about. He can't speak, so he had to show you. He meant no harm. Why can't you understand that?"

"He claims to have meant no harm in Norgard, but harm was done."

"Do you see this cord?" Malaky pointed to the white cord tied around his waist. "It represents Air. All four colors assigned to chaplains of different ranks. Green, blue, red, and white. Earth, Water, Fire, and Air. The four elements the Gadyeni gave humans mastery over. The first Elementals were priests, devoting their lives to serving the Creator. They were pacifists who vowed to harm no one. But no one learned to be a perfect Elemental in the span of a few weeks. It took them years to perfect their abilities.

"And yes, people got hurt. Did that mean they were expelled from the priesthood? No. Only those who refused to learn from their mistakes were forced to leave. You boy, do you refuse to learn from your mistake?"

Lok shook his head. It was a mistake he never wanted to make again.

"There you have it," Brother Malaky addressed the Council. "That ought to be grounds enough to give him and his mentor a second chance."

"The Academy is not an ancient priesthood," replied Scholar Lucan. "Times have changed, and we cannot afford—"

"Can you afford an Elemental Thane with no control over his abilities to be loose in the world where he can only cause more damage?" Brother Malaky's eyes widened, as though surprised by his own words.

The Council members whispered to one another. Lok shifted uncomfortably from foot to foot. The very idea of being expelled and forced to leave his new home terrified him.

I will learn control. I promise to do better.

After what felt like hours, the Premier spoke. "Brother Malaky, we have given your words great consideration and found that they have merit. The young Thane, Lok Tolman, will be given a second chance to study underneath Scholar Kuno for three months. If he does not show better control over his abilities and emotions, he will either accept a new mentor or be asked to leave. Lok Tolman, is this clear?"

Lok nodded.

"And Scholar Kuno, consider this a probationary period. Your future at this Academy depends on your success."

"I understand, Premier Scholar."

"This reprimand hearing has been adjourned." The Council members filed out of the Chamber one by one, each studying Lok as they passed, expressions ranging from curious to frightened to abject disapproval.

Lok caught Zandon's eye as the young man left with his mentor. Zandon gave him a weak smile that didn't reach his eyes. Yes, he was afraid of him. Yes, they were still friends. Lok never wanted to see his friends afraid again.

The crowd of spectators exited the Chamber, leaving Lok and Kuno alone with Brother Malaky.

"I want to thank you for defending Lok," said Kuno.

"It was the least I could do. You two helped me the other day."

"What of your visions, if I may ask? Have you found any explanation for your newfound abilities?"

"None," Brother Malaky sighed. "I keep seeing images, flashes. This boy, for example. Sometimes when I look at him, I see him wearing a Scholar's cloak trimmed with green and a seat on the Council. Other times, I see him surrounded by flames, cities burning in his wake. I feared that if he were expelled, it would lead him on a path of destruction."

Lok paled. He didn't want to hurt anybody. He didn't think he could. *What about Dane Kanton?* Lok recalled throwing a burning log at the man's head. Two burning logs. And that other guard had fallen into the fire. Or had the flames jumped on him? That part was a blur. But it was all done to protect his friends. No thought had been in his mind other than to help.

"Don't worry," said Malaky. "Right now, I only see the Scholar's cloak."

"Holy Brother," said Kuno as they exited the chamber and headed down the stairway, "I was wondering if you'd help me with Lok. As you said, chaplains during the Thousand Years War were comprised mainly of Elementals. Are there any texts at your Chapel that concern Elementals?"

"I can check once these Scholars agree to let me go. I would be honored to help an Elemental." He smiled.

Lok returned the expression, a weight lifting off him.

"I hope you don't mind, Brother, but what do you see when you look at me?"

The chaplain's smile faded into a frown. "I see you wearing a military uniform. An odd one that's completely black with red trim and golden buttons going down the coat."

"That's... odd," replied Kuno. Lok agreed. He could not imagine the bookish Scholar as a soldier.

"My thoughts exactly. Do you have any relative in the army?"

"No. I'm an orphan."

"I've been having a lot of odd dreams about soldiers." Brother Malaky averted his gaze to the steps, his shoulders slumped. "Sometimes, I wonder if Teyrnas is due for another war."

40

Ravens in Flight

King Logan sat alone in a private study with Queen Gallia, a small room on the palace's ground floor with no windows and only one door. He had given explicit orders not to be interrupted under any circumstances. He wanted this meeting over with.

"Not even a single guard?" Gallia asked, smirking as she sat opposite him at a small table.

"I can defend myself."

"So I hear, Raven King."

Logan frowned. "Since when do you address me by my formal title?"

"Because I find it curious. Remind me of its origin."

"I thought you wanted to discuss peace, not history." Logan did not have time for this. The sooner Gallia left, the better for both of their kingdoms. And he still had Callum and Realta Haar to deal with. If they and that stable boy truly were Esme's family... Carwyn's family...

"History is paramount to our discussion." Gallia flashed him a smile. "Indulge me."

If he had to. "The great Thane Balthazar always kept pet ravens, used them as messengers. People began referring to him as the Raven King. My ancestors inherited the title from him."

"So, you claim you're descended from Balthazar." A curious tone entered her voice.

"Correct. Now, are your talks of peace serious, or—"

"I find that very interesting."

"What? Balthazar?" What did ancient history have to do with their present situation?

"I find it very interesting that you claim to be the descendant of a man who never had children."

Logan fought the urge to roll his eyes. "Scholars have never been able to verify that. And it doesn't matter. He was a Thane king. I'm a Thane king. That's what matters."

"So, you merely usurped the title."

"My ancestors chose the title."

"The real ones or the imagined ones?"

Logan's eyes narrowed, studying the woman. "What's your game, Gallia?"

"Pardon?"

"You spend the first year of your reign threatening me, wanting to finish the war your father lost thirty years ago. Then you send a messenger advocating for peace. What's changed?"

"My mind," Gallia said quietly. The sharp glint in her eyes softened. "If you think for one moment that I'd sacrifice the lives of a thousand men to reclaim a few square miles of land, you're out of your mind. Who cares if your father won a bit of land from my father? There are no cities in that area. No resources. Just grassland. Nothing to want, only something to have. War with you would be pointless."

"You really want peace." Logan's eyes widened in surprise.

Gallia nodded, but something was off. The slight frown, the hint of worry in her eyes. What was troubling her?

Logan changed tactics. "Why bring up Balthazar? Everyone in Nowan hates Thanes."

"Hate is an inaccurate word. The common people fear them more than anything else."

"Because your predecessors taught them to fear us."

"No," Gallia replied, the frown deepening. "Don't you read history, Logan? Seven hundred years ago, Thanes ruled this entire realm. Every Northern kingdom bowed to their wills. Those west of the Vogel Mountains had it easiest. Their kings and queens remembered their original purpose. That their abilities were tools to protect humankind, not weapons. Those in the east cared little for ancient history and warred against one another, trying to take what the others had.

"Teyrnas and Nowan were one kingdom back then. The king fathered twin children, a boy and a girl. The son ruled in Caslana, and the daughter ruled in Teyrnas. Both were Thanes, but the daughter made alliances with the west and broke away from her brother's kingdom. The brother was enraged, planned to go to war against his sister, but his human servants poisoned him with Assassin's fern berries. The lead servant established his own kingdom, one in which normal humans were free to rule themselves."

Logan fidgeted. Assassin's fern berries. Small and red, just like cranberries. His father had loved those damn things. Yestyn didn't know the difference when Logan substituted them for their poisonous counterparts.

"Does this tale bother you, Logan?"

"Not particularly, no. You're talking about Merart and Emitia, children of the last true king of Caslana. Emitia hated her father, viewed herself more as Balthazar's daughter. That's why she called herself the Raven Queen and named her first born son Balthazar. So, in a sense, I am descended from Balthazar. Not the one out of legend, but the first king of Teyrnas."

Gallia smiled. "You do know your history."

"As do you."

They lapsed into silence. Logan's throat itched. Too bad he didn't request a pot of tea to be brought in before the meeting started. But he didn't want to take a chance that Gallia would arrive first and slip in a poison. That would have solved several of her problems. Morgan was next in line for the throne, but he was only twelve. Isla would have to rule as regent until the boy came of age. Isla had a good head on her shoulders and good diplomatic sense. Only one thing stood in her way. Her self-doubt. A handful of inaccurate visions had caused her to doubt her Thane abilities, and that doubt bled into other aspects of her life. Should either kingdom declare war, Isla would be at a complete loss.

"What's on your mind, Logan?"

"Future possibilities."

"Do those possibilities include peace between our lands?"

"How serious are you? I won't be tricked like my grandfather."

Gallia's eyes hardened. "Interesting how you choose to bring up Tudur now."

"Why shouldn't I? He wanted peace and died because of it."

Gallia scoffed. "Peace? That man didn't want peace. He wanted subjugation. The entirety of Nowan to pay a yearly tribute to him. Refusal would have meant more bloodshed. My grandfather found a better way. He discovered Tudur's weakness for whores, the younger the better. So, he enlisted my aunt to play the part, and she killed him in his sleep." Gallia laughed. "One of the greatest military minds of his time defeated by a seventeen-year-old girl."

Logan grinned.

"What? No outbursts?"

"We've wondered for years who killed Tudur. Many theories ranging from a paid off servant to an assassin taking advantage of secret passageways. My sister always favored that theory. No one stopped to consider one of his mistresses."

"Why not? Are you prejudiced against female assassins?"

"On the contrary, I'm good friends with a female assassin." Logan smiled, seeing the confusion on Gallia's face. "It's just, my grandmother was ashamed of Tudur's behavior and worked to keep it quiet. We knew he had mistresses, but no names or dates."

Yestyn was no better than him, a small voice whispered in the back of Logan's mind. No denying that. Both men routinely slept with other women, not even bothering to hide the fact from their wives. Carwyn had been furious when he had discovered this, confronting their father and earning a beating for it. Logan merely accepted it, vowing never to treat his own wife in the same manner. Though there was no true love between him and Isla, he had never once cheated on her. Of the four of them, only Carwyn had found true love.

What time did Carwyn die? Mal's words echoed. Logan shoved the thought into the far recesses of his mind. Their brother was dead. Nothing, and certainly not wishful thinking, could bring him back to life. And where on Eltriar was Mal, anyway? It wasn't like him to wander off.

"It seems we both have a lot on our minds today," Gallia said, pulling him out of his thoughts. How long had he been silent?

"And not on each other," Logan hazarded a guess.

Gallia bit down on her lower lip, smudging her red lipstick. Logan reached into his pocket and handed her a handkerchief. He always kept one close by out of habit. That first year after Carwyn's death had been difficult.

"Thank you," she replied quietly, wiping away the makeup.

Her lips were very pale, almost bloodless. "I didn't know you wore a necklace."

"What?" Logan looked down. His brother's necklace, the one with two ravens in flight, had found its way outside of his shirt. He gently touched the pendant, wondering if he ought to leave it in view. He had always thought it had been buried with Carwyn, until he saw it hanging around Realta Haar's neck. Could she and Gareth really be Carwyn's children?

He wondered what Carwyn would have said to Gallia, had he lived to take his rightful place on the throne.

"Was it a gift?" Gallia asked.

"It was."

Clearing her throat, Gallia asked, "Would you really want another war with Nowan?"

Another war. The second in his lifetime, the first during his reign. Most wars between Teyrnas and Nowan lasted five to ten years, sometimes longer. Morgan was only twelve now, but in six years, he'd be fighting age.

An image flashed in his mind. Him and Gallia declaring war on one another. Soldiers preparing for battle in the Caslan Valley. Morgan standing on the front lines, dressed in a dark blue uniform and armor emblazoned with ravens. A sword by his side. The timid boy, now a man, rushing towards the enemy. A sword finding the weak point in his armor, stabbing him through the ribs, destroying his heart. Morgan laying in a pool of his own blood, sightless eyes staring at the sky. His first born, dead.

"No," Logan replied, digging his nails into his palms. "I don't want war."

"But what if war comes to you? What if you are forced to fight?"

"And who would force me? You? I thought you wanted peace."

"I do. It's just..."

The doors burst open, slamming against the walls. Serena stood at the threshold, panting, her hair slick with sweat.

"I said I didn't want to be disturbed!" Logan yelled, jumping to his feet. Serena, the physical proof of Yestyn's infidelity, staggered into the room.

"You ought to have better control over your siblings, Logan."

He ignored her. "Well, what do you have to say for yourself?"

"She's going to betray you," Serena replied, breathless and leaning against the table.

"What makes you say that?" Gallia asked, rising from her seat. Her blue eyes were like ice.

"Explain yourself, girl." They were getting somewhere. Perhaps not a guarantee of peace between their lands, but a step in the right direction. Neither of them wanted war. That much was clear. They were so close! Why did Serena have to interrupt them? Why did this girl always have to ruin everything?

"The kings of Tirshay and Tarod are in her rooms. They're planning a war against Teyrnas. You have to believe me."

"How absurd," Gallia scoffed. "Two monarchs in the palace with no one knowing? How did they get in? An underground passageway?"

Serena looked to Logan, her blue eyes, the same shade of blue as Carwyn's, pleading.

"Answer the queen, Serena." He didn't have time for nonsense.

"I don't know. But Eskandar is here. I recognize him from a portrait."

"Eskandar is a very common name in the River Mallr region of Nowan," replied Gallia. She turned to Logan. "There is a man in my retinue by that name, but he's hardly a king."

"Who is he, then?"

"One of my footmen. What did Eskandar say, young miss?"

"He argued with the king of Bran Maro. Insulted him."

Logan felt his face growing warm. Bran Maro? What game was this girl playing?

Gallia smiled. "I find that hard to believe. Eskandar is a mute, and not very bright. His only insults are rude hand gestures."

"No, that's not true. I can prove it!"

"You'd better," Logan snapped.

"Realta, she…" Serena looked around the small room and out in the corridor. Her eyes darted like an animal caught in a trap. "She was right here!"

Logan balled his hands into fists. Why hadn't he turned away that girl and her father the moment he suspected they were related to Esme? His own curiosity had gotten the better of him, and now he was paying for it.

"This can be easily proven," said Gallia, collecting herself, a wave of calm washing over her. "Where were these kings?"

"They were in your rooms." Serena glared at her.

"Then it's settled. We will go to my rooms and check. What do you say, Logan?"

That this girl is going to cost me dearly. "Very well. Lead the way, Your Majesty."

Gallia glided out of the room, amused by this whole ordeal. Logan walked slightly behind her, right beside Serena. He grabbed the back of the girl's hair, causing her to wince. Gallia did not seem to notice.

"You listen very carefully, girl," Logan whispered through his teeth. "If you're lying, you can forget about eating at my table and attending court functions."

"But, Logan—"

Logan yanked her hair. Serena's eyes watered. "I was very close to negotiating peace with Her Majesty when you barged in. Ruin this for me, and you will spend the rest of your life regretting it." Let his promise to Nell Molyns fall into the Abyss. Teyrnas' future was more important than one bastard.

They arrived at Gallia's rooms. Logan moved in front of her and entered without knocking. A handful of servants occupied the main room, none of them busy at any task. None of them dressed like royalty, either.

"Eskandar!" Logan yelled. A man in his late forties with the brown skin tone of a Southerner rose to his feet and bowed. Logan walked towards him. "Is your name Eskandar?"

The man nodded.

"Why don't you speak?"

The man pointed to his throat and shook his head.

"May I speak, Your Majesty?"

Logan turned and saw a woman with graying brown hair done up in a bun and very pale skin. She wore a simple purple and white dress with House Toutain's silver keys over the heart. A dress befitted a servant.

"You may."

"Eskandar was born without the ability to speak, and he cannot write, I fear."

"And what is your name?"

"Lucia Bazel," she replied with a curtsy.

"She is my handmaid," Gallia explained.

"No, she isn't," Serena cried, pointing at Lucia. "Her name is Kenda. The kings were taking orders from her."

"What is this child talking about, Your Majesty?" Lucia asked Gallia, clearly very confused.

"That's an excellent question," Gallia replied, shooting a glare at Logan.

"Serena, if this is your idea of a joke—"

"It's not a joke! They're plotting against you!" Tears leaked from her eyes.

"What's going on here?" asked a man emerging from an adjacent room. He was around Logan's age with brown hair and different colored eyes. One dark brown, the other blue. He wore simple trousers and a laced shirt. His gaze shifted from Gallia to Logan.

"Nothing to worry about, Deen," replied Gallia, waving her hand at the man as though he were an insect.

"He's the king of Bran Maro!" Serena yelled, frustration boiling over.

Deen laughed. "Who's this girl? Some kind of jester?"

"Who are you?" Logan asked Deen, his patience hanging by a very thin thread.

"Her Majesty's personal musician," Deen replied. He removed a reed flute from his pocket.

"Are there any other accusations against my people you wish to make, young miss?" Gallia questioned.

"But it's the truth," she stammered. "Realta was here. She—"

"And where is Realta now?" Logan loomed over his bastard sister.

Serena shook her head. "I don't know. She was right behind me. You have to believe me!"

Logan looked around the room. At the mute servant, the maid, the musician, and finally at Queen Gallia herself. She had her hands clasped in front of her, limbs and shoulders tense. She glared at Logan, eyes as cold as the River Nerin in midwinter. Any flexibility, any chance to negotiate, had departed from her expression. This was a woman who did not tolerate being falsely accused.

Fury seizing him, Logan backhanded Serena across the face, sending the girl to the ground. Serena laid on the floor, holding her bruised face and crying.

"Deal with her as you like, Your Majesty," he said to Gallia, every muscle in his body seething. "Please know that I had no knowledge of these accusations or her reasons for saying them. I hope that peace between Nowan and Teyrnas is still an option."

"The option might be on the table, but I must first discuss this matter with my advisers. I don't tolerate lies about myself or those in my service."

"I understand, Your Majesty." *Damn that bastard bitch to the Abyss!*

"Please," Serena whimpered, raising to her knees. "Logan…"

Logan kicked the girl in the face. Serena's head smacked against the tiled floor. She let out a pitiful groan. "Never address me by name again."

He gave Gallia a low bow. "I apologize for everything."

"Your apology has been acknowledged."

Logan exited the room, his head low. Carwyn's necklace caught his eye. Taking the pendant gently in his hands, he tucked it back into his shirt. He already had too much on his mind without thinking about his brother.

41

One of Nine

Realta ran beside Serena, but the other girl was faster. Far faster than her. She fell behind as Serena rounded a corner, disappearing behind another before Realta had a chance to see whether she had gone left or right.

Heart pounding against her ribs, she leaned on the wall. Her breathing came out in ragged gasps. A stitch threatened to form in her side.

"Hello there, Realta."

She turned and saw Val walking towards her. Val. He was part of Queen Gallia's entourage. Did he know about the foreign monarchs?

"Have you been running?" Val asked, giving her a concerned look.

Realta nodded. Her throat was too dry for her to speak.

"Come with me. I believe there's a sitting room around here. You can rest up there."

No, I have to warn the king. Queen Gallia is going to betray him, and you might be part of it! Realta mentally screamed as Val took her by the arm and led her away. She was too tired to fight back, to run.

What is this about? Val's voice echoed inside Realta's skull. Her skin crawled. *Now, Little Dreamer, don't be frightened. This is just another form of talking.*

Get out of my head!

Val paused, a hurt expression on his face. "If you insist, Realta. But please, rest for a moment. Just long enough to gather your thoughts."

The sitting room was quite small, the same size as her bedroom. There were no windows, the only light coming from a lantern hanging overhead. In the center was a round table with three chairs and a kettle of tea and cups. Steam rose from the kettle. Had Val planned on running into her?

"Please, sit." Val motioned as he took the opposite seat.

Despite her better judgment, Realta sat, her legs feeling like water. She was so tired. She shouldn't have run so hard. *This is wrong. I have to warn the king.*

"King Logan can care for himself," Val replied, pouring both of them a cup of tea. He took a sip and grimaced. "A bit hot for my tastes. Anyway, I wanted to discuss our experiment. Did you have any dreams about Ambassador Ekene?"

"Yes," Realta replied. Her throat was so dry, it was painful to speak. She took a sip of tea. Ginger-root tea with hints of honey and blackberries. Not too bitter, not too sweet.

"And?" Val leaned forward.

Realta racked her mind, trying and failing to recall all the details. One image stood out clearly. "I saw him as a child, in a schoolhouse. He was studying Lowyrnic history."

Val smiled. "I knew it! I knew you'd be able to do this. Realta, there has been something I've wanted to tell you since the moment we met." He inched his chair closer to hers. "Perhaps it will be easier to explain this way. Have you ever heard of the Gadyeni Cycle?"

Realta shook her head. "I've heard of the Gadyeni, but not any cycles."

"Well, according to the Cycle, the Midnight King arrived on Eltriar thousands of years ago with the intent to rule humanity. The Eight Gadyeni, viewing themselves as explorers and protectors, were appalled by this. So, they appealed to the Creator, asking for permission to intervene, and permission was granted. The Gadyeni fought alongside the humans and banished the Midnight King from this plane of reality. They then created the eight types of Thanes so people would be better equipped to defend themselves."

"What do you mean by 'plane of reality'?"

Val grinned, a teacher excited for his pupil to learn. "This universe is far more complex than we perceive, Little Dreamer. There's the world that we experience through our senses: hearing, sight, smell, touch. But there is also the world we cannot perceive, one that is in between and all around us at the same time. An endless void of nothingness that one can become trapped in for all eternity."

Realta's eyes widened as an icy chill ran down her spine. "The Abyss. Are you talking about the Abyss?"

"Yes and no. The Abyss, as you know it, can only be accessed after death. Same with the Realm of Stars. The Nothingness is different. It was where the Midnight King was trapped for five thousand years."

"Was trapped? You mean he escaped." Realta glanced at the door, trying to remember if Val had locked it. She didn't want to be here anymore. She had to warn King Logan. Was Val just wasting her time by telling her all this?

Val nodded. "And he was enraged. He took revenge on the Gadyeni by attacking the peoples of Eltriar, but not outwardly. He tricked them into attacking themselves and each other, planting lies and doubts in their minds. Then he appeared in the flesh to finish the job. Well, not flesh exactly. Anyway, his war against Eltriar lasted a thousand years. You've heard of this part, right?"

"A little bit."

"A little is better than none. The Eight Gadyeni tried to stop him, but he had millennia to plan, to think of every possible move the Gadyeni could make and how to counter them. His plan was damn near perfect. So, the Gadyeni once again went to the Creator for permission, this time to choose champions to fight the Midnight King. The Creator agreed.

"The Eight Summit Thanes were selected, men and women who had achieved the highest potential in their abilities. Balthazar, a military genius gifted in all eight abilities, was chosen to be their leader. They were known as the Nine. Together, they defeated the Midnight King, banishing him back to the Nothingness. But the Gadyeni Cycle, written by Farsight Scholars, claims that the Midnight King will escape again. And again and again until he is defeated once and for all.

"Three and a half thousand years have passed since that war ended. And I fear that the Midnight King walks Eltriar once more."

Realta broken out in a cold sweat. "How do you know?"

"Because the Nine Thanes are being selected again. I am one, and so are you."

"I..." She swallowed a lump in her throat. "I don't believe you."

"I know it's a lot of information to take in, Realta. It took me years to accept my fate. Don't fight it. That will only make things worse."

"How do I know any of this is true?" Val was part of Gallia's entourage. If he was planning to betray the king, then this was nothing more than a stalling tactic. What he was saying was impossible. Ridiculous!

Val sighed. "Realta, you only saw those monarchs as they truly are because of me."

"What did you say?"

"Syleck, Eskandar, Ayrdeen, even Kenda. They were all dressed as servants when you and Serena spied on them. I allowed you to see them as they truly are. If I was going to betray Logan, why would I do that?"

"I don't know." The air had grown colder, the lantern light dimmer. Had Val slipped something into that tea? No, he had drunk it, too.

"Ambassador Ekene is one of the Nine as well. The only hope for humankind to survive a third attack from the Midnight King is for us to join forces and find the rest of the Nine. It will take time, and it will mean leaving your family behind."

Realta shook her head. "No. I can't leave my father."

"Why not? You were planning to attend the Academy. You'd have been separated from him there."

"Stop reading my mind!"

Val raised his hands, palms flat. "I'm sorry. It's a reflex. Besides, your father and I are almost the same age. I can look after you like a father looks after his daughter. Everything will be all right, Realta. Trust me."

Realta's face grew red hot. How dare he even suggest that! Did he think she could just throw away the last fifteen years and allow him to usurp Callum's place in her heart? "I already have a father."

Val exhaled through his teeth. "You are not a child anymore, Realta Haar. Sometimes we have to do things we don't want to do. Stop thinking of yourself and think of the world!"

"But how? How am I supposed to defeat anyone? All I have are these dreams."

"Your dreams are the key to the past. Dream of the original Nine. Learn their tactics, see their mistakes. I don't want to force you, Realta." The sitting room door opened. A tall figure dressed in all black entered. Realta paled. Dane Kanton locked the door and sat in the third seat, his blue eyes leering at her as the light cast shadows on his scarred face. "But I will do what I must."

"What is... What is he doing here?" Dane Kanton had been stripped of his title and banished from the city. How did he get inside the palace? Why was he with Val? A sickening thought crept into her mind. Had Kanton been working with Val and Gallia this whole time?

"Oh, Captain Kanton has been a great help to me, and I to him. At first, we only wanted him to kill Logan's bastard sister and blame it on your father, the younger brother of Prince Carwyn's dead lover. Rumor claims King Yestyn had her killed shortly after Carwyn's death to tie up loose ends. Rumor isn't always correct, however. It would have been a twisted sort of revenge that was meant to destroy what's left of Logan's sanity. He'd be in no position to negotiate peace with Gallia, lashing out like a bloody animal. War would have been the only option."

Tears streamed down Realta's face. "Why?" Why would Val wish to destroy her father's life? What had Callum done to deserve that?

Val gave her a warm smile. "The monarchs of the Eastern Coalition hate Thanes. They see us as a threat to their power structure. If they discovered that the Midnight King has escaped his imprisonment, they would take the matter into their own hands, and the world would be lost because of their arrogance. But if they are too busy fighting each other, they won't be paying attention to us. We can defeat Alberik once and for all."

"Fighting each other? Why would they fight each other? I thought they were allies."

"For now. A number of strings still need to be pulled. But you see the necessity of this, don't you, Realta?"

"No. Why can't we reason with them?" Logan and Gallia's peace talk was scheduled for today. They could come to an agreement. Stop this madness before it began.

Val slammed his hand onto the table, causing the cups and kettle to clatter. "These people will never see reason. Never." He leaned forward, mere inches from her. "Here's a lesson I learned when I was your age. Trust is a luxury that Thanes cannot afford. We can only trust one another. Normal humans will betray us every single time."

"My father is normal. He'd never betray me."

"Give him time." Val snapped his fingers. Kanton stood and grabbed Realta by the arms, forcing her to her feet. "I had hoped you'd come willingly. The palace is about to become a very dangerous place. I will drag you with me if I need to. Captain." Kanton shoved Realta towards the door.

She struggled, jerking her arms and kicking Kanton's legs. This man hadn't taken her in Lothian, and he wasn't going to take her now! She kept kicking, but his grip was too strong. Her arms were going numb.

Serena, I hope you warned your brother.

But Serena didn't know about Val. Didn't know that Kanton was back in the palace. She had to do something!

Furtively glancing around the room, Realta's eyes landed on an unlit candlestand on a side table by the door. If she could just reach it, get one hand free...

The candlestand inched forward. Realta reached out her hand. It was so close. The candlestand rocked back and forth and shot through the air, sailing over her head. Metal slammed into Kanton's face. He screamed, letting go of her. Sensation rushed back into her arms.

She turned the lock and flung open the door, wondering how she had done that. No time to think, not until she was safe.

"Realta, wait," Val cried.

She spared a glance at the two men. Kanton was on his knees, cradling his bleeding forehead. A sizable gash rested above his eyebrow. Val stood beside the table, one arm outstretched towards her, his face pleading, pained.

"It doesn't have to be this way," he said. "I don't want to force you down this path, but fate has chosen us. We cannot run from fate."

Wanna bet?

Realta dashed down the hallway, turning a sharp corner. She

heard feet running behind her, gaining on her. She ran faster, her sides aching and tears running down her face, blurring her vision. She would not let Kanton take her. She wouldn't!

A strange tugging sensation forced her onward, telling her which way to go. Turning another corner, she saw a group of people. All of them had dark skin. The party from Jemayrt!

"Help me!" Realta cried. The group froze, their expressions ranging from confusion to shock. Ambassador Ekene held out his arms, and Realta ran into them, clinging to the diplomat. That warm, comforting sensation surrounded her.

"What happened, child?" asked the ambassador.

"Isn't she one of Queen Gallia's servants?"

"She has a servant's mark on her wrist."

"No," Realta said. "I'm not her servant. Please, you have to help me!"

The pursuing footsteps halted. Realta glanced over her shoulder and saw Val standing less than a pace away.

One of the men in the ambassador's group, a slender man in his mid-twenties, rushed towards Val, moving so fast Realta almost missed it. He got behind Val and grabbed him by the back of his hair. His other hand held a dagger to Val's throat.

"Kill me and kill the world!" Val yelled.

"It's that madman," said Scholar Adanna, taking a step back.

"What have you done to this girl?" Ekene demanded.

"I told her the truth, same as I told you, Chinasa. We are three of Nine."

"Silence!" The ambassador spoke in Jemayrti to the man holding the dagger. The man nodded and released Val, keeping a watchful eye on him. "You are to stay away from us. Disobey this order and Ezri's knife will find its way into your heart."

"You and Realta are both acting very foolish." Val's eyes were like ice. "But in time, you will have no choice. Alberik has returned for a third time. We—"

"Enough! I have no patience for your blasphemies. Get out of my sight."

Val sighed and gave Realta a pained smile. *Not everything in life is easy, Realta. See you soon.* Shoving his hands into his pockets, Val sauntered away.

"Thank you," Realta whispered, letting go of the ambassador. She felt kind of silly being this close to a diplomat.

"Think nothing of it, child. That man has been a thorn in my foot ever since we arrived. We can escort you back to your quarters, if you wish."

"Actually, can you help me find my father? He's one of King Logan's servants. His name is Callum Haar." Realta knew she ought to find Serena and the king and warn them about Val. But what he said about Callum, how he had planned to frame him for murder... The creeping feeling that something terrible had happened to him pervaded her mind. He hadn't been in his room.

"Of course, child." The ambassador extended his hand. Realta took it, and, followed by the rest of the Jemayrti group, they headed away from Val.

42

Secondary Plans

Motes of dust floated in the light streaming in from the stable's windows. Horses whickered quietly to one another, every now and then stamping a hoof. Serena laid curled up in a corner in the very back, far away from everyone and everything. She cried silent tears, cradling her broken face with her hands. She wished she could disappear. Fade away into nothing.

"Serena?" said a friendly voice. Serena opened one eye and saw Gregor Pym approaching. "My girl, what happened to you?" asked the older man, kneeling beside her. "Smoke, your nose is broken! Who did this?"

"Logan," she managed. Her throat ached from crying.

Gregor's face paled. "But why would your brother do such a thing?"

"He hates me." New tears stung Serena's eyes. She had only wanted to help her brother, to be a good sister. Those kings must have heard her and Realta and managed to disguise themselves in time. Gallia had feigned ignorance, and Logan had believed her, the queen of Nowan of all people! Serena's reward was a kick to the face.

"No, he doesn't, Serena. Your brother loves you very much." Gregor placed a comforting hand on Serena's shoulder, causing her to flinch. She instantly felt guilty. Gregor had never hurt her. The man had always been kind to her. Kind, like the father she never had.

"He never loved me." For a brief moment, Serena thought things would be different, better. Logan had invited her to eat at the reception. And not at some table in the corner. She had sat right next to the king. A place of prominence. It had just been another one of her brother's tricks. A ploy to get what he wanted.

Gregor sighed. "I remember when you were born. Nell had

been so afraid. We'd all heard the rumors, that Yestyn sent his bastards over the mountains. She didn't want to lose you, and when Carwyn learned the truth and confronted the old king..." He swallowed a lump in his throat. "Well, when Nell learned of her illness, she gathered her courage and told Logan everything. Do you remember that day? Logan picked you up and carried you to your own room, right in the family's quarters. He truly loved you as his sister. Do you remember?"

"No." Serena only remembered her mother's funeral. She hadn't been allowed to visit her deathbed. She was just six years old, after all. Sarra, Malaky, Isla, and the old queen had stood next to her, assuring her that she would be cared for. Logan, crowned king three months earlier, didn't spare a single glance at her.

Serena sat up, wiping the tears away from her face. Her hands came away bloody.

"Here." Gregor handed her a tattered handkerchief.

She cleaned some of the blood off her face. She gingerly touched her nose. Yes, it was definitely broken. She winced as she straightened out the bone. That would do for now. She stood and walked towards the horses.

"What are you doing?" Gregor asked, walking beside her.

Serena inspected the horses one by one. She selected a black stallion named Moon Dancer. The animal was one of Logan's fastest, absolutely perfect. The one she should have stolen the first time.

"Serena, speak to me, lass. What are you thinking?"

"If those rumors are true, I have to find them." She went over to the supply rack, selecting a recently oiled saddle and reins. If she left now while Logan was furious with her, the man would not bother sending the Guard after her. She'd be free to cross the Pass, find her real family.

"Serena." Gregor stood between her and the horse. "I know you want those rumors to be true. But where will you know to look? How will you know they're Yestyn's bastards?"

"I'll recognize them." Serena still had that drawing Callum Haar had given her. A man with sharp eyes and a warm smile. His brother-in-law. *My half-brother.*

Gregor placed a hand on Serena's shoulder. "Are you sure about this? I doubt Logan will allow you to come home a second time."

She looked towards the palace with its white walls and ornate gardens. Her eyes drifted to the second floor. To the servants' quarters where she'd been born. Where her mother had died. "That place isn't my home. And Logan isn't my family. You are. Please tell the others that I love them. Thank them for caring for me and my mother."

Gregor embraced Serena with a crushing hug. "You take care of yourself, my girl. And for your sake, I hope you find them."

Serena broke away from Gregor. Picking up the supplies, she went to saddle Moon Dancer.

A long shadow entered the stable. Panic flooding her, Serena dropped the supplies and backed into the stall door, trapped. Had Logan come to stop her a second time? The panic faded as she recognized Callum Haar in the doorway. By his side were Realta, Shasta, and a man wearing a tattered, gray cloak.

"Thank the Creator we found you," said Shasta. Stepping over the saddle, Serena went to her. "We've been searching everywhere."

"I can't stay any longer," Serena replied. "You know what he did to me?" She pointed at her broken nose. Realta placed a hand over her mouth while Callum and Shasta grimaced. The cloaked man stood as still as a statue.

"Serena," Realta said, collecting herself, though her eyes lingered on Serena's nose. "Dane Kanton is back." Gregor cursed under his breath. "He's working with Queen Gallia. And that adviser, Valentin, isn't just an adviser. He's a Minder."

"That's impossible. The Nowani hate Thanes."

"He tricked them into thinking he's normal. And we were right about Gallia's servants. They really are monarchs. Val caused us to see them as they truly are. That's..." She shifted uncomfortably. "That's why your brother didn't believe you."

"That man is not my brother."

"Oh yes, he is, Serena O'Kelwyn," replied Shasta. "He shows love no better than a viper, but you are still his sister. Nothing changes that. I've had my suspicions about those servants from the moment they arrived."

"Why?"

"They only act like servants when they're certain someone is watching. The rest of the time, they're as haughty as spoiled nobles."

"Have you told Logan or Isla?" Shasta had acted as the king and queen's unofficial adviser for years. They always gave her word credence, no matter how strange it seemed. Shasta's assumptions were rarely wrong.

"Not yet, and for that I apologize. Had I warned Logan, he might have believed you."

"So what are we supposed to do about it?" Serena asked.

"Other than running away?" Callum replied, studying the riding equipment.

Serena hung her head. "It seemed like my only option."

"What if you go to Logan now, Shasta?" asked Gregor. "Would he believe you?"

"Logan is not in the right mood for counsel. Perhaps in a few hours. I fear there are many factors at play, but we have gained new allies. Realta, would you care to explain?"

Realta told Serena about her meeting with Val, how the man explained his plot against Teyrnas and his plans to turn the Eastern monarchs against each other. How he had roped Dane Kanton into his schemes. Serena paled when she heard Val wanted her dead with Callum as her supposed murderer. All in an attempt to shatter Logan's mind.

She then explained how she ran away from them. That the Jemayrti ambassador and his entourage had been at the right place at the right time.

"Ambassador Ekene promised to protect me from them. He even helped me find my father and Shasta. And he's a Thane, too," she added with a smile.

"That's good," Serena replied, but she couldn't help feeling that Realta was withholding information. A couple of times, she began to say something, but quickly corrected herself. Serena did not pry. She knew how creepy it was to be around Kanton.

"I warned the ambassador to tread lightly where Queen Gallia is concerned," added Shasta. "We don't want another person to fall victim to her schemes."

"What if Gallia doesn't know the whole plan?" Realta asked. "Val told me he lets Gallia think his plans are hers. She probably doesn't know Val is going to betray her. Is there some way we could warn her, too?"

"One step at a time, child. First, we must show Logan the error of his ways. Then, see that peace, even temporary peace, with Nowan is obtained. I doubt we will ever be able to convince Gallia that her lover is also a backstabber."

"Lover?" Serena raised an eyebrow.

"It wasn't hard to figure out," Shasta replied curtly.

"But what if things go wrong?" asked Gregor. "What then?"

"We've considered that. Thing morning, Master Kel and I showed Master Haar the entrances to the underground tunnels and told him where each one leads. Serena, how familiar are you with these tunnels?"

"I know where to find the northern one." The northern tunnel followed the underground river to the Academy in Norgard. In fact, the entire city of Teyrnas was built on top of a subterranean lake with tributaries from both the Nerin and Wallach rivers. They were designed to be used in warfare, both for civilians to evacuate the city and for soldiers to move in and out unseen.

"Tell me its location. Now."

"It's underneath a basement in the main kitchen. The basement next to the pantry. There's a trapdoor in the back right corner."

"Excellent. Master Pym, should the worst come, lead the servants and any nobles still in the palace into that tunnel. I know Queen Isla will assist you."

"Shall I spread the word now?" Gregor asked.

"Only to those who can keep their mouths shut. This is a worst-case scenario. We won't know the outcome of Logan and Gallia's peace talks for a few days. The last thing we want is for our plan to reach her ears."

Gregor nodded. He walked towards the stable door, glancing at Serena.

"I'll be here when you get back," she replied.

The older man smiled. Giving the cloaked man a respectful nod, Gregor continued towards the palace.

"Is there a safe place for us in the meantime?" asked Callum, placing his hands on Realta's shoulders. "I don't want that psychopath anywhere near my daughter."

"I will tell the guards to be on the lookout for Kanton. But Realta's account bothers me. If Valentin can alter people's clothing, he might be able to create Illusions to alter faces. Kanton may no longer look like himself. We must tread lightly."

Serena's eyes widened. "Callum, what did you say to me after I lied about my age? The day you found me in the barn?"

Callum furrowed his brow. After a moment, he said, "That if you're twenty-one, then I'm an Averillian spice merchant."

She turned to Realta. "What did you do to me when we first met? The very first thing?"

"I hit you on the head with a pail," she replied sheepishly.

"Shasta, what was my favorite story when I was little?"

"The myth regarding Ilana and Nalani's race across the sky. Your mother read it to you every night for a year."

Callum smiled at Serena. "That was a test, wasn't it?"

"I had to be sure."

"You have our father's intelligence," said the cloaked man, removing his hood. The left half of his face was a network of scars. And his eyes were the same clear blue as hers. "Thankfully, that's the only thing we inherited from him."

"Who are you?" she asked, a tremor entering her voice.

He stepped into the stables, leaning on a crutch. "I don't expect you to recognize me. My name is Kel. My son was supposed to travel with you, but he changed his mind at the last second."

"Gareth?" she asked. She barely recalled the boy. Those few days had been a terrifying blur.

"And we met a long time ago. On the day you were born."

"You were at the palace? But how... Are you Yestyn's bastard, too?"

Kel smiled. "Unfortunately, no. I'm legitimate."

Serena's heart leapt into her throat. Why hadn't she seen it immediately? This man was almost identical to Logan. The same hair and eye color, the same shape of the jaw, the same bony frame, though this man was much thinner than her brother. Their brother.

"Who are you?" she repeated more forcefully.

"I was Prince Carwyn O'Kelwyn, heir to the Raven Throne, until Yestyn decided that he'd had enough of me. I survived his beating, and my wife arranged for us to escape the city. We should have taken you with us. I am so sorry we didn't."

"Everyone thinks you're dead," she replied, tears stinging her eyes. "Logan hates me because he thinks you're dead."

"He never hated you." Kel placed a bony hand on her shoulder. "Logan only hates that Yestyn killed me to cover up the truth. But I see a lot has changed since then. Logan isn't the young man I grew up with, but he is still a good man."

"How do you know?"

"I have my sources." He gave her a sly smile. "But those sources agree with Realta. The Eastern Coalition poses a legitimate threat to this country, and we have to find a way to stop them."

"How?" Realta asked.

"We form a plan," replied Shasta, "to help your brother—"

"Don't call him that."

Kel grimaced. Shasta studied Serena, her eyes settling on her broken nose. "Very well," she continued. "King Logan is in more danger than he realizes. Realta, continue assisting Queen Gallia for as long as she allows. Learn all you can about her plans. Callum, offer your services to Lord and Lady Lyr. They're staying at the palace for another week. Gain their trust. Logan has always listened to Lady Sarra's council in the past. Master Kel, continue to act invisible. And Serena, avoid the king. You can't afford any more trouble. I want you to spy on the guard."

"Are you serious? How am I supposed to do that?"

"Logan has entertained the idea of making you a spy for years. Do you remember last summer when you were tasked with cleaning the guardsmen's armor?"

"That was a punishment." Serena had wandered into a meeting between Logan and the Merchant Council of Kereu. They had been discussing trade routes and financing a new fleet of boats using new research from the Academy. It had taken a good fifteen minutes before anyone noticed her presence. Logan, furious, had forced Serena to work at the guardhouse all summer.

"And what did you learn?"

"I learned everyone's names and where they were from." Light dawn on her, Shasta's point becoming clear. "And their work schedules."

Shasta nodded. "You're a fast leaner and good listener. I have a hunch Kanton is near the guards, hiding among their ranks. Find him, if you can."

"I'll try. But what of you, Shasta?"

"My task is the hardest: getting Logan to see his mistake."

"Good luck with that," Kel muttered.

"How much longer will Queen Gallia be here?" asked Realta.

"A few days at least. Perhaps all of this is unnecessary. She and Logan might come to an agreement in that time."

"No." Realta shook her head. "Val wants the Eastern Coalition and Teyrnas to go to war. He will find a way to make it happen."

"Another precaution we must take. Guards your thoughts. Powerful Minders don't need permission to enter minds. We cannot allow him to know our plans."

Serena and Callum nodded. Realta paled, as though she were going to be sick. What else had that man done to her?

The clocks chimed twelve.

"We have no time to waste," said Shasta.

43

Research

The sun had sunken below the horizon, bathing the stone walls in purple light by the time Charity arrived at the Academy. The grand campus with its towering buildings and lush green gardens welcomed her despite the late hour. She hadn't realized how much she missed this place until she laid eyes on it.

The carriages came to a halt in front of the stables, nestled in the corner between the southern and eastern gates. Charity jumped down from the passenger's seat and rounded the vehicle, meeting up with Scholar Maryn. She and the other Scholars were stretching their legs.

"Do you need any help unloading?" Charity asked.

The Scholar smiled, shaking her head. "We'll leave everything in the carriages until morning. You can head inside. I'm sure you want to see your friends."

Charity felt uneasy about leaving such valuable equipment out in the open, but no one could get inside the gates without the guards' permission and no one at the Academy had a reason to steal. Taking a second look, all the Scholars seemed worn out by the day-long journey. She bid Maryn and her colleagues good night and went inside the main building.

Though the sun was down, many Students, Scholars, and Journeymen moved about the ground floor, some with books and paper tucked under their arms and others in small clusters of friends. Charity scanned the faces until she spotted two familiar ones. Evelyn and Coryn. She ran over to the sisters, waving.

"Charity!" they exclaimed, greeting her with an embrace.

"What was it like?" asked Coryn.

"Amazing! There were dozens of nobles and dignitaries, and we were given a tour of the palace. And the king loved Scholar Maryn's invention."

"The king?" Evelyn looked at her in shock. "You actually met King Logan?"

"Yes," Charity beamed.

"Jaim is going to be so jealous," Coryn smirked.

"What else did you do?" Evelyn asked.

"I assisted Scholar Maryn at the exhibition and ate at the king's reception..." The king's reception. Dane Kanton appeared out of nowhere. Charity had frozen, not wanting to face the man but unable to look away. That night in Lothian repeating in her mind, awaking to screams and running into the dark forest. Kanton, the left side of his face covered in burn scars, had stared at her and Callum with such hatred.

But then the king intervened. Kanton had told him that she was dead, but there she was, alive and well. The king banished Kanton, stripping him of his rank and title. Charity was grateful that the king had publicly ousted Kanton, though she'd been terrified and confused, forcing to relive that night once more.

"Charity, are you okay?" asked Evelyn. She and her sister wore faces of concern.

"Yes," she replied, pushing those dark thoughts away. "The king gave me this." She reached into her dress pocket and pulled out a handkerchief. A simple linen square with a pair of ravens embroidered in one corner.

"He just gave it to you?"

"Um... Yeah." Charity did not want to admit she'd been crying her eyes out. That would only lead her to explain Kanton's schemes and thinking about that night again. She wished she could forget it. Besides, Realta and Callum were alive, and Realta would be at the Academy in a few days. Not to mention her best friend was a Thane, too. It was wonderful!

"Do you know where Lok is?" She wanted to share the good news with him.

Evelyn and Coryn exchanged uneasy glances.

"Charity," Evelyn began, her voice level. "Lok got in a lot of trouble the other night."

"What do you mean?" Trouble? Lok Tolman had never been in trouble in his life.

"Zandon suggested they go into Norgard, just for a few hours.

Relax a bit. They didn't mean to do anything wrong, they just..."

"Lok accidentally started a fire," Coryn finished. "The tavern owner thought it was intentional. Lok, Zandon, Jaim, and Ivar all got reprimands from the Council."

"What does that mean?" Charity racked her brain. Reprimands? She vaguely recalled Scholar Roseen mentioning those as a form of punishment, but that she didn't have to worry about them. Reprimands were very rare.

"Each student is allowed to have four during their course of study," Evelyn explained. "After the fifth reprimand, they're expelled and aren't allowed to enter any Academy in the world. Jaim and Ivar have one. Zandon has two. But the Council gave Lok three."

"Three?" she yelled, aghast. A handful of heads turned her way. "For a fire?"

"A few people got hurt, and the Council tried to change Lok's mentor. They thought Scholar Kuno wasn't doing a good job, so they gave him a new one. Tried to, anyway."

Evelyn described how Lok created a wall of fire, seven feet high, according to Zandon. The Council interpreted it as a deliberate act of violence, a cause for immediate expulsion. Zandon and the others were certain Lok was going to be expelled when a chaplain witnessing the reprimand spoke to the Council on Lok's behalf, convincing them to give him a second chance.

"They agreed," Evelyn concluded, "so long as the chaplain helps Lok."

"So, he has two mentors now?"

"For the moment. Charity, they gave Lok three months to get his abilities under control or they'll kick him out."

Charity frowned, her face burning. "That's not right. They can't do that."

"Yes, they can," replied Evelyn, her voice grim. "When I was a first year, there was this student named Ailyssa. She was a Manipulator Thane. Her ability wasn't very strong, but she had a tendency to Manipulate objects at people when she got angry. One day, she got in an argument with another student in the workshop. She sent a jar of nails flying at his face. Ailyssa was expelled, and Padraig lost an eye."

A chill went down Charity's spine. Lok would never hurt someone intentionally. He was kind and caring and... *He threw a burning log at Kanton.* The man's clothes had caught on fire. But that was different. It was self-defense.

"I know it seems unfair," Evelyn continued, "but the Council has every right to expel someone when the rest of the Students are in danger. We all like Lok, but he needs to be careful and learn control."

"I understand. Where is he? Am I allowed to speak with him?"

"Of course. But he's been keeping to himself lately."

"He might be in the library," said Coryn. "I saw him there with Scholar Kuno yesterday evening."

"I'll go check on him. Meet up with you later?"

"Yeah. We'll be in the common area until curfew." Evelyn and Coryn went on their way.

Charity climbed the eastern stairway towards the library. She had trouble wrapping her head around everything. She had been gone for three days, and in that short span, Lok's time at the Academy nearly ended. What if she had been here? Could she have calmed Lok down, preventing him from causing the fire? Or maybe talked him out of going with Zandon? She sighed heavily. These thoughts were meaningless. The past was done. She could only help Lok's future.

There were a surprising number of people in the library. Students and Journeymen sat in small groups of blue and gray. Scholars moved about, carrying books and tomes and speaking with their colleagues. Nobody paid much attention to her.

If I wanted to study without being seen, where would I go?

She pictured the library's layout. There were a handful of tables towards the back, opposite from the archives, that were rarely used. The ideal place to go unnoticed. She quietly made her way there.

Two people sat at the furthermost table, one with a white cloak and the other with a blue one. Several books and papers littered the table. The candle on the wall flickered behind its glass casing.

The man with the white cloak glanced up at her and smiled. "Good evening, Charity. How was your trip?"

Lok spun around in his chair, shock and disbelief spreading over his features. He stood, knocking the chair to the floor, and gave her a hug, wrapping his long arms around her. He was trembling.

"Evelyn and Coryn told me everything," she whispered. "I'm so sorry."

Lok retrieved his notebook and pencil from the table. *"I didn't mean to start that fire. I was just so scared. I overreacted."*

"There's nothing wrong with getting scared, Lok."

"If I may," said Scholar Kuno, rising from his chair and standing next to Lok. "There is something wrong with getting scared if you can manipulate fire but not control it. Lok was lucky this time. We both were," he added, voice faltering.

"Is there anything I can do to help?"

"How fast can you read?"

Charity furrowed her brow, not following. "Very fast, if it's interesting."

"Well, I don't know about interesting," said the Scholar, selecting a book from the pile. "But the more we know about Elementals, the more we can help Lok."

Charity read the book's title: *Religion in the pre-Academic World, a Comprehensive History of Ceremonies and Rites Dating to the Time of the Thousand Years War,* by Scholar Urik of the Lowyrn Academy in the Year 1109.

"It's a bit dated, but Scholar Urik was known for his thoroughness."

"I don't see what religion has to do with controlling fire."

"The ancient priests and chaplains were all Elementals. I had hoped to find texts describing their training methods, but no luck yet."

"I'll do my best," she replied, seeing the Scholar's reasoning.

The three of them sat down at the table. Charity opened the book to the first page. The print was quite small, perhaps half the size of the print in the Academy's textbooks. She flipped through the pages. Same print size on every page. All five hundred of them. Great.

"Don't you want to tell Lok about your trip first?" asked Kuno.

"Oh, right!" She had completely forgotten. She relayed the details of the exhibition and reception to him, the same ones she had given to Evelyn and Coryn. She then told him about Realta and Callum's side of events. How Kanton had posted fake charges against them, causing the king to take them prisoner. The king, realizing Kanton had lied, used Charity to expose him and promised to release Realta and Callum soon.

"Wonderful! Is Realta coming to the Academy?"

"I'm pretty sure."

"I feel like I'm missing something," said Kuno, eyes narrowing. "Kanton gave your friends false charges? Are these the same friends you were separated from?"

"Yes. Well, Realta's our friend. Callum is her father."

"Okay? I thought you said Kanton was just passing through your village. Why didn't you tell me this?" Kuno asked Lok.

The young man cringed and wrote, *"It's complicated."*

"I have time." Kuno closed his book. Charity glanced at the cover. *Thanes at War: Military Tactics Derived from the Eight Thanes.* That sounded a lot more interesting than her book. Maybe she could persuade him to switch.

A figure in a brown chaplain's robe bustled into the small corner, a stack of books in his arms. "Okay," said the chaplain, "I have Scholar Zula's *Treatise on the Eight Thanes*, Scholar Mathi's *On the Preservation of Abilities*, and *The History of the Thousand Years War and the Gadyeni Cycle* by..." He glanced at the title. "Jowan of the Averillian Chapel. Huh, never expected anything like this to come out of Averil. Oh, we have a newcomer. Good evening, Student."

"Good evening, Chaplain." The chaplain was in his mid-thirties with the red and purple earrings of a Learner and Empath Thane. His clear blue eyes danced in the candlelight reflecting off his glasses. Charity studied him, wondering where she had seen his vaguely familiar face before. Had he always been at the Academy?

"Brother Malaky, this is Charity Loy. She grew up in the same village as Lok."

"Nice to meet..." The books slipped out of Brother Malaky's hands, thudding unto the floor. His eyes widened. At first, Charity thought he was looking at her, but instead the chaplain stared into space. Scholar Kuno rushed to his side, propping him up so he would not fall. Charity tried to put the symptoms together.

Was the chaplain having a seizure?

"Three of the Nine in one city with the Fourth nearby! The Wardens of the Night come for them! Tell them to run. Run!"

The words sent chills down her spine. This was definitely not a seizure.

A group of curious Students and Scholars gathered near the table. Scholar Kuno motioned them away. This was none of their concern.

Brother Malaky collapsed, placing his hands on the table for support. Sweat beaded on his forehead.

"What did you see this time?" Kuno asked in a gentle voice.

"Three figures composed of light in Teyrnas," he explained, breathing as though he had sprinted a mile. "A fourth near Caman's Pass in the Hinterlands. The fourth was surrounded by night figures, cowering in fear. The other three..." Brother Malaky shook his head. "They're together, but against one another. Or two against one. That part of the vision is fuzzy."

Kuno helped Brother Malaky sit down. He then collected the fallen books, taking them up with care and inspecting them for damage.

"What's happening at Caman's Pass?" Charity asked. She gripped her Student's cloak to keep her hands from trembling.

"Nothing to trouble yourself with," Brother Malaky replied, rubbing his temples. "I'm afraid this was a very bad introduction, young miss."

"But my parents and sisters live in Vala. It's only fifteen miles from the Pass. Are they in danger?"

Brother Malaky met her gaze. That mixture of patience and hidden pain reminded her of Kel. "No, I don't think so. I got the impression of a young male."

"What about the other three? And the Wardens?" She'd never heard the term, but surmised they were not people she wanted to run into.

Lok nudged Charity. He wrote, *"I will explain it to you later. A lot has happened since you left. But I'm glad Realta and Callum are all right. I was worried about them."*

Light dawned on her. "Maybe that was part of the problem. You were always worried, and that made it hard for you to control your ability."

"That's a good observation, Charity," replied Kuno. "I'm ashamed I never thought of it."

"Two males. One female."

"Pardon?" Charity asked the chaplain.

"The other three. Two of them are male and the third is female. That's all I know. I'm sorry."

"That's all right. I..." Recognition clicked. "You look like King Logan!" Those blue eyes, partially hidden by glasses, were the same shade of blue as the king's. His face was angular, though not quite as thin as his brother, and his hair was closely cropped in the style of chaplains. Had it been longer, she'd have seen the resemblance sooner.

Kel's face appeared in her mind. The face that shared many similarities with the king and this chaplain. His warning not to ask certain questions rang loud and clear.

"I should hope so. I'm his brother. How do you know what my older brother looks like?"

Because he looks like my friend's uncle. "I was at his exhibition. With the Scholars."

"Damn, I forgot about the exhibition." Brother Malaky winced. "I'm sorry. I shouldn't curse. How did Logan look?"

"He seemed well. And your sister was there, too. And Serena," Charity added quietly. The king had acted friendly towards his bastard sister at the reception, but Serena had seemed on edge, uncertain.

"Serena came home?" He let out a heavy sigh. "That girl is better off on her own. I suppose there's a reason for that, though."

The clocks chimed nine times. Charity heard several people get up and leave. Lights out for Students was in one hour.

Kuno collected the books. "I don't want to keep either of you here past curfew. We'll resume tomorrow evening. So long as your studied don't suffer." He shot a glance at Lok.

Lok nodded solemnly. He and Charity stood. The chaplain stood as well.

"I must retire soon. The Council wants a record of every blasted vision, and if I don't write this one down, they'll be livid. Good night, Students Lok and Charity. Good night, Scholar Rudi."

"Kuno," he corrected, frowning.

Brother Malaky grimaced. "Sorry. I need to sleep." The chaplain walked away from the table with a book tucked under his arm.

"I don't know what to make of that one," said Kuno.

"He's a Farsight as well as a Learner and Empath?" Charity questioned.

"So it seems."

"But he only has two earrings."

Kuno sighed. "This world is very strange sometimes, Charity. But the strangeness always makes it interesting." He opened the book on military history and began reading. Charity and Lok took that as their cue to leave.

"What about Dane Kanton?" Lok wrote as they headed down the hall.

"The king kicked him out of the Guard and banished him from the capital."

"Good." Lok's face was hard. He had no sympathy for that man. Charity did not blame him.

"Realta's a Thane, too," she whispered, not wanting anyone to overhear. "A Dreamer."

Lok started, eyes wide. He quickly wrote, *"But there aren't any more Dreamers."*

"There weren't any more Elementals until you," she replied with a smile.

Lok nodded. He faced away from her, lost in thought. Entering the Students' quarters, he wrote, *"I need to practice controlling fire, but I don't want to do it in front of Brother Malaky. Will you help me during free hours?"*

"Why don't you want to practice around the chaplain?"

Lok bit down on his lip and shrugged. *"He's weird in a bad way. I don't trust him. And don't tell him about Realta's ability. Maybe Kuno, but no one else."*

She recalled Lok making a similar request regarding his own abilities. It wasn't unreasonable. Realta would tell the Scholars once she arrived. As for the chaplain, Charity hadn't had enough time to form a real opinion about him yet.

"Okay. I'll help."

44

Blue Roses

Realta rubbed her tired eyes as she helped clean Queen Gallia's quarters. The last two nights, she had gone to sleep intending to dream about Val, hoping to discover more about his plan. Both attempts ended in failure. The first night, she dreamed of a thin man with slate gray hair and wearing a black cloak. His skin was stark white, the shade of freshly fallen snow. He sat beside a fire in the middle of the woods. He didn't notice her until the very end of the dream. All he did was smile and say hello. A second later, Realta awoke.

The second night, she didn't have any dreams. She doubted she got more than an hour or two of sleep. Anxious thoughts plagued her mind. The sense that she would never leave the palace. That she would never be free. She suspected Val's handiwork.

"Are you all right, dear?" asked Lucia. The mild-mannered servant bore little resemblance to the radiant queen she had seen the other day. Realta had trouble remembering they were the same person. But that was the point, wasn't it?

"Just a little tired," she replied.

"Don't let Her Majesty hear that. She will think you're being overworked by House Kelwyn."

"She cares a lot about her servants?" It was as much a statement as a question. Realta had never once heard Gallia raise her voice to a servant, not even if they made a mistake.

Lucia nodded. "Of course. The Nowani aren't barbarians."

Realta glanced over at the closed door. The queen and Val had disappeared into the room an hour ago. Deen, the man with different colored eyes, sat outside the door, playing a simple tune on his reed flute. So far, he had ignored Realta.

"Lucia, how long have you been a servant?" Shasta had advised her to question the supposed servants, searching for holes in their stories without being too obvious.

"I started working as a maid when I was sixteen."

"Why?" Realta quickly added, "If I may ask."

Lucia gave her a patient smile. "You're a curious one today. To be honest, I never had an education and wasn't able to learn a trade. This was my best option. What about you, dear?"

The tattoo on her wrist itched. "I didn't have a choice," she replied quietly.

"And if you did have a choice? What would you be?"

"I don't really know." Realta had always been fascinated by her father's stories about being a guide. Traveling through Caman's Pass was always an adventure. But nervous got in the way. She was fine with people once she spent time with them and got to know them. The first day was always the hardest. And any number of accidents could happen while crossing the Pass. Wild animal attacks, mountain slides, raiders. She understood what to do in those events, but doubted she'd actually be able to face them.

Then she learned the Scholars were arriving in Vala during Autumntide. Her thoughts had shifted to the Academy and all the stories she'd heard from her aunt and uncle. She always wondered what it would be like to attend a real school.

"What about you?" Realta asked. "Do you ever wish you could be something different?"

Lucia let out a soft giggle. "Like what?"

"A queen."

The reed flute stopped. Realta's face grew warm as Lucia stared at her, dark eyes narrowing. Had she gone too far? The servant laughed. Deen resumed playing.

"Such a silly thing to ask! Whatever brought it on, dear?"

Realta shrugged. "Being in the palace, I guess."

The door opened, and two large men, each one built like a boulder, entered the room. They went directly towards Lucia and Realta. She was certain they were part of Gallia's guards, but neither wore a uniform.

"Is everything all right, boys?" Lucia asked them.

"Just checking on the horses," said one. He had a long scar running down the right side of his face. He turned to Realta. "Is your name Realta?"

She nodded.

"One of the guardsmen told me to give you this." He handed her a blue rose. "Said his name was Colm."

"Thank him for me, if you see him again," she replied, holding the rose so that the thrones didn't prick her fingers. Shasta has created a code for Serena. If she saw Kanton in the guardhouse, she was to talk to Colm, placing the word 'red' in the sentence. Colm would then give Realta a red rose. They wanted to raise as little suspicious as possible, so they had enlisted Colm. The young guardsman was nearest to Realta in age and became easily flustered when questioned. Too flustered to give away their true intentions. Everyone would assume it was a simple crush.

A white rose meant no danger at all, while a blue rose meant Serena was suspicious but could not yet prove anything. Realta had been hoping for a white one.

"Aunt Lucia," said the second man, lowering his voice. "Can I speak to you in private?"

"Of course, Chayton. It will only be a moment, dear." Lucia and her nephew went into one of the side rooms reserved for servants. The other man stormed out of the quarters.

Realta carefully placed the rose on a side table. So, Kanton might be hiding among the guards. Then again, he might not. She hated being caught in uncertainty.

"Is he your sweetheart?"

Realta turned and faced Deen. The morning light illuminated half of his face, making his blue eye brighter and the brown one darker.

"Not really. He's just nice."

"Nice is better than mean. And you seem kind of young to have a sweetheart, if you don't mind my saying so."

"I don't mind. Can you play other instruments or just the flute?"

"Oh, I can play dozens," he replied, turning the flute over in his hands. "My mother loved music. Insisted that I learn."

"You have a lovely accent. Why doesn't Queen Gallia have one?"

Deen smiled. "Her Majesty was raised in central Nowan. I come from the east, near the border with Bran Maro. It's a beautiful country. Open fields filled to bursting with wildflowers. A sky that seems to go on forever. Perhaps you'll be able to see it someday." He started playing again, a low, slow paced tune.

The hairs on the back of Realta's neck stood on end. "What do you mean by that?"

Deen lowered his flute. A wry smile crossed his face. "She hasn't told you yet?"

"Told me what?"

"Well, Queen Gallia has taken a liking to you. She's going to ask King Logan to transfer your services to her."

"What?" The blood drained from her face. The queen wanted to take her away? Back to Nowan? She would never see her father again!

"Nothing is set in stone yet. Oh, don't be upset. Nowan is a wonderful country. You will never have to live in fear of Thanes again."

The servants' door banged open, causing Realta to jump. Lucia briskly walked towards the door guarded by Deen.

"Move."

Deen, a puzzled look crossing his face, stood and pulled his chair to the side. "Cos chendosta?"

Lucia shot him a glare and rapped on the door. Val answered it.

The messenger scowled. "What part of don't interrupt—"

"I need to speak with Gallia."

"Wait until we're done."

"Chayton has brought a matter to my attention," she yelled, her face taking on a shade of red.

Val acquiesced. "Fine." He allowed Lucia to enter and closed the door behind her.

Deen shook his head and muttered something in a language Realta did not understand. Repositioning his chair, he sat and resumed playing.

Chayton is a Cuchasi, Val's voice echoed in her head. *He saw your Aura. I'll try my best to smooth things over, but you need to run. Now, Realta! Run!*

For once, Realta did not mind Val being inside her head. She rushed towards the door, throwing it wide open, and sprinted down the hall.

✳✳✳

The warm, spring air felt good on Serena's skin. She stood atop the palace walls along with several members of the Guard, Colm including. Serena had not been keen on letting Colm into their plans. The greenblood guardsman was a good man, but not one hundred percent reliable. Shasta, however, had insisted. The more people on their side, and the more people to give evidence of Gallia's schemes to Logan, the better.

The head of the palace guard, Captain Lewys Glasco, was conducting a surveillance drill. All members of the guard assigned to wall duty were to report to their stations with as little noise as possible, without wasting a second. Once there, Glasco instructed them to observe for fifteen minutes and report their findings to him. Nothing more.

"They're very obedient," commented Rimond, the head of Queen Gallia's bodyguards. Serena knew him as Syleck, the king of Tirshay. She was amazed that Captain Glasco, who made it a point to learn about foreign leaders and their military tactics, did not recognize the man. And here he was, running drills right in front of him at Logan's insistence as a sign of trust. Serena wanted to scream.

"We only recruit the best," Glasco replied.

"And how often are drills done?"

"Until they are perfected."

"And if the unexpected happens? How do they respond?"

Captain Glasco smiled, splitting his face in half. "Serena, double time!"

Serena rolled her eyes but did as instructed. Shasta, with Serena in tow, had informed Glasco that Logan wanted his sister working in the guardhouse. This assignment was to be half punishment and half practice, should the girl choose to join the guard. Glasco readily accepted, and some of the guards had nicknamed her "Little Marsh", after their former colleague. Cupping her hands around her mouth, she yelled, "Gael, Brenan, O'Tyre, Galandar, Atkyn!"

The five men turned to Serena, their expressions ranging from alert to annoyed to readied anticipation. A half second later, the other dozen guardsmen drew their swords and attacked the named men. The five quickly drew their own swords and fought off the others, matching them blow for blow and dodge for dodge.

The purpose of double time was to train guards to fight against larger numbers. A handful of names were called at random, and the others attacked quickly and without mercy. Captain Glasco ordered them to carry dulled weapons during drills, so major injuries were rare. Normally, the only injuries were bruised egos and the occasional sprained wrist or ankle.

Captain Glasco raised his fist in the air and yelled, "Attention!"

The fighting ceased. The men, breathing hard and sweating, sheathed their swords. Serena studied the five she had selected, the ones she suspected might have been replaced by Kanton. She'd hoped watching them fight would narrow down the list.

O'Tyre and Gael were the least likely suspects. O'Tyre belonged to a minor noble family and would be missed. And Gael, while the same height and weight as Kanton, was not nearly as skilled as the disgraced guard. Atkyn also had the same physical features, but the man had favored his left hand during the drill. Kanton was right-handed.

That left Brenan and Galandar. Both men were loners, rarely interacting with their fellow guards. Sure, Kanton might be impersonating one of the more outgoing men. He was a Learner after all, but Serena thought that would be too much work. Thanes grew fatigued just like normal people. Valentin would not be able to keep the Illusion going forever. She doubted the man would risk an Illusion fading in front of multiple people. Serena had to switch tactics.

"Excellent," said Rimond, clapping. "These men are better trained than I ever expected."

"We only want the best."

"Tell me, are any of the men Thanes?"

"Show of hands!"

Six of the guardsmen raised their hands. They then removed their helmets, revealing their ringed ears. Three Learners, one Minder, one Manipulator and Minder, and one Empath.

"How often do they rely on their abilities?" Rimond asked, rubbing his chin and casting dubious glances at the men.

"As little as possible. Men who rely too much on their Thane abilities neglect their sword forms and exercises. Being able to read the enemy's mind won't help if he cuts off your head."

Rimond laughed. "Excellent point."

Serena seized the opportunity. She rammed into Brenan, pinning the man against the wall, and snatched his dagger. The large man reacted quickly, grabbing Serena by the shirt collar and whirling her around. He clapped his hands on Serena's shoulders, threatening to crush her collarbones.

"What in the name of the Abyss are you doing?" Brenan yelled. Using his left hand, he backhanded Serena across the face. Her already broken nose burst alight with new pain.

"Brenan, report!" Glasco bellowed, storming towards the man, Rimond on his heels.

"The bastard tried to steal my dagger, Captain."

Glasco cornered Serena and whispered, "Now why would you do a foolish thing like that?"

Serena shrugged. Warm blood trickled from her nose. She had learned what she needed and felt no need to explain her actions. She had never been a model princess, even a bastard one.

The captain sighed. "You are already on very thin ice, girl. Do you want word of this reaching your brother?"

"No, sir."

"Then stop being foolish and do as you are told."

"Yes, sir." She handed back the dagger to Brenan. The man scowled, returning the weapon to his belt.

Captain Glasco called for everyone to fall into line and led them down the wall to the guardhouse entrance. He and Rimond talked about battle strategies.

And he calls me foolish.

"Everything all right, Serena?" asked Waltyr Rosser, one of the guards who had escorted Kanton out of the palace.

"Not really." Four names on her list of five crossed out, and she had her doubts about Galandar. Perhaps this was a mistake. Kanton could be masquerading as a servant or a stable hand. Stars above, he might not even be in the palace anymore.

"I know your brother sent you to the guardhouse as a punishment," the Waltyr whispered. "But no one knows exactly why."

"He thinks I lied to him."

Waltyr scratched his head. "That's a bit steep for a mere lie."

Serena let out a heavy sigh. "He thinks I lied about Queen Gallia."

"Oh." Waltyr peered over the wall towards the city. Sounds of carriage traffic and people calling out to one another rose from below. "May I pry further?"

"No."

Waltyr nodded. Serena glanced over the side of the wall, the side leading towards the River Nerin. They were too far away to see the water, but Serena knew it was there. And beyond that, a new life. She might never find the rest of Yestyn's bastards, but she would be free. All she had to do was help Logan one last time, despite how much she resented him.

Glancing downwards, Serena spied a small figure in a purple dress running into the guardhouse. A second figure, a medium-sized man with dark hair, ran inside after her.

"Realta?"

"What's that?"

Panic rose in her. Had someone discovered their plan? Serena ran through the line of men, past Captain Glasco and Rimond. The captain and several disgruntled guards called after her. Serena did not slow down for a second. A horrid thought invaded her mind: they were too late. Gallia, or worse, Valentin, had discovered their plans and was hunting them down.

Rushing down the winding stairs, Serena heard a scream.

45

Illusions

Alone in his private study, King Logan gazed down at the gardens. Sarra, Lord Lyr, and their two children walked along the flower-lined path, Kaden and Shandri running ahead and doubling back every couple of paces. Callum Haar walked beside the two adults, hands clasped behind his back. He and Sarra were talking amicably with Lyr adding a word here and there.

It made perfect sense. Sarra and Esme had gotten along wonderfully, as though they were sisters separated at birth. This man was Esme's younger brother, the link to all those lost years. The servant's tattoo on his wrist meant nothing to her.

"I've been a fool," Logan said, turning to face Shasta. The woman, though light on her feet, had never been able to hide her presence from him. Isla, surprisingly, was there, too. The queen had lapsed into another of her silent periods, avoiding all unnecessary interactions. She stood quietly beside Shasta. Her green eyes were wide, like those of a frightened deer.

"In what way?" Shasta asked, folding her hands in front of her.

"I knew Haar and his daughter were related to Esme the moment I saw them. The resemblance was obvious. And the girl..." Logan fought back bitter tears. "She looks just like Esme when Carwyn and I met her." He sighed. "I never should have listened to Kanton."

Shasta studied him with her sharp, brown eyes. Isla remained a silent statue.

"Well? You have nothing to say?"

"I have nothing to correct," Shasta replied. "You have been a fool, in that regard. But you were distracted at the time, and still are."

Logan stole a glance out the window. The three adults had retired to a bench while the children examined the flowers.

"Why did I add to his tattoo? What was I thinking? That man

will never walk free."

"Tattoos can be removed."

"They leave behind scars. People will question him every time they see it. And the girl. She's only a few years younger than... A few years older than Morgan." Logan struggled to think about his bastard sister. The girl was well meaning and did her best to stay out of the way. But Logan had been so close to making a peace deal with Gallia. Until Serena's interruption. "Was I too harsh on Serena?"

"You broke the girl's nose by kicking her in the face. You tell me, Your Majesty."

Logan grimaced. That tone in Shasta's voice made him feel worthless, like a piece of dirt stuck to the bottom of a horseshoe. "I don't suppose she'll ever forgive me." The old king had abused all four of them, Carwyn getting the worst of it. Yestyn had Manipulated objects at his head, blaming him for things that were not his fault, or worse, punishing him for Logan's or Mal's or Sarra's mistakes. And the last beating had killed Carwyn. Was it any wonder his mind didn't always work correctly? He had hated that man so much he resorted to murder. Yestyn, in Logan's broken mind, had gotten exactly what he deserved. When would Logan get what he deserved?

"I'm going to have their tattoos removed this evening. Please inform Gilnyn."

"Will that be enough to ease your conscience?"

"It's a start." If only everyone he met was as honest as Shasta.

"And what about Gallia?" Isla asked timidly. "Have you convinced her to meet with you again?"

"I was waiting for the right time. Shasta, would you mind delivering a message for me?"

"Of course, Your Majesty."

"Tell Gallia that I apologize for the other day's unfortunate mistake. And tell Serena that I went too far. She's a good kid. She doesn't deserve to be treated that way by anyone."

"I will deliver the first message, but you ought to deliver the second one yourself. If I may, that mistake, as you call it, has me thinking. How often has Serena lied to you?"

Logan frowned. "Never. I've never heard her lie."

"So why would Serena lie about Queen Gallia's entourage? What does she have to gain by that? The girl knows her history. The bloody wars that have plagued our nation. Why risk starting another one?"

Logan sat down on the divan next to the window. He weighed Shasta's words carefully, observing their logic flow.

"Nothing. Serena has nothing to gain by lying." He locked eyes with Shasta. "What have you heard?" He then looked to Isla. "Have you seen anything?"

As Isla opened her mouth to reply, the study's door burst open. Queen Gallia stood at the threshold, her eyes burning. Her messenger and her Cuchasi stood by her side.

"Who gave you permission to enter my rooms?" Logan demanded, storming towards her. Isla placed a hand on his arm. This is not the time to be rash, the gesture said. "Your Majesty," he added.

"I want an explanation, Kelwyn," Gallia replied, her voice harsh and low.

"My bastard sister can be impulsive. She—"

"Not her. Realta."

Logan raised an eyebrow. What he wouldn't give to trade Illusions for proper mind reading. "I don't understand."

Gallia scoffed. "Don't understand? You send a mousy, little servant girl into my quarters, knowing I would take pity on her. She looked so terrified of her Thane master, afraid of what he would do to her with his Thane powers. You knew I'd want to help her. That I'd make her part of my retinue. You thought you were so clever!"

"Queen Gallia, would you care to explain what you're talking about?"

"You hid a Thane right under my nose, and now you dare lie to my face!"

"What?" Logan turned to Shasta and Isla. The head of servants stared at Gallia, mouth agape. Isla's face grew ashen.

"Don't act like you didn't know," scoffed Val the messenger. Logan felt a sudden urge to punch that smug look off his face.

Gallia shot him a sideways glare. Val muttered and took a step back. The queen continued, "The girl is a Thane. Another one of my Cuchasi saw her Aura as plainly as I see your face."

"But Realta isn't a Thane."

Gallia smiled. "That's what you wanted me to believe, isn't it? When Shilo first observed her, you were right outside the door, casting one of your Illusions. You made it impossible for her to see the girl's Aura. But Illusions don't last forever."

"I swear, the girl is normal. She..." Logan never thought to have Realta tested. Esme had been a normal person. He was mostly certain that Callum, another normal human, was the girl's father, not Carwyn. But what of her mother? Was she a Thane? Fire and smoke, why didn't he ever think of that?

"Chayton, come here," Gallia said. A man appeared in the doorway. The man's head nearly touched the door frame, his board shoulders almost too wide to fit through. His muscled arms could easily snap Logan's bony limbs like twigs.

Logan steadied himself. If need be, he could create an Illusion of himself for Chayton to attack while he, Isla, and Shasta fled.

There will be no chance for peace if it comes to that. The Teyrnian people would not take an attack on their king and queen lightly.

"Chayton," Gallia turned to face Logan, "tell the king about the girl."

"The little girl with braided, black hair?"

"Naturally."

"She had a black Aura around her. I'd never seen anything like it. But the girl is definitely a Thane. I wouldn't lie."

A black Aura? This was insane. There was no such thing as a black Aura.

"Valentin."

The messenger stepped forward, a wicked smile on his face. "According to historical texts, a black Aura denotes a Dreamer Thane, thought to have died out two centuries ago. Dreamers have the ability to see past events as they sleep and can focus their dreams on specific people. However, Dreamer must be in close proximity to those people. How clever of you Teyrnians to lie about their demise only to hide them among servants. Through Realta, you could have learned anything about Queen Gallia."

Logan suppressed a laugh. "A Dreamer? Really?"

"I don't want another argument, Logan," said Gallia, exasperation leaking into her voice. "I want an explanation."

"An explanation? Fine. Dreamers really are extinct. The Scholars haven't recorded one in generations. And if I wanted to learn your secrets, I'd have my brother-in-law do it. He's one of the most skilled Minders in the capital."

"Are you calling my most trusted Cuchasi a liar?"

"If he's your most trusted, why have the other one read the girl?"

Gallia's face reddened.

Isla placed a hand on his shoulder. He was treading on thin ice. Take the next step carefully.

"I know of a way to settle this. Where is Realta? We'll hear the truth from her."

"Realta ran away the moment Chayton discovered the truth. I sent one of my men after her."

Logan paled.

Screams sounded from the garden. Logan rushed to the window, pushing it open. Below, he saw another man, equally as large as Chayton, fighting Callum. The larger man circled Callum like a wildcat getting ready to lunge at its prey. Sarra grabbed the two children and ran for cover, calling for the guards. Lord Lyr stood several paces away, his dagger unsheathed and his face drained of blood.

The large man bore a striking resemblance to Chayton.

"What are you doing?" Logan demanded, whirling around to face Gallia.

"It's obvious the girl's father is in on the plot. He must be apprehended immediately."

"The girl's father is innocent! He's just a farmhand. He did nothing wrong." As Logan spoke, he knew every word was true. He had sensed something was off about Kanton's testimony. The man had proven himself to be untrustworthy. Why hadn't he taken half an hour to give Haar a proper trial?

"So says you." Gallia stormed out of the room. Shilo followed, but Val and Chayton stood guard at the door.

Shasta and Isla inched closer to Logan. Isla had that haunted look in her eyes that meant she was having a Farsight.

Heart leaping into his throat, Logan looked out the window as

Gallia's lackey lunged at Callum.

***

The man had come out of nowhere. Callum didn't hear him approach until it was too late. He berated himself. A mistake like that could mean life or death for a mountain guide. His quiet life on the Loy farm had made him complacent. Fortunately, the man's hold on Callum's neck was weak, easy to break out of. He saw a blur of fabric from the corner of his eye. Heard children crying.

The man, no older than twenty-five, sneered and lunged for him. Callum ducked and landed a blow on the man's shoulder. It might as well have been a mosquito bite for all the good it did. The man punched wildly, coming dangerously close to Callum's head.

"Hey!"

The man and Callum glanced over at Lord Lyr. The nobleman had his dagger drawn and stood in a fighting stance common among beginning students. Callum doubted this man had ever been in an actual fight.

The younger man glared at Lord Lyr. Callum seized the advantage and landed a blow on the man's right ear, followed by a punch to the jaw. He stumbled, disorientated and off balance. Callum jabbed him in quick succession: jaw, rib cage, jaw. The man wavered but did not fall.

"Bloody Thanes!" he screamed as he charged Callum at full speed. Callum cursed under his breath. Any man back in the Hinterlands would be unconscious by now. Bracing himself, he jumped out of the man's way at the last second.

He now stood side by side with Lyr. The nobleman was pale and sweating, his dagger held in a weak grip. Callum's breathing began to hitch. That punctured lung was coming back to haunt him. He needed to end this fight. Quickly.

"He wants to kill you," said Lyr.

"I hadn't noticed," Callum replied sarcastically.

"He's working under Queen Gallia's orders."

That Callum did not know. Why would the queen want him dead? He hadn't said more than a few sentences to her. And Real-

415

ta was working for her.

Oh, Great Creator.

Realta.

The man charged but froze in mid-step, eyes fixed on something between Callum and Lord Lyr. Callum studied the small field. Nothing stood between them. The man stumbled, falling to his knees. He raised his hands over his now terrified face.

"Please, please, don't hurt me." The man glanced to his side, trembling. He squeezed his eyes shut. "No! No!"

Lord Lyr ran towards the man and sunk the dagger into his chest. The man collapsed to the ground with a quiet thud. Lyr pulled out the dagger and cleaned off the blood on the grass. He looked as though he were going to vomit.

Callum held out his hand and helped the nobleman to his feet. "It was us or him. Isn't that the justification?" asked Lyr.

Callum nodded. "What happened to him?"

"Are you happy now?"

Callum and Lyr glanced upwards. King Logan and Queen Isla were leaning out of a third-story window, Logan speaking to someone inside the room.

"Callum Haar is dead. See for yourself."

A muscular man, who was nearly identical to their attacker, appeared in the window. Glancing downward and seeing Callum alive, the man's eyes widened, his face contorting into a scowl. His eyes drifted to the fallen man. Blood drained from his face. "Huritt!"

Logan tapped the man on the shoulder, causing him to turn. The king made an odd motion. He grabbed the air an inch in front of his face and pulled diagonally, grinning like a madman. The wildness in the king's eyes reminded Callum of Healer Zall.

The big man screamed and backed into the windowsill. He lost his balance, flailing his arms but unable to find a handhold. He fell out of the window and landed on the ground with a sickening thud.

Callum rushed to the man's side. Glassy, dark eyes stared up at nothing. Blood trickled from his mouth and nose. Callum stood and looked up at the king and queen. Shasta Cray appeared in the window.

"Darrys, Callum, are you all right?" he asked.

"Yes, Your Majesty."

"Go to the guardhouse and have them lock down the palace grounds. Apprehend Queen Gallia if need be."

"What's happening?" asked Callum.

"Haar, go find your daughter. Get those tattoos removed and leave! Lyr, tell the guards that we are at full alert."

"Are we at war?" Lyr asked.

"Not yet," replied Isla. "There's still time. Hurry!"

Lord Lyr took off running, leaving the gardens behind. Callum cast a final glance at the two dead men, whispering a silent prayer for their souls. He ran after Lyr.

46

A Change of Face

Realta ran across the courtyard, her lungs burning. Val's warning had given her a good head start, but Deen must have sensed something was off. The man had chased her down the labyrinth-like hallways and stairs, never more than two or three paces behind. Twice, he'd been within inches of catching her, but a guard or a servant had stopped him, wanting an explanation. Neither time had slowed him down for long.

The entrance to the guardhouse loomed in front of her. Just a few more steps. She would be safe. She hoped.

How had this happened? Had Val been distracted, causing his Illusion around her to fade? He never warned her that this was a possibility.

A sickening thought crept into her mind. Val had purposely allowed the Illusions to fade as revenge for not joining him.

She ducked inside the guardhouse, the cool shade enveloping her. The square antechamber had no furniture save for weapons cases and a collection of swords and arrows hanging on the walls. To her left was a doorway leading into the guardhouse proper. To her right, a spiral staircase.

Two hands grabbed her from behind. Realta let out a scream before Deen clamped a hand over her mouth. He wrapped his other arm around her waist.

"Think you could hide forever?" Deen sneered. "Logan must think he's so clever, hiding you among us."

Realta tried to tear away from his grip as her eyes darted around the room. There had to be something that she could use. That she could grab. That she could Manipulate. Realta hadn't used Manipulation since her encounter with Kanton, and still was not sure how she had done it.

Deen began dragged her out of the guardhouse.

She kicked at his legs, searching for any object close by. There on the table! A small knife. It didn't look sharp, but it would do.

Focusing all her effort on the knife, Realta pictured it hitting Deen in the head. A glancing blow just hard enough for him to lose his grip. The knife shuttered, moving an inch. Then another. The knife flew through the air and struck Deen on the head. The man screamed, letting go of Realta. She rushed to the stairway, sparing a glanced over her shoulder. She paled.

The knife had slashed Deen across the forehead. Blood poured from the wound, covering his eyes and cheeks. He frantically wiped the blood from his eyes, sputtering and cursing. The image reminded Realta of Ander, knocked unconscious from a blow to the head. A blow Serena had delivered in a desperate attempt to escape. She always wondered why Serena hadn't hid or talked her way out. Now she understood.

Shouts arose from the top of the stairs, accompanied by the clanking of metal armor. A set of twenty guards, headed by Serena and trailed by Syleck, entered the antechamber. All twenty men froze, seeing Deen's bloodied face. Syleck took a halting step towards his co-conspirator but stopped himself in time. Realta doubted anyone else noticed.

"Are you all right?" Serena asked, rushing to Realta's side. She nodded, thankful to be surrounded by a crowd.

"Is she all right?!" Deen sputtered. "Look what she did to my head!"

"Did you really do that, young miss?" asked a man with graying hair. The insignia on his uniform, a flying raven, identified him as a captain.

"He was chasing me. I didn't have a choice."

"She's lying."

"No, she isn't," said Serena, her eyes burning. "I saw you chasing her."

"I saw him, too," said one of the guards. Two of his colleagues nodded in agreement.

"Care to explain yourself?" the captain asked Deen.

"The girl is a bloody Thane. Logan sent her to spy on us."

The sound of rasping metal sent a shiver down Realta's spine. Half a dozen guardsmen had drawn their blades. Their eyes were fixed on Deen.

"What is the meaning of this?" Deen asked, taking a step back.

"You would dare hurt a Thane?" one man demanded. Realta noticed that he and the other five all had earrings.

Deen's eyes shifted from blade to blade. "I wasn't going to hurt her..."

"Why do you accuse King Logan of spying?" asked the captain. "He has no reason to. He wants to make peace with your queen."

Deen scoffed. "My queen."

"Men, apprehend him and take him for questioning. I want the truth out of this one."

The guards moved towards Deen. He shot a glare at Realta, then shifted his gaze towards Syleck. He looked at him expectantly. The older man made no move to help, his face like stone. Deen fell to his knees and placed his hands over his head.

"I surrender!"

Syleck gasped. He noticed Realta staring at him and closed his mouth, clenching his jaw.

"My real name," Deen continued, "is Ayrdeen Akardal the Second, King of Bran Maro. I surrender to King Logan of Teyrnas and admit to plotting against him with Queen Gallia of Nowan."

The guards looked at each other, their expressions ranging from confusion to shock. Realta and Serena also exchanged confused glances. They had wanted to expose the monarchs' plot, but this seemed too easy.

"Captain Glasco," said Syleck, placing a hand on the man's shoulder. "I'm afraid that Her Majesty's personal musician is addled. He gets into these strange moods, thinks he's another person. These states can last weeks at a time. Please, allow me to take him back to Her Majesty's quarters so I can tend to his wound and see that he doesn't cause any more trouble. Come along, Deen."

Syleck moved to lift Deen to his feet.

"Touch me and I tell them everything." He glared at Syleck, white hot anger in his brown and blue eyes. "Do you want me to tell them about you?"

"Captain Rimond," said one of the guardsmen. Realta thought his name was Waltyr. "I'd like to help you escort this man to his room. My grandfather suffered from the same condition. I know it isn't easy."

"Why?" questioned Deen. "So you can change your face again? I saw you do it once. Are you going to take my face this time? You're just like her!" He jabbed a finger at Realta. Blood dripped down his face, staining his shirt dark red. "Bloody Thanes!"

"Calm down, son," said Captain Glasco. The Thane guardsmen murmured, growing agitated.

"Captain, I surrender. Take me to Logan. Don't touch me!" he yelled as Waltyr inched closer. The guard took a healthy step back, resting his hand on his sword hilt.

Serena tugged on Realta's sleeve. The girl's face was deathly pale.

"What's wrong?" Realta whispered, even though everyone's attention was on the supposed madman.

"Waltyr was raised in an orphanage. He never knew his grandfather."

Realta studied the guardsman, a pit forming in her gut. The man was the same height and build as Kanton, but his hair was light brown instead of black, eyes brown instead of blue. No, that wasn't quite right. Waltyr blinked. For a split second, the brown eyes had shifted to blue.

"If that's him, then where's..." Realta thought of what Deen had said, the man's specific words. He feared Waltyr would take his face. He must have witnessed Val creating his Illusion, the moment he placed it everyone's minds. If that were the case, then where was the real Waltyr? She feared the man was no longer alive. Val was smarter than to allow two copies of the same man wandering around the palace.

"We need to go."

Serena and Realta walked along the perimeter, ignored by the guards. Deen continued to claim that he was a king.

Just before they reached the door, two men ran up to the guardhouse: her father and Lord Darrys Lyr. Callum ran up to her, catching her in an embrace.

"Thank the Creator you're safe," Callum said.

"Are you okay?" Realta asked. Callum's breathing was labored. Sweat coated his brow.

"Lord Lyr, you look as though you've seen a Shade," said Captain Glasco. The nobleman was as pale as paper and seemed to be on the verge of fainting.

"Captain, King Logan has ordered the guard to be on full alert. Lock down the gates. No one is to enter or exit the palace grounds without his written permission. Queen Gallia has betrayed us."

"See! I told you."

"Who are you?"

"I am the King of Bran Maro, and I surrender."

Lord Lyr raised a thin eyebrow. "Very well. On your feet. We'll sort this out."

"I will escort him to the dungeons," said Waltyr.

Realta opened her mouth to protest, but Syleck beat her to it.

"This man is ill," he insisted. "And Queen Gallia would never betray King Logan. We're here to negotiate peace."

"Tell that to the two men who attacked my family, the king and queen, and Master Haar. You will find their bodies in the gardens." Lord Lyr swallowed, fighting back the urge to vomit. He addressed Waltyr, "You and two others will escort this man to the dungeons."

"No," Deen screamed, his face a mask of terror as Waltyr and another guard grabbed him by the arms, pinning them against his back. "He's going to steal my face!"

"There has been a mistake," Syleck pleaded with Lyr. "Please, allow us to speak with Logan. Clear this up."

Lyr and Glasco exchanged wary looks. The nobleman replied, "Only with a contingency of guards present and you stripped of weapons. If you please, captain."

Glasco nodded. Two guards removed Syleck's belt knives, placing them on the table. The captain, along with half a dozen guards, went with Syleck to the palace, hands on the hilts of their swords. None of them were pleased. The rest of the guards left for their posts.

"Father, that man, Waltyr, we think he's Kanton."

"Are you sure?" He looked at the departing group, brow furrowed.

Realta and Serena nodded.

"What are they talking about?" asked Lyr.

Callum explained Kanton's presence in the palace to Lyr, as well as his alliance with Val.

"So, this Valentin can create Illusions that cover an entire person? It's not that I don't believe you. It's just…" He paused, collecting the right words. "Logan has never been able to affect more than one person's mind at a time."

"Val claims he's as powerful as a Summit Thane," Realta added.

Lyr shook his head. "I don't see how that's possible. Full alert." He rubbed his forehead. "I have to get my family out of the palace."

"Shasta Cray is preparing to evacuate everyone through the tunnels," said Callum, "heading for the River Wallach. Find her and the rest of the royal family and go."

"But what about you and your daughter?"

"We can't run with these on our wrists." Callum rolled up his sleeve, revealing two diamonds filled with diagonal lines.

"We will wait for you as long as we can. It was an honor meeting Esme Haar's brother. I never knew her, but she and Sarra were good friends. I'm grateful that she was able to start a new life after…" He faltered.

"I'm glad to hear it."

Lyr gave Callum a quick bow and sprinted towards the palace.

"Where is Gilnyn?" Callum asked Serena.

"He's usually in the dungeons," Serena replied, her face pale. The dungeons were the place Kanton took Deen. They had no choice but to head in the same direction and risk coming face to face with him.

A horn sounded overhead. They exited the guardhouse and looked up at the wall. Guardsmen ran back and forth, shouting orders. More horns sounded, their calls sharp and urgent.

"What's happening?" Callum called, cupping his hands around his mouth.

"Riders have been spotted near the Eastern Gate," replied one guard. "They're flying Nowan's flag."

"Soldiers?"

"We don't know."

"We can't wait to find out," Realta said, anxiety creeping into her mind.

Callum nodded. Running across the courtyard, they raced for the palace. And the dungeons.

47

What Must Be Done

Logan Manipulated the doors open, slamming them against the walls, his black cloak trailing behind him. Queen Gallia spun on her heels, her face pale. A servant, her handmaid if he recalled correctly, stood at her side. He had expected to find that messenger here. The man had sneaked away while Logan was dealing with Gallia's thugs.

Once he had warned Lyr and Haar about the betrayal, he, Shasta, and Isla parted ways, Shasta and Isla going to evacuate everyone and Logan to confront Gallia.

"How...?" Gallia's eyes widened.

"Did you really think I wouldn't be able to handle a single guard?" he asked, circling the room, walking steadily towards her. He heard no movement from the adjacent rooms. That did not guarantee they were empty. He searched for objects to Manipulate, just in case. A candlestand, a vase filled with water, a set of pens on the writing desk.

Queen Gallia composed herself, standing straight. "I had hoped it would buy me some time."

"Time for what? A coup?"

"I didn't..." She gave the servant a sideways glance. The older woman did not look pleased. "I never seriously thought peace between our nations was feasible. This was the only way to ensure the safety of my people."

Logan scoffed. "Safety? Gallia, how many times in the past year have I threatened you or the Nowani people?"

"You sent warnings to me the moment I was crowned. That I shouldn't dare seek another war with Teyrnas."

"I did warn you. But the threat went both ways. Soldiers on both sides always die in battle. I didn't want that for either of us. Your father was a bloodthirsty, old fool. The last thing I wanted was for you to end up the same."

Gallia's face flushed dark red. "My father was a great man."

"Your father was responsible for the bloodiest war in the last century. Six years of continuous fighting and for what? A little extra land that ended up falling to Teyrnas anyway? Do you have any idea how many people died? How many soldiers I witnessed return home with missing limbs?"

Gallia bit down on her lip, tears glistening in her eyes. Her anger ebbed away.

"That war ended thirty years ago," replied the servant, far more causally than Logan expected. "You cannot possible remember—"

"It ended thirty-four years ago. I was six years old. My father took me and my brother to visit a military hospital. He wanted us to see the effects of war firsthand. It was the best thing that man ever did for me." Images flashed in his mind. Countless rows of wounded soldiers lying on cots, all covered with bloodied bandages. A soldier, no older than twenty-five, dying from a chest wound. Carwyn bursting into tears and Yestyn hitting him for being a coward. Logan grimaced. "It made me value peace."

"You say my father was bloodthirsty?" Gallia questioned. "Then how do you explain thirty years of peace?"

"Peace with Teyrnas. Cedric filled his time by fighting in the East. Have you forgotten that part of history?"

"But good came out of those wars. The East is unified now."

"In what way?" Logan asked, standing inches from the queen. He noted a bead of sweat near her hairline.

"A peaceful way. I had hoped Teyrnas would join us."

The servant shot Gallia a glare. The queen wilted under her gaze. "Kenda?"

She stared at Logan, eyes widening in a mixture of anger and shock. Gallia bit down on her lip, smudging her makeup.

"It wasn't that hard to guess," Logan continued. "There are only two queens east of the Vogel Mountains. Queen Gallia Toutain of Nowan and Queen Kenda Hento of Galion. My sister, she..." Logan wished he could kick himself in the face. "She claimed the kings disguised as servants were taking orders from a queen."

Serena, will you ever forgive me? Logan doubted it. He had treated her the same way Yestyn had treated all of them.

Queen Kenda of Galion eyed Logan coolly, the facade of a humble servant melting away. "So, those little spies of yours actually accomplished something. I'm impressed. But it's too late, I'm afraid."

"For peace? No, Your Highness. My negotiations with Gallia are still ongoing."

"And when the guards on the city walls see a force bearing the flags of five nations, how will they react? Who will loose the first arrow?"

Logan narrowed his eyes. "That's impossible. The guards won't attack a foreign body without orders from me." He turned to Gallia. "You want peace. I saw it in your eyes, heard it in your words. It doesn't have to end this way."

"I'm sorry, Logan. Thanes have hurt our peoples too much for too long. You will always find your way back to power. I..." Fresh tears flowed down her face.

"What did you do to her?" Logan questioned Kenda. For years, he had heard of King Cedric's strong-willed daughter, a brave girl who insisted on learning to fight alongside her male cousins. A woman skilled in every hand-held weapon under the stars ought to have the courage to stand up for herself and make her voice heard. Even if her opponent was another queen. The woman standing before him was little more than a frightened child.

"We made her see reason. It took a while. She has her father's stubbornness. But Gallia sees the truth now."

"Or what you made her believe was the truth."

"Tell me, Logan the Raven King, where are the rest of Her Majesty's servants?"

Logan glanced around the room. No one had emerged from the adjoining rooms, not even a bodyguard or that damn messenger. The spacious quarters were empty, save for the three of them.

"You said your guards would not loose an arrow without your orders. What if that arrow did not come from one of your guards? A man on the wall wearing a dark blue uniform, yes. But not your man."

Logan's heart dropped. "Are you insane? That will start a war!"

"That's that point. More of our soldiers are positioned throughout the city, waiting on our signal."

Rage boiled in Logan's veins. Not once had he threatened Nowan or Galion or any of the other Eastern countries. There had been no need for war. How dare this woman force it!

Logan's eyes shifted to the vase. Focusing through his anger, he Manipulated it across the room. The queen fell to the ground, shards of broken glass littering the floor.

"What did you do?" Gallia cried, crouching at Kenda's side. Logan saw she was still breathing. The blow hadn't been strong enough to kill her.

"What you should have done the moment she tried dragging you into this lunacy."

Gallia shook her head in disbelief. She placed a hand on the back of Kenda's head. The hand came away bloody. Damn. He'd have to take her to the infirmary and then sort out this mess. He reached down to help her.

Gallia flinched, staring at him as though he were a wild animal. "Don't touch her!"

Logan backed away, seeing the horrified look in her eyes. He had lost count of the number of times he had seen that same look in his mother's eyes. "Gallia, I didn't mean to hurt her that badly. You and I need to talk."

"No."

"That army isn't here yet. There's still time."

"No," she said slowly, "you meant to hurt her. You could have used an Illusion, but you didn't. You threw a vase at her head!"

"To protect my country."

"And I can't protect my country, too?" Gallia cried. A single sob racked her body. Gaining control of herself, she stood and met Logan face to face. "Do you have any idea what I've been through this last year? The sacrifices I made to keep my people safe from..."

"The other monarchs forced you into this plot, didn't they?"

She averted her eyes, biting down on her lip. She nodded.

Logan sighed, looking down at the unconscious queen. "Help me get Kenda to the infirmary and stop the attack. Then, we can talk. We can find a way out of this."

"Okay," Gallia said after a moment. She bent down and

grabbed one of Kenda's arms. She froze. Standing to her full height, she glared at Logan. Her blue eyes were like ice. "I will never help a Thane."

Fire and smoke! "Gallia, there aren't just Thanes living in Teyrnas. There are normal people, too. If anything, help them."

"Helping them is the same as helping you. I will never help a Thane."

"That's right, Gallia."

Logan spun on his heels and saw Valentin standing in the doorway. The slim man leaned against the door frame, arms folded and smiling.

"You should never help a Thane," Val said, walking closer. "Thanes are the reason your country was oppressed for centuries. Until one brave human said enough. We won't stand for your tyranny any longer." He smiled wickedly.

"We won't stand for your tyranny any longer," Gallia mimicked, directing the words at Logan as though Valentin were not there.

"What are you doing to her?" Logan questioned. Reality dawned on him. "Stars above, you're a Thane!"

"You catch on slowly." Val crouched down beside Kenda and placed his fingers on her neck. "Damn. Still alive. That would have been a legitimate reason for war."

"I don't want war!"

"This isn't about what you want, Logan," said Val, standing and looming over Logan, his gray eyes flashing. "It's about saving the world."

"Come again?" Was this man insane? How did one save the world by starting a war?

"I am One of Nine. So is Realta, and so is Ambassador Ekene. Fate has brought us together for one purpose. The Midnight King walks Eltriar again. We cannot have you monarchs getting in our way while we deal with him. Think of this war as a distraction."

"You really are insane. The Midnight King was destroyed thousands of years ago. The Nine Thanes are long dead."

"The original Nine. The Gadyeni are making their selections as we speak. There is nothing you or I can do to stop them."

Logan eyed the set of pens on the desk. He didn't want to kill

Val, but if he had to maim him in order to stop him, so be it.

"Pens, Logan?" Val laughed. "Pens aren't real weapons. If you want to kill someone, use a knife."

Logan winced as sharp metal slid between his ribs. The air rushed out of his lungs and a coppery taste flooded his mouth. He saw a dagger buried to the hilt in his right side. Blood seeped from the wound.

"See?" Val smiled. "Knives are much more effective than pens."

Logan collapsed to his knees and then fell on the floor, his face next to Kenda's. He placed all of his focus on the pens, willing them to move. Energy drained out of him. The pens didn't move an inch.

Val removed the knife and placed it into Gallia's hand. He unceremoniously grabbed Kenda underneath the arms and hoisted her to her feet. She groaned. Logan coughed. Blood splattered onto the carpeted floor.

"It didn't have to be this way, Logan," Val continued. "But you just keep insisting on peace. So unlike your father. And then Serena and Realta had to spoil the surprise. If you'll excuse me, I must go collect Miss Haar. The world will be lost without her. As for the bastard, well," Val shrugged. "Like brother, like sister."

No! Don't you touch my sister, you son of a bitch!

Logan's vision grew blurry, images fading into splotches of color mixed with gray. He heard Val's voice.

"Your Majesty, are you all right?"

"What? What happened?"

"I saw Logan attack you and Queen Kenda. Thank the Creator you had your father's dagger."

"I... I stabbed him?!"

"He left you no choice. Come, help Kenda get to the Audience Chamber. Syleck and Eskandar are waiting for your orders. Ayrdeen's gotten himself into some trouble, I'm afraid. I will help him and meet up with you as quickly as I can."

"Yes, do so. Val, wait. What about King Logan?"

"I fear he's dead, Your Majesty."

"I thought I heard him cough."

"That was just a reflex, his death throes. You did what you had to, Your Majesty."

Footsteps faded as Val, Gallia, and Kenda exited the room. Logan opened his mouth to scream, to reason with Gallia one last time. The only sound that came from his throat was a raspy breath. His vision faded from gray to black.

48

Prisoners

Realta, Serena, and Callum made their way to the dungeons, passing bewildered servants along the way. Word of the approaching army had spread like wildfire, and some reported having seen soldiers in foreign uniforms in the palace itself. Many were preparing to evacuate, carrying what they could to the tunnels. The halls grew steadily emptier as they neared the palace's lowest level.

Racing down the stairs, Realta heard voices, a man shouting that he was a king. A pit formed in her gut. They were not far from the dungeons now. Not far from Kanton.

"Where's Gilnyn?" asked Callum as they reached the bottom of the stairway.

"This way," Serena replied, leading them away from the voices. This portion of the dungeon was well kept, with the floors swept clean and furniture in good repair. Realta had vague impressions of it from her first night in the palace. The tattoo on her wrist was the only indicator that it had not been a nightmare.

Serena jolted back the moment she stepped inside Gilnyn's work quarters. She clamped her hands over her mouth as the blood drained from her face.

Callum steadied her. He and Realta peered inside the room. On the floor laying Gilnyn Scannail with his throat slit. Dark blood pooled around his body. Lifeless eyes stared up at Realta in horror. She turned away from the sightless gaze, holding onto the door frame for support.

"He killed him," Callum said in a low voice. "Kanton killed him so we can't escape."

"What are you talking about?"

Realta jumped, spinning around to face the voice's owner. Colm, the young guard who had played an unknowing part in their plan, stood off to the side. He gave the group a quizzical look.

"Where's Waltyr?" Serena asked.

"He went upstairs, said something about finding you, Master Haar. Didn't say why, though. It's my turn at prisoner watch. What's wrong?" he asked, walking towards the door. He gasped, turning as white as newly fallen snow when he saw Gilnyn's body. "What...? Who...?"

"Colm, look at me," Callum ordered. Colm tore his eyes away from the body, trembling. "How long have you been down here?"

"Just a few minutes," he stuttered. "Waltyr had me and Iain escort that madman here. Ector was on guard right before me."

"What about Waltyr? Did he leave your sight long enough to do this?"

"Maybe. I don't know. Why would Waltyr kill Gilnyn?" he asked, running his fingers through his light brown hair. "He never did anything wrong."

"Because it wasn't Waltyr," Realta replied.

"I don't understand."

"Colm," said Callum, "how many prisoners are down here?"

"Just the madman, the one who thinks he's a king. And Captain Kanton."

"What?" they said as one.

Colm took a deep breath, steadying himself. "Couple of nights ago, Jaidan and Quillan were doing the rounds, found Captain Kanton walking in the gardens, trying to get inside the palace. They questioned him, asked how he got inside the walls when he attacked them. He called them insane. He nearly broke Quillan's arm. Then Waltyr comes running, helps them arrest him. He said for them to put Kanton in the dungeons. The King Logan would deal with him after Queen Gallia left. It sounded like the right thing to do."

Realta's heart sank. No wonder the guards weren't looking for Kanton. They believed they had already found him.

"Take us to him," said Callum.

"What about Master Scannail?"

Callum glanced into the workroom, grimacing. "We will take care of his body once everything is sorted out. Now, Colm. We don't have much time."

Colm nodded and led them to the other side of the dungeon. Of the dozen cells, only two were occupied. The first one contained Deen, the king of Bran Maro. He sat calmly on the bench, giving Realta and Serena a quick nod as they passed. Most of the blood had been wiped off his face, but the gash on his forehead still bled. He would definitely need stitches. In the other cell sat Dane Kanton. Every detail about the man was perfect. The shade of blue in his eyes. The burn scars crisscrossing the left side of his face. Everything perfect except the look of utter defeat on his face.

"Captain Kanton," said Colm. The man made no reply. "Captain Kanton, Callum Haar is here with Realta and Serena. They've got some questions for you."

No movement.

Realta stepped forward and said, "Waltyr, is that really you?"

The man gazed up at her with mournful eyes. "Can you see me?" he asked in Dane Kanton's voice.

"I see you as Kanton, but that's not the truth, is it? Val tricked everyone into thinking you're him."

Waltyr stood and pressed his face against the bars. Realta shrank back. *This is not Kanton. He only looks like him.*

"Please, you have to help me. No one else believes me."

"Tell us what happened," said Callum. "Quickly."

"The Nowani messenger, he walked up to me while I was on guard duty. We got to talking. Just small stuff. He said I ought to reward myself with a drink." He grimaced. "Should have known he drugged it. Next thing I knew, I was walking to the guest quarters, but it was like someone else was moving my legs for me. I couldn't break out of it.

"He led me to a room. Captain Kanton was there. I tried calling for help, but I couldn't speak. Then the messenger had me and Kanton stand face to face. I blinked, and Kanton had my face, and I had his. I didn't feel anything. It happened so fast. I blinked again, and I was out in the gardens." His eyes glistened. "Quill and Jaidan attacked me. I tried telling them I wasn't Kanton, but they didn't believe me. And when I saw him wearing my face and telling them to lock my away, I didn't know what to do. Please believe me."

"I believe you," said Deen. "I saw the whole thing."

Realta walked over to the foreign king. "Why didn't you tell anyone?"

Deen sneered. "I don't speak to Thanes."

Callum rushed towards the cell. His eyes held that cold anger that appeared every time he was about to get into a fight. "Then why don't you speak to me?"

Deen sighed. "Very well. I knew something was strange about Gallia's messenger but could not put a finger on it. Seeing him steal faces made it obvious that he's a bloody Thane. Of course, I couldn't just say that. Gallia would think I'm mad, and Kenda would say it was just another excuse not to go through with the plan. All that woman wants is blind loyalty. Syleck refusing to help me apprehend that girl was the last straw."

Callum nodded. "Colm, let Waltyr out of that cell and help evacuate the palace. Those armies will be here any minute."

"Should I warn Logan?" Serena asked. Judging by her tone, speaking to her brother was the thing Serena wanted to do.

"I'll find him. He might know a way to get these tattoos off. Realta, you and Serena wait in the tunnels for ten minutes. If I'm not back by then, leave."

"No."

"Realta—"

"We're supposed to leave together."

Callum placed a hand on her shoulder. "I know this isn't an easy decision, but I've survived worse. Go to the Academy. You'll be safe there."

Tears brimming her eyes, Realta embraced her father, not wanting to let him go, not knowing how long they would be separated. "I love you."

"I love you, too. And Serena, you will always have a place in our home. I'm sure your mother would be very proud of you."

Serena gave a quick nod, fighting back her own tears.

"Pardon, but what about me?" asked Deen, wrapping his hands around the bars.

"You stay here."

"But you said the palace is being evacuated. Am I just to hope that Gallia knows I'm down here?"

"Seems like it."

Colm and Waltyr joined them in front of the cell. Waltyr's black hair started to fade to its normal light brown. The blue eyes grew darker. Whatever Val did to create the Illusion was wearing off. Realta hoped the same was happening to Kanton.

"You can't do this to me. I'm a king." He slammed his hand against the bar.

"You're a king who surrendered."

"He has a point," said Colm. "If nobody but the guard knows he's down here, he could starve."

"Syleck knows he's here," said Serena.

Deen scoffed. "That old tyrant hates my guts. Seeing the guard carry my off must have made his day."

Realta shook her head. "We can't leave him to starve."

A smile appeared on Callum's face. "Your Majesty, let's make a deal. I will let you out if you apologize to my daughter."

"Excuse me?"

"Not only did you insult her, but you also chased her halfway around the palace, from what I heard. I don't appreciate people manhandling my daughter. And neither does she."

"She's a Thane and a spy. And she attacked me." Deen pointed to the bloody gash along his forehead.

"In self-defense. Are young girls not allowed to defend themselves against men twice their size in Bran Maro?"

"Of course they can defend themselves." His eyes hardened. "But Thanes..."

"Colm, you and Waltyr leave. There isn't much time left."

"Do you want the keys?" Colm asked, removing a key ring from his belt.

"That won't be necessary."

"Okay, fine!" Deen exhaled through his teeth. "Realta Haar, I apologize for chasing you out of Gallia's rooms, and for placing you in a position that required you to use your..." He grimaced. "Your Thane abilities to defend yourself. And I apologize for speaking to you so rudely a moment earlier. Do you accept my apology?"

"Yes." She smiled. She did not like the idea of leaving the man to starve. Even if he was responsible for the current invasion. Perhaps they could use his knowledge to counteract it.

Callum took the keys from Colm and released Deen. The man slipped out of the cell and froze. "Now what? The others won't exactly welcome me back with open arms."

"You're coming with me to find King Logan. Waltyr, Colm, help evacuate the palace. Make sure no one gets left behind. Realta, Serena, you need to run and run fast."

Realta gave her father one last embrace. Serena joined her, wrapping her arms around both of them. She wondered what life would have been like if Kel and Esme had brought Serena to the Hinterlands with them. She would have loved having another cousin.

"We will find each other again," said Callum. "I promise."

Wiping a stray tear from her face, Realta turned to Serena. "Lead the way."

They ran from the dungeons to the palace above.

✳✳✳

Horns sounded overhead. Val smiled. The first arrow had been fired. Teyrnas was at war with the East. He glanced around the Audience Chamber, studying those present. Eskandar and Syleck spoke to one another in furtive whispers, wondering why Ayrdeen had betrayed them. Kenda sat in a chair, her head bandaged. She half listened to the whispers and half contemplated her next move. The deaths of her nephews, the children of her illegitimate half-brother, had thrown her for a loop. And Gallia stood by the windows, looking at the city and the walls.

Poor woman. She truly had wanted peace with Logan. And she would have gotten it if that bastard had not barged in at the wrong moment. Perhaps the girl was more useful alive than dead. Still, it would have been interesting to see Logan's reaction.

A large hand clamped down on Val's shoulder. Rolling his eyes, he faced Dane Kanton, disguised as Waltyr Rosser, a loyal guardsman who had served House Kelwyn for nearly twenty years. The man was furious.

Val pulled him aside and asked, "Something troubling you?"

"Where in the name of the Abyss is Haar?" he said through his teeth.

"I'm sure he's still around. Assuming you took care of that?"

"Scannail's dead." Kanton grimaced. He had taken no pleasure in that task. From what Val had gleaned, Gilnyn Scannail was the rough around the edges sort who liked everyone once he got to know them, and vice versa. A shame he got in the way of Val's plan.

"Good. Now all you have to do is wait. I will ensure that you get a stab at Haar soon enough."

Kanton frowned.

"Not a fan of puns?"

"It's fading."

"Pardon?"

"Whatever you did to me. It's fading. Look."

Val studied Kanton's face. The light brown hair was turning darker. Hints of blue bled into the brown eyes. The smooth face became angular, scar tissue forming at the edges.

"Nothing lasts forever." Val smiled. He had perfect control over Illusions, and the minds of those who saw them. He could drop the Illusion, like he did with the one covering Realta's Aura, or make it appear to be fading away. It was more fun that way. And he had already gotten rid of the one surrounding the real Waltyr. Realta was a clever girl and deserved to be rewarded every once in a while.

"You think this is funny?" Kanton roared. All four monarchs turned their attention to him and Val.

"What's his problem?" asked Syleck.

"A little crisis of loyalty. Nothing more," Val assured them. He pretended to touch up the 'fading' Illusions. The time wasn't right for Kanton's big reveal. Let the others see Gallia's personal messenger spend an odd amount of time with the man. Let them be shocked as the Illusion disappears before their eyes. He wondered which would be the first to figure it out.

All in good time.

"Bloody Teyrnians," Eskandar spat. "Almost as bad as those bloody Marish." He directed that part to Queen Kenda. Including Bran Maro into their plans had been her idea. The Queen of Galion gave him a sideways glance.

Yes, fight each other. You're doing wonderfully.

The hard part, getting them all to agree to war with Teyrnas, was over. They would fight side by side for a month, maybe two, and then they'd turn on one another. That war could last years, decades. Plenty of time for him to find the others and defeat the Midnight King. He smiled, thinking of the glory.

Ayrdeen surrendering had been a surprise, though. Val didn't worry too much. The man was in no position to command his army, leaving them in a state of confusion. Eskandar, already prejudice against Bran Maro, would use this as propaganda for his own army, inflaming matters within the Coalition. A part of him wished he could be here to see it.

"Val," said Gallia, eyes fixed on the ornate, stained-glass window, "can I speak with you for a moment?"

"Of course, Your Majesty."

Kanton grabbed Val's shoulder, yanking him back. "Don't you dare go back on your deal. I gave up everything for you people."

"I wouldn't dream of it."

Kanton released Val. He walked over to Gallia. Furtive whispers passed between Syleck and Eskandar. Had they finally realized that he and the queen were lovers? Logan's head servant had figured it out in a matter of days.

"Is everything all right, my dear?" Val asked. A hundred guardsmen scurried along the palace wall like ants, helpless to do anything significant.

Gallia sighed. "Are we doing the right thing?"

"Yes. You know in your heart that this is right. The time of Thanes is over."

Gallia shook her head. "That little girl was a Thane. She never did anything to me."

"She spied on us."

"Having her wait on me was your idea."

He shifted from one foot to the other. Sometimes Gallia was too smart for her own good. "It seemed like a good idea at the time. A way to get underneath Logan's skin."

Tears spilled down Gallia's face. "I didn't want to kill him."

"He left you no choice."

"There is always a choice. My father taught me that. I think, in the end, he regretted that war."

"Nowan was being threatened by Thanes." *Don't you dare crack up on me now, Gallia.*

"Was it?" She faced him. "I found a history book. It belongs to Logan's son. It read that King Tudur died in his sleep of a weak heart, the war taking too heavy a toll. But Logan and I know for a fact that he was killed by my aunt. Yes, he was in bed. Yes, he was asleep. But it was no heart attack. Why teach the lie?"

"Because it's embarrassing. A mighty king killed by a teenaged girl? Think about it."

"I have thought about it. Learning that their former king was killed by a Nowani might lead children to resent us. Even hate us. I don't agree with covering up the truth. But this way, the war caused his death. An ambiguous thing instead of a person. After Tudur's death, Queen Lyneth signed a peace treaty with my grandfather. Tudur had been the only one standing in the way of that treaty."

Val rolled his eyes. "Wars and treaties are never determined by one person. Real life is more complicated than that."

Gallia glanced at the other monarchs. "Maybe so."

Val sighed. This next part was not going to be easy. "Gallia, I've been meaning to bring this up the last couple of days. But there was never a good time. I have to leave soon."

"Why?"

"There's something I need to do. Something very important."

"Can I help?"

Val gave her a pained smiled. "No. It's something I must do on my own."

"Will you come back?"

"I'll try," he lied. "I don't want to make any promises I can't keep."

Gallia nodded. "I understand. Be safe out there." She stood on her toes and gave him a light kiss. Val sighed. He did not want to leave her. He felt he could grow to love her, but he could never reveal his true self. The second she discovered he was a Thane, his life and everything they had built together would be over.

Val walked away from the window and motioned for Kanton to follow him. Once they were in the hall, Kanton asked, "Now what?"

"We have work to do."

***

"How many more?" asked Kel. He and Isla stood in the pantry, helping the servants evacuate through the tunnels. Isla's two children, Morgan and Mannix, sat on a wooden crate, huddled together. Both boys had been terrified of the scarred man who had barged into their room, telling them they had to leave. Isla, thank the Creator, had arrived moments later, assuring the boys that this strange man was a friend. Nobody to fear. They eyed Kel warily.

Isla peered into the hallway. "Hundred and fifty. Maybe two hundred."

Kel groaned. He knew the palace boasted a large number of servants, but he never remembered it being this many. Horns sounded from the wall, causing the hairs on the back of his neck to stand on end.

"Tell them to hurry," he replied.

As Isla continued to usher them through the small opening, two figures fought their way through the crowd. Gareth and Gregor Pym. Gareth immediately rushed to Kel's side. The poor boy was trembling. Kel wondered how well he would manage three days traveling underground.

"I'm sorry, Your Majesty," Gregor addressed Isla, "but nobody has seen King Logan. A few say they saw him near Gallia's quarters, but that was half an hour ago."

Isla wrung her hands, sparing a glance at her children. "Are you certain? Maybe he's with Shasta or instructing the guard?"

Gregor shook his head solemnly. "Most of the guard has been overrun. Captain Glasco and at least thirty others are dead. Some sort of ambush. And I've not seen Shasta in ages."

"Could he still be with Gallia?" Kel asked. Logan's stubborn streak rarely allowed him to cut his losses and move on.

Gregor shrugged.

Isla rushed to the door. Kel reached out and grabbed her by the shoulder.

"Where are you going?"

"I have to find him," she replied.

"Let me go."

"I don't think that's a good idea." Isla eyed his leg brace and crutch.

"I know every inch of this place, and I'm pretty good at looking unimportant." He took a deep breath, steadying himself. "If the worst has happened, these people need their queen."

Isla glanced upwards, holding in her tears. "I don't want to think about that." A second horn sounded. "Carwyn, go quickly. I... I have a feeling you'll be safe."

"I'm glad to hear that. Gareth, stay here with Isla. If I'm not back in time, go with her."

"No."

"Son, this isn't a discussion."

"Why can't I go with you?"

Kel let out a heavy sigh. "Because I promised your mother that I would keep you safe. And the safest thing for you is to get out of the city. You see those two boys over there?" He pointed at Morgan and Mannix. "They're your cousins. In the same way that Realta is your cousin. So I'm ordering you to go with your Aunt Isla to the Academy and wait until I get there."

Gareth studied Isla, chewing his lower lip. "Can I trust you?" he asked her.

"Of course, you can, Gareth."

"Then tell me what you saw."

Her face paled. "Pardon?"

"You saw something. Tell me what it was or no deal."

Isla swallowed a lump in her throat. "I saw you with a dagger in your hand and a hawk resting on your shoulder. And I saw a crown on your father's head."

Kel grimacing, squeezing his eyes tight. *Farsights are always vague. You can't know for sure what it means.*

Gareth merely nodded. "Okay. Deal." He turned to Kel. "Do you promise to meet us at the Academy?"

"You have my word."

Gareth embraced him. "I love you."

"I love you, too, son. More than anything." Kel had given up everything for this boy and his mother. He would do it all again in a heartbeat.

Kel headed for the door and froze. At the threshold were Lord and Lady Lyr with their two small children. Sarra locked eyes with him. Horror filled him, realizing that the hood of his cloak was down.

"Carwyn?"

"Sarra, I..."

She took a step closer. Kel tried to back away, but a wooden crate blocked him. She gently touched the scarred half of his face.

"It's true. Malaky was right," she said in a quiet voice.

"I'm sure you hate me."

She frowned. "Hate you? Why would I hate you?"

"Because I ran away. Yestyn, he..." Damn, how could he even begin to explain?

"You did what we all dreamed of doing."

"Living on a farm in the middle of nowhere?"

"Being free." Sarra glanced at her husband and children. The boy and girl clung to their father, averting their eyes from Kel. "Shandri, Kaden, this is—"

"Kel," he interrupted. "My name is Kel. Your mother and I knew each other a long time ago."

Sarra gave him a pained look, but he didn't have time for an official family reunion.

"Have either of you seen Logan?"

"No," replied Lyr, studying him dubiously. "Not since..." His eyes widened. "Stars above, you're—"

"It's impolite to read minds without permission, Lord Lyr," Kel replied. He ambled towards the door, his left leg growing stiff. He hoped it would not give out on him now.

"Where are you going?" Sarra asked.

"To find Logan."

"Be careful," replied Lyr. "Nowani soldiers are everywhere. We barely escaped them."

"Good to know. Follow Isla. She knows what to do." Kel slipped out of the pantry, concealing his face under his hood.

49

Escape

Realta and Serena raced up the stairs, taking them two or three at a time, nearly tripping over themselves, hurrying as fast as their legs could carry them to the ground floor. Dozens of people clogged the narrow hallway, impatiently waiting for their turn to enter the tunnels and bringing what little possessions they could carry. All of them wore faces of terror and confusion. A few mentioned Nowani soldiers roaming the halls.

Realta scanned the crowd. She never knew the exact number of servants at the palace. There was no way to tell how many had escaped.

"Serena!" A little form pushed his way through the crowd. He grabbed hold of Serena, not wanting to let go.

"Mannix, what are you doing here? I thought you already left."

"Mother and that scary man brought us here. They were helping people through the tunnels, but then he left to find Father. And I left to find you."

Another form made its way towards the back. Morgan, his face pale, slowed when he saw Mannix with Serena.

"What did Mother say about wandering off?" the crown prince asked. "Her Farsight said we need to stay together."

"That means Serena, too, right?" the boy asked.

Morgan frowned. Realta was amazed by how much he resembled his father. "She didn't say."

Serena bit down on her lip.

"But that doesn't mean she can't travel in the same direction as us."

"Serena is coming with us!" he cried out in joy.

"Not..." Morgan sighed. He lowered his voice and said, "Mannix, she isn't really... What I mean is..."

"It's complicated," Serena added quietly.

Mannix glared at them. "That's what everyone says. Why can't anyone give me a real answer?"

The crowd shifted forward, creating a gap between the end of the line and them. Realta peered down the long hall. Men shouting, too far away for her to understand the words. A horn sounded outside, sending a shiver down her spine.

Serena got down on her knees and looked Mannix in the eye. "Mannix, you know how some people call me a bastard? That's because King Yestyn was not married to my mother. She was just a servant. Your father is only my half-brother."

Mannix's face contorted, tears glistening in his eyes. "No, that's just something people say."

"They say it because it's true. My mother died before you were born, and—"

"No, you're my real aunt!"

"Listen to me, Mannix." Serena placed her hands on the boy's shoulders. "I love you just as much as if I was your full-blooded aunt and you my full-blooded nephew. And that means Morgan loved you even more. He's your older brother. And the entire time you're away from home, you listen to him and your mother. Promise?"

"But you're coming with us, right?"

Serena opened her mouth to speak, but no words formed.

"Serena, we need to go," said Morgan. The crowd had dwindled to only a handful. Of those remaining was Gregor Pym, ushering people through the narrow opening. The older man bit down on his lip as the last servant passed through. He looked at Realta and the royal children anxiously.

"We'd best get going, Prince Morgan," Gregor said.

"Come along, Mannix. Mother is waiting for us." He tugged on his younger brother's arm. Mannix wrapped his arms around Serena's neck.

"I'm not leaving without Serena."

Serena sighed. Holding onto the boy, she stood and walked over to Gregor Pym. Mannix screamed as Serena forced him into Gregor's arms.

"Care for him the way you cared for me."

"I swear by the Gadyeni, I will, dear."

"Wait. Where's Father?" asked Morgan. He glanced down the corridor. "Didn't that man come back with him?"

"No. I haven't seen Kel or the king," Gregor replied.

"My father went to find him, too," said Realta. Fear crept into her mind. Shouldn't Callum be here by now?

He said to wait ten minutes. It can't have been ten minutes yet. There was still time.

A form appeared at the end of the hallway. A tall man with black hair dressed in plain clothes. Callum! He had made it. The figure stalked closer. Realta's heart sank. This man was too thin to be Callum. His gray eyes flashed at her.

"Running away, Realta?" Val questioned. "That's not very mature."

"Who are you?" Morgan asked.

"You need to go," Realta whispered to him.

"There's really no point in whispering, Little Dreamer. I can read your mind."

"Then read that I want nothing to do with you." Realta motioned for Morgan and the rest to enter the tunnels. The prince crept towards Gregor Pym. Serena stayed by Realta's side.

"He isn't wearing earrings," said Morgan, incredulity lacing his words. "He claims to be a Minder, but he isn't wearing earrings."

"They don't suit me." He held out his hand. "Come, Realta. We don't have much time."

"Gregor," said Serena, "take Morgan and Mannix now!"

"What about Father?"

"I'm afraid that King Logan is no longer with us." Val smiled. "He put up a good fight. I'll give him that."

Realta felt like she was going to be sick. The king was dead? Then where were her father and uncle? What was taking them so long?

"I told you, Realta. I will watch over you. You don't need Callum anymore."

"It's a lie," said Gregor, Mannix whimpering in his arms. "Logan isn't dead. You're a liar!"

"If you don't believe me, feel free to go into Gallia's quarters. You will find your precious Raven King's body lying in a pool of his own blood."

Morgan bit his lower lip, suppressing a cry. Gregor went pale. Serena stared at the messenger in shock.

"You want to me to with you?" Realta questioned, glaring at Val, at this murderer who claimed he wanted to save the world.

"Of course."

"Then let them go." She pointed at Gregor and the two princes.

Val smiled. "Very well. But Master Pym, lock the entrance from the inside. I don't feel like chasing people through tunnels today."

Gregor looked at Serena and Realta, his expression pained. They both nodded. It was okay. This was part of the plan. The older man then ushered the two children into the tunnel. Once inside, he closed the door. A bolt clicked into place.

"Life is so much easier when people do as they're told," Val said, crossing his arms. "Now, Realta."

Realta turned on her heels and ran, Serena one step behind her. Val screamed, his rage hitting her like a wave. His footsteps echoed against the empty walls, chasing them every step of the way into the palace's courtyard. The very place they wanted him to go.

✳✳✳

Soldiers dressed in foreign uniforms patrolled the upper floors, hands on their swords, ready to draw. Callum peered around the corner. The few servants he questioned said that Logan was last seen entering Gallia's quarters. He motioned for Deen, the supposed king of Bran Maro (he'd get the truth out of him once they had time), to follow. He had expected the man to run the moment he was freed, but he had stayed with Callum this whole time. Loyalties could change disturbingly fast.

"Mind explaining to me where those soldiers came from?" Callum whispered, making his way down the hall.

"Did you see the size of Gallia's entourage?" Deen replied. He wiped a drop of blood away from his eyes. The dried blood around the wound had cracked. "Dozens of servants and guards. Very hard to keep track of all those people, especially with those Scholars and nobles leaving. Half of them slipped out and went into the city. They snuck others through the Western Gate, had them hidden in the slums until the right time."

The Western Quarter. The place Esme and Kel claimed he had been beaten and robbed, left for dead. Nobody in Vala had questioned that story. Few had ventured from the Hinterlands, believing cities were more dangerous than villages. How would they react if they learned the truth, that Kel had been attacked right here in the palace? How would Logan react, learning he had survived?

More soldiers appeared. He and Deen slipped into Gallia's quarters. They were empty save for a figure lying in a dark pool on the floor. The figure wore black trousers and shirt, as well as a black cloak. Callum cursed under his breath.

"By the stars, is he dead?" asked Deen.

Callum approached the body, mindful of the blood, and placed his fingers on the king's neck. "Not yet. He has a pulse, but it's very faint."

The doorknob turned. Callum grabbed Deen and forced him into an adjoining room. He closed the door, leaving a small sliver open. His heart raced. Deen breathing down his neck did not help.

A tall figure dressed in dark blue entered. He turned, revealing burn scars on the left side of his face.

Where have you been hiding? Callum wondered as Dane Kanton inspected the room. The former guardsman walked over to the king and kicked him in the ribs.

"Serves you right," Kanton muttered. Eyes scanning the room, he yelled, "Callum Haar! Val told me you'd be here. Show yourself. Fight me like a man this time!"

He wanted another fight, did he? Callum quickly sized up the man. Fighting him at night had been a challenge. Too little light to see properly and too little time to think. He could take him in a hand-to-hand fight. The advantage of a surprise attack belonged to him this time. But what if Kanton pulled a weapon? The scar on his chest burned.

Callum felt a tap on his shoulder. Deen pointed to himself. Callum raised an eyebrow. Did he want to fight Kanton or merely talk? Either way, that would give him time to get Logan out of here. He stepped aside.

Deen threw open the door and jumped into the room. Kanton drew his dagger but relaxed, recognizing the foreign king.

"What are you doing here?" Kanton's eyes narrowed.

"You're going to steal his face, aren't you?" he asked, pointing at Logan.

"What are you talking about?"

"I saw you steal that guardsman's face. Don't deny it!" Deen circled Kanton, forcing the man to turn away from Callum. Taking his cue, Callum rushed towards the fallen king. Logan was still breathing. Barely. Callum inspected his body. A knife wound gaped in his side.

A shadow blocked the main doorway. Callum's eyes darted towards it, expecting to see a guard or soldier. Instead, it was Kel.

"You really have gone mad, haven't you?" Kanton questioned Deen. "That's why Syleck let them arrest you."

"Bloody Thanes. First, you read our minds and burn down our villages. Now you steal our faces!"

Callum motioned for Kel to remain at the door. The king was not a heavy man, but he doubted he could carry him without Kanton noticing. An object caught his eye. Sticking out of the king's boot was a small dagger, no longer than Callum's hand. He removed the blade and waited for Kanton to move closer.

Deen swung his fist at Kanton, missing him by inches. Kanton responded with a knife slash, cutting the king of Bran Maro's arm. A shallow wound. Callum motioned him to move closer. They needed to end this fight now.

Giving Callum a small nod, Deen lunged at Kanton, grabbing hold of his arm and flinging it. The knife slipped out of Kanton's grip. Deen shoved the man backwards. Callum swung the dagger as hard as he could, slashing it across Kanton's hamstring. He screamed in agony and crashed to the floor. Deen snatched up the knife and stood beside Callum, breathing hard.

"You bastard" Kanton yelled, seeing Callum crouching beside him. White hot hatred burning in his eyes. "I'll kill you!" Kanton tried to regain his footing, crying out as he put pressure on his ruined leg.

"I wouldn't try standing on that leg for at least a month," said Kel, striding into the room. "Granted, even if that muscle heals properly, you might not be able to fight again."

Kanton stared at him in confusion. "You? But you're—"

"Supposed to be dead? I know." Kel leaned on his crutch, glaring at Kanton. "What did you hope to gain by bringing my son and niece here? Did you want my brother to be on edge this whole time, hoping he'd say the wrong thing to Queen Gallia? Or did you just want to punish me for not being dead?"

Kanton swallowed, the blood draining from his face.

"Does Logan know you were there when Yestyn beat me? That you were the guard assigned to attend to him that day? Does he know you stood by that whole time and did nothing? That the smirk on your face was the last thing I saw before losing consciousness?"

"You didn't expect me to stop him, did you?" Kanton spat. "You got what you deserved, you ungrateful bastard!"

Kel swung his crutch and hit Kanton in the face, his nose exploding in a spray of blood. Kanton laid on his back, groaning.

Callum placing a hand on Kel's bony shoulder. The man was trembling.

"I take it you have a long history with him?" asked Deen, studying Kel.

"Too long," Callum replied. He reached down, grabbed Logan underneath the arms, and lifted the man to his feet. Deen rushed to Logan's side, supporting him.

"What?" Logan murmured.

"King Logan, do you remember who did this to you?" Callum asked. He and Deen slowly walked towards the door. Kel peered into the hallway. He gave them the all clear.

"Valentin Gardyner. Where's my family?"

Kel nodded.

"They're safe," Callum replied. "Everyone has evacuated."

"You don't know that," Deen said in Marish.

"Shut up," Callum said in the same language. Deen's different colored eyes widened.

"What?"

"Try not to speak, Your Majesty," said Callum. He and Deen supported the king as Kel led them to the servant's stairs. "We'll get you someplace safe."

***

Realta's breath began to hitch as they reached the courtyard.

The carriages belonging to the Jemayrti ambassadorial party waited in front of the stables, horsed and ready to leave. Exactly as planned. *Not exactly. Callum isn't here.* She waved towards the ambassador.

Chinasa Ekene, dressed in all white expect for his red necklace and bracelets, returned the gesture. Shasta Cray stood beside him. Her part of the plan had been to inform the ambassador about his role, to which he readily agreed. Realta and Serena had acted as though they were evacuating to the Academy along with everyone else, drawing Val in the wrong direction. They would then head for the courtyard, where they hoped to lose him in the confusion.

"Realta!" Val called after her. He was only twenty paces away. She steeled herself, forcing her legs to move faster.

"Hurry," said Ambassador Ekene, helping them into the first carriage. She and Serena climbed in with Shasta. The ambassador sat up front with the driver. The driver snapped the reins, and the horses took off for the open gates.

"He's kidnapping the king's sister!" Val yelled. The guards at the gate looked at one another in confusion. Shasta instructed them to let the carriages pass, no matter what. The guards stood in front of the gate, weapons drawn.

"Fools," Shasta muttered.

Both carriages came to a halt. Her mind racing, Realta and Serena peered out of the window. Val had caught up to the guards. He slowed to a walk, not even out of breath. This wasn't supposed to happen. They should be outside of the palace grounds.

What would Val do to her and the ambassador? Would he control their minds, force them to cooperate in his mad schemes against their wills?

How do you know he isn't already doing that?

Realta shivered, pushing the thought away. No, she was still free to make her own decisions. This was real.

"Explain yourselves," the guards demanded of Val and Ekene.

A knife flew through the air. Val ducked out of the way, causing the blade to land in one of the guardsmen's chest. He fell to the ground without a sound. The other guard rounded on the ambassador.

"Whose knife was that?"

"My bodyguard's. But he didn't mean—"

"This is an act of war!" Val yelled, pointing at the Jemayrti.

Arrows rained down from the walls, sticking into the ground. The guard ran for cover. One landed on the roof of the carriage, sticking halfway inside. Soldiers dressed in black uniforms trimmed with white lined the wall. They fired another volley, striking down the second guard moments before he reached the gate. Some came very close to hitting Val.

Ekene shouted at the driver in Jemayrti. The carriages sped through the gate.

"You idiots! Stop shooting!" Val ordered. He ran out of the gate, but stopped, knowing he could never catch up to them.

Realta sat down on the bench, shivering. She struggled to believe it. Their plan had worked. They had escaped.

Escaped? Val's voice rang in her head. *You think you've escaped? There is no running from your destiny, Little Dreamer. Fate won't allow you to escape me!*

"Realta, what's wrong?" asked Serena.

"He's in my head!"

"Speed up," Shasta called out. The carriages raced through a city erupting in chaos. People ran in every direction, screaming and crying out for loved ones. Buildings burned, collapsing in on themselves, ashes billowing in gray plumes. Soldiers in different colored uniforms, some black with white, others red, and bearing foreign banners, flooded the streets. One regiment crowded people into frightened groups. A man broke away from the group, running down the street. An arrow landed in his back.

None paid attention to their carriages. They were only a few among thousands trying to flee.

"His influence will fade once we're far away enough," Shasta assured her. "Did your father make it out of the palace?"

"I don't know," she said quietly. Callum was supposed to meet them at the tunnels. Why wasn't he there?

"Val said that Logan is dead," said Serena, her eyes fixed on the floorboards.

"It was a lie," Shasta replied. "Minders know how to get under your skin."

Serena shook her head, not looking at anyone or anything.

We are Two of Nine, Realta. The Midnight King walks Eltriar again. The statement, the surety in Val's words, echoed in her mind.

She stole a glance out the window. The bars of the Southern Gate were warped and twisted. Dark marks coated the stone archway. They passed through it with easy. Before them laid open country, flat land extending towards the horizon. Other carriages soon joined theirs, riding as fast as their horses could run.

Glancing eastward, she saw a large army comprised of thousands, men on foot and on horseback. Siege weapons loomed in the distance.

"We were too late," Serena said, tears escaping her eyes as she gazed at the armies.

Realta's heart sank. If they had acted sooner, would they have been able to stop this? Somehow convince Gallia to call off the attack? She doubted it. This attack had been months, if not years, in the making.

As the city grew smaller behind them, Realta said a silent prayer for her father and uncle's safety. Callum had survived crossing Caman's Pass a hundred times. He would survive this.

Riding far into the night, Realta drifted into a dreamless sleep.

Epilogue

Charity sat on a low bench in the Academy's gardens with Zandon and Jaim, a large tree providing them with ample shade. Lok stood a short distance away, surrounded by a dozen lanterns, the first of which was lit. The lanky Thane looked at them for permission to begin.

"Now!" Charity shouted.

Taking a deep breath, Lok split the first lantern's flame in half. He cautiously lifted one half, gliding it through the air to the second lantern, lighting it. He repeated the procedure with the third lantern, and the fourth, and the fifth. Each time, his actions grew a little faster, the flame gliding a little smoother. A smile crossed his face.

Charity said a small prayer of thanks. The key to Lok's ability was control. As long as he had control over his emotions and the flame, there was no danger.

"He's really getting good," said Zandon, observing Lok light the ninth lantern.

"Yeah. The candlelighters will be out of a job soon," replied Jaim.

A moment later, the twelfth lantern was lit. Lok beamed a smile at the group.

"Wonderful!" Charity and the others clapped. Lok blushed. The three-month time frame the Scholars placed on him had terrified him, made him doubt his own ability to learn. This little exercise was the confidence boost he needed.

"Lok, that was amazing," said Scholar Kuno, walking up to the group. Lok nodded to his mentor in thanks. Taking a deep breath, Lok lowered his hands and exhaled. All twelve lanterns extinguished as one. Kuno's jaw dropped.

"I had come here to admonish you four for skipping class, but I think I'll let it slide. Whose idea was this?"

"Charity's. One hundred percent," said Jaim as they walked over to the Scholar and Lok.

Charity blushed. "You said that the ancient Elementals were

chaplains. The chaplains in our village were always calm and collected, even as they went about daily tasks. I just asked Lok to imagine he was a chaplain lighting candles for the day."

"Charity, that's ingenious," the Scholar remarked. "Perhaps we ought to switch titles."

"Hey, I got the lanterns," said Jaim.

"Did you use your Thane ability to carry them?"

"Well, not all of them, Scholar." He dug into his pocket for some coins.

Kuno laughed quietly. "I'm just pulling your leg, Jaim."

"So, do you think the Scholars will really kick Lok out?" asked Zandon. The question had been on everyone's mind, but none of them wanted to speak it aloud.

"If he can maintain this level of control, then they have no reason to expel him," replied Kuno, placing a comforting hand on Lok's shoulder. Tension melted away from him.

Charity spied movement from the corner of her eye. Baltyn the guardsman, his large Deirow Hawk flying overhead, ran towards them.

"Hello, Baltyn," Charity said, waving.

The guardsman gave her a half-hearted wave as he stopped to catch his breath. The hawk circled down and landed on his shoulder.

"What is it?" asked Kuno.

"Scholar," he said between breaths, "we've just received word that the city of Teyrnas is under attack."

"What? By whom?"

"By Nowan."

Kuno cursed under his breath. A knot formed in Charity's gut.

"And Tirshay, and Tarod, and Galion, and Bran Maro."

"What?!"

Zandon and Jaim exchanged terrified looks. Lok stepped closer to Charity, his hands shaking. Charity's heart sank. Realta, Callum, Kel, and Gareth were all still in the city. And it was being attacked by not one, but five countries?

The palace walls are thirty feet high. They'll be safe, she tried and failed to convince herself.

"Slow down, Baltyn," said Kuno. "Are you sure this information is correct?"

"I swear by the Creator's true name. Two riders just arrived, one of them half dead from an arrow in his back. They told us everything. The other guards have gone to warn the rest of the Scholars and the Council."

"Fire and smoke, how could this have happened?" Kuno rubbed his forehead.

"It seems the Eastern nations made a pact of some sort. The riders didn't have any more information."

"What about us?" asked Charity. "Will we be safe here?"

"Academies are neutral areas. No one would dare attack one," Baltyn assured her. "But worst case, everyone will evacuate along the Wallach and stay at the Lowyrn Academy until the fighting ends."

"But that's only worst case," Kuno added.

"What about the Garrison?" asked Zandon. "Are they recruiting?"

"Zandon, you have your studied to focus on."

"I'm eighteen, Scholar. Old enough to fight."

Kuno placed a hand on Zandon's shoulder, locking eyes with him. "You're from West Bridge, right? Do you have family there?"

"Yes, Scholar. My parents and cousins."

"Write them before you make this decision. We don't have all the facts yet, and I don't think the Council will appreciate Students leaving to join the Garrison without warning."

"No offense, Scholar, but I don't care what the Council thinks."

Kuno sighed. "Sleep on the decision, if nothing else." He then addressed the rest of the group. "I suggest you go to class. There's no need to fear."

"Not yet," muttered Jaim.

They walked towards the Academy Proper, Scholar Kuno leading the way. Baltyn ran off to warn others. Charity studied Lok's pained face.

"Are you scared?"

Lok nodded.

"I'm sure everyone's all right. Realta probably got out of the city. Callum can beat anyone in a fight, and we both know how smart Master Kel is. I bet they're all heading to the Academy right now." Her voice faltered on the last sentence. Who was she trying to convince? She did not have any evidence that her friend was heading this way, or that she had gotten out of the city in time.

She glanced back at the Academy walls. A cold wind blew in from the east.

＊

Westermor hadn't meant to kill Argys. But the man kept hitting him and hitting him. He just would not stop, even with Mida pleading. West had fought back for once. Was that such a bad thing?

He sat on the floor of an old mining office on the Lowyrn side of the Vogel Mountains. They had decided to rest there for the night. Or rather, Argys has decided. Now Argys was nothing more than a pile of ashes and charred bones. Mida cowered in the corner opposite from West. She had finally stopped screaming. She had such an awful scream. It hurt West's ears.

Sitting on the floor in the darkened room, West tried to think. Thinking had always been hard for him. Mida said he had hit his head as a little boy, and he had the scar to prove it. Right below his hairline. He didn't remember how it happened. But he remembered Mida and Argys talking. Argys had been saying a lot of crazy things about the people they were supposed to meet. That they were all insane and West was a mistake. He should have died with his mother.

And then the hitting began. West's body ached all over, especially his head. He lost count of how many times Argys had punched his head.

That single candle was the only reason he was alive. West had tried telling Argys he could control fire. Fire and water. He had told that nice boy he had met in the forest last month. That boy was just like him. West had never met someone just like himself before. And his girlfriend was nice, too.

"You little fool," Mida finally said, her voice hoarse. "He was our only chance of finding the Wardens. Now what am I supposed to do with you? You monster!"

Mida was lucky there was no more fire.

The small room darkened, even though the sun had set hours

ago. Shadows, as black as pitch, crept into the corners, making them darker than a stormy night. The hairs on the back of West's neck stood on end. He wrapped his arms around his legs and winced. Everything hurt so bad!

One of the shadows stood up, growing taller and thinner. It walked towards the center of the room. Mida screamed. The shadow studied West, cocking its head. West trembled from head to foot.

Returning to its corner, the shadow tore it open, revealing more shadows beyond. But beyond into what? West looked for the trees surrounding the office building, but there were none. Only a dark nothingness.

A man with black hair and gray eyes stepped out of the nothing place and into the room. He shook hands with the shadow. The shadow stepped into the nothing and disappeared. The room returned to its late evening lighting, moonlight streaming in through a dirty window.

"What are you?" Mida cried.

"Be quiet," the man ordered. Mida did as she was told. Good. West did not want to hear her talk any more. She had called him a monster.

"That was very rude, wasn't it?" said the man. He crouched down next to West. "Her calling you a monster."

"You heard that?" he asked.

The man shook his head, smiling. A friendly smile. "No, I heard you thinking it. That's my gift. I read people's minds, just like you control the elements, Westermor."

"You know my name!" He sat up, absolutely amazed. He had met a man a long time ago who did guessing games for a penny each. If he won, you paid a penny, but if you won, then he gave you five pennies. Mida said he was a fraud. Mida said lots of mean things.

"Yes. And I know that a lot of people have hurt you. I came here to help you, West. My name is Val, and we are Two of Nine."

Val helped West to his feet, mindful of the pains in West's ribs and legs. It hurt to stand on his right leg, a sharp pain shooting up from his ankle.

"How did you get here?"

"Oh, the Ullmhir helped me. Have you ever heard of the Ull-mhir?"

West shook his head.

"They are these creatures that live in a world that's parallel to our world, and they can travel here, but only as shadows. And sometimes they help people go from one place to another very quickly. For a small price."

"You mean money?" That's what Argys always meant by 'price'.

Val laughed, a warm, happy sound. "No, the Ullmhir have no need for money. They take something different. They take memories."

"Good memories?"

"Good, bad. It doesn't matter to them. They like memories. They help them see what life is like on this side."

"So where are we going?" West asked. Val was leading him out of the abandoned building. Mida didn't even look up. That was fine. Mida was always mean to him. Well, not always. But it was hard to remember the not always.

"We are going to find the others who are like us."

"The Nine?"

Val smiled. "Yes. You catch on quick, West."

West frowned. "No. I'm stupid."

"Only because people say you're stupid. I bet you're really smart and don't know it."

"Really?" Smart? Him? But he couldn't even read!

"Yeah." Val lowered his voice. "Do you want to hear a secret, West?"

"Yes, Val."

"I'm not speaking Marish. I'm speaking Teyrnian. But because of my ability, you can understand me, and I can understand you."

"Wow!" The nice girl in the forest had tried to teach him Tey-rnian. West only remembered a few words. Mida had been very angry at him. He never understood why. He thought learning was a good thing.

"Let's not think about Mida any longer, West. She will never hurt you again."

"Good."

They walked along the dirt road, the pain in his ankle lessening a little with each step. Up ahead, West saw lights from the nearby village. There was always lots of fire and water in villages.

"How are we going to find them?" West asked. He knew how to count to nine, but he did not know what it meant to be One of Nine. And how did you know if a person was a Nine?

"We're going to find them one by one, West. And the first one is a little girl named Realta Haar."